WELCOME BACK TO LAKEWOOD

A SUMMER DANCE NOVEL

LYNN SWANSON

Go to www.lynnswansonbooks.com to see other books by Lynn Swanson and to arrange for school visits, study guides, readings and book signings.

Welcome Back to Lakewood is the second book in the *Summer Dance* series by Lynn Swanson. To make the story come alive, the author suggests readers listen to the music from the dances in this book, including *Giselle* by Adam, *Double Violin Concerto by Bach*, *Third Piano Concerto & Serenade for Strings* by Tchaikovsky, *Slavonic Dances* by Dvořák and *Poupée Valsante* by Poldini/Kreisler

————

© *Lynn Swanson, Silver Spring, Maryland 2015 USA copyright registration for "The Collected Works of Lynn Swanson": TXu 1-769-577 ISBN: 1466317337 ISBN 13: 9781466317338 Library of Congress Control Number: 2011916633 CreateSpace, North Charleston, South Carolina*

Welcome Back to Lakewood
Copyright © 2015 Lynn Swanson
Silver Spring, Maryland
All rights reserved

ISBN: 1515160807
ISBN-13: 9781515160809
Library of Congress Control Number: 2015914656
CreateSpace Independent Publishing Platform
North Charleston, South Carolina

————

————

The author has referenced several passages from *The Nikolais/Louis Dance Technique* by Alwin Nikolais and Murray Louis and has relied on it extensively to refresh her memory of the technique.

————

Front Cover Photo by Jess Stone

Acknowledgments

A *grand révérence* and a bouquet of flowers to:

Joy Ellis of Footlights Dance & Theatre Boutique for encouragement that has put *Summer Dance* and *Welcome Back to Lakewood* into many dancewear stores and into the hands of many young dancers.

———

A special bow and two roses from my bouquet to Jess for his creation of space for me to write Welcome Back to Lakewood

Dedication

Welcome Back to Lakewood is dedicated to all the kids who dance and to all the dancewear store owners who make sure the kids have what they need to do what it takes.

and

In Loving Memory of Susan Jill Robinson

Table of Contents

PART ONE

PART TWO

PART ONE

CHAPTER ONE

"What is Your Name?"

Sara looked around the cabin and pulled the shiny Lakewood Dance Camp brochure out of her pocket. She stared at herself on the cover wearing last summer's skater ballet costume and holding her beautiful bouquet of flowers as she accepted her second place win. That had gotten her a full scholarship back to this year's camp. Her heart jumped as she remembered the thrill of dancing on the big outdoor stage on the lake. Then it fell as she remembered the troubles she had to face with Robin. *Oh, well,* she thought, *we ended up friends.* But she wasn't really sure.

She looked over the bunks that were all still empty. She knew enough to get here early this year to grab the one she wanted and get settled in. As a scholarship winner she got to choose any cabin she wanted. As a graduate of middle school, she got to choose to be in the Intermediate Division or the Senior Division. She had decided to stick with Intermediate, figuring she would have a better chance of being a standout. Besides, she didn't relish being pushed beyond her limits. Last year was quite enough of that. Also, Robin had won the first place scholarship and would be in the Senior Division. So she had everything figured out. Problem was she couldn't win another scholarship in the Intermediate Division, but she had that figured out, too. Next summer would be the summer her mom could pay for dance camp since her brother got to go to soccer camp this year. But what she was really after was a scholarship to a real professional ballet school like Lin had won last year. She wanted it so bad that she hadn't told anyone. She had a plan. So what could go wrong? Right on cue, the old screen door squeaked open.

"Robin!" Sara exclaimed, staring at the tall strawberry blonde standing in the doorway.

"In person," Robin smiled, letting go the handle of her suitcase and dropping her expensive dance bag. She walked with those long legs of hers right over to the lower bunk next to the front window that Sara was about to claim. She sat down and swung her feet in front of the space under the bed where Sara planned to stash her pointe shoes.

"Why are you in Pavlova cabin? Aren't you in Senior Division this year?" Sara asked, hoping her luck wasn't giving out already.

"Yep," Robin said. "I'm on my way to Tallchief cabin, but thought I'd stop by and give lucky old Pavlova cabin a looksee. Fancy meeting you here. What cabin are you in?"

"This one," Sara replied, but she was thinking of the name Tallchief. She remembered reading in a dance magazine that Maria Tallchief was a beautiful Native American ballet dancer from many years ago, but she couldn't remember any of the details.

"No way," Robin said. "You should be in Senior Division."

Here we go again, Sara thought. Robin was still making judgments about people. "I chose Intermediate that's all," she said. "You chose Intermediate last year when you were fourteen."

"I was in Intermediate," Robin said, "but it wasn't my choice. They made me because of something they thought I did. But this year there is no stopping me."

Sara remembered the rumor that Robin had gotten demoted from Class A to Class B two summers ago because she went off grounds with David, the lifeguard. She was about to speak when Robin stood and picked up her dance bag.

"Is Erin coming?" Robin asked, walking to the door.

"No," Sara said sadly. "She wanted to stay in New York to dance." Sara realized she felt a bit frightened to be at camp without Erin, her best friend from last summer. The bunk she was choosing belonged to Erin last year and she thought of the secret red tin they kept under there all summer. She wondered if it was still in the rafters of the old cabin in the woods where they left it on the last day.

"New York—that's where I'll be dancing next summer after I win the scholarship to the New York City Ballet school this year," Robin bragged. "That's who's coming to perform for us, you know, and to give us master class." Robin stood there staring at Sara as if to say "Just try to get it away from me."

"Yeah, I know," was all Sara could get out before Robin grabbed her suitcase and went out the screen door, letting it slam behind her. But Sara really hadn't known which company was coming. How did Robin always know everything?

"See ya!" Robin shouted as she headed to the Senior Division grounds.

5

New York City Ballet, Sara thought. Excitement raced through her heart and filled her head with visions of famous Balanchine ballets Miss Abbey had shown them on film at her home studio. Those gorgeous plotless dances that the master George Balanchine had come from Russia to create. She knew he had died many years ago but that his ballets lived on in the great company he had created and directed in New York. She could see herself standing on the big outdoor stage at the end of summer receiving a scholarship award to the company's summer program. Then she thought of how long Robin's legs were and how tall, graceful and smart she was. The door squeaked open again and Sara quickly threw her bedroll and dance bag on Erin's old bunk.

"Hi!" There was another tall girl with long red hair standing in the doorway. But it was dark, brownish-red hair and thick hanging down her back, unlike Robin's light, fluffy strawberry blonde hair.

"Hi," Sara answered as she began putting her boxes of pointe shoes under her bunk. "I'm Sara Sutherland."

"I'm Leah Bennett," the girl said confidently. She threw her bedroll onto the top bunk at the back wall of the cabin. Sara suddenly remembered Becky on that top bunk last summer flicking the light bulb chain off and on to get them to get up and go horseback riding. No horses this year, she promised herself.

"How old are you? Where are you from?" Leah asked as she started to unpack her suitcase.

Oh, no, Sara thought, *another Robin who asks millions of questions.* But before she could answer, a medium-sized girl with light brown hair came in.

"Hi!" the girl said with a great smile. "Where do I go?"

6

"Anywhere that's left," Sara answered. She watched as the girl put her bedroll on the bunk under Leah's. Then the door opened again and two girls came in loaded with dance bags, pillows, bedrolls and suitcases.

"I'm Brooke, that's Mary," the taller one said.

"Hi!" everybody answered as they continued unpacking.

"Over here," Brooke motioned to Mary, and they took the bunks next to the big side window, Mary on the top, Brooke on the bottom. Just as they tossed their bedrolls down, a shy looking wispy girl with very long light hair came in. She stood at the door quietly staring at them.

Sara waved her over to her bunk. "Looks like you're above me."

The thin girl wandered over and threw her bedroll on the bunk over Sara's. She quietly told Sara that her name was Shannon like maybe Sara should already know, and then she busied herself unpacking. Leah finished getting organized first, then sat on the floor, which it turned out was her favorite place to plop. "OK, everybody," she said. "Let's exchange information."

One by one as the girls finished unpacking and laying out their bedrolls and pillows they sat on the floor with Leah. "I'll start," Leah said. "I'm Leah Bennett. I'm from Indiana and I'm fourteen." She nodded to Brooke.

"I'm Brooke Blanchard. I'm from Florida and I'm thirteen." Next was Mary who had come in with Brooke and had the bunk over her.

"I'm Mary Henderson. I'm from Florida, too, and I'm twelve and a half."

"We dance at the same studio," Brooke explained. "We both got scholarships from our teacher to come here." *They must be really good,* Sara thought. Everyone here seemed to be the best at their home studio.

Next was the tall wispy quiet girl. "I'm Shannon St. Pierre from France. I'm thirteen."

"Really?" Leah asked. "From France?"

"Yes, that is true," Shannon said with a slight French accent. "But, I am also from New York City."

"Explain please," Leah said. Sara was already impressed.

"Well, you see, my father is French and does business in Paris. That's where I was born. My mother is Irish from New York, and that is how I got the name Shannon St. Pierre and that is why I live in France sometimes and in New York sometimes."

"Are your parents divorced?" Brooke asked. Sara's heart felt this question deeply, of course, because her own parents were divorced.

"Yes," Shannon answered. "But we get along with it OK. I have a younger brother who lives most of the time with my father. I live most of the time with my mother. It is OK."

Wow, Sara thought, *divorced with a younger brother just like my own family. And, like Erin, she probably takes dance classes in New York City.* She just had to ask. "Do you take classes in New York City?"

"Oh, yes, I do," Shannon replied. "I take at the school of the New York City Ballet."

"Oh my gosh," Sara exclaimed. "Do you know Erin Christopher?"

"Yes," Shannon smiled. "I certainly do know her. She is in my classes."

"She was my best friend here last summer!" Sara smiled. "Does she know you are here?"

"Yes, of course she knows," Shannon said, walking over to her suitcase. She pulled out a long empty roll of paper and unfurled it. "She sent this with me for you and for all Pavlova cabin."

"A banner!" Sara exclaimed. "A banner!" She explained how last summer they had hung a paper banner with all their names and accomplishments on it.

"Cool," Leah said. "We'll hang it later. Let's finish our info exchange." Shannon put the paper roll on her bunk and sat down in the circle. Leah nodded to Sara.

"I'm Sara Sutherland from Michigan and I'm fourteen."

"And you won second place in last year's scholarship competition," Leah announced taking this year's Lakewood brochure out of her pocket and pointing to the picture of Sara. The girls all clapped and congratulated her. "So, that means you can't win in our division this year."

Oh, Sara thought, *Leah is happy that she won't have me to compete with for one of the three scholarships to next year's camp.* "That's right" was all Sara said. Leah nodded to the last girl in the circle, the one who had the bunk under Leah.

"I'm Charleigh Stevens from Colorado and I'm thirteen."

"WHAT is your name?" Leah asked, looking bewildered.

"Charleigh," the girl said.

"Charlie?" Leah asked.

"No. Charleigh. C-h-a-r-l-e-i-g-h, Charleigh."

"Sounds like *Charlie* to me," Leah said.

"No. It's Char-leigh," Charleigh said patiently. "Like Shar-Lee."

"Charlie," Leah replied with a smile.

"OK. *Charlie*," Charleigh sighed. "I've always had this problem with my name. It took me until I was five to learn how to write it."

"I've always had trouble with my age," Leah said. "I'm really only three years old."

"What?" Mary said. I thought you were fourteen."

"I was born on February 29 in a leap year, so I've only had three birthdays that have actually fallen on February 29. It took me until I was ten to figure it out." Everybody was laughing when someone knocked on the frame of the screen door. Before they could answer, a large woman walked in and towered over them.

"Hello, Pavlova dancers!" the woman said. "I'm Julie Hess, your counselor. Give me a wave when I read your name." One by one she read their names off a list, pronouncing Charleigh as "Charlie" making everybody laugh again. "Did I get something wrong?" she asked.

"Private joke," Leah said, still laughing.

"Well here's something private for you," Julie said. "Since Pavlova cabin is all here and accounted for, get your bathing suits on and head down to the lake for your swim test. I'll check with the lifeguard to get the results. Remember: there's no going on the raft, no swimming outside the buoys and no taking a boat out unless you can float or tread water for twenty minutes. I want to see a swim star on all of your ID badges."

Sara shuddered at the thought of the swim test, remembering how she barely passed last year and how David, the lifeguard, had to jump in and save her. Robin never forgave her for that and always thought Sara was trying to steal her boyfriend. It didn't help that David stole a kiss from Sara at the ice cream party. But then, Robin had been dancing with Hank. Sara grew warm thinking of Hank and wondered if he would be at the boys camp across the lake this summer. She could still feel the kiss he gave her on her cheek on the last night of camp. Julie Hess's voice interrupted her thoughts. "OK. Let's go. Down to the lake!"

"I don't swim well," Shannon whispered to Sara as they pulled on their suits.

"Don't worry," Sara said. "There will be a handsome lifeguard to save you if you drown."

CHAPTER TWO

"It's Not a Boy"

Sara ran with Shannon down the path to the intermediate beach staring through her sunglasses at the dock. There were several girls sprawled on beach towels, but David was not in the lifeguard chair.

"Whoa," Sara said, stopping.

"What is it?" Shannon asked.

"The lifeguard," Sara said. "It's not a boy!"

"Yes, I see that," Shannon said. She started to walk again. "Come on. Let's get this over with."

Sara kept her eyes on the lifeguard as her soft bare feet followed Shannon's. The woman in the chair looked at her watch, got up and blew her whistle. "OK, time is up for you!" she shouted as she pointed to a bedraggled looking swimmer. It was true, then. She really was the lifeguard. Sara looked across the lake toward Will-O-Green, the boys camp, but saw no movement except for some sail boats tied to the dock moving with the waves. *David*, Sara, thought, *where are you? Hank*, she thought excitedly, *where are you?*

"Hey! You two need to check in with me," the lifeguard shouted. Shannon was already waist deep in water. She waded over to the dock. Sara walked between the sun bathers to the lifeguard.

"I'm Heather Scott," the muscular young woman announced, shiny with sunscreen. She wore an official shirt with a red cross and the words "Intermediate Lifeguard" on it. They told Heather their names and cabin, and Sara dropped her towel and jumped into the water next to Shannon. Heather wrote their names on her clipboard, looked at her watch and hollered "OK. Time starts now for Sara and Shannon!"

Here we go again, Sara thought, swimming out close to Shannon and hoping she would have more endurance than she did last year. Twenty minutes could seem like four hours when you had to float or tread water the whole time. The wind was strong and the water cold and a bit choppy. Sara was thinking June 27 was too early in the northern Michigan woods for the lake to be warm enough for her to stay in long. Then a big wave slapped her in the mouth and she started coughing.

"Be careful out there! Keep your mouth closed!" Heather yelled at Sara.

Great, Sara thought. *I am already not doing too well at Lakewood. What else will I have to overcome from now until August 22?* Suddenly all the auditions and rehearsals for class placement, dance parts, the student concert, and the mid-season and final performances loomed in her mind. She shivered, not from the cold, but from her fear and passion. *I just have to win a summer scholarship to the New York City Ballet school*, she thought. *I just have to.* Then Heather was shouting again.

14

"If you girls are from Senior Division, you are not allowed here at the intermediate beach," she yelled at two girls strolling up the dock. Sara looked over and saw Robin and her friend from last summer, Hillary.

"She's strict," Shannon said, treading next to Sara.

"Thank goodness," Sara said, watching Robin and Hillary turn and walk toward the beach. She didn't need those two hanging around. Sara quickly swam farther out toward the line of buoys, but Robin spotted her and waved. Sara waved back thinking that Robin must have been disappointed not to find David here on the dock with his summer bleached hair, big smile and ready arms. Then Hillary waved and they took off.

"Wait up," Shannon shouted, swimming after Sara.

"Oh. Sorry." Sara realized she had been lost in her thoughts and swimming fast.

"Who are they?" Shannon asked.

"Trouble," Sara couldn't help saying, feeling relieved they had gone.

"The tall one looks like the girl on the cover of the Lakewood brochure who won first-place Intermediate Scholarship last year," Shannon said.

"She is," Sara said treading faster as more waves rolled in on them. "I wonder how many minutes have gone by," she said, wanting to change the subject. No need to explain it all. She wanted a fresh start.

"She certainly is tall and pretty," Shannon said. "Is she a good dancer?"

Sara thought of something Erin might say right now. "Yes, and so are we. We just have to know it." Leah and Charleigh swam up to them all smiles.

"This is a cinch," Leah said. "I can't wait to go on the raft tomorrow."

"Good luck with that after class placement auditions all morning," Sara said, remembering how exhausted she had been after last year's. She was suddenly glad to be taking the water test today instead of tomorrow, and she relaxed a bit and let her arms float out from her. She dipped her head back into the cold water.

"She's a team swimmer," Charleigh offered, nodding toward Leah. "She swims backstroke for medals in her home pool in Indiana."

"Oh, wow," Shannon said. "Show us your stroke." Leah did a few backstrokes. "Beautiful," Shannon exclaimed. "I wish I could swim like that." Then her head disappeared under the water for a second. It seemed too much for her to talk and stay afloat at the same time. Leah quickly grabbed her and got her head above water. "Oops," Shannon struggled to say. "Guess I better concentrate."

Heather hadn't missed a thing. "Hey! Are you OK, Shannon?" she yelled through a megaphone.

"Yes," Shannon said, giving Heather a wave.

"Well, spread out a bit ladies," Heather shouted. "You need to pass on your own without help."

Leah and Charleigh swam backward away from Sara and Shannon, and Sara kicked her legs into some slimy seaweed as she moved away from Shannon. She left her near the string of buoys in case Shannon had to grab on, but stayed close enough so she wouldn't feel abandoned. But Heather would have none of it. "Move away from the buoys, Shannon!" she yelled. Shannon floated over toward Sara.

"Let's go over closer to the dock," Sara suggested, remembering how glad she was to have been near David last year when she went under in the last few seconds of the test. If anything happened to Shannon, Heather would be nearby. Brooke and Mary were there splashing and laughing.

"Hey, you guys," Brooke said. "Can you do this?" She did a backward somersault and came up smiling.

"No thank you," Shannon said. "I'm having enough trouble keeping my head *above* water."

"Watch this," Mary said and went down headfirst raising straight legs with pointed ballet feet high in the air.

"Cool," Brooke said. "Mary and I are on the water ballet team at our club. Mary had a solo this year. I was in the group number." Sara imagined in Florida you could swim in an outdoor pool year-round. She also imagined that Mary and Brooke came from families who had more money than hers did and could afford three or four dance classes a week as well as country club dues. Sara had spent all winter again giving dance lessons and babysitting to earn enough money for her pointe shoes, but this year she was sure she had brought enough to last through all the rehearsals and performances.

"Ten more minutes for Sara and Shannon!" Heather yelled pointing at them.

"Merci," Shannon said, slipping into French to say thank goodness. Sara and Shannon floated around Brooke and Mary for a while enjoying their tricks and water ballet. Then Leah and Charleigh swam over.

"We're pretending to ski downhill underwater," Leah said. "Charlie skis the slopes of Colorado. Like this!" With that Leah went underwater and pretended to ski, moving her bent legs back and forth.

"It's easier in the water," Charleigh laughed.

Now Sara realized that Charleigh must have lots of money, too. She knew it cost a lot to buy skis and all the clothes. She wondered about Leah's family. She already knew Shannon lived a rich and exotic life. It occurred to Sara that any one of these girls could afford to pay for classes at any major ballet school they could get into. *Me? I just* have *to win a scholarship to one*, Sara thought again. *I just have to*. She imagined herself doing pliés at the barre in a big New York City Ballet studio.

"OK. Time is up for Brooke and Mary!" Heather hollered. The girls climbed onto the dock and went to Heather to get stars on their ID badges. Sara had hoped that she and Shannon would make it through without incident. But then Shannon went under again and had to grab onto the dock post to pull herself up. "Time is up for Leah and Charleigh!" Heather called. Sara wished she and Shannon had gotten in the water earlier so they could get out now. "Five more minutes for Sara and Shannon!" Heather yelled. Sara was getting tired and didn't have the other girls to entertain her now. Several girls from other cabins were still in the water, but this was not the time to meet and greet. There were eight weeks of camp ahead to do that. Besides with fifty intermediate dancers she wouldn't be able to get to know all of them. She concentrated on keeping her head above water with an eye on Shannon. She looked across the lake to Camp Will-O-Green again and saw a couple of boys getting into one of the sailboats. Sara remembered how Paul and Hank had won the sailboat race last year in the Will-O-Way. She laughed to herself remembering how they had called themselves Salty and

Skipper and took the trophy from David in his Red Clipper fair and square. That had made David jealous and prompted him to flirt with Sara to get back at Hank. It had gotten very tangled up before Sara figured it all out and the summer ended peacefully. She looked at the boys again getting into the sailboat. No, they were not Paul and Hank. These boys were more slender.

"I am so cold," Shannon said, breaking into Sara's thoughts. "And your teeth are chattering."

Sara realized she was very cold and looked toward Heather. She wasn't even looking at her watch. "Can't be too much longer," Sara said, thinking of how much she wanted a hot shower. She thought of how Erin had helped her last year and suggested to Shannon that they relax by floating on their backs. They tried it, and their long hair floated out wet and pretty around their heads. Sara's dark strands seemed to dance with the lightness of Shannon's. Shannon taught Sara a little French song, then they made up a song with French words Sara knew from ballet like plié, relevé, tendu and arabesque. It was nonsense, but it passed the time. Finally, when Shannon's lips were turning blue, Heather called them in.

Sara had never been so happy to see a star. It was totally honestly won. No doubt about it. Shivering with their towels wrapped around their shoulders, Sara and Shannon ran up the path to Pavlova cabin and into the unknown summer.

CHAPTER THREE

"Opening Session"

Sara and Shannon got to the dining hall on the hill above the lake just as the dinner bell stopped clanging. They stood in line on the steps of the porch waiting to get inside for the cafeteria food. Excited dancers talked about where they were from, which cabin they were in and if they passed the water test. Sara heard "Oklahoma," "Wisconsin," "Nebraska," and "California". When she heard "Tallchief cabin," she looked behind her and saw Kathy Jacobs about five girls back. Kathy had won the third place Intermediate Scholarship last summer and had almost beat out Sara for a part in the special dance for four in *Les Patineurs,* the skaters ballet. She also understudied a senior dancer in *Les Sylphides* in a complicated part. She was nice and Sara liked her, but she looked about three inches taller and about five pounds thinner. More serious competition, Sara thought, looking down at her own body that was maybe one inch taller than last summer. So Kathy was in the same cabin as Robin. Sara wondered which cabin Hillary was in.

"I smell bread baking," Shannon said, sniffing. "Ummmm... and chocolate."

They were hungry after the swim test. Sara felt her stomach growl and remembered how her mom had sent chocolate chip cookies in the red tin last year. "I smell spaghetti," Sara said. "That's what they had last year on the first day. I remember it clearly because after that it was mostly dancer food like salads and chicken and lean meat and vegetables. This is our welcome meal."

"Do they have *des pâtisseries* for breakfast?" Shannon wanted to know.

"English please," Sara laughed.

"Pastries," Shannon smiled. "You know, like croissant."

"Not really," Sara said. "Mostly toast and scrambled eggs."

They moved up farther in the line just as lightning struck above the lake. Thunder roared and rain pounded the old roof covering the cement steps they were standing on. The girls under the tall pine trees behind them screamed and pushed forward. "Move up," Leah shouted in the doorway. "Hurry!" Leah always seemed to organize everything. Sure enough, she got the dancers in front to move forward and suddenly Sara was inside the beautiful wood dining room. Her eyes found the Pavlova table at the edge of the intermediate section and she saw that Brooke and Mary were already there with trays of food in front of them. She spotted the Tallchief table directly across the aisle from them and there she saw Robin and Hillary drinking tall glasses of lemon water and laughing. So, Sara thought, Hillary was in Tallchief with Robin. She had suspected as much. She pictured them sharing bunk beds near a window so they could peek out to see if any boys

22

were roaming. She was relieved not to be in the same cabin with them this year and happy to have Shannon at her side. Sara strained to see the director's table with Miss Sutton and all the dance teachers, but a big support beam blocked her view. She could make out the old piano with music sheets on top and the podium where the teachers would speak after dinner.

The rain was blowing hard against the windows when Sara and Shannon finally walked with their dinner trays to Pavlova table. Leah had made her way there and soon Charleigh joined them so the table was complete. Now Sara could see Miss Sutton and four young teachers at her table. The only one she recognized was Mr. Moyne. She looked at her cabin mates and tried to imagine what the summer held for each of them. As Sara finished the last of her chocolate cake and milk, Miss Sutton rose and walked to the podium. The noise and applause rose to the rafters. Miss Sutton seemed taller than Sara remembered and her hair, pulled neatly back away from her face, seemed darker. But when she began to speak in her lovely British accent Sara felt reassured in Miss Sutton's familiar presence.

"Welcome to the fifty-first summer of Lakewood Dance Camp," Miss Sutton said into a microphone on the podium. More screams and applause filled the room. "How many returning dancers do we have?" Sara was proud to raise her hand along with so many other campers. "Ah, I recognize some of you," Miss Sutton said. Sara thought Miss Sutton smiled her way, but she wasn't sure. "Welcome to all of you. Remember as you compete for class placement, for dance parts and for scholarships, we look at more than just dance technique. We look for growth in character as well as in dance. The qualities we look for in our scholarship winners are leadership, cooperation, enthusiasm and improvement." Sara repeated the important words to herself and thought she would write them at the top of the Pavlova banner. She had a better idea of how to fulfill those goals than she did last year, but she knew it wouldn't be easy. She touched the lucky locket from her dad hanging around her neck and dreamed of dancing in New York.

"What a handsome man," Shannon said, looking toward Mr. Moyne. But Miss Sutton was introducing one of the young women.

"Miss Lee will be your modern dance teacher," Miss Sutton said as a slim young woman in jeans and Lakewood T-shirt took the podium. Her hair was dark and short. As Miss Lee said hello and said she looked forward to having them in class, Sara wondered how difficult her classes might be. She wished she could have taken modern at her home studio, but Miss Abbey did not offer it. *Please let me remember everything Miss Casey taught me last year*, she thought, knowing that winning a summer scholarship to New York was on the line. She tried to feel herself going off balance and raising her bare feet in flexed position. *I think I remember*, she thought. Then another young woman was at the podium.

"Oh, maybe that's our ballet teacher," Shannon said. Shannon seemed to feel an automatic affinity for the woman. Somehow Sara felt squeezed out of the competition before it had even begun. Sure enough, Miss Sutton introduced Miss Alexander as the guest ballet teacher. It would be Russian technique again this year for her students. The tiny woman had a sandy blonde ponytail, and luckily, had no Russian accent.

"Hello dancers," Miss Alexander said. She even smiled. Sara remembered how long she had to wait to see Madame smile last summer. Maybe Miss Alexander wouldn't be as exacting as Madame had been. Maybe it would be more fun. Maybe Sara would feel lovely and light and like she was flying in the air in Miss Alexander's class. She remembered feeling that way in Yuri's master class last year and how she had yearned to dance for him for the rest of her life. "We will work hard for improvement this summer," Miss Alexander said. "See you tomorrow in auditions."

Just as Sara was adjusting to the idea that early in the morning she would actually be in the huge studio on the lake auditioning for class placement, Miss Sutton was saying that she had a surprise for them, that a new class had been added this year. It was Dance History, and Miss Meisner would be their instructor. Sara watched a woman a bit older and a bit heavier than the other teachers walk over to the podium in a long blue skirt and sandals. Her brown hair was curly all over her head. She told them it would be an interesting summer for her because she usually taught college students, but that she looked forward to it and was eager to get started. "We have a lot of ground to cover," she said. "And, by the way, I brought a lot of dance books with me for you to borrow." Sara couldn't imagine having time to read a bunch of books at Lakewood no matter how much she liked the subject matter. She remembered all the rehearsals that were added to their regular classes last year, the choreography she had to prepare for the student dance concert and all the stress surrounding the final performance. She vowed to take it one day at a time. Now it was Mr. Moyne's turn. As he took the podium Sara sighed, feeling like she was once again high over his head in her special part in the extraordinary ballet *Les Sylphides* last summer. It had been so special. This year she hoped to have an even bigger special part in a ballet.

"Hello to all," Mr. Moyne said with a smile. His black hair curled onto his forehead in the moist air. "I hope you all brought your tap and character shoes." Sara liked his tap and folk classes, but knew he was a wonderful ballet dancer, too, and she pictured him on the stage last year with Miss Casey performing *Romeo and Juliet*. She giggled as she remembered watching them rehearse in the secret studio in the basement of the dance building. Then she cringed as she recalled how Robin and Hillary had almost got caught behind the old door that stuck. "I am planning a folk dance for the intermediates for the final performance," he smiled. "It's your turn, so be ready!" he said.

What? Sara thought. *"We're doing a folk dance for the big final performance? But that's what the juniors did last year. I'm supposed to be in a ballet with pointe shoes on for the final performance, not in character shoes for a folk dance.* She couldn't believe her problems were starting already. If she couldn't be seen dancing in a ballet in pointe shoes how could she win a scholarship to the New York City Ballet for next summer? Before she could adjust to the news, Julie Hess was handing her sheet music for the Lakewood camp song.

The old piano keys played the introduction, Miss Sutton motioned for everyone to stand, and Sara sang along:

Lakewood, Lakewood nestled fair
Among the leaves and northern air.
We come to you to dance and share,
to grow and learn, to teach and care,

26

to make new friends and build new paths,
which lead us on to dreams that last.
And when the summer's days are through,
we'll think of our return to you
and never once throughout the year
forget our friends made steadfast here.

Sara felt a lump in her throat and wished Erin were next to her. Just then Shannon smiled at her. "The next time we sing this song will be in at closing ceremonies on the big outdoor stage on the lake," Miss Sutton said. *And all the scholarship winners will be announced*, Sara thought. "We'll see you at class placement auditions in the morning." Again, the old dining hall rafters shook as the dancers cheered and clapped. As Sara and Shannon picked up their trays, Sara's stomach tightened thinking of the morning auditions. As they passed their trays through to the kitchen, she worried about making mistakes and about difficult rehearsals. She worried about dancing in a folk dance for the final concert instead of a ballet. But as they ran through the sprinkling rain to the cabin in the tall pines, Sara remembered she had a whole summer ahead of her to find magic at Lakewood.

CHAPTER FOUR

"Audition"

"Wake up, everybody! Wake up!" It was Leah making sure Pavlova cabin got to the eight o'clock audition on time. "Rise and shine, leap and pointe," she smiled from her top bunk, her long hair falling around her shoulders. *How could she be so alert so early*, Sara wondered. But she knew she would soon be used to the early morning routine. It was just that she had stayed awake so long last night trying to remember all the Russian body positions and arabesques in case they were asked to do them this morning. Miss Alexander had looked smart and quick last night like she might expect miracles immediately. Sara looked out the window to see rain still dripping from the trees. She put her feet on the floor, looked above her and saw Shannon still asleep. She gave her a little nudge, then made her way to the leotards she had thrown into the old chest of drawers near the bathroom and grabbed her favorite black one. She chose brand new pink tights and got her hair back into a bun as tightly as she could. It was still humid outside, which always made Sara's hair curl around her face. When the last brown strand was fastened she found her dance bag and made sure her cleanest ballet shoes were inside along with the pointe shoes that she had broken in just right for this morning. Not too hard or too soft.

"Hey, wait for me!" Mary said, as Brooke started out the door to breakfast. Mary grabbed her raincoat and took off. Charleigh stood at the bathroom door waiting for Leah to come out. When she did there was confusion.

"No, Charlie, you can't wear that," Leah said, looking at Charleigh's royal blue leotard. Charleigh pushed past her into the bathroom.

"Why not?" Sara heard Charleigh say through the closed door.

"What is she wearing?" Shannon wanted to know as she brushed her long light hair.

"Blue," Leah told her.

Shannon went to the bathroom door. "Charleigh, you have to wear black to audition. It says so in the brochure. Did you bring a black leotard? You can borrow one of mine."

"Of course I brought black, but in my home studio royal blue is the color the advanced class wears. Anyway, I didn't read that I guess."

"Well, hurry up and change," Leah said. "I'll wait for you."

"No, Leah. You and Sara go to breakfast. I'll wait," Shannon said. "I'll use the bathroom while you're changing," she told Charleigh through the closed door.

"OK, let's go," Leah said to Sara who was putting her locket in the drawer.

Leah walked so fast through last night's rain puddles that Sara could hardly keep in step let alone talk. It wasn't until they were sitting alone at Pavlova table drinking juice and trying to get some eggs down that Leah spoke. "We have about ten minutes. Tell me what this audition will be like."

Sara saw Shannon and Charleigh coming into the dining hall. "Well, you can't choose where you stand at the barre. It's alphabetical. It's a long class. It was hard last year. They really push you here. They'll divide us into two sections, Class A and Class B. Class A is the higher level, but they combined all fifty of us last year for the final performance and everybody got pretty good parts."

"Let's get over there and warm up," Leah said, picking up her tray. Sara wanted to wait for Shannon, but she still hadn't learned enough about Leah. So as Shannon sat down Sara got up.

"We'll see you in the dance building," Sara told Shannon and Charleigh. "Hurry." As the girls approached the studio, the sun began to shine over the lake. Sara looked across the water to the boys camp. Then she remembered her question for Leah. "That pool you swim in at home where you do the backstroke," she began. "Is it at a private club?"

"Right," Leah laughed sarcastically. "A private club right at the YMCA, and it's for sure not in Paris," she said, opening the door to the dance building. Sara led the way downstairs to the locker room. It was filled with strangers hanging up their street clothes and slamming locker doors. Sara smiled at a few familiar faces from last summer, but there was no Becky and no Danielle. "Let's get up there," Leah said. Sara shut her locker door and ran up the old steps behind Leah. *YMCA-Leap-Year-Leah*, she thought.

"Wow! What a huge room," Leah whispered. "Are you kidding me?"

"I forgot how big it was myself," Sara said, looking over the dancers warming up at the barre and stretching on the beautiful wood floor. It looked like twice as many dancers with all their reflections in the wall mirror. They squeezed in at the barre and Sara started to do some pliés but felt her stomach turn over. "I think I ate too fast," she was saying to Leah when Miss Sutton entered the room with Miss Alexander, Miss Lee and Mr. Moyne. They all carried clip boards with evaluation forms. *Here we go*, Sara said to herself. The accompanist took his place at the piano and the dancers quickly stood at attention wherever they could find space. Sara did not see Shannon or Charleigh.

"Good morning, dancers," Miss Sutton said. She looked up at the big clock on the wall. "We need to get started on time so the Senior Division can start on time," she said. "We'll take the barre together, then break into small groups for center-floor exercises and pointe work. You will know before you leave whether you are in Class A or B. When I call your name, go to the piano and pin a number to your leotard."

Sara could already feel Miss Alexander's careful eyes on them searching for potential. She stood as tall as she could and made sure her tights were straight. As she was pinning audition number 45 to her leotard and trying to figure out where her place would be at the barre, she saw Shannon and Charleigh checking in with Miss Sutton. *Oops*, she thought. *I forgot to tell them to never never be late to anything.* Before she knew it Sara was performing plié and tendu, degagé and rond de jamb at the Lakewood ballet barre next to Shannon St. Pierre. She almost lost her focus on petit battements thinking of how her foot had nearly tangled with Robin's during barre

32

exercises last year. After grand battement, the high leg lifts to the front, side and back, the portable barres were removed from the center of the room and Miss Sutton called them center-floor. *Whew*, Sara thought, glancing at the clock, *I made it through the first part without incident. Now the real dancing begins.* Mr. Moyne, Miss Lee and Miss Alexander took seats with their backs to the mirror still making notes on their evaluation forms.

"Take a deep breath," Miss Sutton directed to help them relax. It didn't seem to help Sara much. She felt stiff and tense and wished Miss Sutton had led them through some stretches at the barre like Miss Abbey always did at home. "Take a minute to stretch on your own while we divide you into groups." Miss Sutton went over to talk with the teachers.

"Hmmmm....," Sara whispered to Shannon as they stretched quietly on the floor. "They're going to rank us already." Charleigh had gone across the room to Mary and Brooke. Sara saw Leah making her way over.

"The barre was standard," Shannon said softly. "Nothing extraordinary."

"You guys looked good," Leah said, sitting on floor with them. "I thought your leg was going to hit the ceiling in grand battement, Shannon."

"Oh, thank you," Shannon replied, pressing her chest to the floor between her long, outstretched legs. "But, you know, it is *how* you do it, not *what* you do that counts." Sara vowed to remember that when she danced this morning. Right now she could use a drink of water, but continued stretching like everyone else.

When they were assigned to one of four groups, Sara found herself dancing with Shannon and Leah along with twelve other girls she didn't know. Charleigh was in the second group and Mary and Brooke in the third. "First group," Miss Sutton said, pointing to Sara's group after she had taught the class a beautiful slow and lengthy movement. It was filled with balances on one leg, high arabesques and even a plié in fifth position all the way to the floor with one foot moving into passé on the way up. It finished with a simple and elegant port a bras, or movement of the arms, with the arms ending circled high overhead. Sara liked the slow adage work, but planned to place herself in the back line until she had the feel of the combination.

She ran with her group out to center-floor and waited in the poised position Miss Sutton had requested. The piano music started and she took a deep breath. As she moved through the adage piece by piece, she tried to watch herself in the mirror to make sure her lines were correct, to breathe in at the right moments, to make a flow of the exercise. She tried to pretend she was dancing on the stage in front of a large audience, but then a girl in the front line turned the wrong way. It was jarring and Sara worked hard after that just to perform the sequence correctly. Finally she stood with the group in the end pose with her arms circled above her head.

"Next group," Miss Sutton said, and Sara's group ran over to stand against the barre.

"That was hard," Leah said, breathing deeply.

"Stay warm," Shannon advised. "Our muscles could get cold waiting for our next turn." Sara did a few demi-pliés now and then while she watched the other groups go through the combination. She hoped she would have a chance to do it again. A second chance would let her expand all the movements to really fulfill the wonderful music. She watched the teachers make notes on their boards.

When each group had done the adage combination, Miss Sutton consulted with the teachers again. Sara was getting nervous as the teachers glanced at the different dancers and nodded their heads as they talked. Then Miss Sutton turned and asked Sara's group to come center-floor. She would have her second chance! But Miss Sutton asked them to change lines, so this time Sara would be in front. If she forgot the movements she would have to try to sneak a look into the mirror at the other girls. The music began and Sara took an extra deep breath and flowed through the movements easily this time. But they weren't done yet. Miss Alexander asked that they repeat the adage, reversing the movement. Oh, oh. Everything would be backwards. The group turned to face the other corner of the room and switched feet, so they would begin with the left foot in front this time instead of the right. There was no time to think it through. Halfway through the movement Sara was facing one of the girls in her line when they were supposed to be facing the same way. *One of us is wrong*, Sara thought. She quickly looked in the mirror and saw that Shannon and Leah had done it her way, but it left her feeling a bit shaky.

Miss Sutton looked toward the other teachers again. Miss Alexander waved Miss Sutton over and pointed toward the group saying something Sara couldn't hear. Miss Sutton spoke again. "Sara come forward. Number 44 come forward." That was Shannon. "Please do it again to the second side." Sara and Shannon glanced at each other knowing that they had been called forward either because they were making mistakes or because Miss Alexander like the way they danced the adage.

Sara felt every eye in the classroom on them as they danced. When they finished, Miss Alexander praised their breathing, head positions and balance, but showed them how to extend the energy of the slow movement. "You should go on forever, graining with your arms, legs, rib cage and eyes into the infinity of space." It was an intention, she said, that the audience would see. It was a way to express and fulfill movement. She demonstrated it for them, then asked them to do it again to the other side incorporating her corrections. "Better. Thank you," Miss Alexander said when they were done, allowing Sara and Shannon to return to the group. As Miss Sutton demonstrated the next set of movements, Sara felt a bit worried about being singled out for attention, but then she remembered what Erin had told her last year, that it meant the teacher saw potential in you.

The set of quick allégro movements they were to do next was complicated with lots of changes in direction. Be careful, Sara told herself. Watch carefully. But Leah was pushing past her rather forcefully to get to the front of the class so she could see Miss Sutton clearly, or so Miss Alexander would see her clearly. Sara hung in the back of the class as they practiced the combination so she could try to understand it and take it into her body. Jump into the air, change feet, land in fifth, chassé right, pas de bourrée under, pas de bourrée over while turning, two more jumps in place and repeat the whole thing to the other side without stopping. Miss Sutton watched them do it and clapped her hands to keep them in rhythm. It was very quick. Sara knew she had to be sharp and clear in the movement and get her pointed feet completely off the floor.

"First group!" Miss Sutton said, moving out of the way. Sara stayed in the back line, but Shannon and Leah went right up into the front line. It didn't matter, because when the group had done it once to each side, Miss Sutton motioned for the front line to split and go to the back and that left Sara's line in front. The piano kept playing until they had changed lines four times. Sara was exhausted. No one had made a mistake as far as she could tell, but there were obvious differences in how each dancer fulfilled the fast combination.

When each group had performed the allégro, Miss Sutton asked Leah to do the combination alone. Leah beamed with confidence and enthusiasm as she totally conquered the tricky movements. Everyone applauded when she finished. She didn't even look tired. No wonder she had pushed her way into the front line. *Wow*, Sara thought. *YMCA Leah can do more than swim.*

Sara was perspiring now and noted that they had been dancing for more than an hour and a half. They still had to get through pirouettes and a big waltz combination across the floor. She was hoping they wouldn't have to show body positions, especially Russian ones. The pirouette combination led by Mr. Moyne was slow and meant to show control. During warm-ups Sara had seen some girls doing a bunch of quick pirouettes in a row. Now they were taken by surprise when asked to do two perfect slow turns ending with the free foot at the knee. But Sara knew from last year to expect this and had practiced them at home. She wasn't prepared, however, when Mr. Moyne told them to change into their pointe shoes to repeat the turns. *Here goes*, she thought. *This will separate Class A from Class B.*

They were allowed a few moments to do some slow rises onto pointe at the barre before Sara's group was called to center-floor. The piano music begged them to stay slow and in control. Sara remembered Madame telling her to pull up last year and working with her to bring her arms and shoulders around quickly to the front and how to use her head to spot the turns. She could also hear Miss Abbey from her home studio coaching her to push her standing heel forward as she turned and to keep her free leg pushed back at the knee. She was thinking all of this at once not sure which to emphasize when she almost fell out of one of her turns. She pulled up extra hard at the end and saved it. "Next group!" was all Mr. Moyne said. When she heard his voice she thought of how he had whispered in her ear last summer telling her to breathe in as he lifted her in her special part in *Les Sylphides.* The thrill of that moment on stage in her beautiful white costume gave her confidence.

The long waltz combination was Sara's favorite part of class, and she loved the movement Mr. Moyne created for them. It was full of big slides, leaps, jumps and turns in the air, and Sara felt exhilarated, forgetting how tired and thirsty she was. As she waited next to the barre for one of the other groups to finish the combination, she looked at the lake through the tall windows. She saw some of the boys out in sail boats and squinted to see if Hank was one of the boys, but all she got was sun in her eyes. *Pay attention*, she told herself. She had been in class over two hours now. Shannon and Leah were whispering at the barre, looking hot and tired. There was no air conditioning in the dance building and the heat was rising in the woods surrounding the studio. Sara eyed the water fountain just outside the classroom and couldn't wait to feel the ice cold water slipping down her throat.

"For the last part of class," Miss Alexander was saying, "I'd like the first two groups out here on the floor." Sara ran

38

out into the middle of the floor with the others and waited for instruction. "I'd like to see you do sliding chugs all the way across the room. Begin by facing each other in straight rows, put your upstage arm out and your downstage arm back. Lift your upstage leg into arabesque, lower your head and simply scoot your standing foot forward. Do NOT let your back leg fall even a half inch. It must remain straight and high. The lines will pass through each other." She demonstrated the scooting movement with perfect technique. Her feet were beautiful. She was exact, but soft.

Of course, you had to lead with your heel and maintain a good turned-out position while performing this movement, and it is difficult to keep good balance on tiny-soled pointe shoes. The music began and Sara could feel her body trying to fall apart. Her front arm wanted to come down, her back leg wanted to fall, her head wanted to come up. She was tired and struggled to maintain control. The music was a bit familiar, but she couldn't place it. When the lines had successfully passed through each other, Miss Alexander called the next two groups. Sara watched in fascination as the dancers passed through each other to the other side of the room.

"Wow. That is beautiful," Leah said.

"Yes," Shannon said. *"Giselle* is a wonderful ballet."

That was it. *Giselle*! Miss Abbey had taken her class to see National Ballet of Canada perform the second act of *Giselle* last winter. It was one of the old fashioned romantic ballets with long white costumes and a laurel of white flowers in the dancers' hair. And they wore wedding veils over their faces at the beginning because it was about young girls who died before they had a chance to marry. Miss Lee's voice interrupted her thoughts.

"First two groups please," Miss Lee said. Sara pulled herself up tall and anticipated closing bows and a then quick run for the drinking fountain. But it wouldn't be that easy. "We'd like to see bourrées across the room facing front. Right arm overhead, left arm to the side in á la seconde. Take your favorite bow at the end, then sit quietly on the floor. First two groups line up in four rows and begin from stage left. Let's go."

Sara and Shannon put themselves in the second row, and Leah placed herself in the front line again. The music began and Sara tried hard to remember everything Madame had taught her last year about the tiny little running steps on pointe. She pulled herself up using all the muscles in her torso, pressed her shoulders down and tried to pull her body up out of her pointe shoes. As she started across the big room, she could see Madame stopping her, telling her "You pull up but not OUT of your shoes. Do again." She thought of striving for good turn-out so both her heels would show to the audience. Most of all she tried to look like a scholarship winner. She smiled gently in spite of how tired she was and kept her arms soft, the right one circled overhead, the left out to her side. Finally it was over. With the rest of the class, she took a step to the right, put her left foot back, her arms to her sides, and curtsied to Miss Lee, but her eyes were on Miss Alexander who was marking her evaluation form and watching the dancers at the same time. Smart and quick.

"We call that pas de bourrée couru in my school," Shannon said in perfect French as they sat watching the next groups move across the floor.

"In Paris or New York?" Leah wanted to know.

"Both," Shannon said. "It just means little running steps." She sat against the wall under the barre. Her hair looked even lighter under the sun coming in the window. It made Sara miss Erin.

Soon the weary girls were left to wait while the teachers went into Miss Sutton's office to decide how they would divide the dancers in half for the summer. Sara took off her pointe shoes and wiggled her toes. She saw no blood, but she knew she would see some before the summer was out. She stretched out on the floor on her back, legs bent to rest the small of her back, and thought of water. She spotted Mary and Brooke across the room chatting quietly with some younger girls. She saw Charleigh in the center of the room making new friends. She felt her stomach growl and hoped lunch was ready for them in the dining hall. She waited for the teachers to come back.

Finally the door to Miss Sutton's office opened and the dancers stood up. Sara quickly found her soft ballet slippers and slipped them on. She pushed some loose hair back and pulled up her tights. She tried to look as straight and tall as she could. "When you hear your number," Miss Sutton said, "please stand on the left side of the room." *Here goes*, Sara thought. *My fate for the entire summer will be decided by dancing and competing with the girls in my class.* She just had to win a summer scholarship to the New York City Ballet. She just had to.

"Number 45." Miss Sutton called Sara's number first! Everyone watched while she walked to the left of the room. "Number 10." That was Leah, and she ran over and stood next to Sara. Several numbers were called and then number 44, and Shannon walked over. The three smiled at each other.

41

Sara was so excited. Soon there were twenty-four dancers in their group, and Miss Sutton began calling the numbers of the twenty-six girls who were to stand on the right side of the room. Mary, Brooke and Charleigh were called to that group and hugged one another and jumped up and down, delighted it was over and that they were together. Sara felt so hot, and her feet felt so sore.

"Class A," Miss Sutton announced, motioning to Sara's group. "And Class B," she said, opening her arm to the others. Thank you, dancers," Miss Sutton said. "Good class. Please put your numbers on the piano on your way out and pick up a schedule. Make sure you have the right one. We'll see you in class tomorrow morning. Intermediates: Go to lunch and rest. Seniors: Come in." Sara saw Robin, Hillary, Kathy Jacobs and the other senior dancers crowding the doorway, staring at them. But Sara was staring at nothing but the drinking fountain.

"Come on, Shannon," Sara said. "Hurry." They threw their numbers on the piano, grabbed Class A schedules and were the first ones to gulp the ice cold water. Sara took a paper towel she found at the back of the fountain, wet it and slapped it on her forehead. Shannon laughed and stuck one on her forehead. Then they pushed through the seniors and ran down the stairs to the locker room.

Camp Lakewood
Intermediate Division
Class A
June 27 – August 22

Monday	9 am-10:30 am Ballet Studio B Miss Sutton	10:45 am-Noon Tap Studio C Mr. Moyne	Noon-1 pm LUNCH	2:30 pm-3:40 pm Modern Dance Studio A Miss Lee	3:45 pm-5 pm Folk Dance Studio C Mr. Moyne	5:30 pm-6:30 pm DINNER	7 pm-8:30 pm Rehearsal may be called
Tuesday	8:30 am-10am Pointe Studio B Miss Sutton	10:45 am-Noon Folk Dance Studio C Mr. Moyne	Noon-1 pm LUNCH	2 pm-3:30pm Ballet Studio B Miss Sutton	3:50 pm-5:15 pm Modern Dance Studio A Miss Lee	5:30 pm-6:30 pm DINNER	7 pm-8:30 pm Rehearsal may be called
Wednes-day	9 am-10:30 am Ballet Studio B Miss Sutton	10:45 am-Noon Tap Studio C Mr. Moyne	Noon-1 pm LUNCH	2:30 pm-3:40 pm Modern Dance Studio A Miss Lee	3:45 pm-5 pm Folk Dance Studio C Mr. Moyne	5:30 pm-6:30 pm DINNER	.7 pm-8:30 pm Rehearsal may be called
Thurs-day	8:30 am-10 am Pointe Studio B Miss Sutton	10:45 am-Noon Folk Dance Studio C Mr. Moyne	Noon-1 pm LUNCH	2:30 pm-3:40 pm Ballet Studio B Miss Sutton	3:45 pm-5 pm Modern Dance Studio A Miss Lee	5:30 pm-6:30 pm DINNER	7 pm-8:30 pm Rehearsal may be called
Friday	9am-10:30am Ballet Studio B Miss Sutton	10:45 am-Noon Tap Studio C Mr. Moyne	Noon-12:45 pm LUNCH	1 pm-2:30 pm Pointe Studio B Miss Sutton	2:40 pm-3:40pm Modern Dance Studio A Miss Lee	3:50 pm-5 pm Folk Dance Studio C Mr. Moyne	5:30 pm-6:30 pm DINNER No rehearsals
Saturday		10:30 am-Noon Dance History Miss Meisner Music Library	Noon-1 pm LUNCH		Rehearsal may be called	Rehearsal may be called	5:30 pm-6:30 pm DINNER

Sunday No classes/Rehearsal may be called week of performances
Breakfast is served between 6 am and 8 am Monday-Friday
Breakfast is served between 7:30 am and 9:30 am Saturdays and Sundays

CHAPTER FIVE

"Things are Certainly Different"

"Miss Sutton!" Sara exclaimed from her bottom bunk after lunch. "Look at this schedule. We have Miss Sutton for ballet!" She was astonished because Miss Sutton had taught the seniors last year. This could only mean one thing: Miss Alexander would be teaching the seniors. *A lucky break*, Sara thought. This meant she wouldn't have to do all those strange Russian body positions.

"So?" Mary said. "So do we."

Sara looked around at the tired bodies of dancers who didn't care much at this point who their teachers would be starting tomorrow. Even Leah admitted her muscles were a bit sore. "My classes at home are only an hour and fifteen minutes," she said, sitting on the floor. "And I only dance three times a week." She put an apple from the dining hall into one of her pointe shoe boxes she had stored under Charleigh's bunk. Sara noticed Leah's were on the left and Charleigh's on the right. She looked under Brooke's bunk and saw that Brooke and Mary had done the same thing.

"Shannon," Sara said, "where did you put your pointe shoes?"

"In the closet," Shannon said quietly from her bunk over Sara.

"Why don't you put them with mine under my bunk?"

"Oh, no. That's all right," Shannon said. "They're fine." She looked too tired to move.

Sara lay back on her bedroll and felt the peanut butter and jelly sandwich she had gulped down for lunch kind of rolling around in her stomach. She stared at the Class A Intermediate schedule. She would be able to escape the sharp eye of Miss Alexander. She knew she could dance well for Miss Sutton. This was all turning out very well. The rest of the schedule was like last year's except for Dance History on Saturday mornings. *Good*, she thought. *Maybe that will mean not so many Saturday rehearsals.* But she wondered if they would have written exams or papers to write for Dance History.

"I had no idea they'd have us dance so much," Brooke said, looking at her Class B schedule.

"I know," Mary said, "I wanted more time to swim."

"I wanted more time to ski," Charleigh said. Everyone laughed.

"I wanted more time to sleep," Shannon said, plumping the pillow under her head.

"Come on," Leah said. "Let's put up the banner. Where is it, Shannon?"

"Oh, it's in the closet in my suitcase," Shannon said wearily. "I'll get it later."

"I'll get it," Leah said, standing up.

"No," Shannon snapped. "I'll get it later."

46

Leah stared at her for a minute. Sara wondered what was going to happen, but then Leah sat back on the floor. "Well, let's *do* something," she said.

"Guess I'll take a shower," Charleigh said, getting off her bunk.

"I'm going for a swim," Mary said, slowly getting up. She went out to the clothes line to get her bathing suit.

"OK, me too," Brooke said. Charleigh let them go into the bathroom first to change, then she went in and turned on the shower. Sara could hear the water surging out of the shower head and thought it might be nice to take a shower, too. Or maybe she'd go out on the raft. But then she had a better idea. She saw that Shannon had fallen asleep. She'd need to make sure Leah was occupied.

"What are you going to do?" Sara asked Leah. Yesterday she had sounded so eager to go out on the raft.

"I think I'll walk around and try to find the junior and senior cabins and maybe the indoor theatre and the music library." They had to walk past the big outdoor theatre on the lake to get to the dance building, so she had already seen that.

"There's a huge costume room, too," Sara told her. "It's down the hall in the basement of the dance building. It's an amazing place filled with rows and rows of gorgeous costumes. We'll get to choose some for our student concert."

"Student concert?" Leah said, wrinkling her nose. "I didn't see that on the schedule."

There's a lot that's going to happen that isn't on the schedule, Sara thought, remembering the student concert, all the extra performance rehearsals, the horseback ride, the boys' party, and the secret cabin in the woods. "Not everything is on that piece of paper," Sara said. "Just a warning."

"Well, I'm off," Leah said, letting the screen door slap behind her.

Sara looked up at Shannon sleeping peacefully, and put on her shoes. She tip-toed out the door and closed it quietly. She took the path under the tall, swaying fir trees up to the lookout bench. "Wow, look at that," she said out loud, gazing across the bright blue lake to the dense forest beyond the boys camp. She thought of the little deer she and Erin had seen last year when they thought they were lost forever, the horses in the barn, the red tin still in the old cabin. She sighed and began to feel some energy coming back into her body. She couldn't believe it had been a year since she sat on this bench and sobbed because her whole life seemed like a disaster. Robin had twisted her foot when she fell through the plank over the stream because Sara shined a flashlight in her eyes, and that had changed everything for Sara. She had to dance Robin's special part in *Les Sylphides* that she wasn't ready for. She felt pushed beyond her maturity and, although she had triumphed, she was so happy to be in Intermediate Division again this year and to feel confident knowing what to expect. She could be a leader from the beginning. *Leadership, cooperation, enthusiasm, improvement* ran through her head like someone was whispering it to her. At the same time she felt something ghostlike and wispy around her neck and realized she had left her lucky locket in the drawer. She understood that she would have to show cooperation, enthusiasm and improvement along with leadership. Still, she smiled remembering how Miss Sutton had called her number first for Class

A that morning. The leadership part was going to be easy this year, especially with Miss Sutton as her teacher.

Sara touched her neck and looked across the lake where a few boys were gathering wood. She stood up and walked toward the cluster of pine trees that hid the start of the secret path to the boys side. She looked at her watch. She had plenty of time to get down the path, check out the camp and get back up to the bench before anyone knew she was gone. She pushed her way into the underbrush, fern and low-hanging tree branches and was soon lost in the silent green covering as she followed the narrow dirt path. As it wound around the left side of the lake and continued downward, Sara felt the dry path turn mucky and was glad she had worn shoes. *This is where Erin got the picker in her bare foot last summer*, she remembered, *and where she got the poison ivy*. Sara's feet seemed to run downhill by themselves and then she smelled mint and felt the coolness of the stream. She looked downstream and spotted the plank across the water. She listened, but heard no one. She looked around and saw no one. The plank looked safe, and Sara laughed to herself remembering how Charlie the "axe man" who had built the new plank had suddenly appeared last year and frightened her. A wind came up and blew the thick trees overhead and she scurried onto the plank. She knew when she got to the other side she would be off-limits, but she just had to find out if Hank was here.

Sara ran quickly across the plank and jumped onto the slimy bank almost onto a snake. "Ahggggg!" she yelled, jumping back. But the garter snake slithered off as quickly as it had appeared. *Why do I always forget about snakes?* Sara thought, climbing the path upward to the boys camp. Soon she was hiding behind a tree trunk. When she peeked around the tree she saw the big fire pit filled with charred logs, row boats and sail boats tied to the dock, some boys out on their raft, and a couple boys leaping around on the grounds. Then she heard piano music coming from the old horse barn. *What was going on?* She ran and hid behind more trees until she made her way farther back into the woods to the barn. She could still smell the leather saddles and horse manure from when Hank had taken her into the barn last summer. But when she looked up she was surprised to see a big sign over the barn door that said "Woodlake Dance Barn." *What?* she thought, mystified. Then she heard a man's voice yelling out a ballet combination and the music seemed to get louder. "Keep the battu clean and high in the air!" The voice said. "And land softly on your knee. Stay in control on the way down." Landing on your knee was a movement for boys. *Could this be a boys dance camp now?* She heard applause signifying the end of class and pulled back behind the tree trunk as the boys began to file out of the barn. *The dance barn*, she thought. Unless Hank had gone from training to be a camp counselor to training to be a dancer, he would not be here. She stared at the handsome young men making their way to main camp, dance bags over their shoulders. It was almost too surprising to take in. As soon as the teacher and accompanist left the barn, Sara came out from behind the tree and started back down the path to the girls' side of the lake. "Lakewood, Woodlake," she mumbled to herself as she crossed the plank. Clever. But no Hank.

As Sara took the fork in the woods upward toward the lookout bench, she heard footsteps cracking on fallen branches. She looked around quickly, but saw no one. She continued her ascent, but then she heard it again. She stopped. Then she heard Robin's voice. "The old cabin looked just the same," Robin said. "Yeah, acorns and all," Hillary said, laughing. They had already been to the secret cabin in the woods! Sara jumped off the path and hid in the brush to let Robin and Hillary go ahead, and when she saw them, she gasped. Robin was carrying the red tin. Her red tin. The red tin she and Erin had left up in the rafters of the old cabin. She honestly could not remember if Robin and Hillary had known about the tin last year. She and Erin had kept it a secret stashed under Erin's bunk behind all of their pointe shoe boxes. Maybe they thought it had been left in the cabin by deer hunters. But one thing was certain: if they had been to the secret cabin, they had been to the boys camp, too.

As soon as the girls passed and Sara knew they had probably gone past the lookout bench, she got back on the path. She sat on the bench picturing the mementos she and Erin had stored in the red tin: the dance programs, the dried flowers, the poem from Hank. She was going to share the empty tin with Shannon this summer, but now it was gone. She thought about the boys dance camp, the barn converted to dance studios, the music coming from the building where the horses had been stabled. The absence of Hank. The summer felt like the gift of a fresh start at the same time it felt like she had been robbed. Things were certainly different.

CHAPTER SIX

"First Lesson"

One thing that was the same was the way sunshine flooded Studio B in the morning. As the seniors made the ceiling rafters shake dancing in the large studio above them, Sara smiled as she stood at the barre and saw the sun painting the wood floor in that familiar crystal-morning clarity. She was glad to be downstairs in the smaller studio with Shannon next to her and all the dancers wearing any color leotard they wanted today. Miss Sutton entered the room and Sara quickly placed her left hand on the barre and moved her feet into first position ready to begin pliés. Then she noticed some of the dancers were in fifth position, including Shannon, who had placed herself first in line at the barre. When the class turned to the other side, Leah would be first. It was a responsibility Sara always avoided. Some dancers caught on to an exercise the first time, but Sara was always afraid she wouldn't. Better to be safe.

"Good morning, dancers, Miss Sutton smiled, her long legs in black pants that matched her leotard and glistening hair. She took roll, introduced the accompanist at the piano, and they began. Miss Sutton did not use a cane to push against their feet and legs as Madame had, but her succinct words with sharp British accent had the same effect. "Press the knees back." "Push the heel forward, *forward.*" "I want a perfectly flat back as you come up from the port a bras over to the floor." "Press your heels into the floor on the count of five, not six." "Keep the leg turned-out in balençoire, this is not just a leg swing! You are ballet dancers." As they neared the end of the barre exercises, Sara was perspiring.

"Morning Coffee," Miss Sutton requested from the accompanist. *What could that possibly be?* Sara wondered. "This is a little warm-up I created for the hip. If done correctly, it lets you feel the difference between being turned-in and properly turned-out. Begin in fifth position. Left hand on the barre. Give me sur le coup de pied, fifth position, retiré, fifth position, throw the leg high to the side, plié bending the thrown leg and crossing it turned in over the standing leg, then throw the leg out to the side again and back into fifth position. Four times each side." The accompanist played the introduction to a fast tango and they began. What a mess. Miss Sutton stopped them in the "middle of the muddle". Clearly some of the dancers did not know that sur le coup de pied meant to place your foot near your ankle and that retiré meant to point that foot at the knee. And of the girls who did understand it, some placed the foot in a wrapped position just above the ankle and some placed it in front of the ankle. Of the dancers who knew to place the foot at the knee, some placed it under the front of the knee while others placed it at the side of the knee. No one seemed to have the timing right. Even with Shannon leading, the class fell apart.

"Sara," Miss Sutton said, "center-floor." Sara could feel her heart beating quickly. *Please let me do it correctly*, she thought, wondering if this was part of her responsibility as a scholarship winner. She was glad Madame had taught her how to place her foot properly near her ankle and knee last year. The tango music began and Sara went through the exercise with no barre, trying hard to keep her posture straight and her turn-out secure. She remembered to use her torso muscles to keep her balance, and her arms rounded to her sides. "Good," Miss Sutton said. "But do it again and bring both feet completely flat on the floor when in fifth position. A bit faster," she told the accompanist. Sara was nervous as she tried to keep her balance, perform all the fine points perfectly and keep up with the music. "Now these corrections are for everybody," Miss Sutton said. "Really wrap that foot around the upper ankle," she said. "And keep the knee pressed back hard with the heel coming forward more on the retiré." She watched carefully as Sara wrapped her foot and then pressed her knee back as she pointed at the side of her knee. "Good. Now everyone again," Miss Sutton said. As Sara returned to the barre, feeling a bit dismayed about her performance and the responsibility of being a scholarship winner, Miss Sutton opened a window letting in a little breeze off the lake.

Miss Sutton led them through the English version of three arabesques that were completely foreign to Sara. *Oh, great*, Sara thought, trying to keep her balance. *No Russian body positions, but strange English arabesques.* Shannon seemed to catch on quickly to the English style and did the arabesques all perfectly and gracefully. She never seemed nervous. Always poised. And Leah, once again, led the class in the allegro.

She seemed to be the queen of fast footwork. It was amazing. She understood the combinations the first time Miss Sutton explained them. Her jumps were clean and her beats were quick and clear. By the time Miss Sutton ended the class in grand revérénce, Sara was relieved it was over.

The locker room was buzzing with confusion. "I didn't know half that stuff we did at the barre," someone said.

"She goes too fast. How can she expect us to get it so quickly?" someone else said.

"I'm not used to those arm positions," another girl said practically in tears.

Sara knew it would get harder, but somehow easier at the same time. "Come on," she said. "We only have five minutes to get to tap class." She threw her ballet slippers into her locker, grabbed her tap shoes and led the way down the hall to Studio C.

Mr. Moyne greeted them at the door. There was music with a strong beat playing in the studio behind him. Sara couldn't wait to just have fun in his class. "Sara," Mr. Moyne said as she approached him. Shannon walked past her into the classroom. Sara smiled at Mr. Moyne, but was still a bit embarrassed about how long it had taken her last year to coordinate the lift with him in her special part in *Les Sylphides*. "Good to see you. Nice to have you back at Lakewood."

Sara felt special. "Thank you," she answered.

"I have a nice solo in mind for you in the folk dance for the final performance or maybe a duet."

"Great," Sara said. She remembered how beautiful the Junior Division costumes were for their folk dance last year. Long ribbons hanging down their backs, bright skirts, flowers in their hair. Still, no matter how good the part she got, it wouldn't be on pointe. She was starting to think she should have enrolled in the Senior Division. She just had to stand out in ballet to get that New York City Ballet scholarship. Maybe she had already learned her first lesson.

CHAPTER SEVEN

"Change is Good"

"Finally," Sara said. "Salad for lunch! Dancer food." She smiled, taking a big bite of the grilled chicken from the top.

"Yuk!" Leah said. "I'd rather have a hamburger."

Sara thought she'd like to lose a couple of pounds to look taller. But she could hear Miss Abbey saying to eat healthy foods *always*. Nothing wrong with chicken salad and iced tea, she told herself, but then she couldn't resist a bit of ice cream for dessert. When Sara had almost finished, Shannon nudged her arm.

"Grab a pear from the big bowl on the way out," Shannon said. "Let's go."

Sara was in no rush. Modern dance class didn't start for over an hour and she wasn't looking forward to it. "What's the rush?" she asked, listening to Brooke, Mary and Charleigh talking about how much they loved their morning classes. They laughed and seemed to take everything so lightly. Leah finished two peanut butter cookies and left, saying she was going out on the raft.

"Come on," Shannon coaxed again. They cleared their trays, grabbed pears and walked back to Pavlova cabin. No one was there. Shannon went to the closet and brought out her suitcase. She opened it and brought out the blank paper banner, then she reached back in and brought out a bright blue tin. It was round and shiny and the same size as the red one from last year.

"This is for you," Shannon announced. "Open it before someone comes."

Sara popped the lid open, pushed back the shiny tin foil and stared at home made chocolate chip cookies. "Wow," Sara whispered. "You made these?"

"There's a note under the foil at the bottom," Shannon said, glancing out the big side window to see if the other girls were coming.

Sara quickly found the note. "It's from Erin!" The note said, *"I hope you & Shannon enjoy the cookies and fill the tin with this summer's memories."* She wasn't ready to tell Shannon about the secret path, the old cabin, the taking of the red tin. She thought it might be better to keep it to herself all summer. But now they were the official Blue Tin Club. They each took a cookie and were chewing when the door suddenly swung open.

"Mail call!" It was Julie Hess, their counselor. She barely looked at them; just threw a couple of letters onto the chest of drawers and shut the door again. "Everybody passed the water test!" she shouted as she walked off the porch steps.

"That was close," Sara said, putting the note from Erin in the tin. "Hurry. Put your pointe shoe boxes next to mine. We'll put the tin behind the boxes." Shannon took the suitcase to the closet and returned with several boxes and Sara helped her shove them under the bunk. Then she hid the blue tin behind them. They put their pears on the chest of drawers and looked over the mail. Nothing for them. One letter each for Mary and Brooke. She put the letters on their beds and turned to Shannon. "Want to put up the banner?"

Erin had sent thumbtacks and different color markers. Sara helped Shannon tack the long, blank paper along the outside of the bathroom wall where it had hung last year. They stood back and looked at it. "Soon it will be filled with stick figures and notes and pictures," Sara said. "Ura!" She yelled, raising her arm. "Ura for Pavlova cabin! That means—"

"Hoorah in Russian," Shannon said. "Erin told me." Sara was wondering what else Erin had told her when Leah came in dripping under her beach towel.

"Hey, the banner's up," she smiled. "Great!" She grabbed a red marker and walked toward the banner. "Do you mind if I write my name on it?"

"Well," Shannon said carefully, "why don't we wait until everyone is here?"

"Oh," Leah said, dropping the red marker. "Sure." She seemed OK about it and went into the bathroom. Leah certainly seemed happiest when she was the one organizing things. Sara liked her a lot and admired her energy and her dancing. By the time all the other girls returned to the cabin, it was time for Sara, Shannon and Leah to go to modern dance class. *Here we go again,* Sara thought, trying to remember what it felt like to dance with bare feet, to let her body go off center and to roll on the floor. She thought how well her modern dance piece for the student concert had finally turned out last year, especially after she and Erin had joined forces with Robin and Hillary. She could move that way again, she told herself, and be even better this year. But when she got on her modern leotard and footless tights and took her place on the floor in the big studio, she was confronted with another change.

Miss Diane Lee had studied for many years in New York learning the Alwin Nikolais method of modern dance. "Wipe your slate clean, she told them as they sat cross-legged on the floor, backs straight. "This technique is completely different from anything you have ever been taught. Clear your mind of any other type of movement you have done."

How many ways were there to move? Sara wondered. She thought she had learned most of them in Miss Casey's class last year.

"You will learn the difference between thick and thin, heavy and light, fast and slow, large and small, wild and tame. You will learn how to work on the periphery, with volume, touching body parts, with rhythmic interplay. You will learn sculpturing and pulsing." Sara tried to visualize these things.

"You will learn to fill this room with the effect your body has on space and you will understand the effect of space on your body. You will learn to move across the floor using a specific type of energy and you will learn how to put together movement phrases. You will learn the Nikolais warm-up sequence and memorize it. We will begin."

They spent an hour learning the first half of the warm-up movements with Miss Lee demonstrating, talking about them in detail and walking around the class coaching individual dancers. Miss Lee explained that once they had mastered the correct technique for the complete series of warm-ups, the class would be expected to perform all of them, from stretches to a plié series center-floor within forty-five minutes and without her help. The rest of the class would be spent on learning and executing a concept of Nikolais movement vocabulary. In the last part of class Miss Lee sat on a stool in front of the mirror beating a small drum and calling out the warm-ups they had learned so far. Sara didn't know if she should concentrate on doing each movement as accurately as she could or focus on just remembering them in correct order. Leah and Shannon seemed to know the order of the sequence already. Sara did the best she could and got through it watching other people out of the corner of her eye. *So far, so good,* she thought when Miss Lee excused them.

"Let's go to the music library tonight and see if they have any paper or notebooks," she said to Shannon in the locker room. "I want to write all this down before I forget it."

"You won't forget," Leah said cheerily as she slammed her locker door shut and put on her character shoes for folk class. "Hurry up," she said. "Five minutes to get to folk class."

"Just let your body remember it," Shannon said. "It's called muscle memory."

"I know what it's called," Sara said. She sat on the bench and strapped on her character shoes. "I just have trouble doing it." It seemed like a strange technique. After all, it began with slapping your own face, neck, chest and thighs to awaken the sensitive parts of the body. *Strange,* Sara said to herself. *Strange.* But, as her mom always said, "Change is good." *Right,* Sara thought.

CHAPTER EIGHT

"Miss Sutton's Challenge"

Folk dance was exhausting after the tension of Miss Lee's class. Mr. Moyne's energy seemed high, his taped music lively, and the patterns across the floor a bit confusing. "This line goes inside that line," he corrected as the dancers wove in and out of each other. They wore long, full practice skirts and he showed them how to twirl in them. Sara was glad folk class would be in the morning tomorrow. She always danced better early in the day.

After class she sat on the locker room bench and watched Shannon put her things into her dance bag. Their first full day of the summer program was over. It wasn't going be as easy as she had hoped, scholarship winner or not. She unfolded her Class A schedule and saw that ballet class wasn't until two o'clock in the afternoon tomorrow. She'd have to save some energy after pointe and folk in the morning. She realized she was starving and hoped there would be something delicious for dinner. The six cabin mates sat at Pavlova table too tired to talk while they ate. Sara's concession to trying to eat less was that she ate only half a piece of apple pie. She looked over at Robin and Hillary who were sipping their lemon water for dessert. *I wonder what they did with the red tin*, she thought. Then she remembered the pretty blue tin Erin had sent and didn't care.

"Let's go to the music library," Sara said to Shannon. She still wanted something to write her modern dance notes on. Sara had a little trouble finding it, although she had told Shannon she remembered exactly where it was. By the time they got there it was closed. "Great," she said. "I really have to write that stuff down tonight."

"Never mind," Shannon said. "Let's go down to the beach and I'll do it with you."

So they spent the next hour in the sand going over all the movements they had learned that day. When Sara finally lay down in her bedroll that night she went over them in her mind again wearing her lucky locket, but kept messing them up. But when Julie Hess called "Lights out!" at ten o'clock, Sara was already asleep.

In the morning she had to wake up Shannon for their eight-thirty pointe class. Everyone else was gone. By the time they got to the dining hall, breakfast was being cleared away. They would have to get up earlier from now on. They drank some juice and ate peanut butter toast on the way to the dance building. Sara pushed extra pins into her bun as they made their way down the hall to Studio B. Miss Sutton was just about to close the door. Shannon took her place at the end of the barre. Sara ran across the room to get a spot in the middle of the barre, but no one moved to let her in. She went quickly to end of the barre. Like it or not, she would be second leader this morning. She watched Shannon closely when they did each movement on the first side, then tried hard to remember it when they turned to do it on the other side. But during the quick tendu combination she realized she had forgotten to take off her locket. She lost her focus for a second and made a mistake, throwing off some of the dancers behind her who must have been relying on her.

"Leah," Miss Sutton said quietly, pointing Sara's way, "move to the end of the barre." Sara cringed as Leah took a place in front of her. So much for leadership today. The rest of the barre went smoothly and Sara managed to take off the locket before they started the center-floor movements. Miss Sutton worked them hard on bourrées again and had them work in pairs doing a little battu step in a circle, arms up, their hands touching. The music reminded Sara of the bourrées they did in the audition class. Then Miss Sutton had them try the chugs across the room, one line at a time. They finished the class with arabesques en pointe, then took their bows. "See you for ballet this afternoon," Miss Sutton said. "Be on time." Miss Sutton was too English-polite, Sara thought, to look at her and Shannon when she said it, but Sara knew it was meant for them.

Folk, as Sara suspected, was much more fun for her in the morning. Mr. Moyne seemed to love her dancing, and placed her in the front row. When he tried some new steps, he organized the first line of the first group to include Sara, Leah, Shannon and a girl named Alene Kay. The four worked well together and were almost the same height. Alene's hair was the same color as Shannon's, and she was just as poised. Shannon invited Alene to have lunch at Pavlova table, and Charleigh agreed to eat at Baryshnikov table in Alene's place. Charleigh made lots of new friends and Sara learned that Alene was from Chicago.

"Chicago," Sara said to her over a tuna fish sandwich. "There is a girl in the Senior Division named Robin Stewart from Chicago."

"I know," Alene said. "She dances at my home studio. She's kind of our star."

Sara could hardly believe it. First Shannon dancing with Erin in New York and now Alene dancing with Robin in Chicago. Sara looked over at Robin and caught her eye. Robin waved at them, then went back to her lunch.

"Small world," Brooke said, shrugging her shoulders. Mary giggled. Alene and Leah said they wanted to practice the Nikolais warm-ups with Sara and Shannon before their two o'clock ballet class, so they found Studio C open in the dance building and took off their shoes to begin. Just as they got started, the office secretary, Mrs. Lane, came to the doorway.

"What's going on?" Mrs. Lane wanted to know.

"We're practicing modern dance," Leah said, looking up at her.

"Sorry. Not allowed. You have to get special permission to use a classroom during the day. Do you have a note?"

"No," Leah said. "We didn't know."

"Well, now you do," Mrs. Lane said, pointing to the doorway. She was not smiling. "And, by the way, you are supposed to leave your shoes upstairs at the front door or in a locker. You should know *that*." She stared at them like they were regular people, not dancers. Like they hadn't won a scholarship or paid a lot of money to come here. *Cooperation*, Sara thought, *cooperation*. Feeling leadership, she apologized for them all. They grabbed their shoes and left quickly, Mrs. Lane watching them until they got to the top of the stairs.

It would be onward through the afternoon of ballet and then modern dance without the benefit of extra practice.

Sara was careful to place herself in the middle of the barre for ballet and totally enjoyed the class. She liked Miss Sutton's large waltz combinations and felt almost as wonderful as she had in Yuri's master class last year, light and joyful. After leaps across the room but before they took their bows, Miss Sutton asked them to sit on the floor. "I have exciting news," she began. "Some members of the New York City Ballet are coming to Lakewood in four weeks." The girls who hadn't known about this gasped in delight. "They will be performing a Balanchine piece from their repertory and the seniors will perform Act Two of *Giselle* for them. Sara knew it would be in the small indoor theatre named for Balanchine where last year's performance of *Les Slyphides* had been. She sighed, remembering the San Francisco Ballet's inspiring performance there of the Second Act of *Swan Lake*. How handsome Yuri had been on the stage, how wonderful a master teacher!

"There might be room for a few of you to be in *Giselle*," Miss Sutton said, looking around at them. Sara tried to look enthusiastic. She would give *anything* to be in it. "We'll see. I will give you some more movements from the ballet and see how you do. Grand révérence now." As Sara took her bows she thought about how great class had been, but then remembered her mistake in pointe class this morning and being caught in Studio C trying to practice modern. She wondered if Mrs. Lane knew her name.

There was no time to worry about it. She had just enough time to get upstairs to Studio A, brush her hair into a pony tail and pull her tights back to expose bare feet before Miss Lee began beating her drum. Here goes, Sara worried as she sat up tall on the floor with the bottoms of her feet together and began the Nikolais warm-ups. Miss Lee called out each exercise, but it was up to the class to remember how to do each of them, and when they got to chest lifts from a flat back position, Miss Lee began walking around the room. "Lift from the sternum," she shouted, drumming louder to keep them in count. "Not the lower rib cage." She bent over to help someone. Sara tried to feel the difference. "Use a sharper gesture when lifting the chest," she said. "Roll forward over your legs smoothly and come up with a *straight* back, arms in front of you." Sara tried to show the difference between a rounded back and straight back as Miss Casey had taught her last year. Miss Lee was next to her. To Sara's surprise, she complimented her. "Good," she said. "What's your name?" Sara told her and Miss Lee moved on to another dancer. *Hmmm...,* Sara thought, m*aybe quality could triumph over memory.*

Miss Lee taught them the rest of the warm-up exercises before the end of class and charged them with remembering the entire sequence for the next day. Over dinner when Leah and Shannon complained about how difficult class had been, Sara realized that she had actually enjoyed it in spite of her fear. But who knew what would happen tomorrow.

CHAPTER NINE

"The Cookies and the Missing Locket"

At eight-thirty every night the counselors lit the torches along the grassy bluff above the lake. Sara and Shannon sat on the dining hall steps and watched the orange flames dancing in the cool breeze. "Just think," Shannon said, "our first class doesn't start until nine o'clock tomorrow morning. We can sleep in."

"Problem is," Sara said, "breakfast ends at eight."

"I refuse to be prisoner to that rule," Shannon said. "Especially when they don't even have croissants or coffee au lait."

"This is the woods of northern Michigan," Sara reminded her. "Not Paris."

"I will start keeping food in the cabin," Shannon said.

"Where will you keep it?" Sara wanted to know. "Don't you want some good hot food before you start dancing for four hours?"

"I will keep it in the blue tin," Shannon stated with resolve. "I need my sleep. An apple, a pear, some brie will be OK."

"Brie?" Sara laughed. "I think the cheese will be cheddar from Pinconning, Michigan. And we don't keep food in the blue tin, only memories like flower petals and dance programs."

"Whatever," Shannon replied, waving her hand in the evening air. "But let's go to the cabin now and offer the cookies to everyone so we don't eat them all. We must be thin." Sara wanted to wait until they could be alone in the cabin so the tin would remain their secret. Shannon didn't seem to understand.

"We are the only members of the Blue Tin Club, Shannon," Sara stressed. "We put special items from the summer into the tin, then at the end of camp we go someplace secret and divvy the things up between the two of us." She still wasn't ready to tell Shannon about the secret cabin in the woods.

"Then let's go to the cabin now," Shannon said. "The girls usually stay outside walking the grounds or visiting other cabins until about nine." She got up and began walking down the steps. Sara followed her. Shannon was right. They were alone to retrieve the tin and to put the cookies out on the chest of drawers. They looked good sitting on top of the tin foil next to the pears. The girls lay on their bunks waiting for their cabin mates to get back so they could see their happy faces when they found the cookies. Shannon was engrossed in a book written in French and Sara thought about the English style arabesques, the chugging step, and the Nikolais warmups. She knew now that it was pronounced "Nik-o-lie." She got up to get her locket for good luck, but when she opened the drawer, it was gone. She suddenly remembered taking it off in Miss Sutton's class that morning and putting it on the floor under the barre where she had been standing. She looked at the clock next to the cookies and the pears. It was almost nine. She was pretty sure that last summer the dance building was locked at nine. She had to sneak in and get the locket before someone found it in the morning. "I'll be right back," she said to Shannon, and took off out the door.

There was only one light on in the dance building. She took off her shoes and put them near the front door. She'd have to go all the way downstairs, through the locker room, and down the long hall to Studio B. As she padded quietly down the hall, she heard music. The secret practice room! But when she stopped and listened again she knew it was coming from Studio B. She walked quietly toward the music and her locket. The door was closed, but she heard a man's voice. It was the teacher's voice from Woodlake Dance Barn. She pressed her ear against the door. Now she heard Miss Alexander speaking. She couldn't quite make out what they were saying, but, for sure, she wouldn't be able to get the locket. She tip-toed back down the hall, through the locker room and up the stairs. She slipped into her shoes without tying them, and ran along the side of the building toward the back. Though it wasn't completely dark outside, a full moon floated over the lake lighting the trees and grounds around her. She tried to hide among the wild brush as she made her way to the Studio B window.

The window was a bit too high. Sara quickly looked around and found a big rock to stand on. When she peered in she saw Miss Alexander in pointe shoes dancing quick steps with the man. She ducked when she thought they looked her way. Then she shoved the heavy rock over so she could see the part of the barre where she had stood that morning. There, on the floor, was the locket glistening in the light of the room. It looked so close, yet Sara knew there was no chance of getting it back tonight. She'd have to be the first one in the studio in the morning. As she walked back to Pavlova cabin, she took a moment to gaze at the torches in the darkening sky. She thought of how David had tried to kiss her on the dock after the student concert last year when Hank was inside dancing with Robin. She looked across the lake and felt relieved that it looked like she would have no boy trouble this year. She would be able to focus completely on dance.

When she got back to the cabin the girls were eating the cookies. "Oh, good," Leah smiled. "You're here. Where were you?"

Sara thought fast. "I went back to get my class schedule. I left it in one of the lockers, but the building was closed."

"Is this it?" Brooke asked, taking it off Sara's bunk.

"Oh, I didn't see it there," Sara said, putting it in her dance bag.

"OK," Leah directed. "Everyone on the floor. We're going to start the banner now." Leah looked at Shannon who produced the color markers. She must have agreed.

"Here's the plan," Leah said. "Everybody pick a color." She threw the markers in the center of the circle and quickly grabbed the red one. Mary and Charleigh both went for the bright pink, and Mary let Charleigh have it. By then Shannon had the green, Brooke had the blue and Sara had the yellow. That left purple for Mary. "Now everyone write their name on the banner. All achievements will be posted under each name."

"Wait," Sara said. She walked over to the banner and wrote across the top in all different colors: *Leadership-Cooperation-Enthusiasm-Improvement*. Now they would know what they were working for. Then she wrote "Ura!"

"What does that 'ura' mean?" Mary asked.

"That means 'Hoorah' in Russian," Sara answered. "We learned it from our Russian ballet teacher last year. And Pavlova cabin had a lot to hoorah about. We had two scholarship winners and great performances. We also learned to work together for good results." As soon as the words were out of Sara's mouth, she got the wispy feeling around her neck again. And after they had all written their names on the banner and most of them were asleep, Sara knew the feeling was the special necklace of pearls. The dance spirits of old had found her again. "Good night," she said dreamily to Shannon who was still reading her book.

"Good night," Leah mumbled.

CHAPTER TEN

"Mrs. Lane Adds Trouble"

"Where did you go last night?" Shannon asked Sara at the ballet barre in the morning. Her plan had worked to eat a pear for breakfast, but her eyes still looked sleepy.

"I came here to get my locket. I left it under the barre in pointe class yesterday, but when I got here the building was already locked." She wasn't sure if she should tell Shannon about Miss Alexander and the boys' teacher rehearsing. She didn't know if she should tell her about the dance camp for boys.

"Oh," Shannon said. "Did you get it this morning?" Sara had been the first one in the room, but it was gone.

"Nope," Sara said, wondering where it was and if she'd ever see it again. After tap class on the way to lunch Shannon suggested they put up a sign in the locker room about the lost locket. Sara did not want to do that and risk Miss Sutton finding out that she had worn it to class in the first place.

They went out on the raft after lunch. They had over an hour before their modern class. "Do you have a boyfriend in Paris?" Sara asked.

Shannon smiled. "No, but I have a friend who is a boy in New York. He dances in my ballet class and he takes classes at the Nikolais school."

"What's his name?"

"Jackson," Shannon answered. "He's here this summer, too. Right across the lake." So Shannon knew all along that it was a dance camp for boys over there! "He is getting a modern class from Miss Lee there, too."

"We're not allowed over there," Sara said. "It's off-limits."

"Of course, I know," Shannon said. "We could maybe take a boat out in the lake, though?"

The pendulum began to swing inside Sara. The boys, the dancing, the boys, the scholarship…. "Maybe," she answered before easing off the ladder into the lake.

Her third Nikolais class was more difficult that the first two. Miss Lee sat on her stool beating her drum and counting, expecting them to go through the complete set of warm-ups entirely on their own. Sara tried to follow the others to make sure she was with everyone, but it was too hard to put your head down where it was supposed to be and see other people. Besides, she wanted to look good, like she knew what she was doing. If only she could find a way to write all these exercises down. She promised herself she would go to the music library for paper before dinner that night, right after folk class ended at five. Meanwhile, she enjoyed the concept they learned in class on carving volume in space. It was fun learning to focus attention inside her own personal space, rather than smiling for an audience. It was interesting and challenging to pretend to watch her hands, legs and arms expressing circles of space getting larger or smaller. She could carry it along with her foot, her elbow, her hand. She could pass it to the dancer next to her. She loved learning to walk in lines across the big studio frontward, switching to walking sideways and then backward, shifting her weight so it was always over the balls of her feet. She loved the demands Miss Lee made on them to be in a state of readiness, with their bodies prepared to move in any direction at any time, alert and clear. She loved learning to walk at different heights and with different energies. If only she could stop making mistakes in the long warm-up exercises, she might have a chance of impressing Miss Lee. You had to look good in every class to win a scholarship. It was all based on the teachers exchanging information, even the guest teachers.

In folk class Mr. Moyne already seemed to be setting choreography on them for the final performance. He kept trying out different floor patterns from zig-zag lines to circles and squares. The steps were easy. Sara didn't see anything demanding enough to warrant a scholarship win. Toward the end of class, he had them sit under the barre and called Sara out along with Shannon, Leah, Alene and a girl named Keera. He played a certain part of the taped music and demonstrated a tricky pattern of quick steps and turns for them to try. He brought tambourines out of the closet and showed them how to tap them over their heads while performing the steps. Sara thought it showed promise to be entertaining, but it didn't seem hard. Then he asked half the class to stand and perform a swaying step behind Leah, Shannon, Alene and Keera, leaving Sara out. Finally, the remainder of the class was asked to make a line in front of the four. Eventually, the line behind and in front of the four girls made a circle and danced around them while they twirled. All the skirts were flying with the lively music. Then Mr. Moyne taught Sara some steps that might become the first part of her solo. It was a nice way to end the day of classes.

Sara put her character shoes into her locker, threw her dance bag over her shoulder and headed toward the stairs. She had to get some paper at the music library before it closed.

"Hey," Shannon hollered after her, "wait for me." But Shannon was too slow. Sara had to get over there.

"I'll see you at dinner!" Sara told her, running for the stairs. But in the hall upstairs Mrs. Lane appeared in the doorway of her office.

"Sara," Mrs. Lane said. Sara stopped on her heels. So Mrs. Lane did know her name. She waited for something awful to happen.

"Is this yours?" Mrs. Lane held up her locket.

"Yes," Sara nodded, happy to see it.

"Come into my office," Mrs. Lane said, motioning for Sara to move past her. Sara found a chair in front of her desk. The phone rang and Sara had to wait until Mrs. Lane finished a conversation with the seamstress. "Sara," Mrs. Lane began. But then Mr. Moyne came to the door and asked Mrs. Lane something about his schedule for tomorrow. Sara looked up at the clock. She'd have to walk all the way across camp, get the paper, and make it back quickly if she was going to get to the dining room in time for dinner. And she was starving, as usual, after a full afternoon of dancing. "Sara," Mrs. Lane began again. Sara saw Shannon and Leah walk out of the building on their way to dinner. "You know, the rule is that dancers aren't allowed to wear jewelry to class."

"Yes. I know. I had it on the night before and forgot to take it off." She wondered how Mrs. Lane knew it was hers.

"Well, for a scholarship winner, you certainly are forgetting a lot of things." Especially the Nikolais dance warm-ups, Sara thought, eager to get the paper to write them down. But she remembered *cooperation* again and said she was sorry. Again.

"It was a good thing I found your name inside the locket, so I knew it was yours. Shall I keep it for you for the summer, or can you remember not to wear it to class?" Sara didn't like to think of Mrs. Lane fooling around with her special locket, but she was polite. She had to get out of there.

"I'll take it. Thank you for returning it to me," Sara smiled, holding out her hand. But Mrs. Lane answered the phone again and held up her finger to indicate Sara would have to wait. Sara looked up at the clock again.

"All right," Mrs. Lane finally said to Sara, handing her the locket. "Now hurry to dinner." She stood at the door watching Sara, who had to turn right toward the dining hall now instead of left to the music library.

That night after she had thought through the Nikolais warm-ups in her bunk and everyone else was asleep, she quietly put her locket in the blue tin.

CHAPTER ELEVEN

"Miss Alexander's Visit"

Sara felt stronger, sharper and sturdier in Thursday morning pointe class. She could anticipate some of Miss Sutton's combinations and was beginning to understand her expectations. She was getting used to the barre and center-floor, the music and the tempos. She was looking forward to Mr. Moyne's folk class next, and was even resigned to star in his final performance choreography. Then Miss Alexander paid a visit.

"Everyone. Everyone!" Miss Sutton said, clapping her hands. The dancers stood still and the music stopped. Miss Alexander came into the room, nodded to Miss Sutton and sat on a chair next to the piano. The trusty clipboard was in her hand again. Sara looked at Shannon, but Shannon was paying close attention to Miss Sutton. Sara knew Miss Alexander was scouting for high-level intermediate dancers for her production of *Giselle*. After all, Sara knew, just being a senior didn't automatically make you a better dancer than a very good intermediate. She stood tall, fastened some loose hair and listened.

"Small groups," Miss Sutton said. She pointed at Shannon, then at Leah, Alene, Sara and Keera. "First group," she announced. "The rest of you form groups and be ready." The class divided itself quickly behind the first group. "Miss Alexander *might* invite a few of you to dance in *Giselle*," she said cautiously. "First group center-floor." But instead of asking for a familiar step, Miss Sutton demonstrated a movement kneeling on the floor with the front foot turned out. "Now show me a beautiful port a bras," Miss Sutton said, placing her left arm to the side and lavishly sweeping her right arm all around her body from the side, over her head, leaning her body backward, opening the arm and letting it flow back to the side. The music was soft and romantic. Sara thought it would be easy to make a big circle around her head, but Miss Sutton pushed them to fulfill the sweeping movement and she demanded complete unison. "You must show that you can be totally and exactly together," she said, moving Shannon's arm into place. "The arm is here on the count of three and here on six. Be aware of the dancers around you. Stay together." Sara saw Miss Alexander marking her chart, and tried to make her port a bras large and to show a softness of the arm that she thought Madame would demand. "Next group," Miss Sutton said.

Sara watched Miss Alexander as she observed the next groups, trying to figure out who she might choose, but there was no clue. She smiled a bit at Sara's group during bourrées in a big circle, but Sara couldn't tell if it was for the entire group, or just one or two of them. Finally, they performed the difficult scooting step. "Keep your foot on the floor turned-out," Miss Sutton coached. "Lead with your heel. Keep that back leg up." Sara was trying so hard to move forward without losing her turn-out or dropping her arabesque leg that she felt stiff. She wished she could look at the dancers next to her to make sure she was moving in unison with them and to see Miss Alexander's face. She just kept looking at the floor and scooting. When her line had passed through the line coming toward them and she lifted her head, she saw a worried look on Miss Sutton's face. Sara saw some feet scooting on the floor without much turn-out and more than one leg bobbing up and down. She could just hear Madame making a funny comment like, "You not pump. I don't need water. I need dancer." She was so giddy from being tired and the pressure of dancing in front of Miss Alexander that she almost giggled out loud. Miss Alexander was still watching the dancers closely, but was not making so many marks on her chart. Perhaps she had made her decisions.

When the class assembled for grand révérence, Sara ran quickly to the front row with Leah and Keera and tried to stay exactly with them through each bow. Unison was, apparently, important for *Giselle*. In the mirror, she saw Shannon behind her standing next to Alene. Sara pulled herself up tall and felt the whole class moving with her in every breath she took. She felt a surge of confidence, but she saw that Miss Alexander was watching Shannon. Then the piano music stopped and Miss Sutton excused them.

All through folk Sara tried not to think of pointe class and *Giselle*, but she worried about the scoots and the bourrées, the port de bras and the grand révérence. She wondered when the list of chosen dancers would be posted on the bulletin board next to Mrs. Lane's office. Being in that ballet might be not only a magnificent experience, but her only chance at getting the summer scholarship to the New York

City Ballet school. She thought of how much her dancing had improved last summer after dancing in *Les Slyphides* and was sure it was the most important thing that helped her win the second place scholarship back to Lakewood.

"Sara!" Mr. Moyne shouted across the room. "You missed your entrance. Pay attention. Again please." He stopped and started the recorded music. Sara wondered why he had begun his choreography for the final performance so early in the summer. He kept giving her steps, then changing them. She was sure today would be no exception. She got it right the second time and he was happy, but by the end of class he had changed her steps all over again. "Try this," he said, demonstrating a click of the heels and pretending to spread a full skirt like the one Sara wore. She obeyed and tried to smile. How would she ever be able to make this part look bigger and more difficult than it was? She was starting to feel trapped in a technique level beneath her abilities and felt again that she had made a mistake in choosing to be in Intermediate Division. Then she thought of taking class next to Robin each day and some of the older dancers and she wasn't sure. Winning a part in *Giselle* was her only answer.

"You better start paying attention in there," Leah said on the way to lunch.

"Come on," Sara said to Shannon. "Let's go see if the music library is open." Leah headed to the dining hall. When they got to the library there was a sign on the door that said it was closed for lunch. "Unbelievable," Sara said. "My paper luck is so bad."

"I'm hungry," Shannon said. "Let's go eat before *they* close for lunch. We can try again later." As they stepped off the porch of the old building Sara thought she saw a boy walking on the path that led through the Junior Division grounds, but when she looked again she saw nothing but trees.

At lunch Sara overheard Robin and Kathy talking about *Giselle*. "I want to dance the part of one of the attendants," Robin said. Sara remembered there were two attendants to Myrtha, one of the lead roles.

"I know," Kathy said, "but there are so many senior dancers who are sixteen, even a few who are seventeen. We're only fifteen."

"What does that matter?" Robin said. "We're good and I want to be seen in order to get that scholarship to the New York City Ballet school." Sara had almost forgotten how much Robin wanted the same thing she did.

"We're going swimming," Mary said. "Come on, Brooke."

"Wait for me," Leah said. "I'm going to start doing laps." The three left and Charleigh walked to the music library with Sara and Shannon. As they got near the Junior Division grounds Sara kept her eyes open for boys but didn't see any.

"Hello," Miss Meisner greeted them from behind a creaky wood desk. She looked at her watch. "I have a Dance History class in five minutes. What can I help you with?"

"Do you have any spare paper?" Sara asked.

"Oh, yes. Here you go," Miss Meisner answered, holding out a couple of small recipe cards she took out of her desk drawer. "That's all I found in here. I use movies and slides for my classes. And books, of course. The cards are for checking out the books, music, and dance films."

Sara took the cards and thanked her. "Great," she said. Shannon and Charleigh went out on the raft, and Sara sat on her bunk with the little recipe cards writing down all the Nikolais warm-up exercises she could remember. She wrote

87

as small as she could, but ran out of room way too soon. When Shannon got back she told Sara she had skipped a couple here and there, so they weren't in the correct order. By then it was time to get to ballet, then immediately to modern class. On the way to the dance building, as Sara tried to get the order of the warm-ups straight by repeating them to Shannon, Leah came up behind them on the path.

"No," Leah said. "The lower back twist comes before the spine release swings."

"I will *never* get these," Sara said, feeling angry that Leah caught on so fast and that Shannon was so poised and calm. But in class she managed once more to get through the exercises by staying in the back line and following other people when she drew a blank, but she was sure that Miss Lee noticed. She enjoyed learning more new concepts and moving across the floor leading with a different body part each time. At the end of class Miss Lee gave them a homework assignment.

"You will have an assignment each day now," Miss Lee announced. "For tomorrow create a short movement phrase showing the use of two separate body parts, changing energy and time. It must have a beginning, middle and end. Change levels to make it interesting. The lights will stay on in the large studio for you until nine." So, that was it, Sara thought. Instead of practicing the order of the warm-ups at night, she'd have to create movement phrases.

On the way out of the building the girls checked the board to see if the *Giselle* list was posted. "Not yet," Leah said. She pretended to tap dance all the way to dinner.

CHAPTER TWELVE

"Miss Alexander's Choice"

"Well, let's get to the dance building," Sara said to Shannon after dinner. "We have to create our movement phrase for modern tomorrow." They thought it would take them about a half hour to complete. But it was after eight before they were satisfied with what they had. Leah came in and worked across the large studio from them. Several other girls took up additional space in the room. By eight-thirty Leah and the others left and Sara and Shannon decided to stay a bit longer and perform their movement phrases for each other. When they went down to the empty locker room Sara heard music again coming from Studio B. "Follow me," she said to Shannon.

They moved quietly down the hall and found Miss Alexander dancing with the boys' teacher. The door was wide open. The girls ducked behind the door. "Come on," Shannon whispered. "Let's get out of here." They clearly were not supposed to be down there. They walked quickly back to the locker room, gathered their things and went up the steps. It was getting dark outside.

"Shannon," Sara said, grabbing her arm. "We can watch them from a window." She took off around the side of the building and found the rock not exactly in the same place she had left it. Shannon helped her drag it over some big pine-cones closer to the window, and they stood on it. "I love that music," Sara whispered, not knowing what it was.

"Everyone loves the music from *Tarantella,*" Shannon said.

Shannon knew so much about dance, Sara thought, envi-ous that she got to dance in New York. Sara pretended she knew the pas de deux. "Yes. I adore *Tarantella,*" she said with false authority. She turned to face Shannon causing the rock to wobble, and Shannon slipped off. Her big toe must have been under the rock because when Sara moved over on the rock to help her, Shannon's toe got smashed.

"Ow!" Shannon yelled, pulling her toe out as Sara jumped off the rock.

"Come on," Sara said, helping her off the ground. They better leave fast. Shannon cried a little and limped all the way back to the cabin. She missed ballet Friday morning and Mrs. Lane came into the room to explain to Miss Sutton that Shannon was visiting the nurse. Shannon arrived in time to watch tap with her left big toe taped up. *Not again*, Sara thought, n*ot again*. She could not believe that she had caused another dancer to hurt herself. She remembered how long it took Robin to recover last year and how she couldn't dance in pointe shoes for the San Francisco Ballet. But Shannon had no crutches and made it up the stairs alone.

When Sara tried to apologize, Shannon said it wasn't her fault that she fell off a rock. It sounded so funny that they started laughing, then they looked up and saw a crowd of girls in front of the posted list of names for *Giselle*. Sara stood on tip-toe to see above some heads. When she realized the names were in alphabetical order she dropped down to S. She saw "Stewart, Robin" and then "St. Pierre, Shannon" and finally her own name: "Sutherland, Sara." There were no designated parts yet.

"We made it! We made it!" Sara said excitedly to Shannon. Then she heard Robin's voice behind her.

"We made it too," Robin said confidently to Kathy Jacobs and Hillary. Then she looked down at Shannon's foot and said "Oops. Fall off the porch?" Sara remembered that is what Robin told everybody last year about her own injury.

"No. A rock," Shannon answered. Robin looked at Sara like she knew something. Sara remembered how the rock had not been in exactly the same place where she had left it. She looked up and saw that Leah had not made it into *Giselle*. She and Shannon were the only intermediates invited. Leah probably would have made it if allégro had been part of the audition. She was so good at the fast steps. Sara glanced at the board again and saw that rehearsals would begin Monday evening at seven o'clock. "Let's get to lunch," Shannon said. "I can't walk too fast, and pointe starts at one 'clock."

In pointe class Miss Sutton said she was sorry to hear about Shannon's toe and asked everyone not to dance on the lawn or take any chances. "Your body is your instrument," she reminded them. She congratulated Sara and Shannon for making it into *Giselle* and everyone applauded. Shannon watched class from a chair in the corner, but didn't seem to be in much pain, and Sara was glad Miss Sutton did not include bourrées or chugs across the room today. She had energy left for Miss Lee's Nikolais class. Poor Shannon. After working so

91

hard on her movement piece last night, she wouldn't even be able to do it.

After the warm-up exercises, Miss Lee began calling dancers out to perform their individual movement phrases. From watching several dancers and listening to Miss Lee's comments, Sara was afraid that she had missed the mark on the assignment.

"Focus. Focus. Keep your eyes focused on your movement," Miss Lee coached Sara when she performed her phrase. "If that is your elbow leading, I really need to see that!" Sara was asked to do it again, and she tried to incorporate Miss Lee's comments. After watching everyone else's movement phrases and dancing several combinations across the floor with sudden changes of direction, Sara's head was as full of new material as her body was tired.

"Your homework assignment for Monday is to create a phrase that uses a single body part, one that you did not use for your last assignment, and to express stretching, graining your body from inside out toward at least one corner. Practice your focus and changing levels!" With that, Miss Lee excused them. Sara felt exhausted and still had to go to folk class. Friday was the longest day.

After the predictable folk class, Leah walked to dinner with Sara and Shannon.

"I'm sorry you didn't make it into *Giselle*," Shannon said to Leah.

"I'm sorry you hurt your foot," Leah said. "How did that happen?" Sara gave Shannon a warning with her eyes not to tell.

"Oh, I was just standing on a rock in the woods and slipped off," Shannon said.

"What woods?" Leah wanted to know.

"We took a path up to a lookout bench," Sara decided to say. "We'll take you there after dinner." This seemed to satisfy Leah. No harm could come from showing her the lookout bench. It was better than telling her about the rock and the window. Shannon looked surprised. She didn't know about the lookout bench yet.

During dinner Brooke and Mary announced that they were preparing a synchronized swimming show. "We want you to be in it, Leah," Brooke said.

"No," Leah said. "I really don't do that kind of thing. Backstroke only. How about Charlie?"

"What?" Charleigh said. She had been talking with a girl at the table behind her.

"We want to put on a water ballet," Mary told her, "but Miss Hess says we have to have more people. Will you be in it, please?"

"Pleeeease?" Brooke smiled. "We'll teach you some cool moves. It will be easy and fun."

"Sure," Charleigh said. "As long as Grace can be in it, too." Grace must be her new friend at the Baryshnikov table behind her. The girls agreed and the four of them began to make plans to meet at the beach for practice every day they could.

Sara wished she had extra time like that for fun, but now she would not only have to practice the sequence of Nikolais warm-ups and create a movement phrase for Miss Lee's class each day, but also go to *Giselle* rehearsals after dinner for the next three weeks. *Three weeks*, she thought. *Just three weeks until I perform in front of the New York City Ballet dancers.* She felt a nervous pinch in her stomach, but her mind was filled with images of long white costumes, lines passing through each other in arabesque scoots and the beautiful formations they would make on stage in the little Balanchine theatre in the woods. It was her chance to win the scholarship to New York.

CHAPTER THIRTEEN

"A Banner Day"

After dinner Friday Sara led Shannon and Leah up the path through the tall pine trees to the lookout bench. "Be careful," she cautioned them. "Don't twist your toe on a pine cone."

"Don't worry," Shannon said, moving along tenderly.

"I started to walk up this path the day I went out to explore things," Leah said, pushing brush away from her leg. "But I got beyond the Senior Division cabins and decided there was nothing up here." When they got to the top she seemed nearly dumbfounded by the beauty of the scene. "Wow!" she said, trying to take in the expanse of the blue water and miles of thick green forest.

"Belle, Belle," Shannon said, slipping into French again. "Beautiful!" She sat down on the bench.

"What kind of camp is that over there?" Leah asked, shielding her eyes with her hand.

"It's a boys dance camp this year," Sara told her, watching some boys walking around on their grounds. "Last year it was like a fitness or wilderness camp. They had horses and everything." That was all she wanted to tell them. "If we sit here long enough we can see the sun go down over the lake," Sara said, remembering the boys' party last year. Nobody thought that was a good idea. Shannon wanted to get back and rest her foot. Leah wanted to practice her back stroke before the beach closed at eight. *And*, Sara thought, *we have our first Dance History class in the morning*. She looked again at the boys across the lake and then they headed back to Pavlova cabin.

Sara woke up shivering in her bedroll Saturday morning. *Oh*, she thought, *this up north Michigan weather can change so fast*. She curled up on her bunk thinking of hot chocolate and oatmeal and toast and eggs and pancakes. It all streamed by in her head, but she was too cold to put her feet on the floor. She heard the shower going and envied the girl who was already in the warm water. She knew it wouldn't be sleepyhead Shannon. *Probably YMCA-Leap-Year-Leah*, she thought. She peeked at the clock, then went back to sleep. When she woke up the clock said 9:30. She had missed breakfast! Then the heavy wood door opened and Shannon came in with an apple, muffin and hot chocolate for her.

"Merci! Merci! Sara exclaimed. Shannon smiled as Sara ate the little breakfast on her bunk. "I was out like a light." She wondered where everybody was.

"Charleigh, Brooke and Mary are having a water ballet meeting at the boat house with Grace," Shannon said. "Too cold to go in the lake. I don't know where Leah went." Then the door opened and Leah appeared. Her shoes were mucky.

"Howdy," Leah said casually. She took off her shoes and threw them out on the porch. Sara looked out the window and saw that it hadn't been raining. It was sunny and the trees were blowing hard in the cold wind.

"Where were you?" Sara asked Leah as she headed toward the bathroom.

"On a path," Leah said. "It led off from the lookout bench. It started going downhill fast and I stepped in muck and saw a snake, so I came back. It's dark and cool in there. I smelled mint." She went into the bathroom. *Leah was almost to the stream*, Sara thought. She did *not* want her to find the secret way to the boys camp and to the secret old cabin beyond. It was bad enough that Robin and Hillary knew about them. What if she needed a place to go alone to practice or to think about things?

"Better get dressed, Sara," Shannon said. "We have to get to Dance History." Sara took a long shower, brushed her hair out straight over her shoulders, put on jeans and her heavy blue sweater, and the three girls walked across the grounds to the music library. They took seats in the middle of long rows of cold folding chairs.

"We begin." Miss Meisner said, rolling down a map of Western Europe. "People expressed their thoughts and emotions through movement long before they had speech. But let us begin where dance was used as a form of entertainment. The origins of ballet can be traced to the early court dances in France and Italy." She used a pointer to show the two countries. It reminded Sara of Madame's cane last year. "Any celebration," Miss Meisner continued, "was cause for dancing in the court by all the lords and ladies."

Sara looked around the walls of the room and noticed quotes by dancers. She saw one by Martha Graham that began "There is a vitality, a life force, a quickening that is translated through you into action..." She felt the wispiness around her neck and felt the connection again to dancers who had gone before her. Little white pearls of spirit, she thought, touching her neck. So many dancers had been trained, performed before passionate audiences and then passed away, she thought.

"Around the fourteen hundreds," Miss Meisner said, "dance teachers mastered and taught these complicated dances. In fact, they were called Dance Masters. They were all men, and were revered as the finest dance teachers and choreographers." Sara thought of Yuri and the great master class he gave last summer.

"Does anyone know who the first person was to start a ballet school?" Miss Meisner asked. Shannon raised her hand. "Yes?" Miss Meisner said, pointing to Shannon.

"King Louis the Fourteenth of France in 1661," Shannon said. "It was called 'Academie Royale de Danse'," she said. "The Royal Academy of Dance." Sara noticed a book in Shannon's lap, the same one she had been reading since she arrived at camp. It was a French book of dance history. No wonder she knew so much. "From that," Shannon continued, "came the Paris Opera Ballet, which still exists today."

"Very *good*!" Miss Meisner smiled, her curly hair bobbing as she nodded her head. "King Louis the Fourteenth had a profound influence on the progression of ballet. He was an avid supporter as well as a beloved performer. He was commonly referred to as the Sun King because he appeared in an ornate gold costume as Apollo, god of the sun." After that, Miss Meisner skipped to the early 1800s of the Pre-Romantic Period with the origin of pointe work. "Maria Taglioni, an Italian, is usually given credit for being the first ballerina to dance en pointe, although she did not have the benefit of hard, blocked shoes like you do. Somehow she managed to dance on her toes with just a lot of stiches sewn in the points of her soft shoes." *Ouch*, Sara thought.

Miss Meisner filled the rest of class by explaining the various threads of ballet that came out of France, Italy, Russia and England. "The Italian Cecchetti method, the Russian Vaganova method and the English Royal Academy of Dance method all had their beginnings in this shared history," she said, beaming with pride as though she owned the history itself. "Then there is the Balanchine method, which is Balanchine's own. Though he himself was trained in Russian, he wanted to devise a system of his own in America that would prepare his students for his unique choreography. We will be talking much more about Balanchine and the New York City Ballet as we progress through this course." Sara perked up. She would have to know all about Balanchine if she were going to dance at New York City ballet school next summer and maybe join the company one day. Miss Meisner excused them without giving them any homework. *Yay*, Sara thought. *No homework. I've caught a break!* On the way to lunch they saw some boys coming out of the dance building.

"Jackson!" Shannon yelled. "Jackson Rose!" A tall boy with reddish blond hair turned. He saw Shannon and walked over, dance bag hanging from his white T-shirt and black sweater. A shorter guy with brown curly hair followed him.

"Shannon," Jackson smiled, his blue eyes looking down at her taped toe. "How are you? What happened?"

"Oh, petite problem. Fell off a pine cone," Shannon laughed. "What are you guys doing over here?"

"Partnering class with senior girls," Jackson said. "This is Patrick McCracken." Patrick smiled and his eyes turned to Sara.

"This is Sara Sutherland," Shannon smiled. Sara said hello.

"We have to get back for lunch before it's over," Jackson said. But we'll see you later." The boys took off using the official path to the boys' side that began at the edge of the Junior Division grounds at the right side of the lake.

"So that's Jackson. Jackson who takes class at the Nikolais school in New York?" Sara asked.

"Yes. And with me and Erin at the ballet school."

Sara's head was reeling with missed chances and possibilities. If she had chosen Senior Division she could be doing partnering on Saturday mornings, if she could practice Nikolais warm-ups with Jackson she could look good in that class. If she wanted to have a summer boyfriend, Jackson was *it* with his fair complexion and red-blond hair. And those eyes, Sara thought. Jackson had flowered into her heart and warmed it on a cold day.

After lunch they had the entire rest of the day with no classes. It was too cold to go swimming, and the lake was too rough to take out a boat. Sara thought she would beg people's class schedules so she could write the Nikolais progression of warm-ups on the backs of them. The girls were on their bunks eating the last of the chocolate chip cookies.

"No, I still need mine," Charleigh said, looking up from a dance magazine.

"Me, too," Brooke said. "Try Shannon." But Shannon was at the nurse for a check-up on her toe.

"How about you, Mary?" Sara asked.

Mary was reading a letter from her dance teacher at home. "I don't have the schedule memorized yet," she said.

"Don't look at me," Leah said. "But I have an idea. I volunteer to put my Class A schedule on the wall next to the banner so we can look at it if we need to." She found a tack and put her schedule on the wall.

"OK," Charleigh said, getting off her bunk and fishing her schedule out of her drawer. "I'll put my Class B up." But none of that helped Sara write out the Nikolais exercises.

Shannon came in and announced that she would be ready to dance on Monday, but not in pointe shoes. She'd have to go back for another check-up on Wednesday. Sara hoped they wouldn't have to wear pointe shoes for their first *Giselle* rehearsal Monday evening.

"Hey," Charleigh said. "Let's put Sara and Shannon's achievement on the banner!"

"Oh, yeah," Mary agreed. Leah quietly got the markers out of the drawer. She handed the green one to Shannon and the yellow one to Sara. Under her name Shannon wrote, "Made Giselle". Under her name Sara drew a little stick figure and wrote "Giselle". She used her vivid imagination to see other things under her name like "Special part in Giselle" and "Fabulous eye-catching ballet solo" and "Summer scholarship to NYC Ballet school". But when she backed away from the board and blinked all she saw was a skinny stick figure next to the word "Giselle". She went over to the board again and made the stick figure look more like it was dancing in pointe shoes.

That night she thought of how much she liked Dance History. She pictured Jackson smiling at her. She saw herself dancing with him. She looked at the banner once more. At least, she thought, she had made it into *Giselle*. She decided that it had been a banner first week.

CHAPTER FOURTEEN

"Surprise on Sunday"

"Let's see if they leave the dance building open on Sundays," Leah said at breakfast. "It's still too cold to go swimming, and we could make up our movement phrases for modern dance." She ate two bagel halves with cream cheese and peanut butter.

"What a good idea," Shannon said, tasting a pancake she said was nothing like a French crepe.

"We can try," Sara said, sipping her juice, "but it was closed Sundays last year. No one's around like the teachers or Mrs. Lane, so they lock it up."

"Everyone," Charleigh announced, coming to their table with another stranger, "this is Catherine Eli. She's in Baryshnikov cabin with Grace." *That girl's a friend machine,* Sara thought. They all said hello, then Mary and Brooke went with Charleigh to visit Catherine and her roommates. Sara, Shannon and Leah walked to the dance building and found it locked up tight. They sat on the dining hall steps for a while looking at the lake, and then went back to the cabin. Shannon settled in her bunk to read more of her dance history book. Sara sat up on her bedroll and looked over the recipe cards with her Nikolais notes in tiny, messy handwriting. She had inserted arrows and more messy notes to add the exercises she had forgotten originally. Leah took up the floor creating her movement phrase for Monday.

This is just no use, Sara thought. *These notes are making me more confused. I need a whole big notebook to write them in and a space to practice them full out. If I don't start looking confident and even fearless in that class, my chances are nil for getting that scholarship to New York City Ballet.* She had made it into *Giselle* and planned to do a really great dance on pointe for the student concert, so if she could just conquer modern dance she thought she'd have a chance, even though she'd have to be in a folk dance for the final performance.

"Well, I'm done," Leah finally said. "I'm going to do my laundry." She grabbed a pillow case of dirty clothes and left for the laundry building.

Sara got up and took the foil off the chest of drawers. She went out on the porch and brushed off the cookie crumbs for the chipmunks and put the foil in the blue tin under her locket. It was good to see the locket. It made her feel lucky just looking at it. Suddenly she figured out how she was going to win the scholarship. She put on the locket and pulled her hair back into a pony tail. This was the time to take Shannon to the secret cabin. They could make up their movement phrases there and be the best in class on Monday. They could be alone and help each other create something really good. She looked at the clock. Three whole hours until dinner. She looked out the window and saw Julie Hess walking with some other counselors over by the Senior Division cabins. "Shannon," Sara said. "Put on your shoes and sweater and come with me."

They got to the lookout bench and Sara ducked into the group of tall pine trees and onto the path. She took off down the narrow trail and laughed, so happy to be sharing her blue tin secret with Shannon. But when she got to the fork she couldn't remember where to get off the path. When she felt cooler and started to feel muck, she went back up a few yards. "Where are we?" Shannon asked, frowning. "Are we lost? Aren't we off-limits? My toe hurts."

"Here. I think it's here," Sara said. "Come on." She charged left through the trees and brush until she came to a big patch of fern. She was close. But she couldn't find the cabin. She looked in every direction. Then she looked up at the sky and saw a clearing. "Over here," she said, going uphill toward the clearing. And there it was! It was more ramshackled than she remembered. "Watch out for poison ivy," she warned Shannon, looking down for it herself. When she looked up she thought she saw movement in the cabin window. She walked closer to the cabin, putting her finger over her mouth to warn Shannon to be quiet. They ducked down under a window. Shannon stayed down and Sara peeked inside. It was Robin and Hillary practicing modern dance. They were making up movement phrases! They had stolen the red tin and now they had stolen her idea! They would need to get out of there quickly before being seen. Sara still didn't completely trust Robin. And Hillary was so silly she might spill the beans and get them all in trouble.

"Let's go," Sara whispered. Shannon started to stand up and Sara pushed her back down. They crept away unseen in the bushes. But Sara couldn't find the way back to the path. The woods were silent except for the wind blowing the trees. There were no markers. No clues.

"Look!" Shannon whispered. "A little deer."

"Come on," Sara said, quickly following the deer. She thought it might be headed toward the stream for a drink. It was worth a try. They followed it downhill for a while and then it sensed them and began to leap away through the trees. They kept up as long as they could by watching its bobbing white tail. Just as it disappeared, they saw the stream.

"Wow," Shannon said. "Where are we?" Sara didn't know what part of the stream they were on. She didn't know if they should go left or right or wade to the other side. Suddenly they heard crunching in the brush behind them. Sara's heart beat quickly and she turned around to see three boys coming toward them.

"Hey!" One of them said, smiling. "Boy dancers find girl dancers."

Sara started to breathe again. "Hi," she said.

"We're lost," Shannon said. "Which way to Lakewood?"

"Well, you can go way down to that plank and cross over to your side," the boy said.

Oh my gosh, Sara thought, *we are on the boys' side, completely off-limits!* She looked the way the boy was pointing. If she squinted she could just make out the plank. "Great," she said. "Thanks." She had to get them out of there before a boys' counselor saw them. But when they got to the plank more boys appeared. Sara pretended not to see them, got over the plank as quickly as she could and darted up the path. As soon as they were out of sight and well into the tall pine trees, Shannon stopped. "My toe hurts," she said. "I can't go that

106

fast." They found a tree stump for Shannon to sit on. She was angry. "I can't believe you brought me here," she scowled. "First you get us lost trying to find some old cabin, then you get us more lost trying to find a stream, then we are found by the boys on their side. Off-limits, Sara. We could get sent home."

"Oh, that cabin is more on the girls' side," Sara said, trying to sound confident. "And those boys don't know who we are."

"Yes," Shannon said. "Jackson and Patrick do. I feel embarrassed."

"Jackson and Patrick?" Sara said. "What do you mean?"

"I couldn't go as fast as you over the plank and I saw them. They saw us and waved."

Oops, Sara thought. Her secrets were not her secrets anymore, and Shannon was so angry that it didn't feel like a blue tin secret at all. Somehow she would have to let Jackson and Patrick know that she and Shannon were not allowed over there and ask them not to say anything to anyone. All she had wanted was a place to practice. A space to become a better dancer, a better student, a good friend. Now she didn't even know if she had a friend. She had not only caused Shannon to hurt her toe, but nearly got her caught off-limits.

After she got Shannon back to Pavlova cabin, Sara realized that she wouldn't have a chance to see Jackson or Patrick until next Saturday after Dance History class. And that was only if she could catch them coming out of the dance building at just the right moment. If they got out early and left quickly to get back to their side for lunch, she would miss seeing them entirely. She couldn't risk going back to the stream today. Shannon got into the shower and Sara decided to take out a boat to see if she could row to the middle of the lake and spot the boys. If she did, she could wave them over. She remembered how she and Erin got together with Hank and Paul that way last summer. But when she got down to the lake, Heather was not there, and there was a sign by the boats that said "Closed Due to Weather." She looked out at the choppy waves on the lake and sighed. Seven more weeks of camp, she thought. She touched her locket and turned back to the cabin. Leah came back with her clean clothes at the same time Sara climbed onto the porch.

"What did you guys do?" Leah wanted to know as she put away her clothes.

"Just hung out," Sara said, making sure her shoes were under the bed and out of sight. Once the muck dried off, she'd be safe. She didn't see Shannon's shoes.

"Well, if you haven't figured out your modern dance phrase for tomorrow, I have an idea," she said.

Shannon came out of the bathroom limping. "I don't think I'll be able to dance tomorrow," she said, looking at Sara. "So I am not going to worry about doing the assignment." Sara cringed.

"The laundry building is really huge," Leah continued. "I was the only one there, so I had enough room to practice. Maybe you could go there after dinner. It doesn't close until nine."

So after dinner Sara put her locket under her pillow, went to the laundry building, threw her clothes into a washer and created her Nikolais movement phrase. *And that*, she thought, *is the end of the first week of camp.*

CHAPTER FIFTEEN

"First Rehearsal"

Monday morning was warm and sunny. Sara went to breakfast early and left a peach and scrambled eggs covered in foil on the chest of drawers for Shannon. Shannon sat out of classes all day and didn't speak to Sara much. Sara danced hard and tried to mind her own business. Miss Lee seemed OK with her 'laundry room' movement phrase, though she demanded more clarity in Sara's attempt to lead with her knee. They learned the concepts of moving in thick and thin and the difference between them, then moved across the floor doing the combination of walks she had already taught them, changing direction and levels. Sara was surprised at how much she remembered. But after going across the floor once, Miss Lee added new movements to the combination, and Sara felt lost again. Apparently, Miss Lee would keep expecting the class to remember every single thing she taught them day after day no matter how long and complicated it got. To Sara it seemed like a big pile of movement that kept building brick by brick. If you couldn't remember the bottom movement of brick, the whole thing could fall. And Miss Lee just kept adding more bricks and beating her drum.

"Did you do the warm-ups better today?" Leah asked Sara on the way to folk class.

"No," Sara admitted. "I still don't know them very well. I peek at other people and I look in the mirror at the class whenever I can." She was afraid that she if pretended too well Miss Lee would ask her to lead the class in the warm-ups as she had Keera today. She wanted to remain in the back line. She still needed a way to see them clearly written down and a space to practice them over and over until she never had to look at anybody else. She had to look like a leader. She had to show enthusiasm and improvement to get that scholarship.

Mr. Moyne had fresh ideas in folk class and forgot about most of the steps he had already taught them. Each teacher had a different way of doing things, Sara knew, and this was her least favorite way. While she kept having to remember everything for Miss Lee, she had to keep forgetting everything for Mr. Moyne. Each day seemed like a new start. *Thank goodness for tap class*, she found herself thinking. It was just plain fun for Sara because she had taken tap practically her whole life. That was a class where she could shine without worry.

At dinner, Robin and Hillary came over to Pavlova table. *Oh, no*, Sara thought. *They saw us at the cabin window.* She waited for Robin to say something about it, but instead she said, "Have you guys seen the new posting for *Giselle*?"

"No," Leah said, looking up at Robin. "What about it?"

"There are understudies listed," Hillary said. "They probably didn't want to take any chances on more people hurting a toe." She looked at Shannon as if to say that she knew she had been somewhere she wasn't supposed to be.

"Who are the understudies?" Sara asked. She had a sudden fear that Shannon had been moved out of the corps de ballet to understudy. If so, it would be Sara's fault.

"We aren't telling," Robin said coyly. "We don't tell things." Sara wondered what that meant—that they had seen them at the cabin window but wouldn't tell, as long as Sara and Shannon wouldn't tell they had seen Robin and Hillary there? You never knew with those two. They were so nice at the end of last summer, but now they seemed more like their old selves.

"Let's go," Sara said. Leah and Shannon followed her down the path to the empty dance building.

"Oh, wow," Leah said, staring at the board. She was an understudy!

"Whew," Shannon sighed. Her name was where it had been Friday.

"Great!" Sara said, pointing to the list of understudies. "And Alene is an understudy, too, and Keera." She gave Leah a hug. "Congrats, Leah," she said.

"It probably just means I have to come to all the rehearsals and never get a chance to dance," Leah said. But Sara knew there were possibilities.

"You never know," Sara said, remembering how she got Robin's special part last year.

Back at the cabin, Leah took a red marker and wrote "Giselle Understudy" next to her name on the banner. "There," she said, smiling proudly. "I'll add a stick figure when I get something better." She looked at the clock. "We better work on our Nikolais assignment for tomorrow before it's time for *Giselle* rehearsal," she said. They went to the dance building and worked on their movement phrases downstairs

111

in Studio B until seven o'clock. Then they ran upstairs to the big studio.

Shannon lucked out. No pointe shoes for first rehearsal. She wouldn't have to sit this one out. "I rested my foot all day for this," she said, taking a place at the ballet barre with no tape on her toe. Sara stood next to her and looked around the room at the posters of *Giselle* someone had put up around the walls. The white costumes were dreamy. The dancers floated in a romantic world and a male dancer was holding a bouquet of white lilies and looking sweetly sad. Soon she'd be on the stage in a scene just like that dancing for members of the New York City Ballet. She looked in the mirror and tried to picture herself in one of the beautiful long white costumes. She was so excited thinking about it that she was barely aware of all the seniors who had filled the room.

No parts had been given yet, so Sara knew if it was anything like last year they would try out for solos and special parts tonight. But first Miss Sutton led them in barre exercises to get their muscles warm. Sara noticed how beautifully trained the older dancers were and that most of them were still a couple of inches taller than she was. She pulled herself up tall and lengthened her neck. Miss Alexander watched from a chair near the piano, and after the barre exercises she took over. She explained that Giselle is a lovely village peasant girl loved by Hilarion, a keeper of the game animals used for hunting. But Giselle falls in love with Count Albrecht, who pretends to be a villager but is actually engaged to a Princess. When Giselle finds out Albrecht was only playing a game and that she was tricked, she dances to her death from shock and a broken heart.

The second act, which they would be dancing, takes place after midnight in the land of forest spirits. The corps de ballet, the ensemble dancers, would be the Wilis, all young maiden spirits who died before their wedding day. The Queen of the Wilis is Myrtha and she has two attendants. Albrecht is sorry for what he did and comes to Giselle's grave, but Myrtha and the Wilis prey upon travelers caught in the forest after midnight. They entice them to dance in their magic circle until the victims die of exhaustion. Myrtha forces Giselle to dance for Albrecht so he will follow her in dance to his death. But Giselle's love and forgiveness are more powerful than Myrtha's magic and Giselle saves Albrecht, though she must return to her grave at dawn.

"*Giselle* is a beautiful romantic ballet first danced in 1841 in Paris," Miss Alexander told them. "Since then, every ballerina in the world has wanted to dance the title role and every premier danseur has aspired to dance the part of Albrecht. It is, perhaps, the most romantic of all the romantic ballets, and you are privileged to be dancing it. The wonderful music by Adolphe Adam will inspire you to respect the tradition of this ballet by dancing your very best." Sara felt charged with the responsibility of fulfilling this ideal. She was so happy to be chosen for it and wanted Miss Alexander to notice how good a dancer she was so she would award her a special part to dance in front of the New York City Ballet. It would almost clinch her getting the scholarship she wanted. *Oh, please*, she thought. *Please notice me. Please give me a special part.*

Miss Alexander divided the group into two and taught them the entrance step of simply walking forward out of the wings at the sides of the stage and bending forward to bow low to Myrtha. She taught them sauté arabesques with pas de bourrées going from side to side. She had them lower to one knee and move their arms in the sweeping port de bras Miss Sutton had taught them in class. Leah, Alene and Keera followed along behind with the senior understudies learning everything in case they had to suddenly fill in for someone. Sara loved the music and tried to express the movements as softly and romantically as Madame had taught her last year for *Les Sylphides*. Then the group was asked to sit under the barre, and Miss Alexander called the names of seven senior dancers. "Jennifer Hart, Robin Stewart, Courtney Karlen, Katie Easton, Kathy Jacobs, Stephanie Cook and Ashley Black come center-floor, please." Sara watched eagerly as Miss Alexander found a certain place in the music and demonstrated beautiful, flowing steps for them to try with leaps and attitude en pointe, turns and bourrées. The girls danced it together, then Miss Alexander had Robin and Jennifer try it alone. Miss Sutton coached Courtney and Kathy in the corner until it was their turn. The teachers chatted in whispers and made notes. Sara thought she could do all the steps. *Why doesn't Miss Alexander ask me?* she thought. But she was sure there would be other parts to try. Finally, Robin and Kathy were asked to do it again.

Next, Miss Alexander taught the same seven dancers different choreography with bourrées all the way across the room and an arabesque slowly bending over into penché. Sara became frightened and was not sure, if asked, she would be able to do the slow, controlled movement well. It looked hard. After that, the same dancers were asked to do leaps in different directions all around the room, and turns into leaps in a circle and beats, crossing their ankles in the air. Sara thought it looked enchanting and joyous. Then the boys' teacher she

114

had seen dancing downstairs appeared in the doorway with Jackson. Sara's heart fluttered in surprise and delight. Miss Alexander introduced the teacher as Mr. Peters. "Most of you know Jackson," she said. Jackson's smile made Sara smile and her heart warm.

"Let's have Courtney and Katie try some partnering with Jackson," Miss Alexander said. Mr. Peters led them in some careful lifts and supported pirouettes. Jackson was an attentive and strong partner. *Please give me a chance to dance with him,* Sara thought. After doing the arabesque lifts with Mr. Moyne last year she was sure she could do everything Courtney and Katie were doing. Besides, she knew she and Jackson would look wonderful together with his sandy red hair and her dark brown. She watched the dancers carefully and did a few pliés to keep her muscles warm in case she was called out. But only Jennifer Hart and Stephanie Cook were asked to try. "All right," Miss Alexander said finally. "Let's have everyone out on the floor now."

Wow, is that it for special parts? Sara wondered. Her heart felt a bit empty. For the last half hour of rehearsal Miss Alexander taught them a step moving forward with four scoots, a step leaning backward with one arm moving overhead and four more scoots forward. She had them divide into two groups again and they moved toward each other doing the difficult steps. Sara tried hard to do the chugs as Miss Sutton had taught them, keeping her back leg still and high and her head down into her outstretched arm. She knew her leg wasn't as long as some of the other girls', so she stretched as much as she could. Then Miss Alexander was next to her. As Sara leaned backward, Miss Alexander took her wrist and moved it in a slightly different direction. "Bigger and softer," she said.

115

Sara's heart fell a little more. She wanted to be noticed, but not for making mistakes. Although she knew when a teacher chose you for corrections it applied to the whole class and the attention might mean the teacher saw potential, she did not have a good feeling about it.

After they practiced doing the scoots several times across the room with the lines passing through each other, Miss Alexander called Shannon out and asked her to try some of the steps that the seven seniors had learned. Sara was excited. There was still a chance! She could be called out next. She watched Shannon move gracefully to the lovely music. She was so lithe and poised. *Her face is like an angel's,* Sara thought. She looked in the mirror to see if she her own face could look as serene. Then suddenly it was over. "Thank you, dancers," Miss Alexander said. "We'll post parts tomorrow."

"Rehearsal tomorrow night, same time!" Miss Sutton reminded them. "We only have three weeks to be ready for performance." Sara walked with Leah to the dressing room because Miss Alexander was talking with Shannon and looking at her toe. She wished Madame were here this year. She wished Madame would smile at her for doing something right. She wished she were taller. She wished her legs were longer. She wished her face was like an angel's. She wished Leah would stop chatting. Couldn't she tell Sara was suffering in disappointment?

In her bunk that night Sara reached under her pillow and touched her locket. *Please let me see my name posted tomorrow for a special part*, she wished. She fell off to sleep seeing Jackson lifting her high in the air and smiling up at her as her long white costume floated around them.

CHAPTER SIXTEEN

"A Step Forward, A Step Backward"

Tuesday morning was Sara's fourth pointe class and she not only expected Miss Sutton to notice her enthusiasm and improvement, but she expected some hint from her that after class she would find the name "Sara Sutherland" posted next to Mrs. Lane's office for a special part in *Giselle*. She could still hear the uplifting music in her head and could see the flowing movements of the seniors who had the chance to audition for the special parts. Sara could hardly contain her worries that she would get nothing but a part in the corps de ballet. *Maybe they have a part in mind for me*, she thought, *based on my scholarship award from last year*. After all, Miss Sutton knew the quality of her dancing.

Shannon was quiet on the walk to the dance building. When Sara asked her if she was excited to have been called out to try for a special part last night, she just shrugged, took a bite out of her apple and said, "It was nice, of course." When Sara asked her what Miss Alexander had said about her toe, she said, "Oh, that it had just been bruised. It looked OK to her. She said I should be back on pointe soon." In spite of how simple it all seemed, Sara felt envious and amazed at Shannon's calm reaction. *If I had been given the chance for a special part, I certainly would be more excited about it,* she thought.

After pointe class there was no new *Giselle* posting. After folk class there was no new *Giselle* posting. After lunch there was no new *Giselle* posting. After ballet class there was no new *Giselle* posting. Miss Lee sat on her chair and pounded her drum during modern class and Sara struggled to remember the long sequence of warm-ups again. Week two, she thought, and she just wasn't feeling that much more confident. Her mind kept flitting to *Giselle* and she looked out the open doorway to see if Mrs. Lane was putting up the new posting. "Sara!" Miss Lee shouted her way. "Focus. F-O-C-U-S!" *Oops*, she thought, getting back into the standing drop swings over to the floor and back up. She actually liked doing them, especially on the fourth set when she could push her feet off the floor up into the air. Her well-trained ballet muscles took over and lifted her easily and high. As she stood in relevé balance on one foot at the end of the series, Miss Lee came over to her. She took her hands and pulled her out in front of the class.

"Let's see a complete set of drop swings, Sara," she said. There was no time to think. The drum started and Sara did her best. When she finished and stood on one leg in perfect balance, arms up, the class applauded. Miss Lee nodded and smiled at her. *Wow*, Sara thought, *a step forward*. At least something had gone right in that class, but she still had to perform her movement phrase. She had some trouble recalling it and forced herself to stop thinking about *Giselle* to get through it. Showing the difference between thick and thin, including level changes and changes in direction was a challenging assignment. Sara thought hers was not as interesting as some of the other dancers'. *Oh well,* she *thought, ballet is my life, modern is just something I have to learn to be well-rounded.* They finished the class doing across-the-floor combinations they had already learned, with Miss Lee adding flex-straighten joint-hinge movements, and after class there it was! Sara was exhausted from modern and so hungry her stomach complained as she stood next to Leah and Shannon staring at the posting.

The part of Giselle went to Courtney Karlen and the part of Myrtha to Katie Easton, both seniors. Robin and Kathy Jacobs won the roles of Myrtha's attendants. Sara looked up and down the list for her name. She saw that Jennifer Hart and Stephanie Cook got understudies for Giselle and Myrtha. She saw Ashley Black was understudy for Kathy Jacobs. Then she saw that Shannon got understudy to Robin. That was it. Her name was nowhere. "Congrats, Shannon," Leah said. Sara's heart refused to believe it. Nothing.

"I got nothing," Sara said quietly.

"Of course you got something," Leah said. "You are in the corps de ballet. I got nothing."

"Well," Shannon said, "as understudy you might get a chance to dance in it."

"Yeah, if someone croaks," Leah said, nudging Sara.

"What?" Sara said, annoyed. Then she understood that she had not congratulated Shannon. "Congrats, Shannon," she said from her fragile heart. But she knew what it could be like to understudy Robin.

After a quick dinner of listening to Brooke and Mary talk about their water ballet and Charleigh introducing them to another new friend, they went to the cabin to see if they had any mail. Sara had a letter from Jen Hutchins, her friend back home, who had sent the banner last year. It was filled with news of a party with some of their school friends. Old boys and new boys and boys Jen hoped to meet. It all sounded so far away and unimportant to Sara, but she'd write back to her using the back sides of Jen's paper. She put the letter in her drawer and took a shower until she heard banging on the door. "Come on, Sara!" Leah yelled. "We have to make up our hinge movement phrases for modern."

So, Sara thought sadly. *It will be the same every day: classes till five, quick dinner, practice for modern until seven, Giselle rehearsal until eight-thirty.* When she came out of the bathroom, she saw on the banner in bright green marker under Shannon's name "Understudy Myrtha Attendant in *Giselle*". If her heart had started to mend, it fell apart again. Then she looked at the top of the banner and saw "Leadership-Cooperation-Enthusiasm-Improvement." Maybe there was hope. Maybe she could shine in leadership. *But how,* she wondered. *How could she be seen as a leader without a starring role?* She looked at the word "Cooperation" and it just sounded so boring. Her "Enthusiasm" was lacking.

Sara decided she could try for "Improvement" by throwing herself into creating an outstanding Nikolais movement phrase. The thing about modern class was that Miss Lee used no music. Sara realized how much beautiful music in ballet and even in folk class inspired her. The silence of the practice room tonight made her uncomfortable. It forced her to look completely inward for motion, for the particular movement that would clearly express action from her body's hinges. She tried a variety of flexing and straightening movements in her head/neck and hip/leg, shifting her weight. She pretended

Miss Lee was watching her, and kept making improvements. But then she looked at what Leah was creating and in the last ten minutes threw out what she had and started again. That would have to do for tomorrow. But her heart wasn't in it because of how much more she loved ballet, yet had no special part in *Giselle*. She thought about how she had been called out in front of modern class to do part of the warm-ups, yet couldn't remember the whole sequence. A step forward, a step backward, she thought.

There were no boys at rehearsal. There were no soloists at rehearsal. Just the corps de ballet and their understudies. Miss Alexander must be working with the soloists in their regular ballet class. Not only would Sara not be dancing a special part, she couldn't even watch the other dancers learn their special parts. She felt somehow demoted. Miss Alexander had them dance in soft ballet slippers again while she plotted out various formations and poses they would make throughout the ballet, explaining the story as she went. Miss Sutton pretended to be Giselle or Myrtha or Albrecht, as needed, to keep the plot going. The story was romantic and the music stirring, but in bed that night Sara wished on a star out her window that the whole cast would be at the next rehearsal.

CHAPTER SEVENTEEN

"An Invitation"

"The period from 1830 to 1870 is considered the Romantic Period of classical ballet," Miss Meisner said Saturday morning. There was a white screen behind her for a film to be shown. Sara was impatient because she had thought of a plan she couldn't wait to enact right after class. "Women stole the spotlight dancing in their pointe shoes in ballets such as *Giselle.* The long white tutu was introduced, and ballet went from mythological subject matter to dances with an ethereal, fairy-like quality. Does anyone know what ballets are considered Neo-Romantic ballets? That is, ballets in the Romantic style choreographed after 1870?" Shannon's hand went up. Sara wondered if she was reading her French dance history book after lights-out.

"*Swan Lake* and *Les Sylphides,*" Shannon answered.

"Very *good*," Miss Meisner responded. "Today we are going to watch last summer's performance of *Les Sylphides*. I think some of you in this room were in it." Sara looked around the room. She was the only one present who had danced in it. *Couldn't Miss Meisner mention that?* Her ballet star seemed

123

very dim. The window shades were drawn and she watched the film in awe. It really was terrific. When it came time for her little part with Mr. Moyne she thought she might look awkward, but she didn't. She looked great. Her heart soared with seeing how high in the air she was lifted, then it dropped when she remembered it hadn't been enough to get her something good in *Giselle*. When the shades went up Leah tried to make things right.

"Good job, Sara," Leah said. "That was you at the beginning in those lifts across the stage, right?" The class applauded for Sara. *Leah was great. She could probably lead a revolution,* Sara thought, smiling.

Miss Meisner went on to *Giselle*, and after explaining the plot, which Sara already knew, pulled the shades down again. Sara was fascinated. It was a film of *Giselle* performed by the famous Russian company, the Bolshoi Ballet. It was soft and sad and joyous and exciting all at the same time. Sara noticed all the movements she had already learned and all the ones she had yet to learn. She was amazed at how perfectly together the corps de ballet was. It was a highly important part of the ballet. They were the gorgeous background for the soloists. They were like the scenery itself, like the glue that held all the beauty together. And she had to admit, after watching the steps that Giselle and Myrtha had to do, that she was just not ready technically to do them, let alone express the required emotion through her body. But she thought she could dance one of the attendant roles if she would just be given a chance. She looked at Shannon who would get to learn Robin's part. Then she got another idea. As soon as class was over she would tell Shannon both of her ideas.

124

This time when the shades went up, Miss Meisner passed out notebooks and pens. She had more than little recipe cards after all! Now Sara could write down all the long Nikolais warm-up exercises. Miss Meisner instructed them to take the rest of class to make notes about the Romantic ballets. Sara wrote her name on the front of the book and started writing with enthusiasm. After all, she had seen the San Francisco Ballet perform Act 2 of *Swan Lake* last year, had danced in *Les Sylphides*, and was now going to be in *Giselle*. One of the notes she made was just how important and beautiful the corps de ballet was in all the Romantic ballets. She looked up again at the quote on the wall from Martha Graham and read more of it this time: "There is a vitality, a life force, a quickening that is translated through you into action, and because there is only one of you in all time, this expression is unique." *There is only one of me, I am unique*, Sara thought, even as she knew she would have to look exactly like all the other members of the corps for *Giselle*. As Miss Meisner began to collect the notebooks and people started shuffling around to leave, Sara managed to rip out several blank sheets of paper from the back of the book and stuff them in her dance bag.

"Hurry," she urged Shannon, leaping off the porch of the music library. She took off toward the dance building, and Shannon followed quickly. She had seen the nurse on Wednesday who declared her toe healed. "Now," Sara began. "If we run into Jackson, would you ask him to help us practice the Nikolais sequence of warm-ups?"

"How could he do that?" Shannon said. "He has to get back for lunch. And where would we do it?"

"I'll think of something," Sara said. Now that she didn't have a special part in *Giselle*, it was of utmost importance that she do well in modern. She had to get that scholarship to the New York City Ballet school somehow. She had to be outstanding and be noticed by all the teachers. She could just see them with their clipboards discussing the dancers and deciding who would be recommended.

Sure enough, several boys were coming out of the dance building as Sara and Shannon approached. Sara spotted Jackson and Patrick spotted her. He made a beeline for her and said hello. Sara wished Shannon had Leah's personality right now and would get to the point with Jackson. Sara glanced at his handsome face and felt the flower blossoming in her heart again. Count Albrecht, she sighed to herself. He is going to look wonderful in *Giselle*. She couldn't wait to see him dance the role full out. She nudged Shannon with her elbow. "We were wondering," Shannon began, "if you might find time to do a favor."

"A favor?" Patrick said, looking at Sara.

Shannon said shyly, "Perhaps you could work with us in the Nikolais warm up sequence?" Sara thought she sounded French again. This was no time to sound soft.

"I need help," Sara blurted. "I am new at it and can't seem to remember them all. Miss Lee sits on her chair and beats her drum and..."

"I know," Jackson said. "That is the method. You'll learn them eventually." *Eventually*, Sara thought. *I don't have time for eventually*. Then he pulled some flyers out of his dance bag and handed them to Sara. "I'll make a deal with you," he smiled. "If you pass out these flyers to all the intermediate cabins, I'll loan you my Nikolais book. It shows all the exercises and the complete movement vocabulary."

Sara took the red flyers. "Deal," she said, reading one of them. *"Intermediates: Come to Woodlake Boys Dance Camp Saturday, July 17 at 6 PM for Dinner and a Dance Party!" Just a week from today,* Sara smiled.

"I'll give you the book when you come over for the party," Jackson promised. "See you!" And they headed toward the path to their side of the lake.

After lunch Sara and Shannon threw their dance bags on their bunks, grabbed Leah before she started swimming her laps and visited Julie Hess at her cabin, about three down from theirs and deeper in the trees. She was chatting on the porch with some other counselors. "The boys gave us these flyers to pass out," Sara told them. "Is it OK?"

Julie Hess took one and looked it over. "Oh, yes. We already told their counselor we'd be over. Go ahead and put one in each cabin." So the girls made the rounds delivering the bright flyers. As they edged near the Senior Division, Robin and Hillary came out of Tallchief cabin.

"What are you doing over here?" Robin asked. "Let's see that." Leah handed her a flyer. "Oh, boys' party. We have ours with them tonight." *Of course you do,* Sara thought. Robin always managed to know or do everything first. At least Sara wouldn't have to watch her flirt.

"Have a good time," Sara said and moved on. She still needed to tell Shannon her second idea. As they neared Pavlova cabin Leah took off for the beach and she had Shannon to herself. "Thanks, Leah!" Sara called out to Leah, and then she turned to Shannon. "Listen," she began. "I think we should get started on our dance piece for the student concert. Last year we barely got it done in time."

127

"But no one has even announced a student concert," Shannon said, walking onto the Pavlova porch.

"I know," Sara said. "They didn't tell us about it last year until half way through camp, then we had to perform it two weeks later. "

"Probably for good reason," Shannon said, putting her extra flyers on the chest of drawers. "We already have a tight schedule with *Giselle* rehearsals every evening and finding time to create our Nikolais movement phrases each day. Let's wait until *Giselle* is over before we start something else."

"But, we should do a really strong ballet piece for the concert, Shannon." Sara thought of Lin's performance last year of the Sugar Plum Fairy from *The Nutcracker*. It had helped win her a summer scholarship to a professional ballet school. In fact, she was in San Francisco right now. "It would help you toward winning a scholarship. They only give three in each division, you know."

"Well, where would we practice, and when?" Shannon asked, climbing onto her bunk.

Sara had thought about that. "We could use the secret cabin in the woods when it's empty."

"N-O!" Shannon said. "I am never going back down that trail. Snakes and poison ivy and muck. Besides, it's off-limits."

Sara didn't want to explain how only half the cabin was on the boys' side. She remembered how they had drawn the line across the old linoleum floor with acorns last year. But she also remembered how magical the cabin seemed and how she had led the girls in a circle ritual that helped them rehearse and perform better. She needed magic and she needed a place to create and practice a smashing ballet piece. A New York

City summer scholarship depended on it. Maybe Leah would do it with her. *No*, she thought, *Shannon is a better dancer and has already been noticed by Miss Alexander*. She had another idea. "I know a little practice room in the basement of the dance building," she said. "No one ever goes there. It's not off-limits and it's private. No one could see what we're doing." *Please, Shannon. Please, Shannon*. Sara held her breath.

"I guess that would be all right," Shannon said as she opened her dance history book.

Sara started breathing again. "Good," she said, trying to sound casual. "We can get started right away. Come on, I'll show you the room."

"No," Shannon moaned. "I need to rest. Show me after dinner."

Sara had no choice but to agree. She put one of the flyers on the wall near the banner and one in the blue tin. She found her locket under her pillow and put it in the tin again. Her luck seemed good now and she wanted the locket to be safe. She felt hopeful as she went to the dance building to see how late it would be open tonight. The door was open, but no one was around. Mrs. Lane's office door was locked. There was no sign anywhere telling the hours the dance building was open. She'd have to get Shannon over here immediately after dinner. She began to think about costumes. They'd have to be gorgeous. She went downstairs, through the locker room and down the long hall to the costume room, but it was locked too. She decided to walk across camp just to look at the official path to the boys' side, but when she got as far as the music library she saw that it was open and empty, so she went inside and gazed at all the quotations on the walls. "To be romantic about something is to see what you are and to wish for something entirely different. This requires magic." It was the Balanchine quote she had learned last summer. Yes! That was it, the magic would be in performing part of a Balanchine ballet. That would prove that she could handle the Balanchine technique taught at the New York City Ballet school. And Shannon could help her a lot because she was already learning the Balanchine technique at the school. It was all perfect!

She looked at the dance films on the shelves until her eyes stopped at the Balanchine collection. She saw *Serenade* and *Apollo* and *Allegro Brillante* and *Jewels* and *Concerto Barocco* and *Theme and Variations*. Miss Abbey had shown them some of the ballets, so she knew that *Apollo* and *Jewels* wouldn't be right for them to dance. She took *Serenade* off the shelf and put it in the TV player. Wow! It was beautiful, but required a whole cast of dancers to fulfill the flowing patterns. She put it back and played *Allegro Brillante*. It was *faboulous* but out because there were five men in it. She tried *Concerto Barocco*. Interesting. Mostly women dancers who all wore white leotards with little white skirts attached. Very simple. There was no theme or plot or drama to it. Just crisp, quick movement to Bach violin music. She thought she could do most of the steps. But she and Shannon would have to synchronize their movements exactly. Then she played *Theme and Variations* and was dazzled. The dancers wore luscious short, absolutely gigantic tutus with what looked like flower petals at the top and they had little silver crowns in their hair. The music was a stately Tchaikovsky score. The foot work was just as fast as *Concerto Barocco,* but the two dances and the music were very different.

"Doing some research?" Miss Meisner said, shutting the screen door behind her.

Sara jumped. "I hope it's OK."

"Yes. Do you want to check something out?" Miss Meisner sat behind her desk.

"Can I check out a couple of dance films?" she asked. Miss Meisner let her take both *Concerto Barocco* and *Theme and Variations*. She ran back to the dance building, into the basement and went quickly down the long winding hall, past the costume room, and through the heavy door to the secret practice room. She was able to see through the little window in the door this year without jumping. No one was there. The door opened easily and then her luck got even better. There was a monitor in the room with a tiny screen. It was dusty, but Sara tried it and it worked! They would decide on a dance tonight. She left the dance films on top of the player and ran all the way back to the cabin.

"Where have you been?" Mary wanted to know. She and Brooke were wearing wet bathing suits. "We need you guys to watch our water ballet and tell us what you think."

"Yeah," Brooke said. "Shannon, wake up." She gave Shannon a gentle nudge. "Leah is already down there with Charleigh and Grace."

Sara looked at her watch. They had a couple hours before dinner. She and Shannon went down to the beach and found Leah on the raft with a crowd of girls. Heather Scott was at the end of the dock on her official chair, megaphone next to her, mostly watching the girls inside the buoys who couldn't swim very well. She also kept an eye on some campers who had taken row boats out. The sun was warm and glinting brightly off the water. Sara looked across to the boys' side as she told Shannon about the Balanchine dance films. The boys were doing the same thing as the girls, swimming and boating. But next Saturday they'd be preparing a cook out for the Intermediate girls. Sara pictured herself dancing with Jackson. They settled on the beach and waited for the show to begin. Leah waved at them and when they waved back, Mary, Brooke, Charleigh and Grace performed a lovely synchronized ballet with graceful arms and pointed feet. It amazed Sara how they could tumble backward and stay under water so long. "Ugh," Shannon said. "I would not want that water up my nose." When the performers surfaced and waved their arms, Sara and Shannon stood up and clapped and hooted. When the performers swam over to the beach, they wanted help for the ending of their piece.

"We need a couple more moves," Charleigh said. "We are out of ideas. Got any?" Sara did have one because she had just watched the Balanchine dances.

"How about if you walk into the shallow water at the end, hold hands, raise up your arms and go under each other's arms?" She showed them how to do it, with the girls weaving under each other's arms a few times ending in a straight line again.

"I love it!" Grace said.

"I know," Brooke said. "Let's try doing it on the raft, falling into the water sideways one by one as we finish the movement. Then we can all come to the surface and bow and wave to the audience." They said thanks and swam out to the raft.

Sara watched them go under each other's arms on the raft and fall sideways into the water one by one. They must have practiced it four times. Sara did not like the water much more than Shannon did and wondered how the girls could stay in the water so long. The weather was warm, but not hot. The air was nice and light. Now and then a cool breeze brushed Sara's face. She thought about the boys' party next Saturday. "How old is Jackson?" she asked Shannon.

"I'm not sure," Shannon said. "He's tall and seems mature. I guess sixteen. Maybe you should ask how old Patrick is," she laughed. "He seems to have a crush on you."

"Not really," Sara said. "I don't even know him."

"You don't even know Jackson," she said, throwing a stone into the water.

"I know. But somehow I feel like I already know him." It was true. Sara couldn't explain it. She just felt comfortable around him. Heather Scott blew her whistle and yelled that dinner was in fifteen minutes. The girls started straggling out of the lake. "Come on," Sara said. "Hurry!"

They ran to the cabin and put on practice leotards, then shorts and shirts. They would go directly to the secret practice room after dinner. Sara was brushing her hair into a pony tail when the swimmers came in.

"You guys have to be careful to clear the raft so you don't hit your heads on it when you fall into the water," Leah told them as they dried off.

"OK. Don't worry," Mary said, "We can do it."

"Well, be sure you tell Grace," Leah said.

"We will, we will," Charleigh promised. "But you need to clear the raft for us. We don't want anybody on it during our performance."

"Look!" Brooke exclaimed, pointing to the red flyer on her way into the shower. "A party with the boys!" Charleigh and Mary looked it over with excitement.

"Do we get to go alone?" Charleigh asked.

Sara knew the answer to that one. "No. The counselors go with us," she told them. "But they don't hang out with us. It's cool."

At dinner the girls talked about how they were going to get Mrs. Lane to make them some flyers so they'd have a big audience for the water show. "When is it?" Sara asked.

The girls looked at each other blankly. Grace turned around from the table behind Charleigh. "Let's have it next Sunday afternoon." Mary, Brooke and Charleigh agreed and they decided to ask Mrs. Lane about the flyers on Monday.

A new friend of Charleigh's from the Senior Division came over to their table to chat. Sara heard her say how beautiful the soloists looked learning their parts for *Giselle*. *So*, Sara thought. Just as she suspected, Miss Alexander was teaching their parts in class. *Oh, why didn't I choose Senior Division*, she worried again. No matter. She would dazzle the teachers with her student concert performance.

CHAPTER EIGHTEEN

"Secret Practice Room"

As soon as they finished dinner, Sara and Shannon ran to the dance building. *Please don't be locked*, Sara thought. She smiled when it opened. "They must leave the building open late Saturday nights," Sara said, leading the way downstairs. Shannon followed her through the heavy door and down the dark hallway into the little room.

"It's stuffy in here," Shannon said, coughing a bit from the dust.

Sara climbed onto a chair and tried to open the window to let in the cool pine air, but it was stuck. She jumped down and pushed the film of *Concerto Barocco* into the machine. "Watch this," she smiled.

"Oh, *Concerto Barocco*!" Shannon exclaimed, watching the precise dancers in their simple skirted leotards.

"You already know it?" Sara asked.

"No. I don't know it, but I've seen the company perform it. I love it, but it's too advanced for us."

"Well, how about *Theme and Variations*?" Sara asked, taking out the first film and pushing in the second. The stately

Tchaikovsky music made Sara feel regal. She would love to wear the little crown and the big, thick tutu. Mostly she would love to have the teachers see her doing it. Talk about points!

"Sara," Shannon said. "I don't know if we could do that one, either."

"Not the whole thing," Sara urged. She just had to get her to agree. "Just a portion we think we could do."

Shannon said she thought both ballets were difficult and that she didn't want to look stupid. "Besides," she said. "You need more than two dancers to do those steps where they bourrée under each other's arms, and there's all that really fast footwork."

"Well, we need to choose one of these and learn some of the movements from the film. Enough to put about three minutes together."

"Trois? Trois minutes?" Shannon spoke French again, but trois was also a ballet word, so Sara knew Shannon was astounded that they would be limited to three minutes.

"That's enough time," Sara assured her. "Let's just decide what we want to do." They watched both dances twice, skipping over the parts where men were included. There were nice sections in each dance they could probably do. They took off their shoes and tried some of the steps from each ballet in their socks. They stopped the films over and over and an hour later had only learned about three steps.

"You see," Shannon said. "I told you it would be too difficult for us. What did you do last year?"

"Four of us did a modern dance piece," Sara told her. "But this year I really need to do a strong ballet because I am only doing ensemble work in *Giselle.*"

"Well, you won a scholarship last year doing the modern," Shannon said. "We could do modern."

"NO!" Sara was nearly defiant. Shannon was not hearing her.

"What is the big problem?" Shannon wanted to know, putting on her shoes.

Sara would have to tell her. "I am not eligible for an Intermediate Division scholarship this year. What I am trying for is a summer scholarship to the school of the New York City Ballet where you and Erin and Jackson go."

"But no one has said they are giving a scholarship, Sara. It is best not to wish upon something that is not real. We should concentrate on what is real by just doing well in our classes and doing a student concert piece we can fulfill. If there is even going to be a student concert."

Sara suddenly felt like screaming. Shannon had destroyed her dream. Of course, there would be a special scholarship! Of course there would be a student concert! She stared angrily at the blank monitor screen. She had heard Robin say she wanted the scholarship to the New York City Ballet school. Of course there would be a scholarship.

"Besides," Shannon continued, "as I said, two dancers alone cannot do justice to the intricate movements and patterns Balanchine created for these ballets. We would need at least three."

Sara had an idea. "OK. Three! Let's ask Leah. She's a good dancer and she's really great at fast footwork."

"I must warn," Shannon said, "that we will not look good unless I can teach you how to use the Balanchine arms and hands. It's done with a flourish. And when you do the movements, it's not just the steps, but how you flow in between the steps that count."

137

"I know I can do it," Sara smiled. "I think Leah can do it!"

"Very well," Shannon agreed. "I will try with you, but if it looks bad, I won't be in it."

Sara smiled. It would be good. Without a doubt, it would be good. They sat on the floor and watched both ballets again. Then they looked at each other. "I choose *Theme and Variations,*" Sara said happily. She could just see herself in the big tutu and shiny crown dancing to the Tchaikovsky music.

"I choose *Concerto Barocco,*" Shannon said, like it was a conclusion. She looked Sara in the eyes. "The simple white leotards with skirts will show our precise movements. You will need to lose a bit of weight, and Leah three or four pounds."

Sara swallowed. How dare her suggest she was fat. "What?" she said.

"We must be thin to look perfect in the white," she said. "And to move quickly like birds."

Easy for her to say, Sara thought. Shannon couldn't get much thinner. And Sara wondered how they would get Leah to lose weight, but they'd have to try. She was a whiz in fast steps and they needed her. They watched *Concerto Barocco* one more time, put the film on top of the player and left. Sara tried the exit door that led out of the hallway three times to make sure it wasn't sticking this year. Each time, it opened easily. Someone must have fixed it. They dropped *Theme and Variations* into the return slot at the music library and took the path to Pavlova cabin. The torches had already been lit along the lawn overlooking the placid lake.

Sara was so excited that night she could hardly get to sleep. The boys' party and the promise of their Balanchine performance danced in her head like sugar plums from *The Nutcracker.*

138

CHAPTER NINETEEN

"Explorations"

At breakfast Sunday Sara watched Leah eat two pieces of toast along with bacon and eggs and wondered how she would be able to say something to her about losing weight. But first she would have to get her excited to be in the Balanchine piece with them. She wanted to take her to the secret practice room today to show her the dance, but the dance building was closed on Sundays. It would have to wait until tomorrow night after dinner when they went to work on their Nikolais homework phrases. Suddenly Sara was distracted by Hillary's laughter.

"Last night was SO fun!" Hillary bragged to all within earshot. "We danced right up until ten o'clock. Those boys are so cute." She glanced Sara's way. Sara had forgotten that they were at the boys' party last night.

"Jackson is such a good dancer," Robin smiled dreamily. Sara felt her heart close a bit thinking how Jackson and Robin were about the same height and had the same color hair. She imagined them dancing close to dreamy music. "Wish he lived in Chicago instead of New York," Robin said.

"We could go to the Joffrey school together. Well, maybe I'll dance with him in New York one day," she said like she had a secret. She was *so* after that New York City Ballet summer scholarship.

"Let's go to the lookout bench," Leah suggested. Sara looked out the window and saw that rain was threatening. "Come on!" Leah said to Shannon. So the three dumped their trays and took off. But soon Sara realized why Leah had wanted to go there and it wasn't for the view. As thunder began to sound in the distant trees, Leah headed for the secret path to the boys' side. "Duck in here," she told them.

A frown took over Shannon's face. "No thank you," she said, staying glued to the bench.

"But you don't even know what's in there," Leah protested. "It's a really cool path that I think leads to some water down there. Let's find out." She waited for them at the entrance to the hidden path.

Sara wasn't sure what to do. "I think it might be off-limits," she said. "I mean as soon as you got a ways in, it might be. Certainly not worth the risk of getting demoted or being sent home."

"Well, who would know? It's not like our counselor is watching us." Leah seemed insistent.

"I'm going back to the cabin to read," Shannon said. She started back. *Oh, thanks*, Sara thought.

"Come on, before it starts raining," Leah said to Sara. Then she disappeared into the trees. Sara followed her into the heavy brush. Maybe she could bring her back before they got to the stream. But Leah was practically running. "See? Isn't this cool?" she laughed, bounding around the curve that led deeper down the trail. Sara kept her eye out for snakes, but this time there were none. Soon she smelled mint and her shoes got into some muck. The stream would appear next. "Wow, look at this!" Leah exclaimed. "A stream."

"Now I know we're off-limits!" Sara warned. "I refuse to go farther!" She really didn't want Leah to know you could get to the boys' side simply by going over the plank. After that, she might find the secret cabin. Sara wanted to keep it a blue tin secret. It had come in so handy last year as a place where she was able to bring the girls together in a spirit of cooperation. Plus, she really liked Leah and didn't want her to get in trouble. The more people knew about it, the higher the chance of them all getting in trouble. She turned around hoping Leah would follow, but she kept gazing at the stream. Thunder rumbled overhead. The wind changed direction and swayed the tops of the pine trees. "Come on!" Sara shouted as she started back up the path.

"Go ahead," Leah said, fixed to her spot.

Darn, Sara thought as she made her way quickly back to the lookout bench. By the time she got there it began to rain, so she ran all the way to Pavlova cabin. She found everyone on their bunks reading or chatting. Mary, Brooke and Charleigh were unhappy they couldn't practice their synchronized swim routine. Shannon had her nose back in her dance history book and took it out to stare at Sara as if to say *"Well, what happened? Where is Leah?"* Sara just shrugged her shoulders and threw her shoes off as a huge bolt of lightning cracked overhead. Now the rain was pouring against the windows and pounding on the old tin roof of the cabin. She glanced out the window but didn't see Leah.

Sara wanted to write to Erin on the back of the note she had sent, but it was in the blue tin. She got some of

141

the paper she had ripped out of her Dance History notebook, found a pen and got on her bunk. She'd answer Jen Hutchins first. She got Jen's letter out of the drawer and wrote on the backside of it. There really wasn't much to say. The more Sara danced, the less she seemed to have in common with friends who didn't. She told Jen briefly about getting a banner from Erin, about how the dancing was going so far and a bit about Jackson. That was it. She folded the letter and begged two envelopes with stamps from Mary. Then she settled down to write details to Erin. Lightning cracked and thunder rolled over the lake again and Leah came in soaked.

"Where have you been?" Charleigh asked.

"Just exploring," Leah said, kicking off her shoes. She grabbed a towel, dry clothes and a hairbrush and went into the bathroom. Sara was dying to know if Leah had crossed the plank and found the boys' side, but began her letter to Erin. She told her she had her bunk from last year, thanked her for the banner, the cookies and the blue tin, and told her every detail of everything she could think of that had happened so far, including how hard and interesting the Nikolais method of modern dance was for her. "A BIG challenge!" she wrote. About Jackson, she said "I guess you already know how cute he is. He must be a good dancer, too. He is going to be Albrecht in *Giselle*." She finished by telling her about the boys' party next Saturday. "No horse barn to worry about this year!" she said in closing. "Wish you were here. Send stamps and envelopes." As she licked the envelope, Leah came out of the bathroom. There wasn't a clue on her dry face about exactly how far she had gone.

The rain stopped by dinner time but the paths and trees were soaked and dripping. The torches were lit, as usual, at eight-thirty. It reminded Sara that she only had a half hour to get to the laundry room and create her modern dance movement phrase for Monday. It had to be based on moving on the periphery. "Make lines in space like you're running around the room with a lit sparkler," Miss Lee had instructed. Sara's last two movements needed a lot of correction so this one had to be good. "Want to go to the laundry room and make up our modern phrase?" she asked Shannon.

"I already did mine," Shannon answered.

"Where did you go?" Sara wanted to know.

"I just made it up in my head on my bunk this afternoon," she said.

Seriously? Sara thought. How could she do everything so easily?

"I'll go," Leah said, jumping down from her bunk. "I was going to go, anyway." As soon as they were out the door Sara asked her.

"How far down the stream did you go? I mean it was lightning and everything."

"Oh, I walked a bit and saw a plank across the stream, but then a big bold of lightning hit, and I freaked out. I ran all the way back to the cabin," Leah laughed. "I'll wait for a sunny day."

"That must be totally off-limits," Sara said. "Besides, there's probably nothing over there."

"We'll see," Leah said.

The last girl was just leaving the laundry room. They moved the big wooden table to the side of the room and began to work on their movements. Sara tried not to be distracted by what Leah was doing and tried not to look up at the clock. Soon she was moving around the room pretending to make traces in a black night with a colorful sparkler. She could see reds, blues, greens and the blend they made in the air. She enjoyed twisting and turning, pretending to toss the sparkler under her leg and catching it with the other leg, then grabbing it with her other hand making a delicious flow of movement. Before she knew it Julie Hess was at the door kicking them out so she could lock up. But she kept thinking about what she had created as she walked the path back to the cabin, as she brushed her teeth and as she fell asleep. She must have dreamed about it, too, because she had no trouble in class Monday remembering it.

"Yes!" Miss Lee hollered out as Sara finished performing her movement for the class. "Remember that." And for some reason, Sara didn't think she'd have any trouble remembering it. It seemed a part of her, living in her body to be thrown out at a whim. It amazed her. After all, she was the same girl who had so much trouble catching on quickly to ballet exercises that she was frightened to stand at the end of the barre. I'll remember, she thought happily. Shannon smiled at her.

Sara felt like she was riding a little wave of success as she went down the hall to folk class. But when she heard the seniors dancing above her and felt their feet bouncing off the floor over her head she imagined that they were learning a wonderful ballet piece for the final performance. She could see them in flowing costumes moving in their pointe shoes on the big outdoor stage on the lake, all without her. She was going to have to really show off in the student concert ballet, step it up in all of her classes and show a *lot* of enthusiasm and leadership to be in the running for the scholarship to New York. She smiled big when Mr. Moyne handed out the tambourines and focused hard on the new steps he gave her. She could hear Miss Abbey say, "You can make any part look larger by the way you dance it." She vowed to cooperate, to look enthused, to gather all her stage presence and make her part look very large in the folk dance. She'd worry about leadership later.

Sara saw Shannon staring at Leah as she ate two helpings of pasta at dinner. If Sara wanted to make *Concerto Barocco* beautiful, she was going to have to say something. "You must be really hungry, Leah," she said. Shannon looked the other way.

"What? I want to have enough energy for *Giselle* rehearsal tonight," she said.

"Sometimes it works better to eat less for dinner and eat a little apple before rehearsal," Sara said.

"I know, but we also have to make up our Nikolais movement phrase for tomorrow before *Giselle* rehearsal at seven. We're going to need energy." Shannon looked at Leah, then stared at Sara like the Balanchine dream was never going to happen. *Say something*, Sara thought. But Shannon just kept staring. Sara was going to have to be the leader.

"We're not going to do twenty laps of backstroke," Sara said. "We're not even actually dancing full out at *Giselle* rehearsals yet."

"Well, it's not like I'm fat," Leah said. Then she glanced at Shannon. "I mean, I don't want to look like a weasel." Shannon was offended and left. Sara was going to have to fix this.

She took a sip of water and began. "Leah," she said. "Shannon and I want to invite you to dance with us in the student concert. We want to do a quick-moving Balanchine piece and to move fast we are all going to have to be trim."

"*What* student concert?" Leah demanded. "No one has said anything about that at all."

"Well, there is going to be one. The intermediates do one every summer. But they won't tell us until after we do *Giselle* at the end of week four. That's how they did it last year. Then we only had two weeks to prepare. Please believe me!"

"Well, it's only the beginning of week three," Leah said. "And how about I'll believe it when I see it?" she said, getting up. Sara felt so stupid watching her walk away. She had completely failed at leadership.

CHAPTER TWENTY

"Stopping and Starting"

Sara went to the cabin and found Shannon alone. "Let's take Leah to the secret practice room tonight and show her the *Concerto Barocco* film," she said.

"Are you kidding?" Shannon said, pulling some new pointe shoes out from under the bed. "I think we should leave her alone. And, really, Sara. I think we should wait to see if there actually is going to be a student concert."

"But you promised, Shannon," Sara said, feeling let down.

"I said I would try with you, but if it looked bad I wouldn't do it," Shannon said. Then Brooke, Mary and Charleigh came in with paper for flyers. Leah was right behind them.

"Look what Leah helped us get from Mrs. Lane!" Mary said excitedly. "We're going to make flyers tonight for our water show."

So, Sara thought. *Leah is in good somehow with Mrs. Lane.* She remembered the two run-ins she'd had with Mrs. Lane already. She grabbed new pointe shoes from under her bunk and took off with Shannon for the dance building. They created their Nikolais movement phrases for the next day in the big studio before everyone started arriving for *Giselle* rehearsal. The assignment was turning, whirling and spinning, and Sara tried to enjoy creating something from what Miss Lee had taught them in class that day, but she kept thinking about Leah. She really needed her in *Concerto Barocco.*

The entire cast showed up for *Giselle* except Jackson. The principal dancers knew most of their parts and Robin and Kathy Jacobs had learned a lot of theirs. Sara felt like a small speck in the ballet. She watched Shannon understudy Robin. It was clear that if something happened Shannon would have no trouble stepping in for her. In fact, Sara thought, she would look delightful. She watched Leah in the background with Keera and Alene following everything the corps de ballet did in case they had to take someone's part. She realized she was lucky to have her own part even if it was just in the corps, and she started concentrating. The music was dynamic and she strived to fulfill it and to express each movement with grace. But Miss Alexander didn't seem to notice. "OK, dancers," she said. "Everything you know now, full out." Sara arched her feet over the box of her new hard pointe shoes to try to get them broken in more. Miss Alexander started the music from the beginning and Sara pretended to stand in the wings with a white wedding veil over her head. She looked across the room at the other half of the corps de ballet waiting in the make-believe wings.

Sara was amazed at how soft and strong Katie Easton's bourrées were at the opening of the ballet. Sara wondered if she'd ever be that strong on pointe as she watched Katie's Myrtha character do the tiny, slow running steps all the way across the entire room, then repeat them to the other side, arms crossed in front. It had a mysterious and eerie quality. And she was so surprised to see how beautiful and flowing Robin and Kathy's solos were when danced full out in pointe shoes and to the rich music. Miss Sutton wasn't there, so Miss Alexander kept running in pretending to take Jackson's part to keep the story going. Sara actually loved the part where she held one hand in the air with Shannon and danced in a circle. She looked at all the other pairs on both sides of the stage and was enchanted.

In the locker room after rehearsal Sara kept thinking of the secret practice room with the film of *Concerto Barocco* she had left there. Her new pointe shoes had made a blister on one foot and a little blood on the other. As she applied ointment and Band-Aids, Leah sat down next to her. "I was looking in the mirror tonight," she said. "You're right. I didn't need that second helping of pasta." Then she took off. Maybe there was hope.

Walking past the moonlit lake on the way back to the cabin, Sara complimented Shannon on learning Robin's part so quickly just by watching. "Facile," Shannon said in French. She smiled. "Easy. You just have to focus. For example, when you are in ballet, don't think about modern. When you are in tap, don't think about folk. When you are in modern, don't think about ballet. When you are in rehearsal, don't think about Jackson."

When they got to Pavlova, water ballet flyers with wet lettering were drying on the floor. "Did you guys use enough color?" Leah teased, picking one up. "These are really cool. Let's put this one on the wall," she said, tacking it next to the flyer for the boys' party.

"Will you guys help us pass them out tomorrow?" Charleigh asked. "We need to take one to every intermediate cabin so we'll have a big audience Sunday."

"Sure, Charlie," Leah said. "How about right after dinner before we have our *Giselle* rehearsal?" She looked at Sara and Shannon.

No, Sara thought. *That's the only time I have to make up my modern dance movement phrase.* Then she remembered what Shannon had just said. She thought: *When you're passing out flyers, don't think about modern.* She might have to try doing choreography in her head tomorrow night. "OK," she agreed. Perhaps she was learning about cooperation in more ways than one.

Tuesday morning Sara woke up feeling sticky and hot. No breeze came in the window. The sun was already too bright. *Ugh,* she thought. *Up North Michigan Hot Streak.* She was the first one awake and decided to take a cool shower before going to pointe class. Soon Brooke was knocking on the door. "Don't forget about helping us with the flyers tonight!" she said as Sara gathered her dance bag and left. She let the screen door bang a little hoping it would wake up Shannon and Leah so they wouldn't be late for the eight-thirty class. She ate breakfast quickly limiting herself to a bit of cereal and half a peanut butter toast as she pictured herself in the white short skirted leotard for *Concerto Barocco*. The woods was already warm as she made her way to the dance building. In the locker room alone she fussed over getting her new pointe shoes on just right, carefully putting Band-Aids on the sore spots. She was the first one in Studio B and looked at herself in the mirror. She liked the way her feet looked in the pointe shoes, liked the way her hair went smoothly into a tight bun, but she wished her legs were longer and that her hips were narrower inside the dark blue leotard. She wished she knew what the Nikolais assignment would be for tomorrow so she could begin working on it right now, but modern class wouldn't end until almost five-fifteen, her last class of the day. Then she'd have to rush to dinner, distribute flyers and get to *Giselle* rehearsal by seven. She went up on her pointe shoes several times to warm her feet, then tried to bourrée all the way across the room and back pretending to be Myrtha in the opening scene of *Giselle.*

"Softer, softer!" Miss Sutton instructed, coming into the sunny room. Sara quickly came down off her pointes.

"New pointe shoes," Sara said as an excuse.

"Pull up more. Come on, try again."

Sara remembered Madame's harsh criticism of her bourrées last year, and suddenly wished she had not arrived early. But as Miss Sutton watched her move across the floor, she could hear Madame say, "You can do! Yes!" She only made it three quarters across the small room, but Miss Sutton smiled and said it was better. When the other dancers arrived and class began, Sara felt special for having Miss Sutton's attention but realized she had a long way to go to look like Katie Easton. On the way out of class she saw a dance film on the piano. "Balanchine's Tarantella" someone had written on the cover above a picture of a dancer in red and yellow holding a tambourine above her head. A male dancer in a red sash smiled next to her. Changing into her character shoes in the locker room, Sara thought of asking Shannon to peek through the back window of Studio B tonight after *Giselle* rehearsal to see if Miss Alexander and Mr. Peters would be practicing *Tarantella*, but she couldn't, of course. Shannon's toe had just healed from her fall off the rock. She had another idea.

151

After lunch, when Sara entered Studio B for ballet class, the *Tarantella* film was gone. All through class she thought of her idea even though she could hear Shannon saying: *When you are in ballet, don't think about modern. When you are in tap don't think about folk. When you are in modern don't think about ballet. When you are in rehearsal don't think about Jackson.* She was in ballet thinking about all those things and more. After leaps across the floor and bows, Sara was so hot she could hardly stand it.

"The temperature must be ninety-eight and a hundred degrees humid," Leah complained on the way to the locker room. "Guess they don't believe in air conditioning up in the woods." Sara wondered if this would be a good time to introduce her idea, but Leah left quickly. "I'm going to splash cold water on my face and get to modern to practice my movement phrase before class starts." Sara and Shannon followed Leah up the stairs to the big studio. They had about five minutes to run through their assignment before class began. In spite of the heat, Miss Lee sat on her stool beating her drum and the class was expected to go through the entire set of warm-ups as usual. Sara was thinking of the boys' party this Saturday and had more trouble than ever remembering the sequence. Miss Lee looked at her just as she made a glaring mistake. She couldn't wait to get that Nikolais book from Jackson Saturday.

Instead of teaching new dance vocabulary center-floor, Miss Lee went right to having them perform their homework assignments. Sara was glad for the chance to get a drink of water, put her dance towel around her neck and sit under the barre. But Miss Lee called her first along with Leah, Shannon, Keera and Alene. They were to space themselves around the big room and, when Miss Lee said "Go," to perform their homework assignments at the same time. "No matter your movement, stay in your own personal space," Miss Lee coached. Sara totally forgot how hot she was as she moved around turning, whirling and spinning. As she caught the movements of the other girls out of the corner of her eye and felt their motion all around her, she felt like she was part of an energetic performance. When she completed her phrase but no one else had stopped, she started again, moving around the room trying to be the most interesting dancer. Finally Miss Lee shouted "Stop!" and Sara put her arm and foot down and stood still.

That was not good enough for Miss Lee. "I said *stop!*" she shouted again. "Sara, when I said 'stop' you continued moving." Sara didn't get it. *No,* she wanted to say, *I definitely stopped.* "Stop means stop," Miss Lee continued, staring at her. "Move again." Sara was embarrassed and stood frozen. Miss Lee began to beat her drum and Sara started repeating her movement phrase. "Now STOP!" Miss Lee shouted, beating her drum hard in a single beat. Sara quickly brought her foot down, her arms to her sides and stood still. "When I say stop, *freeze* exactly where you are!" Miss Lee was getting frustrated. "Go again." She beat her drum again and Sara moved again. She was right in the middle of a jump into the air while turning when she heard "STOP!" and the big beat of the drum. She froze as soon as she landed on one foot, keeping her arms over head where they had been. "YES!" Miss Lee shouted. She turned to the class. "Can you see the difference?" Sara stood in the middle of the room alone while everyone continued to stare at her. The girls under the barre nodded their heads. "OK. Again Sara. This time change your movement." Sara had to think quickly. She just started making things up using turning, twirling and spinning. "Bigger, Sara," Miss Lee said. "Take up the space in the room!" Sara began to dart into space, running as she turned and spun. Miss Lee beat the drum more quickly. Sara felt like a train racing on a track through space, her feet almost leaving her body. "STOP!" Miss Lee shouted and Sara froze with her head down, her arms out and one knee up. The class burst into applause. Sara was afraid to move. "Yes!" Miss Lee finally said.

Then Miss Lee called the other dancers out and they all practiced moving and stopping until the end of class. "Assignment for tomorrow," Miss Lee said. "Combine a volume study with turning, whirling and spinning. You must show 'stopping' twice in your phrase. Remember, the audience sees the intention of your movement expression. If you don't show a clear intention, you're expressing nothing."

"I'm gonna die from this heat," Sara heard Keera say on the way down to the locker room. But Sara had forgotten all about it. She was still turning, whirling, spinning, and stopping in her mind. Her body felt like it was still moving. It was a good feeling, like she had become the movement itself. She kind of floated to dinner.

"You better eat some more chicken salad, Sara, if you want to get through rehearsal tonight," Leah said. "But first we have to help with the water ballet flyers." She looked up at the clock.

"I am sure we'll have time for everything," Shannon said. "Charleigh, Brooke and Mary have already left for the flyers."

When they got to Pavlova cabin the flyers were sitting on the chest of drawers with a list of which cabins they were to go to. "Hurry!" Sara said. "Let's try to get to the dance building by six-thirty so we'll have a half hour to make up our Nikolais movement phrase for tomorrow." Shannon and Leah followed her as she grabbed the flyers and went out the door. Leah quickly ripped the list into three parts and made sure they each had enough flyers for their cabins. "See you at the dance building," Sara said, running to her first cabin on the list. She got back to Pavlova at six-thirty, threw her last flyer into the blue tin, splashed her face with cold water, grabbed her dance bag and took off for the dance building.

CHAPTER TWENTY-ONE

"The Man in the Hallway"

Sara threw off her shoes at the door to the dance building and was already creating her movement phrase for tomorrow in her head. Jackson and Courtney Karlen were rehearsing in the big studio with Mr. Peters. The romantic music filled the room. Shannon and Leah were nowhere to be found. Jackson was a beautiful partner. He was strong and sturdy, but soft all at the same time. They made a wonderful Albrecht and Giselle. She looked up at the clock. She only had about fifteen minutes left to find a space to choreograph her assignment for modern tomorrow. Then Katie Easton arrived along with Robin and Kathy. They not only got to learn their special parts in ballet class, but got to come early to rehearsal to practice. When Miss Alexander arrived, Sara felt jealous and like a big nobody again. She was sure if she had chosen Senior Division Miss Alexander would have noticed her dancing and let her try out for one of the special parts. Now she felt another decision pressing inside her head. She really needed to get her modern assignment done, especially after today's experience with Miss Lee, but she also really needed to stay here and watch this rehearsal. She felt ballet swell in her heart again as her favorite thing in all the world, where she belonged, what she was striving for.

"Hold her waist securely when she goes down forward over her pointe, but remember to look gentle because you are sorry for what you did and you are trying to win her back and be forgiven. You must express caring and love," Mr. Peters coached Jackson. Sara sighed inside. Oh, how she would love to be Jackson's partner. *Caring and love*, she thought. She felt a whisper around her neck again and reached for her locket, but remembered it was in the blue tin. She looked at the clock but stayed glued to her spot, letting the dancers and music fill her. Robin brushed past her on the way to the drinking fountain.

"I hear you have a solo in the folk dance for final performance," Robin said, smiling. Sara couldn't tell if she was happy for her or rubbing it in that she didn't have a special part in *Giselle*.

"Yeah," Sara smiled back. She decided to rub it in. "It's fantastic. I really love it!"

But Robin was her old self. "*Giselle* is what is fantastic," she said, walking back into the studio. Sara watched Robin's long legs carry her svelte body topped with her strawberry blonde hair across the room until she began warm-ups at the barre. She looked at the clock again. Just ten minutes left to create something for Miss Lee tomorrow. Then Courtney was excused and Miss Alexander called Katie out to work with Jackson and Mr. Peters. Sara was fascinated by the intricate movements and enveloped by the sweet music. She relaxed against the wall to watch. Some of the other corps de ballet dancers arrived looking fresh like they had just had showers and brushed their hair back into neat buns to fight the hot weather. Sara realized she didn't get a chance to shower and also realized that now she had run out of time to do her homework assignment.

"Here you are!" Leah said behind her. She turned to see that Shannon was with her and that both were perspiring from their practice and the heat. "Where have you been?"

"Right here," Sara said. "Why?"

"Why?" Leah said. "Did you finish your homework for modern? Where did you do it?"

"Where did you do yours?" Sara asked.

"Downstairs in Studio B," Leah said. "Where did you do yours?" Shannon looked at Sara like she knew the truth.

"I'll do it later," Sara said, not really knowing how that was going to happen. She stood in the doorway with the gathering dancers as Mr. Peters worked with Katie and Jackson. When they had finished the partnering, Miss Alexander took over and Katie rehearsed the larger part of her role. She was already doing it beautifully. *All of these girls have learned their parts so quickly*, Sara thought, worried that she couldn't have. *Well, no problem,* she thought. *I wasn't asked.* Still, she was sure she could dance the part of one of Myrtha's attendants. Maybe it was that she wasn't tall enough. After all, Robin and Kathy were about the same height.

"Come in, dancers!" Miss Alexander finally called. Sara ran to a place under the barre and put on her pointe shoes. During the barre warm-ups she kept glancing at Jackson across the room. His long legs took deep pliés and his placement of shoulders over hips seemed perfect. *New York training*, Sara sighed to herself, yearning to get there.

The ballet came together more tonight with everyone knowing much more of their parts. Sara kept staring at the group in the mirror, pleased with what she saw. She couldn't wait for all the black leotards to turn into beautiful white costumes. Tonight Miss Alexander brought long-stemmed white lilies and wispy forest ferns for the soloists to use in their roles. They were silk, but looked real. *How romantic*, Sara thought, watching Myrtha dance with the ferns. She felt Myrtha's power as she called her Wilis out of the wings to dance. It was getting exciting. "Not bad, everyone," Miss Alexander said at eight-thirty. "But we'll really have to nail down the rest of the choreography by the end of the week. Then next week we'll focus on expression and style and all the details. Let's hope this sticky weather breaks. Good night, dancers." Sara watched Jackson say good-bye to Courtney and Katie. She watched Robin follow him out of the studio.

"Oh, boy, would I like a swim," Leah said. "Too bad the beach is closed."

"Come on," Shannon said. "Let's go to the cabin, take cold showers and get some sleep."

Sara still had to make up her Nikolais phrase for tomorrow. She was pretty sure the dance building stayed open until nine. "Go ahead without me," she told them. "I'll wait until it clears out here, then work on my movement phrase for modern." She actually wanted to enact her other idea, but it was too late. It would have to wait until tomorrow. Leah and Shannon left and Sara went downstairs through the long hallway to Studio B, but when she got there Miss Alexander and Mr. Peters were just going in to rehearse. She left quickly before they saw her and walked around to the back of the building and found the rock to stand on. The evening was still warm, and the moon was hiding behind the clouds when she looked in the window. Miss Alexander's feet were perfect in her pointe shoes as they arched over in quick echappés a la seconde and in dazzling turns, tambourine overhead. Mr. Peters was on his knee next to her striking his tambourine on his raised knee and his shoulder, then overhead. How energetic their quick moves were as they chased each other joyfully around the room to the exuberant music! How much fun character dance could be! How wonderful Balanchine's choreography! The hands on the studio clock suddenly moved to 8:40, so she decided to go quickly to the secret practice room in the basement to make up her movement phrase for tomorrow.

She was so excited about Balanchine dances when she got into the room, she decided to take a couple of minutes to look at *Concerto Barocco* again. She was amazed once more at how quickly the dancers moved, and she noticed what Shannon had said about the important flow between the actual steps. What energy and grace in a package of precise movements those dancers were! She also noted again how lean they were and how they were able to flit like birds on their pointe shoes. She wanted to learn more of the steps, but knew it must be getting late. She took the film out and put it back on top of the player. She sat on the floor for a minute and tried to get her mind back into turning, whirling, spinning, carving volume and stopping on a dime. When she had thought of something she got up and tried it, changing it several times. She imagined taking up the whole big studio with her patterns and carving of space. She had it and she liked it.

She had no way of knowing exactly what time it was, but had a feeling she better get out of there before they locked the dance building doors. What a long day it had been. She couldn't wait to get to the shower and her bunk. She grabbed her dance bag and turned off the dim overhead light. She opened the door and went quickly down the dark hallway to the exit door. She turned the knob and pulled, but it didn't open. She pulled harder. She pushed the door knob in and twisted harder and pulled again, but it didn't open. She kicked it but it didn't open. She pounded, but no one came. Studio B was way over on the other side of the building. Miss Alexander and Mr. Peters would never hear her. Why would the door stick today when it had opened easily the last time she was here? She sat on the floor to think. She'd have to go back into the practice room, stand on a chair, open the window and climb out. But when she tried it, the window wouldn't even budge. She went back down the hall and pounded some more. "Help!" she cried. "I'm in here!" Suddenly the door flew open and an old man stood there in the shadows. Her heart jumped and she screamed.

"Stop yer hollerin'," the man said. "What are ya doin' in there anyways?"

Sara saw he had a mop and a bucket. She raced past him and slipped on the wet floor.

"Take it easy," he said, helping her up. "You're worse than a foal trying to stand up for the first time." That's when Sara recognized him. It was Charlie from the boys' horse barn last year! He must be the janitor now.

"Charlie, the Axe Man," Sara blurted before thinking. He glared at her. "You fixed the plank over the stream last summer."

"Yep," he said, twisting the door knob. "Looks like I'll be fixin' this door so it don't stick in hot weather." Sara started to leave. "Hold on," he said. "I already locked the

162

door upstairs. I'll have to let you out." He followed her up the stairs with jangling keys. Sara was scared of him and just wanted out of there. Before he let her out he warned that he locked the building at nine o'clock sharp week days. "Eight-thirty Saturdays," he told her. "Don't let me catch you here after hours again."

Sara ran all the way back to the cabin under the dark, towering fir trees, her heart still pounding. She wondered if Charlie would tell Miss Sutton. She was going to have to get more organized and make every minute count if she wanted that scholarship. She was going to have to be exactly where she was supposed to be every second. She jumped onto the porch and pushed past her cabin mates who were all sitting there talking. She grabbed the blue tin, took out her locket and shoved the tin back. She wore the locket in the shower, and she held it in her bunk as she thought about the day's events: the bourrées for Miss Sutton, being singled out in the Nikolais class, passing out the flyers, racing to rehearsal, watching the soloists rehearse with Jackson, the magic of *Giselle*, watching *Tarantella*, getting stuck in the hallway, the scare with Charlie. At least she had her assignment done for Miss Lee. As soon as Erin sent her envelopes and stamps, she'd write her all the details.

CHAPTER TWENTY-TWO

"Costumes"

In ballet class Wednesday morning Miss Sutton had the whole class practice the scoots across the room with Shannon and Sara in the front of each line. As Sara scooted, her arm outstretched and head down, she wondered if Jackson would be at rehearsal that night. She pictured his square shoulders inside his white T-shirt and his soft arms holding Courtney. "Keep your back leg stable in that arabesque, Sara," Miss Sutton called out above the driving music. Shannon looked at her as if to say, *When you are in ballet, think about ballet*. Her eyes darted from Sara's eyes to her neck, then back up to her eyes, then down to her neck. Sara realized she was wearing her locket. She couldn't believe that Miss Sutton hadn't noticed. When the lines had crossed and she reached the other side of the room, she quickly took off the locket and put it in the corner under the barre. She mouthed a thank you to Shannon, took her bows center-floor with the class, grabbed her locket and was happy to get into tap class.

"Really," Shannon whispered to her before Mr. Moyne entered the room. "What are you thinking when you are not thinking? And why all the mystery last night?"

"I'll tell you at lunch," Sara promised. She had fun dancing the time step, double time step and learning part of a tap dance to funky jazz music. At lunch there were too many people around to tell Shannon anything, so they went to the lookout bench when everybody else went swimming. The day was cooler and a breeze swayed the trees and brushed their faces. "I went to Studio B after rehearsal, but Miss Alexander and Mr. Peters were rehearsing *Tarantella* in there, so I went to the secret practice room to make up my Nikolais phrase and the exit door stuck *big* time when I tried to get out. It was really scary. Charlie had to let me out."

"Charleigh?" Shannon asked.

"No. Charlie the Axe Man. That's what we called him last year because he scared us with an axe he used to fix the plank across the stream." Sara pointed toward the path to the boys' side. "He was stable man for the boys' horses last year and he's the janitor this year, I guess. He told me he locks the doors to the dance building at nine weekdays and eight-thirty Saturdays." She didn't mention standing on the rock to watch *Tarantella* rehearsal, how Charlie had yelled at her or her worry that Charlie might tell Miss Sutton.

"Sara," Shannon said gravely. "I think you better prepare your modern dance phrase *before Giselle* rehearsals from now on." She looked at her. "If you ever want to dance in New York, you are going to have to learn how to focus." She glanced at her watch. "You see, right now we would have had time to practice our phrase for modern if we hadn't had this talk."

166

"Well, come on," Sara said. "Let's go." They went right to the laundry room and spent fifteen minutes running through their Nikolais phrases. Modern was their next class, so when it came time to perform her assignment, it was fresh in Sara's mind. Her body remembered every move. Miss Lee called some people out alone and some in groups and Sara got called out alone. She began slowly by pretending to carve space into volume with her arms. Then she stopped. Then she dashed through space turning, whirling and spinning, then she stopped. Then she pretended to carve space with her knee as she spun around. She finished by whirling and carving with her foot. She stopped sharply at the end. There was silence.

"Remember that," was all that Miss Lee said. Then it was over. The rest of class was spent moving across the studio learning legs swings and the concept of momentum. Sara like it because it had a three-quarter time drum beat like a waltz. On the way to folk class Leah told her she liked her movement phrase. Miss Lee had told Leah to remember hers, too. They agreed these were achievements of some kind and deserved to be put on the Pavlova banner. Mr. Moyne seemed to be sticking to the steps he had created for Sara's solo and she found true enthusiasm for them after watching *Tarantella* rehearsal. Tapping the tambourine over her head as she twirled, she pretended she was Miss Alexander in pointe shoes. She imagined Jackson was her partner and they both wore red and yellow costumes and flirted and chased each other around the stage. She could hear the huge audience applauding for them in the big outdoor theatre by the lake. After the whole class practiced what they had learned of the dance with Leah, Shannon, Keera and Alene doing what they knew of their special part, Mr. Moyne excused them for dinner. Sara skipped happily down the hall to the locker room, but met Mrs. Lane half way there.

"Sara, your mother is on the office phone," she said. "I don't know what she wants."

Sara threw her character shoes in her dance bag with her locket, ballet slippers, tap and pointe shoes, grabbed her street clothes and ran up the stairs to the office. Mrs. Lane handed her the phone. Her mom just wanted to know how she was and asked if there was going to be a performance half-way through camp like there was last year. She was excited to find out that Sara was chosen for *Giselle,* but was sad that she wouldn't be able to come to the performance because she had to go to her brother's soccer camp the same weekend. "Always something," she said. "Well, I'll be at your final performance," she assured her.

"Don't worry," Sara told her. "It isn't like I have a special part or something." Her mom said she would tell Miss Abbey about *Giselle.*

Shannon was waiting for Sara at the door. "Is everything all right?" she asked.

"Yes," Sara answered. "She was just checking in with me." But Sara felt disappointed that she wouldn't have anyone to watch her in the big romantic ballet that would be performed in just a week and a half. After dinner she and Leah wrote "Nikolais Remembers" on the banner in their marker colors. Sara wrote the number "2" after hers and Leah wrote "1" after hers.

"What's a remember?" Mary wanted to know. Sara explained, then went with Leah and Shannon to Studio B to choreograph their moving leg swing phrases for tomorrow.

The full cast was at *Giselle* rehearsal, and Mr. Peters was just finishing the partnering practice when Sara took her place at the barre for warm-ups, staring at Jackson. "OK," Miss Alexander said. "Let's run the whole thing from the beginning and see what we've got." Sara took her place in the make-believe wings in her make-believe wedding veil at the side of the room next to Shannon. The corps de ballet understudies followed every step in the corners of the room, and Miss Sutton came in and began to walk around making corrections. But Sara didn't get one correction. Maybe she wasn't doing anything wrong or maybe she just wasn't important enough to get a comment. When they were done Miss Alexander added new choreography including the scoots. *This is it*, Sara thought, *the most important part for the corps de ballet.* She looked in the mirror as the lines scooted toward each other in low arabesque. She thought Jackson was looking at her, but couldn't move her head to see for sure. When it was over, the seamstress appeared in the doorway.

"When you hear your name called, please go downstairs to the costume room for a fitting," Miss Sutton announced. They went in alphabetical order, so almost everybody got called out of rehearsal before Sara. She had a bad feeling remembering last year's disaster when her costume was miles too big and had to be completely taken in for her. She could still hear Robin saying, "It's the incredible shrinking ballerina." But this year Shannon was called out with Sara and they got to go downstairs together. Sara watched Shannon's face as they entered the vast costume room with its rows and rows of fluffy and silky costumes, ribbons, lace and netting.

"Wow," Shannon said. "Je ne sais quoi! I cannot adequately describe it."

Sara was glad for the English translation and smiled. "I know. Isn't it great? We get to choose our student concert costumes from this room." Her eyes swept the rows quickly looking for white leotards with little skirts attached.

"OK, one of you up here," the seamstress said, standing next to the raised fitting platform, measuring tape around her neck. Costumes with long white tutus hung next to her just like the ones in the posters upstairs.

"You first," Sara said to Shannon. She wandered through the rows of costumes while Shannon was being fitted. She saw some white leotards, but they didn't have skirts attached. Then it was her turn. Shannon went back upstairs. Sara closed her eyes when the seamstress pulled the prickly net costume over her head, afraid to see how droopy it would be. But when she opened her eyes, she couldn't believe how perfectly the costume fit. She went up on her pointes and turned around in a circle. "It fits!" she smiled.

"Of course," the seamstress said. "It's yours from *Les Slyphides* last year. Actually, I think I'll take the straps out a bit, you've grown taller."

Sara liked hearing that. She went happily back to rehearsal and watched from under the barre as Robin and Kathy rehearsed their special parts. She was learning their parts in her head, and would offer to step in should she be needed. After rehearsal, she watched Jackson and Mr. Peters walk away through the woods. She could hardly wait for the party Saturday night. On the way to the cabin she and Shannon sat on the steps of the dining hall and watched the torches dance over the lake. "I looked for white leotards for

Concerto Barocco," Sara said. "I saw some but they didn't have skirts attached."

"Well, the costume room is so big, and a student concert still has not been announced," Shannon reminded her.

I am getting really sick of this, Sara thought. "Come with me," she said, getting up. She would take Shannon to the Balanchine indoor theatre in the woods where they would be performing *Giselle* and where they held the student concert last year. When they got there, Sara found all the doors locked, but some dim lights on. They walked around the building until Sara found the window to the Green Room. She pressed her face against the glass until she could make out all the posters from past concerts hanging on the walls. "Look!" she told Shannon. "Proof!" Shannon put her hands over her eyes and pressed into the window.

"Those posters began fifty-one years ago," Sara explained. "Why wouldn't there be one for this year?" Shannon shrugged. "And we better get Leah into the secret practice room," Sara continued, "to show her the film of *Concerto Barocco*."

"Perhaps," Shannon said calmly. "However, I think we should concentrate on *Giselle* right now."

In her bunk that night Sara decided to enact her plan the next day.

CHAPTER TWENTY-THREE

"Leah Sees the Dance"

Thursday morning went quickly. At lunch Sara noticed Leah eating less than she usually did. Mary, Brooke and Charleigh chatted about getting into the water after lunch to practice for their Sunday performance. Alene came over from Baryshnikov table and asked Shannon to go back to the dance building to practice their modern dance assignment for this afternoon. Sara was pretty sure she would remember hers, and she planned to create her new one for tomorrow in Studio B right after dinner tonight before *Giselle* rehearsal. She promised herself she would absolutely *not* watch the soloists rehearse tonight. Miss Lee seemed to stare at Sara lately during the Nikolais warm-up exercises waiting for her to make a mistake. Sara kept following other people and Miss Lee knew it. Her homework assignments had to make up for it until she got Jackson's book. But there was still the important task of beginning work on their Balanchine piece for the student concert. As soon as Shannon and Alene left the dining hall, Sara saw her chance.

"Leah, I want to show you something," she began.

"What?"

"It's in the dance building," Sara said quietly, but the other girls heard her.

"Leah, you said you would watch our water ballet right now," Brooke said.

"Yeah, Leah," Mary said. "We really need you to watch it. Only two more days to practice."

Charleigh got up from the table. "We need to get in the water right away."

But I need to show Leah the Concerto Barocco *film,* Sara thought. She wanted to begin their rehearsals for it next week. "This won't take long," she smiled at Leah. She urged with her eyes, but Leah had no idea what she was trying to say. Then Grace came over.

"Ready to watch us?" Grace asked Leah. "We better get going."

"OK, you guys get your bathing suits on, and I'll meet you down at the beach," Leah said. When they left, she turned to Sara. "What's going on?"

"I want to show you the film of *Concerto Barocco*," Sara said, holding her breath. *Please*, she thought. Leah didn't say anything. "For the student concert."

"Oh, the one they haven't told us about," Leah laughed. "We are *so* busy, Sara, and we don't even know if that is going to happen."

"It *is* going to happen, Leah. And I want to be the best and I want to do this Balanchine dance and—"

"Maybe you should do it alone," Leah said.

"No. No. We have to have at least three. Four would be better. We have to go under each other's arms and make formations. You will *love* it when you see it."

"Sara, I really did promise Charlie and company that I would watch their water ballet today, and I mean what if we waste our time on it and there is no student concert this year?"

"I can show you something in five minutes," Sara said. "Come on!" To Sara's relief Leah must have been curious because she followed Sara as she ran over to the Balanchine Theatre. Again Sara went around to the Green Room window and pressed her face against it. "Look in that Green Room!" she said. Leah looked through the window. "Those are all posters on the wall from the last fifty years of intermediate student dance concerts. You see. They have one every single year."

"What's a Green Room?" Leah asked. "The walls aren't green."

"It's the room where you get a pep talk before performing," Sara told her. "The first one ever must have been green. But look at the posters from each year."

I think I see *you*, "Leah said. "Over there on the far side of the wall." Sara looked carefully. She finally found the poster of herself along with all the other performers from last year.

"That *is* me!" Sara exclaimed, thrilled to see the poster.

"Don't you girls have some place you're supposed to be?" It was Mrs. Lane on her way to the dance building. "The theatre is closed."

They quickly found the path and ran back to the cabins. "Do you believe me?" Sara asked.

"I think so," Leah said.

"Will you watch the dance film then?"

"I guess so," Leah said as she left Sara and headed for the beach.

175

"OK, maybe tonight!" Sara yelled after her. *YES!* She thought. She went into Pavlova to see if she had any mail. No one was there, but she was excited to see a big envelope from Erin on the chest of drawers. She got on her bunk and ripped it open. Six stamped envelopes fell out. One for today and one for each week left of camp! Sara grabbed the letter that was stuck inside. New York in the summer sounded great. Erin loved her ballet classes and was also taking an exciting summer modern dance workshop at the Martha Graham School. She wanted to know the latest Lakewood details, especially if Sara and Shannon had taken a boat out to meet the boys, if Sara had shown Shannon or anyone the secret path or the secret cabin. She wanted to know what was in the blue tin and on the banner.

Sara grabbed some Dance History paper from her drawer and wrote to Erin. She told her everything, including about her folk solo, the bourrées for Miss Sutton, being singled out in the Nikolais class, the water ballet, watching the soloists rehearse with Jackson, the magic of *Giselle*, watching *Tarantella*, getting stuck in the hallway, the scare with Charlie. She finished by telling her that her *Les Sylphides* costume from last year fit her for *Giselle*, and that she was going to get Shannon and Leah to dance in *Concerto Barocco*, and that the New York City Ballet was coming to visit in a week. "Shannon is so smart and pretty and catches on so fast and so does Leah. I really need to step it up. Shannon says I need to focus more. I think I need to see Jackson more. Ha Ha! The boys' party is this Saturday. Miss you. Wish you were here. PS: So far we only have your note in the blue tin, a flyer for the boys' party and a flyer for the water ballet. There's not much on the banner yet." As she licked the envelope, she

176

realized she hadn't put her folk solo on the banner, so with the yellow marker, she wrote "folk solo" under her name with a sigh. She put Erin's second letter in the blue tin, and on her way to ballet class, she threw her letter to Erin into the camp mailbox and pictured Leah in the secret practice room tonight watching the dance film. She wanted to be able to write *"Concerto Barocco* performance" on the banner!

In the locker room between ballet and modern dance, Sara went through her Nikolais assignment in her head. Her body seemed to hold the memory of it with no problem. Now if she could just look good going through the long warm-ups today. She probably should have rehearsed them in her mind instead of writing the letter to Erin, but there was so much to do all the time. Besides, ballet was more important to her and she would have the Nikolais method book in just one more day. Then she would make up for lost time. She got through the exercises again by looking in the mirror at the class and pretending she knew the sequence. Miss Lee called them out in groups to perform their homework assignments of going across the floor doing their own version of locomotion leg swings. Sara enjoyed hearing the three-quarter time drum-beats and watching the other groups, but her own movement phrase got no praise.

Leah got another remember from Miss Lee, along with Keera. It went OK for Sara, but not outstanding. That would come soon, Sara told herself. The new vocabulary they learned was called response to touch. When someone touched one of your body parts, you had to quickly respond by graining toward the touch, then another body part would be touched and you had to respond to that. You couldn't move away from the touch, and you weren't supposed to see where the person was going to touch you. Shannon and Alene were partners, so Sara grabbed Leah. "For Friday," Miss Lee said, "I want to see you and your partner really expressing this vocabulary. Work together practicing, alternating being the toucher and the one who is touched. Don't choreograph anything specific, just get used to working together. This is a favorite of mine and I really want to see you do it successfully."

"Put your second remember on the banner, Leah," Sara reminded Leah after dinner. Leah crossed out the number one and wrote a number two over it. She also wrote "special part in folk dance." Shannon wrote the same under her name.

"What's a remember?" Mary asked again.

"It's when you do a good movement assignment in modern dance and Miss Lee tells you to remember it," Brooke told her.

"Oh, yeah," Mary said. "Now I remember," she laughed.

"We don't have homework in modern," Charleigh said. "It's a good thing, with all the work we have on our water show. I hope we have a big audience."

"You will," Shannon told her. "We passed out all the flyers and I heard some seniors talking about it, too."

"Grace is having trouble with the ending where we fall off the raft," Charleigh said. "Come on, let's go get her and practice it." They left and Leah, Shannon and Sara went to the dance building. They ran into Alene on the path.

In Studio B, they all began practicing the body-part touch improvisation, but Sara could hear the *Giselle* soloists rehearsing upstairs. She kept picturing Jackson so handsome in his black tights, his caring arms holding Courtney. "Sara," Leah said. "You need to respond faster when I touch you. Are you paying attention?" Shannon looked over at her.

Don't think about Jackson when you are practicing in Studio B, her eyes seemed to say. As the ceiling creaked above them, Sara focused more on the Nikolais movement and really got into it after a while, especially when she was the one responding to Leah's touch. Leah was very inventive, touching Sara's toe, her elbow, her back, her forehead. After a while they decided to watch each other, and Sara was intrigued with the ways Shannon and Alene interpreted the vocabulary.

"Let's all do it together now," Sara suggested. "When I holler *switch,* we'll change touchers. So for the last five minutes before *Giselle* rehearsal the four took all the space they could in Studio B practicing the touch and response exercise. Sara felt confident and exhilarated. She was ready for tomorrow. *But now for tonight*, she thought as they headed up the stairs to rehearsal. Jackson was standing at the barre next to Courtney and Robin.

After quick barre exercises to get their muscles warm, Miss Alexander announced that she had heard from the New York City Ballet. "They will arrive next Thursday evening," she smiled. "They will give master class to intermediates and seniors Friday morning. You will perform *Giselle* for them Friday evening, and they will perform *Allegro Brillante* for you Saturday evening. This means we have exactly one week to be ready. Opening places please."

Sara could hardly believe it! She would get to see members of the New York City Ballet performing that gorgeous, wonderful, fabulous *Allegro Brillante*! She had only watched a bit of the film in the secret practice room, but she had loved it immediately. She took her opening position in the pretend wings with images of *Allegro Brillante* floating in her mind. Then she gazed around the room at the beautiful *Giselle*

179

posters. She sighed with joy at how wonderful and magical her own performance would be. As she watched Myrtha dance her opening steps and Albrecht come into the make-believe forest she was filled with happiness that she would be a part of it. Courtney had rehearsed her solo and her variation with Jackson nearly to perfection already and the music seemed to make them all soar. "Pretty good," Miss Alexander said when they finished what they knew of the choreography. They spent the rest of the rehearsal finishing the ballet. It was so sad when Giselle returned to her grave. Albrecht was still so in love with her and was left alone on stage crushing the lilies and falling down. It was the most romantic story ever.

"OK," Miss Alexander said. "You are excused, but you must remember every step. Come Monday night prepared to polish, polish, polish! We move into the theatre Thursday for tech rehearsal."

Wow, Sara thought. *We just have next Monday, Tuesday and Wednesday to practice.* She honestly was relieved that she didn't have a major part in the ballet. She would look perfect in the part she had and hoped everyone would notice. She grabbed Leah on the way down to the locker room. "Leah," she whispered. "Come on. I'll show you the dance film now." They let everyone pass them and once they were all in the locker room, Sara led Leah past the costume room, down the hall into the secret practice room.

"This better be good," Leah said as Sara popped in the film. Sara watched Leah's face. Her heart danced as Leah smiled. "Really cool," Leah said. "Really cool."

"You see what I mean?" Sara said.

"Yeah, it's really fast steps how I like to dance," Leah said. "What is that music?"

180

Sara picked up the film box. "It's Tchaikovsky's *Third Piano Concerto*."

"Does Shannon think we can do it?" Leah asked.

Sara could hear Shannon saying that she would not be in it if it didn't look good. "Yes, she does," Sara said. "But we're going to have to start learning it right away. And you and I are going to have to lose some weight." She waited for Leah's answer.

"Well, OK, but we can't learn the whole thing."

"We don't have to," Sara said. "I think we'll only need about three minutes worth. At least that was it was last year." She wondered if it was getting close to nine o'clock. She didn't want Charlie, the janitor, to find them there. "We have to go now before they lock the building." The hall door opened more easily than ever. Good old Charlie.

On the way to the cabin, Sara could hardly believe it when Leah said, "I sure hope there's going to be a student concert."

CHAPTER TWENTY-FOUR

"Balanchine and Boys' Party"

At breakfast Friday morning Sara, Shannon and Leah made a plan to start learning *Concerto Barocco.* There was no *Giselle* rehearsal tonight, so they would go to the little practice room to begin. "We'll just watch it and decide what part to do," Sara said. But first they had to get through the day's classes. Even though there were no rehearsals Friday evenings, it was the tightest day with no break at all after lunch. In ballet, Sara let Shannon and Leah take the leadership places at the ends of the barre again, but made a mental note that she would soon have to get Miss Sutton's attention by taking one of those places. And she would have to do it without making any mistakes. *First things first,* as her mother would say. First she would conquer memorizing the Nikolais warm-up sequence. Once she got through that a couple times with no blank spots in her mind, she would jump into the ballet leadership position. The announcement of the scholarship winner to New York City Ballet was only a few weeks away.

Tap was so much fun, as usual, and at lunch, Leah only ate a half sandwich and a glass of milk and announced that she had begun swimming extra laps. Pointe class was extraordinary with Miss Sutton bringing Sara, Shannon, Leah, Alene and Keera to the front line to lead the class in their steps from *Giselle.* Sara was surprised to see that the understudies knew all the corps de ballet steps. But then Miss Sutton did something wonderful! She asked Sara and Shannon to try the parts of Myrtha's attendants. Here was Sara's chance! She knew she could do it. Miss Sutton asked the rest of the class to sit under the barre and motioned the accompanist to begin. Sara remembered part of it, but then got confused. After all, she had been concentrating on her own part. But Shannon was amazing. She took her role as understudy to Robin seriously and it was clear she had learned every single step, arm movement and expression in addition to her own part. Sara followed her along, but Shannon was the star. When they finished, the class applauded. Now Sara knew that she probably couldn't just jump in and dance the role if she were asked. Her heart drooped a little, but she told herself this was all the more reason to look terrific in *Concerto Barocco* for the student concert.

Finally it was time for modern dance. Surprisingly, Miss Lee did only some short warm-ups, choosing some from the beginning, middle and end of the long series. Sara got through that with no problem, then threw herself into the combinations going across the floor. She could feel her body moving more smoothly to the unique dance vocabulary and was able to walk, run and stop precisely to the drum beat now and to switch levels from high to low to medium with more ease. Today they focused on turning quickly into a backward walking step, switching to a sideways step, then moving forward again. The second time they did it they had to change levels without missing a beat. Sara was perspiring when she took her place next to Leah under the barre and Miss Lee began to watch their homework assignments.

Sara observed with interest as each couple took the floor to perform their improvisational respond to touch exercise. She could actually see clearly who was fulfilling it completely and who was not, so when it was her turn she was energetic and moved sharply. Leah was a great partner and seemed more responsive than when they had practiced. When they finished, Miss Lee told Sara and Leah to remember the *essence* of what they had done. They finished class by learning a new movement vocabulary called leading the group. When a group of dancers turned direction and you were in the front, it was up to you to do a movement everyone else had to follow until you turned direction and someone else took over. Sara loved it. When she found herself leader she tried to incorporate changing levels while moving on the periphery. Miss Lee said they would work more with leading the group on Monday. Their homework was to come up with some interesting combination of Nikolais dance movements they would do if they were leading.

"That is three remembers for you two," Shannon said in the locker room after class. "I am impressed."

"Modern sure is different than ballet," Sara said. "I've never had a ballet teacher tell me to remember the *essence* of anything."

"I wonder why Miss Lee is asking us to remember things," Leah said.

"She's probably going to have us review the whole dance vocabulary at the end of the summer," Shannon said. "But so far I have nothing to remember." She shrugged her shoulders.

Sara was impatient in folk class. Mr. Moyne was back to changing steps again for her solo. She tried to show cooperation and enthusiasm. She held a vision in her mind of *Tarantella* with its red and yellow swirls of costume and the joyous flirtation. But she had no boy to dance with. "I like that," Mr. Moyne finally told her. "Remember that combination."

Another remember, Sara thought to herself. *I'll have to write all these things down I am supposed to remember.* As it was, she had trouble going to sleep some nights because she went over in her mind the steps and patterns to *Giselle,* her remembers for Miss Lee, and her folk solo, which was changing again. When she mentioned this to Leah and Shannon they said it was all part of the responsibility of being a dancer.

Back at the cabin after dinner Sara couldn't wait to freshen up and take Leah and Shannon to the secret studio to begin practicing *Concerto Barocco.* "Hurry," she said, grabbing her dance bag.

"Wait," Leah said, finding her red marker. "We have to write that we have three Nikolais remembers now."

Shannon handed Sara the yellow marker. "Pavlova cabin is getting lucky," she smiled. Sara crossed out the number two and wrote in a three and they left just as Brooke, Mary and Charleigh came in to get into their bathing suits for their water ballet practice.

"Good luck and be careful!" Leah shouted to them.

Soon the three sat on the floor in the secret basement practice room watching the Balanchine dance. They decided to watch it twice in silence before speaking. Sara's eyes were glued to the dancers as they moved pertly and quickly like birds, yet flowing like a waterfall. Unbelievably, they all agreed to learn part of the first section. "This is going to be great!" Sara exclaimed.

"We'll see," Shannon said. "I think it's going to be difficult."

"I can't wait to try these fast steps," Leah said, standing up. "Come on, let's get started." They played the film over and over trying to learn the first few steps, but they kept bumping into each other. "We look like a comedy act instead of a ballet," Leah laughed.

"I have most of the first steps memorized already," Shannon said confidently. "Let's work on it a bit more, then practice it in the laundry room on Sunday," she suggested. Sara liked the idea, though they would have no film and no music. They started from the beginning again concentrating on the footwork and trying to stay in their own personal spaces. Then Sara realized she had no way of knowing what time it was. It seemed like they had been in there for hours.

"Does anybody know what time it is?" Sara finally asked. It was getting dark outside.

Shannon pulled a little watch out of her dance bag and held it up to the dim light coming from the ceiling. "It's ten to nine," she said. "We better leave. They lock up at nine, right?"

"What should we do with the dance film?" Leah asked. "What if somebody comes in here and takes it or sees it and figures out we have been using the room?"

"Oh, it's OK," Sara said. "No one comes in here. Mr. Peters and Miss Alexander are practicing in Studio B. The other dancers won't come down here. They don't even know about it. I only knew about it because I heard music coming down the hall last year when Mr. Moyne and Miss Casey were rehearsing *Romeo and Juliet."*

"Well, it won't do us any good to take it with us," Leah said. "The laundry room has nothing to watch it on." So they put it on a chair in the room and left.

As they walked back to the cabin, Sara's head was filled with images of Mr. Moyne and Miss Casey's performance in the outdoor theatre on the lake at the end of camp last year. *Romeo and Juliet* had been so touching. She remembered how she had given Hank a flower from her own bouquet at the stage door just as Juliet had given one of her flowers to Romeo when they took their bows. She felt Hank's kiss on her cheek and wondered where he was this very moment. In her bunk that night she ran through the *Concerto Barocco* steps they had just learned, her new folk steps, the entire *Giselle*, and all three Nikolais movement phrases she was to remember. Then she thought of the boys' party tomorrow night and fell asleep thinking of Jackson.

Saturday morning in Dance History Miss Meisner presented the history of the great George Balanchine. "He was born in St. Petersburg, Russia in 1904 and graduated from the Russian Soviet State School of Ballet in 1921. He also studied piano and music composition," she began. *Ah*, Sara thought, beginning to understand how Balanchine was able to choreograph *Concert Barocco* with such flowing musicality. Miss Meisner continued: "He began choreographing dances in 1923 and toured a small group of dancers in Germany, Paris and London. Then, he came to New York in 1933 and began to create his plot-less ballets, great abstract dance compositions that are still being performed by companies today. In the spring of 1941 he created the wonderful *Concerto Barocco* for a South American tour and it was first performed by the New York City Ballet in 1948. Does anyone know the music for that ballet?" Before Sara could get her hand up, Shannon answered the question.

"This is a ballet in three movements to J.S. Bach's Concerto for Two Violins and Orchestra in D minor," Shannon stated. Sara thought she probably only knew it from reading the box the film came in.

"Right again!" Miss Meisner smiled. She continued by naming several of the many ballets Balanchine made for his company, including *Serenade, La Valse, Apollo* and *Allegro Brillante.* "As you know, some members of the New York City Ballet will be here to perform for you Saturday. They will perform *Allegro Brillante,* a dance for four couples and one principal couple to music by Tchaikovsky." Sara could hardly wait. Miss Meisner continued her lecture presenting most of Balanchine's life, including that he was married for a while to ballerina Maria Tallchief, that he introduced the trend of ballet in musicals and operettas, and that he not only trained dancers in his own technique and style at the New York City Ballet school, but travelled the country observing at dance schools and holding many teacher seminars. "Balanchine," she concluded, "was undoubtedly one of our most brilliant choreographers and the only one who had a genius for pure ballet. Now, the shades, please."

Sara jumped up to pull down one of the window shades. She couldn't wait to see what dance film they would get to see. Her heart jumped in excitement when she discovered it was *Allegro Brillante!* It was breathtaking, dazzling, flowing yet precise, lyrical and joyful. When it was over Sara reluctantly

189

moved to put the window shade back up. She wanted to stay in the darkness with the light of the film forever.

Miss Meisner's voice broke through Sara's daydreams. "Balanchine was a staunch believer that neither a story nor stage décor, nor costumes should be allowed to distract from the dancing. He thought that with thin beautiful bodies and simple costumes, the purity of the movement itself would shine through. Although he passed away in 1983, his ballets continue to shine." *And we'll get to see one on stage in the Balanchine theatre here Saturday night,* Sara thought excitedly. But then she remembered that she'd be performing *Giselle* for the New York City Ballet the night before, and didn't feel quite ready. She wanted desperately to be noticed as a gifted dancer in order to get to New York.

"We have to get thin, Leah," Sara said as they jumped off the porch of the music building. She was totally motivated after watching the film. Visions of how wonderful their student concert performance could be took over her emotions. Shannon smiled as they ate salads with tuna for lunch, sipped lemon water, and skipped dessert.

They watched the final rehearsal of the water ballet, went out on the raft for a while and then it was time for the boys' party. Sara remembered how she had worn Erin's big sweater last year, but it was warm tonight so she suggested they all wear their Lakewood T-shirts and jeans. "Great idea!" Charleigh said. "Anything but a bathing suit!" They all laughed, changed clothes, brushed their hair, put on a touch of lipstick and sat on the Pavlova porch waiting for Julie Hess to come for them. As they joined the rest of the intermediates and their counselors and walked the official path to Camp Woodlake, Sara thought of Jackson. When they reached the other side she didn't see him. Boys were everywhere, it seemed, building the fire in the pit, setting up dining tables, bringing out water and soda, but she couldn't find Jackson. Then she heard a voice behind her. "Hi, Sara!" She turned to see Patrick.

"Oh, hi," she smiled, looking for Jackson. But Patrick was alone.

"Can I give you a tour of Woodlake?" Patrick asked. He was cute, Sara thought. Just not Jackson.

"Sure, we'd love that," Sara said, including Shannon and Leah for the tour.

"You go," Leah said. "We're going down to see their boats." She grabbed Shannon and they took off laughing.

Oh, great, Sara thought. Maybe they'd run into Jackson as they walked around. She looked around again, but didn't see him.

"How's *Giselle* coming along?" Patrick wanted to know as he led her up the path toward the office and dining hall.

"OK," Sara said. "We just finished learning the whole thing. Now it will be polish, polish, polish!"

"I know," Patrick said. "I can't wait to see it." He tried to take Sara's hand as they went up the steps to the dining hall, but Sara went up the steps quickly in front of him. "This is where all the eating happens," Patrick laughed as he opened the door for her.

Sara suddenly remembered she had to ask him not to tell something. "Patrick, "she began, "did you see us down at the stream one day?"

"Yeah. I waved, but you left."

"Well, would you please not tell anybody that you saw us down there? It was off-limits. We could get in trouble."

191

"No problem," he said smiling at her. "I saw Leah down there the other day, too."

"Really?" Sara asked, surprised.

"Yeah. For sure. We met on the little plank and she introduced herself. Guess I shouldn't tell anybody about that, either."

"Right," Sara said, glad he had told her. *Interesting. But why wouldn't Leah have said anything about it?* "Thanks. They are pretty strict about where we can go and our scholarships depend on adhering to the rules."

"I heard you won second place intermediate last year," Patrick said.

"Yeah," Sara smiled, remembering the moment Madame smiled down at her while she held her bouquet of flowers.

"That's cool. I got a scholarship to come here this year, too, from Mr. Peters."

"Congrats!" Sara said. "Does Mr. Peters teach at the school of the New York City Ballet?"

"He sure does. We love him. He's a great teacher. Like Balanchine. Loves pure movement."

As they turned to leave the dining hall Sara saw a flurry of activity in the kitchen. Then Jackson appeared carrying a box of lettuce, tomatoes, ketchup and mustard. His blond-red hair shined under the ceiling lights. He actually smiled down at her and said hello. She thought she wouldn't be able to speak, but then a small hello came out. "Oh, I have that Nik book for you," he told her as he walked out the door. I'll give it to you later."

"Thanks," Sara said, listening to her heart beat in her ears. She felt warm and happy. Patrick took her all around camp past the cabins, the beach, and finally over to the dance barn. It was locked, but they looked in the window at the first floor studio with its shiny wood floor, the mirror and ballet barre. Sara saw a piano in the corner and imagined the boys turning, jumping and leaping across the room. She wondered when she would get a chance to partner with a boy. Next year, if she came back, she would be in the Senior Division and would take a partnering class on Saturday mornings. *Oh, wait*, she thought, *I will be dancing in New York next summer.* She pictured herself dancing a pas de deux with Jackson.

She thanked Patrick for the walk and found Leah and Shannon. "How did the private tour go?" Leah wanted to know, sitting in front of the fire. Shannon sat next to her and leaned in for the answer.

"Good," she said. "I asked Patrick not to tell anybody they saw us down by the plank, Shannon."

"You went all the way to the plank?" Leah said, acting surprised.

"Apparently, you did, too, Leah," Sara said. "Why didn't you tell us?"

Leah shrugged. "Didn't think it was important. It was just part of exploring. I was going to tell you." Shannon looked away. She couldn't have cared less. But it bothered Sara, and she wondered if Leah had discovered the secret cabin.

"How far did you go?" Sara asked.

"Just to the other side of the plank," Leah said. "I jumped off almost on a snake and turned back. Patrick and Jackson saw me and we introduced ourselves. That's it. Really."

"Well, we shouldn't go down there," Sara warned. "It wouldn't be worth it if we got caught."

"Silly. It's all silly," Shannon frowned. "Danser, danser! We are here only to dance. Of course, you will not go there."

193

End of story, Sara thought. But she really couldn't imagine not going to the secret cabin at least once more. Magical things happened there last summer. Patrick came over and told them the hamburgers and hot dogs were ready. They followed him up to the dining tables and buffet. Sara looked at the potato salad thinking how thin she wanted to be. She took half as much as she wanted, grabbed carrot sticks, and skipped the hamburger roll. No potato chips, either. She looked over at Leah's plate and was glad to see that she had made good choices, too. They had to get into those little white costumes for *Concerto Barocco*. Shannon's plate held only half a hamburger and some salad. After dinner, they all went into the dining hall to dance. One of the boys acted as DJ and played great dance music. Sara danced with every boy who asked her or danced alone or next to Leah and Shannon. She loved every kind of dancing and threw herself into it, but she kept her eye out for Jackson. Just as Patrick came up to Sara to ask her for the next dance, Jackson came out of the kitchen. She watched as he came over to her in a tight green T-shirt and jeans. His blue eyes smiled down at her as he invited her to go with him to get the book. Sara felt breathless and tried to act poised.

He led her to the dance barn and opened it with a key. She followed him as he darted up the stairs to the second level. He opened the dance studio door with another key. They took off their shoes and went into the studio. "Here it is," Jackson said, taking the big book off a shelf. He handed it to Sara. It was a big, shiny, soft cover book that weighed a ton.

"Thank you," Sara smiled, hanging on to it carefully. She didn't want to leave right away. It was awesome to be in the boys' studio, especially with Jackson. She opened the book. "Where do you think I should start?" she asked.

194

He laughed. "At the beginning."

Sara turned the book to the first chapter and saw the warm-up exercises. There they were, the entire and complete sequence!

"There is a description of how each warm-up is done," Jackson said.

Sara wanted to kiss him on the spot. This was *wonderful*. She could take a boat out or lie in her bunk at night or sit on the dining hall steps and read it. She would devour it and understand the exercises and practice them and memorize the sequence. She would not fail in modern class, she would not be mediocre in modern class, she would be great in modern class!

"Come on," Jackson said, walking to the center of the room. "I'll go through some of them with you quickly." Sara looked up at the clock. She had to meet Julie Hess and the other girls in fifteen minutes for their walk back to Lakewood. She looked in the mirror and saw the reflection of herself with Jackson.

"Great," she said. They got through the first five exercises then the hands of the clock suddenly bolted forward to ten o'clock. Sara's heart was warm with affection for Jackson and all his help when she said she had to go. Jackson quickly locked the door to the studio and they scurried down the stairs. Sara held the book tightly as she watched him lock the door to the dance barn while she put on her shoes. She thanked him and he gave her a little hug.

"Good luck," he called as she ran across the camp and found Miss Hess and the other girls.

"Over here!" Leah shouted to her. Shannon waved from inside the group. Sara felt like she was suspended in air as she

195

joined the girls and they began the walk back through the dark woods. The deep smell of the pine trees filled Sara's nose, lungs, and her heart, cushioning her affection for Jackson. She lay in bed that night thinking how Jackson was just across the lake and she smiled, still feeling his hug.

CHAPTER TWENTY-FIVE

"Water Ballet, Lost Film, Understudies"

S unday morning Sara woke up before anyone else in Pavlova. She wanted to write on the banner "Rehearsed with Jackson!" but she knew it didn't count as a real rehearsal. She tip-toed over to the chest of drawers and picked up the Nikolais book and put it on her bunk. She'd take a quick shower, then begin her study of the complicated warm-up sequence. When she was in the shower she remembered that she had left her locket in her dance bag. She came out of the bathroom, dressed quietly and put on the locket. Then she felt the wisp around her neck again like a whisper of the old dance spirits. She felt warm and lucky. She climbed on her bunk and started to read the Nikolais book, but the sun looked so bright and the day so happy that she took the book and walked over to the dining hall steps.

She looked across the lake but saw no activity at all. She opened the book and the wind took the pages in a flurry. She pushed the pages back and concentrated on the beginning of the exercises. "Oh," she said out loud, "now I get that transition!" Then she heard the door unlock above her head. Soon people were walking past her to breakfast. When Leah arrived, they both went inside.

"Oops, dropped something!" Sara looked behind her. A piece of paper had fallen out of the book onto the floor. She took it from Robin. "Might be one of those secret notes," Robin teased. "How was the boys' party last night?"

"Good," Sara said.

"Did you see Jackson?" Robin wanted to know. "He's such a good dancer."

"Yes," Sara said. "But he was busy in the kitchen a lot of the time." She was not going to tell her how they shared a special time right in the boys' dance studio. That would be kept close to her heart.

"Too bad," Robin said, walking past her.

Sara opened the piece of paper to find a note from Patrick: *Dear Sara, I wanted to let you know how much I have enjoyed meeting you. I wish we'd get a chance to dance together. I bet we could dance a great duet. Maybe we could take boats out and meet in the middle of the lake. If I see you out there, I'll row out. Happy Dancing from Patrick!* Leah was reading it over Sara's shoulder.

"Wow," Leah laughed. "Private tour, private note."

Sara wondered when Patrick had put the note in the book. It must have been there before the party. She wondered if Jackson knew it was in there. She hoped not because that would mean Jackson was trying to help Patrick get to know her. Her heart dropped a little. She stuck the note back in the book and after breakfast put it in the blue tin as soon as she found herself alone with Shannon. "Better get breakfast before it's over," she told Shannon.

"What did I miss?" Shannon wanted to know from her bunk. "What did you just put in the tin?" Sara told her about last night and about the note.

"I am never taking a boat out without you," she told Shannon. "And I'm never dancing a duet with Patrick."

Shannon went to the dining hall and the cabin stayed empty all morning. Sara had no idea where anybody was. She spent the whole time reading Jackson's Nikolais book. It was amazing to see pictures of dancers in New York doing the same warm-up exercises that she had been learning in class. She read the words carefully to understand the exact purpose and intended quality of each movement. Just as she got off her bunk to practice the entire sequence and try to commit it to memory, Shannon called to her from the porch.

"Time for the water ballet!"

Sara glanced at the clock on the dresser. Five minutes to one. They better hurry. "Where have you been?" she asked Shannon as they ran down the cement steps to the beach.

"I found an old hammock across the road in the woods," Shannon said. "I fell asleep there reading my dance history book."

"Across the road?" Sara asked.

"Yes," Shannon said. "Way back near the camp entrance. It's a lovely and quiet place."

"Well, that's because I don't think we're supposed to be there," Sara said. The beach was crowded with campers waiting for the water ballet to start. They found just enough space to squeeze in on the grass above the sand. It was a perfect, warm day for the performance. Sara spotted Leah on the end of the dock near Heather Scott. Not everyone was there as part of the audience. There were swimmers on one side of the dock and the water ballet would take place on the other side near the raft. Heather had to keep her eye everybody, including girls who had taken boats out onto the lake. Sara looked all around, but didn't see the performers yet. She turned to Shannon. "So, how did you find that place across the road?"

"I just decided to go for a walk after breakfast and wanted to see the camp entrance again. Of course, I hadn't seen it since the day I arrived. The camp flags are still flying and the big welcome sign is still there. I looked across the road and noticed how thick the forest was. No one was around, so I went over, walked for a bit on an old trail and found the hammock in a clearing."

"Here come the performers," Sara said, watching Brooke, Mary, Charleigh and Grace come out from behind trees high above the beach. They wore their brightest color swimsuits, and pretty multicolored ribbons dangled from their braided hair. They came together in a line while piano music started from a portable player somewhere on the beach. Everyone applauded as the swimmers gracefully made their way to the warm, sandy beach where they did a few dance steps, then swam out into the water to the raft. They floated around the raft doing synchronized arm movements, then swam into a circle out farther from the raft. Sara was fascinated as the dancers flowed through their well-choreographed and practiced movements. She wondered how they could hold their breath so long under water while showing beautiful legs in the air. Toward the end, they made a chain by lying flat on the water, another swimmer's feet around their necks. Mary let herself go backward paddling deep into the water pulling

200

the others, who went under water one by one. Then Mary surfaced at the place where the last girl had gone under and pulled the whole line of girls up again, back into a line. They all paddled and smiled while everyone applauded for them. Heather turned to watch them and holler her approval through her megaphone. Then she turned back to watch her swimmers and boaters.

Sara couldn't wait to see how the ending would look. The girls swam toward the audience as precisely as a drill team, then waded in to the beach area holding hands. When the music struck a loud note they raised their hands in the air over their heads, bent forward in big penché arabesques, their legs high behind. Then they went under each other's arms on their tip-toes, their wet ribbons dripping. The audience cheered, but that wasn't the real ending. The girls ran into the water toward the raft, swam a fancy crawl stroke in unison and climbed onto the raft. They turned to face the audience in a line across the wet raft. One by one, beginning with Mary and ending with Grace, they went to the edge of the raft and let themselves fall over sideways into the water. Then, as each one surfaced, she climbed back onto the raft and struck a final pose. Sara stood with the rest of the audience and clapped and cheered. It had been a perfect performance. Then she realized Grace was missing. Grace hadn't surfaced yet from her sideways fall off the raft. Someone pointed and Sara saw Grace's head out in the water. Heather turned around, but before she could jump into the water, Leah sprang off the dock and furiously back-stroked out to Grace. Before Heather could yell any instructions to her, Leah had Grace up on the slippery raft. In a moment she was sitting up and breathing fine. Sara realized she had been holding her own breath and let it out.

"Stay there!" Heather yelled to them. She turned to the crowd. "Someone get a boat!"

"Bateau!" Shannon answered Heather in French. "Bateau!" She grabbed Sara by the shirt and they ran to the boat shed to get a rowboat. They rowed quickly out to the raft and soon the frightened girls were safely in the boat. When they reached shore, the anxious crowd cheered. Someone began shouting for Leah and she took a little bow, then helped Grace find a towel for her shoulders.

"Everybody OK?" Heather hollered.

"I'm fine!" Grace waved. Leah turned and gave Heather a thumbs up.

"I was worried about that," Leah said to Shannon. "The raft was slippery and by the time it was Grace's turn to go off it, she couldn't hold her balance and hit her head going in. But she was just stunned a bit."

Heather waved and everyone dispersed. Julie Hess took Grace to Baryshnikov cabin. Back in Pavlova, once Charleigh, Mary and Brooke had taken hot showers and were dry on their bunks, Sara took a red marker and wrote "Life-Saver!" under Leah's name on the banner. Leah looked up from the floor where she had plopped on a towel, waiting her turn for the shower. "Thanks!" she said, getting up. She took yellow and green markers and wrote "Boat Rescuer" under Sara and Shannon's names.

"Come on, you guys," Leah said to the water ballet girls. She handed them each their marker. "Give yourself credit for a great performance."

"We should have been more careful like you warned us," Brooke said.

"Yeah. I feel terrible," Charleigh said.

"Well, we practiced so long and hard," Mary said. "The audience loved it, and Grace is fine." She took her purple marker and wrote "Lakewood Swim Show" under her name. Then she wrote "Grace" under that to include her. Charleigh and Brooke did the same.

Then Julie Hess came to the porch with a stack of sandwiches and milk from the dining hall. She knew they had missed lunch. "Good teamwork in more ways than one!" she yelled, walking away. "Nicely done, everyone. Great rescue, Leah!"

When Leah finally got into the shower, Sara thought: "YMCA-Leap-Year-Life-Saving Leah." She hoped Leah could save her life by dancing well in *Concerto Barocco* so she could get to New York.

After dinner Sara, Shannon and Leah went to the laundry room to begin *Concerto Barocco* practice, but it was full of campers doing their wash. They sat on the steps for a while waiting for the place to clear out, but just as someone left, someone else went in. Sunday evening was clearly the busiest time for the laundry room. "We might as well do our laundry," Leah said, leading the way back to the cabin for their dirty clothes. When they finished drying and folding their clothes and the last girl had left, it was almost eight-thirty.

"Hurry," Sara said, grabbing her pillow case of clean clothes. "We have a half hour left." She shut and locked the heavy door to the laundry room and looked up at the clock. They threw their clean clothes on top of the big table and pushed it out of the way to the side of the room. As promised, Shannon remembered the opening steps to *Concerto Barocco*. She did the steps for them slowly over and over until all three of them could do it in unison.

"It looks OK," Shannon said. "But you must keep your back supported and you must keep your weight over the balls of your feet at all times to be ready to move into the next steps. Try again." She drilled them on the opening position and on the flowing Balanchine style until Julie Hess pounded on the door.

"Nine o'clock!" Miss Hess hollered. "Let's go!" She helped them move the big table back to the center of the room, then shooed them out and locked up.

Before going to sleep Sara wrote down the steps they had learned to *Concerto Barocco* and put them under her pillow with her locket. Sleeping on them would bring her luck.

Monday after lunch Sara needed to find a place to practice a phrase for that afternoon's modern class. If she found herself the leader of the group she wanted to be ready with movement that showed she understood not only how to lead, but how to use pure Nikolais dance vocabulary. She wanted to come up with something using different levels, graining, turning and spinning or maybe using leg swings. She decided to go across the road to find the clear space in the woods that Shannon had found. Before anyone could ask where she was going, she took off running toward the camp entrance. When she reached the small different color flags blowing in the wind surrounding the sign "Welcome to Lakewood," she crossed the wide dirt road into the thick woods. She tried to imagine which way Shannon had gone. She looked up at the trees, but didn't see any clearing. She looked down at the ground and saw what looked like a narrow path. She took it and it turned into a wider path. But then the wider path broke into two paths. *Oh-oh*, she thought. She looked up at the trees again and thought she saw a clearing. She took the fork in the path that would take her there.

Soon Sara saw an old raggy hammock tied between two trees at the edge of a clearing. There was a blackened fire pit too, with sitting stones. She looked all around in the silent space. She was eerily alone. In her head she began to hear Miss Lee's drum beating and she went to the center of the clearing. Dancing on top of dried pine needles, she pretended the whole modern dance class was behind her, that she was suddenly the leader. She tried moving to one side while throwing herself off-balance and she tried carving volume in space. Then she tried a few leg swings flowing into twirling and spinning. Finally she changed levels while pretending to be drawing lines in space with a sparkler. She was having so much fun that she giggled out loud. She was set for this afternoon. She ran back up the path out of the clearing but must have taken the wrong path at the fork. She wasn't good at reversing things. She stopped running and caught her breath. How did Shannon get back? It was getting hot and the heavy pine smell permeated her nostrils. Then the wind blew and she thought she smelled the blackened fire pit. She followed the strong odor of burnt smoke back to the fork in the path. Then she turned around and walked slowly and carefully forward on the other fork. She was relieved when she saw the Lakewood flags across the road. *Welcome BACK to Lakewood*, she thought. She made it back to Pavlova in time to grab her dance bag and catch up with Leah and Shannon on the path to the dance building.

"You smell like pine and smoke," Leah said. "Where have you been?"

"Just went for a walk," Sara said, looking at the ground. But she felt Shannon staring at her. She was sure Shannon knew. Sara hoped they could keep it another blue tin secret.

Sara still hadn't spent enough time using Jackson's book to memorize the Nikolais warm-up sequence, but did them better today. After spending scary time in the woods practicing, it seemed she was not going to get a chance to lead the group. Miss Lee sat on her stool beating her drum. The class kept moving this way and that, the leaders kept changing as the direction changed to face the different walls of the studio, but Sara never seemed to end up in front of the group. Everything moved so quickly that it was all she could do to follow the leader and try to express pure movement. Then, at the last minute, the group changed direction to face the windows looking out over the lake. Sara stepped quickly to the front and before anyone could move in front of her, she began to improvise on the movements she had created in the woods. The trees swaying over the lake, the blueness of the water, the memory of dancing with Jackson inspired her.

"Yes!" Miss Lee exclaimed as Sara led the class in moving forward, backward, changing levels, in turns and spins and finally in leg swings to change direction. Then it was someone else's turn to lead. Sara felt exhilarated from creating the movement and from leading well. Enriched from this, she felt herself move to a higher level of dance expression for the remainder of class. Miss Lee put her in the front line going across the floor learning the new movement vocabulary for the day called undercurves.

For the undercurve movement they had to imagine they were moving continuously on the lower half of a circle. Sara thought how interesting modern dance vocabulary was. There

206

was always something different that stimulated your brain and body in a new way. As she did the undercurves across the floor to the beat of the drum, it felt like a kind of skipping in a sort of down, up, down movement. The homework assignment for Tuesday was to perform a clear expression of undercurves going across the floor while changing directions. It would be a cinch, Sara thought. Something she could create in her mind. On the way to folk class, she got Sara and Leah to agree to watch the *Concerto Barocco* film after dinner instead of working on the Nikolais homework.

They ate a hurried dinner, but when they got to the secret practice room, the film was gone. "Where did we leave it?" Shannon asked, looking around.

"I think I left it on the chair," Sara said, looking under it. Leah looked inside an old cupboard, but there was nothing inside but cobwebs. "No one knows about this room," Sara said, sitting on the wobbly chair.

"Looks like somebody does," Leah said, plopping onto the floor.

"If we lost that film, Miss Meisner will not be pleased," Shannon warned.

"Think, Sara!" Leah said. "What did you do with it?"

"Nothing. Nothing. I am sure I left it on this chair."

"Instead of arguing, I think we should just go over again what we have learned so far," Shannon suggested. Sara felt bad. This whole thing was her idea and it seemed to be falling apart. She looked at Leah who still looked like she needed to lose weight. She looked down at herself and vowed to start cutting her own meals in half. She looked at Shannon who had already begun to move her thin body in the steps she had taught them in the laundry room. Sara and Leah got up and followed her. When they had practiced the steps slowly several times, Shannon increased the tempo by humming the music.

"And this is still slower than we'll actually have to do it," Shannon said. Sara wondered how she'd ever do it really fast and in pointe shoes. But they still had more than two weeks to learn it if she was right about the student concert being announced next week. They worked hard and then trudged up the stairs to *Giselle* rehearsal.

"Ok, dancers," Miss Alexander said. "Everyone in pointe shoes. We'll dance the entire ballet full out tonight." The girls got their pointe shoes out of their bags and sat on the floor putting them on. Jackson and Mr. Peterson arrived. Patrick was with them tonight. He found Sara and smiled. Sara pretended to be busy tying the ribbons on her pointe shoes. *Right,* she thought. *Like I'm ever going to dance a duet with you.*

The beautiful music quickly took Sara from anything else in the world into the make-believe woods of *Giselle*. She watched out of the corner of her eye as the soloists performed. She held her soft poses with the rest of the corps de ballet in circles or straight lines while Giselle danced all around Albrecht, and Myrtha encouraged her to dance him to death. She watched in wonder the slow controlled movements of Myrtha and her wonderful bourrées across the whole room. She was in awe at Giselle's allegro, her devastatingly quick beats and crosses of the ankles in the air. How difficult the steps were, how perfectly Courtney and Katie did them. Jackson seemed to improve with each rehearsal, his leaps higher, his sorrow deeper.

Miss Sutton had arrived after the rehearsal began and now she was applauding. "Nice. Very nice. It is coming along,"

she said. "I'd like to see it again with the understudies dancing." Sara looked at Shannon who didn't flinch. She stood
prepared with Leah, Keera and the other understudies while
their counterparts sat under the barres to rest. Patrick stepped
in for Jackson. He must have learned the role in the boys'
studio. The music began and Sara could tell almost from the
beginning that the magic wasn't there. It was rough, with
the understudies barely getting through their roles, except
for Shannon. She danced Robin's part as if it had always been
hers. Robin was glaring at her like she had glared at Sara
last year. But Shannon was completely oblivious to it and
just danced in her calm and graceful way. The seamstress
appeared at the doorway during the rehearsal and as soon as
it was over Miss Sutton announced they would begin final
costume fittings. As the dancers went downstairs two at a
time in alphabetical order, Miss Alexander and the soloists
worked with the understudies. Miss Sutton took the rest of
the group through the full ballet again, making corrections
as they went. She worked with Hillary on keeping her back
leg up in the scoots across floor. Sara remembered how good
Hillary was last year as a comic skater, but this was a whole
different thing.

When Sara and Shannon came up from their fittings,
rehearsal was almost over. Patrick found Sara on the way out.
"Hi, Sara," he said, touching her arm. Leah and Shannon took
off for the locker room. "Did you get my note?" he asked.

"Yes," Sara said, looking at the dancers going down the
stairs to the locker room, which is where she wished she was.
"Thanks."

"Let's go, Patrick!" Mr. Peters hollered from outside. He
was waiting with Jackson.

209

"See you soon, I hope," Patrick smiled as he made his way out the door. Sara felt uncomfortable as she went down the stairs.

"Don't leave me like that," she told Shannon and Leah. They just laughed.

Back at the cabin, Sara couldn't help talking about the *Concerto Barocco* film. "What are we going to do?" she asked Shannon and Leah. Brooke, Charleigh and Mary were already in their pajamas and in their bunks.

"What's wrong?" Brooke asked. When Sara explained about the missing film, her answer seemed logical. "It's probably back on the shelf in the music room," she said.

"Yeah," Mary said. "Don't worry about it until you check in there."

You guys don't know Robin, Sara thought. She just had a feeling that Robin had it.

CHAPTER TWENTY-SIX

"Film, Photos and Letters"

Tuesday was absolutely freezing. Sara wore thick leg warmers and a sweater over her leotard and tights for morning pointe class. Her feet seemed to take forever to warm up. After lunch she spent some time with Leah and Shannon sitting in front of the fireplace in the great room off the dining hall. It was really for visiting parents and other guests, but Miss Sutton had lit a fire and opened the doors for all the dancers today. Sara finally felt warm near the orange flames listening to the fire crackling. She had ballet class next and then it would be on to modern dance once more, her most challenging class. She closed her eyes, sat back in her chair and concentrated on the undercurve movement with changes of direction she would have to perform for Miss Lee today. She pictured herself moving backward first, then sideways, then forward, then sideways in the other direction. She kept mixing it up in her mind, making it interesting.

In ballet class she felt cold all over again during the barre and was happy when Miss Sutton kept them moving quickly. How she loved the piano music that seemed to carry her high into the air, leaping and turning. She didn't mind at all when Miss Sutton called Shannon, Keera and Leah out to demonstrate a combination to the class, praising their accuracy and style. She was thinking again about modern class. She had studied the warm-up sequence in Jackson's book last night and was ready to test her memory today.

Soon Sara was sitting on the cold studio floor holding her bare feet trying to warm them up. Miss Lee was beating her drum softly as the dancers entered the room, encouraging them to do some stretching on their own to stay warm. Then the sequence of exercises began. Shannon was on Sara's right and Leah on her left. No one was in front of her. It was part of her test. She would try to follow no one today for the first time, but she could look out of the corner of her eye to see Shannon or Leah if absolutely necessary. The drum beat got stronger and Sara got past the part where she often made her first mistake. Then she got past the second part where she *always* made a mistake. Then they had completed the floor exercises and were doing the standing warm-ups. She got through the drop swings that she loved so much, especially the part where her feet got to leave the floor. Then she suddenly forgot what came next. *Darn,* she thought. As they went into the leg warm-ups she had to sneak a look at Leah. "Focus on your own space!" Miss Lee shouted above her drumming. "You should know these by now!" Sara was sure Miss Lee was looking at her. Why did she have so much trouble remembering these? She could hear Shannon telling her again not to think of anything but what she was doing at the moment, but she thought she had been doing that. Maybe there was something wrong with her brain, because she had trouble remembering ballet barre combinations, too. She worried she would never be a real dancer, would never make it to New York. *Oh, well,* she thought. *This is only modern dance and I am going to be a ballet dancer.* Still, she knew Miss Lee would have to give her a great recommendation if she were going to get a summer scholarship to the New York City Ballet.

Sara was relieved when she got to sit under the barre and watch homework assignments. Most of what she saw did not inspire her. Miss Lee seemed bored with them, too, and started calling out four girls at a time. It was more interesting with four people moving in different directions to the drumbeat, all doing movement based on undercurves. When Sara was called out to the floor with a group, she kept the idea of the movement in her head: *"Plié, transfer weight, lift; plié, transfer, lift; plié, transfer, lift…"* She found if she kept saying it in her head she could make it more interesting by moving sharply in different directions. It was difficult, but she managed it. She imagined moving in the bottom half of a circle, just as Miss Lee had explained to them. She was relieved when they began working on overcurves, with the transfer of weight at a high level, instead of low level. It felt more natural to Sara. It was like rising to the top part of a circle, and included leaps. *Wow*, Sara thought. *A new way of thinking of leaps.* She felt like a gazelle rising and falling across the room. She loved doing leaps in bare feet.

For Wednesday, they were to combine undercurves with overcurves. "Remember," Miss Lee said, "for the overcurves begin with little rises, then rises a bit off the floor, then progress to leaps. See you tomorrow."

At dinner, Shannon said she didn't care for under or overcurves. She said, in fact, she didn't care much for modern dance compared to ballet. It made Sara realize that she liked

213

both classes most of the time and that she was looking forward to creating her homework assignment for tomorrow. But first they had to decide what to practice after dinner before *Giselle* rehearsal, their modern assignment or *Concerto Barocco*.

"I wonder what happened to the *Concerto Barocco* film," Leah said as she sipped warm tea instead of eating dessert. "We really need to find it."

Sara said "Let's run over to the music library and see if someone put it back there." They put on their heavy sweaters, went over to the music library and caught Miss Meisner as she was locking up to go to dinner.

"Yes," she told them. Charlie returned it." But when Shannon told her they'd like to check it out again, she told them someone else had checked it out. "Come on in and we'll look," she said. She looked at her cards, then looked up at them. "Oh, yes, Robin Stewart checked it out."

Sara just knew it. *Robin! Great. Just great.*

"The seniors are expected to learn an entire Balanchine ballet and to write an essay on it," Miss Meisner said proudly. "I must say she chose well."

Too well, Sara thought. *Now what would they do?* "When is it due back?" She asked.

"Not for two weeks," Miss Meisner said.

Two weeks. That was about all the time they'd probably have before the student concert. Sara was disappointed and angry at the same time. She wanted to march right over to Tallchief cabin and get the film back from Robin.

"Thanks," Leah said to Miss Meisner. Sara was in a daze. When they got on the porch and Miss Meisner had hurried past them to dinner, Sara spoke.

"I can't believe it! We had it first. We have to get it back."

"We shouldn't have left it in the practice room," Shannon said.

"I thought you said no one knew about that room," Leah said.

Sara told them about how the door had stuck on Robin and Hillary last summer as they were watching a Romeo and Juliet rehearsal.

"You mean we could have got stuck in there?" Leah asked.

"No. Charlie, the janitor, fixed it," Sara assured her. They decided to go to Studio B and create their Nikolais movement phrases for Wednesday. But all the time Sara was trying to make up an undercurve-overcurve combination, she was thinking of how to get the *Concerto Barocco* film away from Robin.

At *Giselle* rehearsal they had a perfect run-through. "Bravo! Bravo!" Mr. Peters hollered out. Miss Sutton smiled. But then Miss Alexander had them perform it again facing the windows instead of the mirrors. Everything seemed to fall apart. Dancers who thought they knew the ballet by heart drew blanks. Sara almost turned the wrong way one time. Someone having the jitters gave everyone the jitters. Miss Alexander screeched the music to a halt.

"We move into the theatre tomorrow, dancers!" she said. "You perform for the New York City Ballet dancers on Friday. Not next Friday. The day after tomorrow Friday! Now get your bearings. *Think!*" Her voice rose higher than Sara had ever heard it. Sara realized she had been thinking of the *Concerto Barocco* film and stealing glances at Robin during the rehearsal. She'd do better in the next run-through. But then the seamstress came into the room with their costumes. Gorgeous long, white gowns hung from a rack she pushed into the room, wedding veils floating above each one. Jackson's costume hung on the end, the dark vest and white blousy shirt swaying on a hanger. A smaller version for Patrick hung next to it.

"OK," Miss Sutton said. "Boys use my office to change. Girls stay here." Sara and Shannon helped each other zip up. When Sara looked into the mirror she saw a mysterious forest spirit under her veil, the long white skirt almost dancing on its own. When she saw all the other dancers in the gauzy white she knew everything had been transformed. Everything would be fine. Jackson and Patrick entered the room and Sara gasped in delight. The V-neck shirt revealed Jackson's chest a bit, and the sleeves flowed as he walked. Even Patrick was stunning as he smiled at her.

"Now," Miss Alexander said, quieting their chatter. "Let's do it again, but put on leg warmers and sweaters. It's still cold in here." Once they were ready they did some barre exercises to warm their muscles again, then Miss Alexander started the music and everything went along OK for a while.

"Hillary!" Miss Sutton shouted when they had finished. "I have told you before not to let your leg drop in the scoots across the floor! We have no time left for you to get it right. Just get it right!"

"I'd like to see Leah take Hillary's part this time," Miss Alexander said. Sara watched a little frightened as Hillary stepped out and Leah stepped in. Leah looked wonderful in her costume that actually was a bit loose from the weight she had already lost. It seemed no one was breathing as the music began again. When they finished, Leah stood in the group quietly waiting while Miss Alexander and Miss Sutton talked in the corner. Mr. Peters went over Albrecht's last movements of the ballet with Patrick and Jackson. Sara was hoping Leah would get Hillary's part, but could imagine how angry Hillary would be if that happened. Then the photographer arrived in the doorway with his camera. Miss Sutton noticed him, looked up at the clock, and ended her conversation with Miss Alexander.

"Pictures, everyone!" Miss Sutton announced. Everyone threw off sweaters and leg warmers. Miss Sutton and Miss Alexander arranged them in poses from various parts of the ballet for the photographer. Sara tried hard to look her best, yet blend in with the rest of the corps. She watched in awe as Jackson, Courtney and Katie posed for special shots, then watched in envy as Robin and Kathy had their picture taken in their roles as Katie's attendants.

Leadership, cooperation, enthusiasm, improvement, Sara told herself. *Be enthused no matter what, show leadership in the part you have, cooperate in your heart, try to improve in dance and as a person.* But she was upset. She still could not quite believe she didn't have a special part in this ballet or even an understudy role for a soloist. She tried to remember that Madame had seen something special in her dancing last year, but tonight that seemed like a long time ago.

Finally, it was over. Sara took off her costume, put her leotard and sweater back on, hung her costume on the rack and ran down to the locker room before Patrick could try to talk to her. She just wanted a hot shower and a warm bunk. She pouted that she had no special part, no movement study prepared for Miss Lee tomorrow and no *Concerto Barocco* film.

"Félicitation, ami," Shannon smiled to Leah on the way to Pavlova cabin.

"What?" Leah said. "I only do the backstroke and I only speak English."

217

"Congratulations, friend," Shannon said. "You stepped in for Hillary. Well done."

"Well, I didn't get the part, I just rehearsed it," Leah answered.

Sara planned to lie in bed and think up her Nikolais phrase for tomorrow. She had already been thinking of how to combine undercurves and overcurves as they walked past the dark lake under the flaming torches. But when they got to the cabin, Brooke said that Sara and Shannon had received letters in the mail. "On the dresser!" she told them. Sara noted that hers was from her mom and threw it on her bunk. While she was in the shower Shannon knocked on the door.

"News! News!" Shannon hollered. "My dad is in New York and is coming here for *Giselle*!"

"Wow," Sara said. She wasn't sure if that made her feel better or worse. There would be no one in the audience for her. "That's great," she yelled through the door. But when she got on her bunk and opened her letter, she had a surprise. Her mother told her that Miss Abbey was coming for *Giselle*. At first Sara felt excited, but then she was worried that Miss Abbey would be disappointed. After all, she had no special part. She nearly cried thinking how her teacher from home would be expecting something more. Then she saw her mom's PS: "Miss Abbey is so proud that you made it into the corps de ballet of a *senior* ballet!" So she already knew. Sara still wasn't sure whether to be happy or sad. She felt under her pillow for her locket and touched the paper on which she had written the first movements of *Concerto Barocco*. She crunched it, knowing it might never happen now. Then she fastened the locket around her neck and went to sleep.

Wednesday morning brought a bright sun and warmth. It felt like summer had returned to the woods. The lake was gleaming and Sara actually felt like floating in it. Maybe she'd take out a boat after lunch. She took off her locket and put it back under her pillow wishing that her dad was coming for *Giselle* instead of Miss Abbey. At breakfast she told all the girls about Miss Abbey coming. Brooke said it was swell, Mary said it was awesome and Charleigh said she was going to bring as many friends to it as she could. "We'll be all be cheering for you!" She said. Shannon said she wished Leah had someone coming from Indiana.

"What for?" Leah said. "I'll just be standing in the dressing room in case somebody breaks a leg."

In ballet, Miss Sutton told the class what a fine job Leah had done standing in for a senior dancer last night. "We must all be ready at all times," Miss Sutton said in that very English way of hers.

In tap Mr. Moyne completed teaching them a whole routine to the most delightful, zany music. Sara felt uplifted by all the fun. But she had to improvise in modern dance. When it was her turn to take the floor to show her homework assignment, she made it up on the spot doing little under-curve steps to the beat of Miss Lee's drum, then switching to small overcurve steps, then doing larger overcurve steps until finally she was leaping all over the huge studio taking up more space than anyone. She was lost in her movements pretending to be riding the top of a sphere like a wild animal in the savannah. Suddenly the drum stopped and Sara remembered how to come to a dead stop. *STOP!* she told herself.

"Sara, that was really good!" Miss Lee announced. "Remember that." At the end of class, Miss Lee announced that they would have no homework assignment for Monday. "Enjoy *Giselle* and the New York City Ballet visit," she said cheerily. But during folk class, Sara felt grumpy again. *Remember that,* she heard Miss Lee saying. *Remember that,* she thought sarcastically, *but don't get a special part in* Giselle. *Remember that, but lose the dance film that could save your life here and get you a summer scholarship to New York. Remember that, but get Patrick's attention instead of Jackson's. Remember that, and have Miss Abbey in the audience instead of your dad.*

"Sara!" Mr. Moyne hollered. "You were to remember your steps. Will we have to start from scratch?"

Oh, there's another one, Sara thought. *Remember that, but get a folk solo instead of a ballet solo for the final concert.* She wanted to turn everything around. Instead, she tried hard to remember the steps Mr. Moyne had taught her. She suddenly thought of watching Miss Alexander and Mr. Peters rehearsing *Tarantella.* She held her heart and her tambourine high and most of the steps came back to her.

They were back in their practice clothes for *Giselle* rehearsal that night. As Sara stood at the barre looking over at Jackson she realized she had not taken a boat out after lunch. They made it through rehearsal without incident. After they finished polishing in certain places and Hillary got yelled at again for letting her leg drop, Miss Sutton announced they would have no regular classes the next day. Sara couldn't believe tomorrow was Thursday and they would be moving into the theatre to set up and practice *Giselle* on stage. The New York City Ballet would arrive tomorrow evening! When they got back to the cabin, Sara used her yellow marker to give herself credit for her fourth modern dance remember and fell soundly asleep.

CHAPTER TWENTY-SEVEN

"Tech Rehearsal Goes Bad"

When Sara woke up Thursday it took her a minute to realize she had no early morning pointe class to rush to and that she would have no classes at all for the whole day. They didn't have to report to the theatre until three in the afternoon, so she just lay in her bunk for a while waiting for Shannon to wake up. All the other bunks were empty. She looked at the clock: 7:45. Breakfast would end in fifteen minutes. She wondered if Shannon had stashed food anywhere. She found an apple and a little packet of peanut butter in Shannon's drawer. She had probably planned to eat them this morning. There was nothing to eat in the blue tin, but looking at it reminded Sara to put her locket in there for safe-keeping for the next couple of days. Then she took the crunched *Concerto Barocco* notes from under her pillow. As she looked over the notes, her mood fell. Without the film she was sunk. But she flattened the paper and put it back under her pillow. She just had to figure out a way to get that film back. She looked at Shannon again who was in a deep sleep. She was on her own. She'd grab an apple from the dining hall and go straight to Tallchief cabin to explain the mix-up to Robin and get the film back.

Tallchief was empty, so she went back to the dining hall. Robin wasn't there. She went to the dance building and looked in the window. The senior girls who had solos and special parts in *Giselle*, including Robin, were rehearsing with Miss Alexander. Sara watched for a while, but it made her feel unimportant. *That could be me in there*, she thought, *if I had chosen Senior Division*. She walked the path to the boat shed in fear that she would not be able to win the scholarship to New York City Ballet and in regret that she couldn't be in the running for a Lakewood scholarship either. *Nothing. I have nothing if I can't perform a Balanchine ballet in the student concert,* she thought. She thought of taking out a boat, but her body seemed to go by itself back up the path to Tallchief cabin. It was still empty, but she spotted the *Concerto Barocco* film on the chest of drawers. She could sneak in and get it and no one would know.

"Can I help you?" Sara jumped. There was a counselor suddenly standing between Sara and the cabin.

"I was looking for Robin," Sara smiled.

"She's at rehearsal," the woman said.

"OK. Thanks!" Sara said. She walked away quickly toward Pavlova.

"Just a minute," the counselor yelled. "What's your name?" But Sara kept walking.

Shannon was still asleep, so Sara took out a boat. The day was already warm and the water glistening. She was happy to be alone to think. She was going to have to talk to Robin. She rowed to the middle of the lake and looked over at the Woodlake grounds. Jackson was so tall she knew she'd spot him immediately if he were out there. She dropped anchor, stretched her body over the seats and let the sun warm her face. When she opened her eyes Patrick was rowing over to her. "Hi, Sara!" he smiled. The wind seemed to make his hair curlier.

"Oh, hi," Sara said. She had forgotten his promise to row out to her and her vow not to go out on the lake by herself. Was there no place she could be safely alone? He dropped anchor next to her, but made no move to get into her boat. Sara thought of last year and how her heart had opened like a flower when she had met Hank on the lake. Her heart didn't do that around Patrick. They chatted for a while, then Sara said she had to get back. They waved good-bye and Sara took the boat back. As she crossed her name off the list at the boat shed she decided to wake up Shannon. At least they could make use of the time they had to rehearse what they had already put together for *Concerto Barocco*.

"No," Shannon said, eating an apple on her bunk. "No. We must rest today while we can. Technical and dress rehearsals are crazy and confusing. We must rest until three o'clock." Leah came in.

"What's going on?" she asked.

"I think we should rehearse what we know of *Concerto Barocco*," Sara pleaded, taking her notes for it from under her pillow.

"Oh, no," Leah said. "I am going to do fifty laps of backstroke this morning. I am trying to lose weight, you know." So that was the end of that.

At three o'clock they entered the theatre through the stage door and were assigned dressing rooms. The corps de ballet was in one room, the soloists in another and the boys were down the hall. It seemed each time Sara was in a theatre she learned something new and today she learned how to help prepare the stage floor. While technicians were talking to each other through headsets to plan the stage lights, and the stage crew set up the backdrop, Sara was given a broom and told to sweep the stage floor. Shannon helped test the curtain ropes. Then Sara and Leah were given wet mops. When they were done, the floor glistened. Miss Sutton walked the floor in socks to make sure there were no rough places that might cause someone to fall. She taped any spot she thought might cause a problem for a pointe shoe. "Maybe one day we'll have a real dance floor," she said. Miss Alexander arrived and placed a box of rosin in both of the wings. The dancers would rub the toes of their pointe shoes in the rosin before dancing in case there were any slippery places on the floor. Sara thought of how she had forgotten to step into the box last summer for *Les Sylphides* rehearsal, but remembered how wonderful her little part with Mr. Moyne was for the performance when they waltzed upstage together and he lifted her high into the air. She stood on stage with her mop imagining the beautiful white costume flowing above her legs at the height of the lift. She heard the audience applauding for her once again.

Miss Sutton's voice came through the loudspeaker. "Tech rehearsal in five minutes! Leotards and ballet slippers. No pointe shoes. No make-up."

"Sara!" Leah yelled from the wings. "Come on!" Sara ran toward Leah, but somehow the mop got in her way and she tripped over it, twisted her right foot and instantly felt a deep pain. She winced and hobbled over to Leah.

"Oh, no," Leah said. "Is it OK?"

"It really hurts," Sara cried. Leah helped her get to the dressing room, then she was on her own trying to get into her leotard and tights. She had trouble lifting her leg into her tights, but was able to step on her foot to get back out onto the stage for rehearsal.

Soon the dancers were ready behind the closed curtains, the music began and Sara was in the middle of the first practice of *Giselle* on stage. But her foot hurt more as rehearsal went on. It was throbbing by the time Miss Sutton stopped them for the second time to get their spacing right. She tried not to limp, but the pain was bad.

"What's the matter with you?" Shannon whispered as they knelt and began their port a bras to the lilting music.

"I think I sprained my foot," Sara said, her face scrunched in pain.

"You should be icing it," Shannon replied.

"Do you have any ice with you?" Sara asked sarcastically.

Then the music changed and Courtney and Jackson made their entrance. Sara prayed that her foot wouldn't swell. She prayed that she would be able to get her pointe shoes on for dress rehearsal. She prayed that no one would notice her limp. She needed ice and an aspirin. Ice was the only thing that would keep the swelling down and prevent further injury. She didn't know what to do. If she didn't dance in *Giselle* tomorrow night in front of the New York City Ballet dancers, how would anyone know how good a dancer she was? If she didn't get off her leg right away, how would she be able to rest it enough to dance tomorrow night? Soon the decision was not hers.

"Stop!" Miss Alexander shouted from the front of the stage. "Your spacing is way off in the first formation. Let's see

225

you spread out and take up the whole stage." As Sara tried to move to open up the space, Miss Sutton saw her limp.

"Sara, are you OK?" Miss Sutton shouted toward the stage from the tenth row. Everything stopped. Everyone stared at Sara. She felt tears, but mustered the courage to speak.

"My foot hurts," Sara said.

Miss Sutton walked up to the stage. "Someone help her down here," she said. Leah came out from the wings and got Sara off the stage onto a seat in the front row. "OK, resume rehearsal," Miss Sutton shouted. "Leah, take Sara's part." From then on Sara was mostly oblivious to what was going on. Someone brought her an ice pack and an aspirin and told her to elevate her foot.

Mr. Peters came over and asked Sara what happened. She explained about tripping over the mop. He patted her shoulder and said, "It's OK. Leah is doing a good job up there." Sara looked up and watched Leah dancing her part. She did look good. As they danced, fog began to appear onstage. It was created from dry ice and made everything look so mystical and eerie, just like a grave in a midnight forest should be. Oh, how she wanted to be up on that stage. She couldn't believe this was happening. She wanted to sob, but held back. Slowly her foot began to stop throbbing and she noticed the beautiful scenery backdrop of the heavy woods. Even without costumes and make-up it was awesome. She watched in delight as Giselle leaped off into the wings throwing the long ferns behind her. Her eyes were riveted to the stage when the corps de ballet performed the scoots across the floor, passing through each other's lines. It was perfect except for Hillary's back arabesque leg bobbing a bit.

226

Miss Alexander let the dancers go through the entire ballet, then made her corrections and comments to them. Miss Sutton had some comments for the lighting technicians, then turned to the dancers still standing on stage. The fog had stopped and Sara could see everyone's healthy feet. "OK, dancers," Miss Sutton said, "take forty-five minutes for dinner and be back here by six. We'll warm up on the stage and begin full dress rehearsal at six-thirty with costumes, make-up and pointe shoes. Leah, nice job standing in! Thank you dancers." Everyone applauded for the good rehearsal and took off for the dressing rooms. Leah and Shannon came down off the stage for Sara. "You stay off that foot for the rest of the day, young lady," Miss Sutton told Sara. "And keep it iced. We'll check you tomorrow." So that was that. In a blink of an eye and one wet mop, that was that.

Sara waited until Leah and Shannon had her safely on her bunk with ice on her elevated foot before letting loose a torrent of tears. She stopped crying when Charleigh, Mary and Brooke came in with a dinner tray for her. "We are so sorry," Mary said.

"It will be OK in the morning," Brooke offered. "You'll see."

"Can you move your toes?" Charleigh asked. Sara tried and found that she could, but it caused pain.

"Oh, stupid mop!" Sara hollered. Mary took the yellow marker and wrote "Stupid Mop" under Sara's name on the banner. She drew a cartoon mop. Sara laughed. Then there was a knock on the cabin door. Sara couldn't believe it when she heard Jackson's voice.

"More ice for the injured," he said, handing an ice pack through the door to Brooke. "Tell her to keep her foot up and iced all night. She'll be OK. Leah and Shannon, you better come back to the dining hall and get dinner." Sara watched them through the window as they headed down the path. Her spirit felt broken, but her heart felt warm.

Jackson must be having dinner in the girl's dining hall to save time. *But still*, she thought, *imagine Jackson coming all the way to Pavlova cabin with ice just for me.* She glanced at the clock. Just twenty-five minutes until they were all due back at the theatre to get into costume and make-up. Everything was going so fast, and without her. Then she fell asleep and didn't wake up until she heard Leah and Shannon come in around nine o'clock.

"What happed? What happened?" she asked. The melted ice pack fell to the floor.

"It went OK," Leah said.

"Very interesting," Shannon added.

"What do you mean?" Sara asked, moving her foot around. The pain had almost subsided.

"Well, they took Leah out of your part, pulled Hillary out of the performance, and put Leah in Hillary's part."

"Really?" Sara was confused. "So which part will you dance tomorrow night?"

"Beats me," Leah said. "Probably neither."

"But they were really upset with Hillary," Shannon said. "I don't think they will put her back in. And Leah is, obviously, the favorite understudy."

"Can you put weight on your foot now?" Leah asked. Then Mary, Charleigh and Brooke came in. They brought a new ice pack from Julie Hess.

"Miss Hess arranged for the nurse to come here in the morning to check your foot," Mary said, putting the new ice under her foot.

"Yeah, so just stay in bed with the ice tonight," Brooke said. Charleigh adjusted the pillow and the ice pack. Sara lay back quietly as the girls got ready for bed. When they were all in their bunks and the lights were out, Sara turned toward the wall and cried softly. Everything was ruined. She had practically no chance now of dancing in the master class tomorrow given by a New York City Ballet dancer and probably no chance of performing for them tomorrow night. That meant practically no chance of getting a scholarship to New York.

"Don't cry, Sara," Mary said in the dark. "It will be all right."

"Yeah, there's the whole second half of summer," Charleigh said.

"And you have a folk dance solo," Brooke said. That made Sara cry more. A folk dance solo in character shoes instead of a ballet solo in pointe shoes. Then she remembered that Miss Abbey would be here tomorrow evening for the *Giselle* performance that she wouldn't even be in. Then she remembered that Robin still had the *Concerto Barocco* film. Then she yearned to sleep with her lucky locket, but it was in the secret blue tin. She took the pillow from under her foot and put it over her head and eventually fell asleep. She slept late and awoke to the nurse knocking on the door. The cabin was empty.

"Don't get up," the nurse said. Then Leah came out of the bathroom drying her hair on a towel and let the nurse in.

"This way to the mop foot," Leah laughed. The nurse touched Sara's foot and asked her to move it. The pain seemed completely gone.

"No swelling and no bruising," the nurse announced.

229

"Really?" Sara asked in delight.

"Really," the nurse said. "Try to stand on it." Sara got up and barely put weight on the foot. "Come on," the nurse coached. "Step on it." Sara did and didn't feel any pain. "Take a few steps," the nurse instructed. Sara was afraid, but did what she was told.

"Wow!" Leah said. "Looking *good*."

"Well, I think it was just minor, but I'll wrap your foot and ankle in tape so you won't twist it."

"Can she dance today?" Leah asked, combing her hair. "We have master class late this afternoon and a performance tonight."

"I know," the nurse said, turning to Sara. "I need to report your condition to Miss Sutton." Then Shannon came in with breakfast for Sara. Everyone seemed to pause mid-air waiting for the verdict. "I'll tell you what," the nurse said. "You wear the tape and ballet slippers for master class and I'll check you again back stage tonight with pointe shoes on. If you can get up on them OK, I think you'll be able to perform."

"After all, you're not dancing Giselle," Leah said.

"Not even dancing Myrtha," Shannon offered.

For once Sara was glad she didn't have a major part. "I'm not even one of the attendants!" Sara said. After a moment they all laughed and Sara realized there wasn't that much at stake as long as she could be seen by a member of the New York City Ballet and dance her best.

PART TWO

CHAPTER TWENTY-EIGHT

"Master Class"

As luck would have it, no one wore pointe shoes for the master class. Sara spent some time warming up in the hall and her foot was moving pretty well. She made sure she stood between Leah and Shannon at the barre for moral support and her pink tights hid the tape, so she mostly looked like everyone else.

"I'm Misty Schaffer, a soloist with the New York City Ballet," the pretty brunette announced. "I'm looking forward to your performance tonight."

Not as much as I'm looking forward to your performance tomorrow night, Sara thought excitedly. But it seemed so far away. She still had to get through this class and try to make it into the performance tonight. Just for a second she thought of how Jackson had brought her the ice last night, then she told herself to focus on class right this minute. Compared to Yuri's master class last year, this one seemed slower and easier. The barre certainly wasn't tricky and Sara began to regain her strength and confidence. But during the hour of center-floor exercises Miss Schaffer made the class increasingly difficult.

As they went on, it was getting harder for Sara to look like one of the best in the class. *Notice me, notice me*, Sara thought as she did perfect pirouettes on her good foot. But the teacher always seemed to be looking the other way whenever Sara did something really well. Then for the allegro combination Miss Schaffer pulled Leah out in front.

"What's your name?" she asked. "Where are you from?" When Leah told her, Miss Schaffer said, "OK, same combination, and follow Leah from Indiana! Try to get as high in the air for the beats as she does. Go for the same cleanness of movement." Sara did OK, but the quick movements were not her best thing.

For the slow waltz combination Miss Schaffer called Shannon, Keera and Alene to lead the class. It was probably the most flowing, lyrical and lovely combination Sara had ever been asked to do. She watched the lead group out of the corner of her eye as she danced and was awed by their grace. She forgot about her taped foot and totally immersed herself in the joy of dancing. The final combination across the floor was a quick, brilliant waltz with changes of direction in the air and a big leap at the end. She smiled as they practiced the movement to the buoyant piano music, then just seemed to take off into the air when they did it for real. But when they were instructed to do it in reverse, half the class messed up. Sara had managed to get through it correctly.

"Whoa," Miss Schaffer said. "Think. Think. Shannon, Keera, Alene and... She pointed to Sara.

"Sara," Sara smiled.

"Shannon, Keera, Alene and Sara, first group. Everyone else make groups of four or five and follow. Watch these four, please." The music began and Sara's body felt light as she

234

danced the combination across the floor with Shannon, Keera and Alene. They took the final leap in exact unison and Misty Schaffer clapped and smiled at them. "*Yes!*" she exclaimed. Sara was back. As she took her place doing grand révérence with the class she beamed in the mirror at her own good performance. As she gathered up her towel and dance bag her foot hurt only the slightest bit. There was hope that she would be able to dance in the performance tonight, and Misty Schaffer would be in the audience to see her along with other members of the NYC Ballet that she hadn't seen or met yet.

But as she walked out the studio door, Robin walked past her going into the studio. She looked down at Sara and said, "Hope you can wear pointe shoes tonight." Sara could honestly never tell if Robin was being nice or being sarcastic. All she was sure of was that they both wanted the scholarship to New York. Before she could think of anything to say, Robin was past her and in the studio for her master class. Sara wanted more than ever now to get that *Concerto Barocco* film away from her. As soon as the performance was over she'd figure out a way. For now, they only had two hours until reporting to the theatre. They would have a warm-up followed by a run-through of *Giselle* in pointe shoes and then would get into their costumes and make-up for the performance.

"You better ice that foot," Leah told Sara on the way to the dining hall.

"How does it feel?" Shannon asked.

"Really good," Sara said, trying not to limp. The truth was it was starting to hurt a bit again. "But I guess I'll ice it for a while after dinner." She looked down at her foot to make sure it wasn't swelling. The tape seemed to be holding it. During dinner she thought again of how Jackson had brought the ice for her. She smiled and said to Shannon, "That was so nice of Jackson to bring ice last night."

"What?" Shannon said.

"That wasn't Jackson," Leah said. "It was Patrick."

"But I heard Jackson's voice and saw him out the window going to the dining hall with you guys." *They must be kidding*, Sara thought.

Shannon and Leah both laughed. "You were wishful-thinking," Shannon said.

"Or hallucinating," Leah laughed. Sara's mood went from joy to dismay in a second.

"Jackson had to stay in the theatre for an extra rehearsal last night," Shannon explained.

"Oh. Well, I'm going to get an ice pack from the kitchen," Sara said, embarrassed.

Leah gently pushed her back into her chair. "Stay put," she said. "I'll get it."

When they were back in Pavlova cabin, Shannon made sure Sara's foot was propped up with the ice, then she and Leah got the markers out and wrote "Master Class with Misty Schaffer, NYC Ballet—Class Leader!" under all three of their names. Sara smiled. She had been noticed.

CHAPTER TWENTY-NINE

"Giselle Performance"

As soon as they got to the Balanchine Theatre Sara carefully tried on her pointe shoes. She wanted to get her foot warmed up slowly before the nurse checked her. She held on to the back of her dressing room chair and gently rose onto her pointes. As chaos brewed around her with the dancers scurrying to organize their costumes and make-up and to get into their leotards, tights and pointe shoes for the warm-up and run-through, Sara stood looking down at her foot. Everything looked OK. The tape gave her confidence.

"Can you bourrée?" Shannon asked. Sara tried a few of the tiny running steps not going far from the chair. The foot hurt a little, but she was determined to keep going, to work through the pain. She could collapse completely tomorrow, but she had to get through tonight. Then she saw Leah in the doorway dressed for the run-through, ready to take her place. Suddenly the nurse, Miss Sutton, and Miss Alexander came through the door. Sara glanced at the clock. Just forty-five minutes until the curtain would go up on *Giselle*. She had to

237

be in it. The dancers all gathered around as Miss Sutton asked Sara to go up on pointe.

"No problem," Sara smiled, not admitting to a tiny bit of pain.

The nurse touched around the tape. "No swelling," she said. Shannon gave a thumbs-up, but Leah still stood ready at the door.

"Let's see you put all your weight on that foot," Miss Alexander said. Sara went down flat on her feet, then up on her pointes again holding her good foot up behind her hurt foot. She could hear Madame shouting at her last summer, *Pull up out of your shoes. Pull up. Pull up.* It worked! She seemed lighter and there was no pain.

"I think it will be OK," the nurse announced. Sara let her breath out. *Hurray!*

"OK, everybody on stage for warm-ups!" Miss Sutton directed.

Sara put her arm around Leah in the doorway and the two walked out to the portable barres together for the warm-up exercises. "I'm glad," Leah said. Mr. Peters led them in pliés and tendus and jetés, and by the time they got to the rond de jambs Sara knew she'd be just fine. She had never felt so happy to be part of simple warm-ups. She watched Jackson out of the corner of her eye. After a while she noticed Hillary standing in the corner of the stage talking to Miss Sutton and Miss Alexander. Soon Hillary left the stage and Miss Sutton motioned for Leah.

"Wonder what's up?" Shannon whispered to Sara as they did stretches with one leg on the barre.

Soon Leah came back to her place at the barre next to Sara. "I'm in, Hillary's out," she said.

There by a thread go I, Sara thought. "I'm glad," she smiled. She helped clear away the barres so the stage hands could cart them off into a room down the hall, then took her place next to Shannon in the wings ready to begin the run-through. The music started and Sara was so grateful to have this practice on stage before the performance. It was easy to fit into the group who had learned to get the formations and spacing correct last night. Miss Alexander let them get through the entire ballet without stopping them. All the instructors applauded when they were done.

"Good!" Miss Alexander shouted to them from the back of the house. "Very nice!"

"Bows now!" Miss Sutton directed. The corps de ballet stood in a line and bowed together. Then Myrtha's attendants, Robin and Kathy, took their bows; then Katie as Myrtha; and finally Jackson and Courtney as Albrecht and Giselle. Sara thought Jackson looked handsome and professional. She thought of how they had practiced modern dance in the Woodlake studio the night of the boys' party. She hoped they would have a chance to be together alone again. Then she saw Patrick smile at her from the wings and give her a thumbs up. She supposed she should thank him for bringing the ice.

"Good work, company," Miss Sutton said. "Be back on stage at seven forty-five sharp in costume and make-up. And don't tangle with any mops!" Sara laughed with everyone else.

The dancers broke into chatter as they headed for the dressing rooms. Patrick was waiting in the wings as Sara tried to make her way off the stage and into the hallway. "Nice to see you dancing," he smiled.

"Yes. And thanks for bringing the ice over to the cabin last night," Sara said as she continued to walk past him.

"You're welcome," Patrick said. "Any time."

"Sure hope there's no other time," Sara smiled. That ought to do it. But he followed her down the hall. Then she felt Leah come up quickly behind her.

"Hurray, Sara," Leah said, grabbing her arm. "We have to get all our make-up on and everything." The two took off for their dressing room. Sara could feel Patrick staring at her back.

Sara sat in her chair in front of the mirror and rubbed the top of her foot. *So far, so good, she thought.* She took her pointe shoes off to rest her feet and put on clean tights. Then she threw on her warm-up pants and pulled on a cardigan sweater. She let her hair down and brushed it tightly again into a bun, then tightened it more with a hairnet and secured it with pins. She put cream on her face and was applying foundation make-up when Hillary came over to Leah's chair.

"Are you happy to be dancing my part?" Hillary asked with a frown.

"I had no choice," Leah answered. Sara stood up.

"Well, it's not right. I worked hard for four weeks on that part," Hillary said.

Then Robin came over. "You're mostly a swimmer, aren't you?" She said to Leah.

Sara felt like pushing her. "No. She's mostly a dancer who knows how to swim."

"Very competitively," Robin said.

"You know all about competition," Sara said. She could hardly believe Robin was the same girl she had finally seemed to make friends with at the end of last summer.

"Everyone back off," Leah said.

Shannon finished tying her pointe shoes and stood up. "Stop!" she said. "We must perform momentarily. Leah dances and that's it. It was not her decision. Leave her alone."

Robin and Hillary turned and Shannon made sure they kept walking away. Sara looked at Leah who acted as though nothing had happened. YMCA-Leap-Year-Life-Saving Leah always seemed to keep swimming a good backstroke, letting the water run off of her no matter what happened. Sara sat back down and applied her make-up. When she found her costume on the clothes rack she began to get excited. She pulled the white, scratchy netting and the soft nylon bodice over her head and Leah zipped her up. She zipped Shannon, and Shannon zipped Leah. They all took a few stitches in the ribbons of their pointe shoes to keep them from unraveling and then Miss Sutton's voice beamed through the intercom. "All dancers on stage! All dancers on stage!"

Sara kept her leg warmers and sweater on over her costume to keep her muscles from getting cold. She did a few pliés on a chair in the wings and then a few tendus to stretch her feet. She went through the entire ballet in her mind, seeing herself in every place she was supposed to be at every moment. Then Miss Alexander called them into a circle in the middle of the stage behind the closed curtains. "This is your ballet now," she told them. "I have given you all I know of it. Now it is yours. Honor its tradition. Protect its beauty by the way you dance it. Now all hold hands." Sara held Shannon's hand on her left and Leah's hand on her right. "Have a wonderful performance," Miss Alexander said. "Places everyone."

Sara threw her leg warmers and sweater onto the chair in the wings and took her place with Shannon waiting for the part where Myrtha appeared in the night forest and waved them onto the stage in their wedding gowns and veils. She tried to pretend she was a Wili who had died before getting married and thought how romantic it was that Albrecht would come into the forest to Giselle's grave to ask her forgiveness. The curtain opened, the music began and Sara heard Mr. Peters walking behind her saying, "Keep your heads, now. Think. Keep your heads." She relaxed immediately and knew everything would be perfect. She heard someone coughing in the audience and suddenly remembered Miss Abbey was out there somewhere and Misty Schaffer and the rest of the New York City Ballet dancers. Her heart tried to flutter away out of her chest, but she heard Mr. Peters' voice again in her head and calmed down. Myrtha came on and did her bourrées all across the stage one way and then the other and showed perfect control in her adage work. They were getting off to a spectacular start. Soon Myrtha waved the corps de ballet dancers onto the stage and Sara felt thrilled to be in the performance and to have Shannon for her partner. They held their right hands together overhead and circled around each other en pointe battu and then took up the stage with the rest of the ensemble dancers in their beautiful formations. The white fog appeared at their feet and became thicker as they continued. When Giselle entered and then Albrecht, they seemed more professional than Sara had ever seen them. The way they looked at each other, the tilt of their heads, the yearning to be together was touching. The way Myrtha and her attendants kept Giselle protected from Albrecht was all danced in the old, dramatic way. Sara wondered how many times this ballet had been danced by how many different companies, and she was so glad to be part of the history. She felt especially poised tonight, like she was in a lovely dream and she seemed to float in the layers of her long white tutu.

At the peak of the ballet with the most profound music, Sara and the corps de ballet performed the scoots across the stage, and as soon as the two lines passed through each other the audience burst into applause. Sara tried to hold a serene look on her face to keep the scene magical and true, but was so excited by the thought of Misty Schaffer out there applauding for her that she felt herself smile just a little. Soon came the part where the chimes announced the sun was coming up and it was morning. Giselle returned to her grave and Albrecht collapsed onto the floor with the white lilies and it was all over. The audience immediately stood up and applauded wildly. As Sara took her bow, she realized all the boys from Woodlake were at the back of the theatre shouting hurrahs. She spotted Miss Abbey and smiled. Then Patrick came out from the wings with big bouquets of flowers for Courtney and Katie. Everyone bowed again and the curtains finally closed. Sara's first thought was that she wanted to perform it again at least three times. It was over so quickly after weeks of work. Back in the dressing room there were programs on all the chairs, one for each dancer. Sara opened hers and found her name as part of the corps de ballet. It was real. It was forever. No one could ever take it away from her. It was part of her life. It was another pearl on her make-believe dance necklace. She touched her neck and put the program on the dressing table.

"Sara!" Shannon yelled from the doorway. "Come here." She held a bouquet of yellow roses with a long white ribbon. "Here is my father." As Shannon introduced them, Miss Abbey appeared with tears in her eyes.

"Sara, Sara," Miss Abbey said. "It was so wonderful. Congratulations!" She handed Sara a perfect bouquet of pink and red carnations with a streaming pink ribbon.

"Ice cream for the dancers!" Mr. St. Pierre exclaimed. Then he said something in French to Shannon, kissed her cheek and left.

"My father invites you and Miss Abbey to go into town with us for ice cream," Shannon said. "His treat. He will meet us outside at the stage door. Hurry up and change."

"Wonderful," Miss Abbey said, following Mr. St. Pierre.

Then Sara remembered Leah. She had no flowers and her name wasn't even in the program. "What about Leah?" she asked Shannon.

"Oh, yes, of course—Leah!" Shannon said, going over to Leah to invite her. Sara gave Leah some of the flowers from her bouquet. Then Leah saw Hillary standing near the door-way and walked over to her. Sara couldn't hear what they said to each other, but saw Leah give the flowers to Hillary.

Sara got her make-up and costume off quickly and went out the stage door with Leah and Shannon. They were greeted enthusiastically by Mary, Brooke and Charleigh. "Congrats, you guys!" "It was wonderful!" "It was awesome!" "So beautiful!" They went on and on in their excitement, and after hugs, went down to see the moon over the lake with Grace and some of the younger boys.

Shannon found Miss Abbey and Mr. St. Pierre in the crowd and they all rode into town in a beautiful car that Shannon's father had leased for the trip. No dancer thinks of weight loss after a great performance, and a lot of ice cream was eaten in delight. When the adults dropped the dancers off at the path to their cabin, everyone was nicely tired out, but still excited. "Your mom will be here for the final performance," Miss Abbey assured Sara.

"Yes, and your mother, too," Mr. St. Pierre said to Shannon as he kissed her good-bye.

"Who is coming for you, Leah?" Miss Abbey wanted to know.

"Oh, probably all the citizens of Indiana," Leah joked. Everyone laughed. The three tired dancers walked under the swaying pine trees and sparkling stars to Pavlova cabin, the torches over the lake dancing in the breeze behind them.

CHAPTER THIRTY

"Saturday Surprises"

Sara woke up Saturday morning to rain smacking the cabin windows and pelting the roof of the old cabin. Everyone else was still asleep. She looked over at the flowers she and Shannon had left on the chest of drawers last night. *It really happened,* she thought. *I was in* Giselle *last night.* She took the program out from under her pillow and looked at her name again. Then she looked at the front of it. "Lakewood Dance Camp," she read, "presents *Giselle"* She could hardly believe it was over. No more evening rehearsals. No more hoping for a special part. No more watching Jackson partner Courtney. The performance had been a huge success. She pulled her bedroll up to her neck and smiled smugly. Miss Abbey had seen her in a high level performance and might give her a great part in her next ballet. Maybe she would get the part of Clara in *The Nutcracker*. She had danced in front of the New York City Ballet members and Misty Schaffer would probably remember how well she danced. Sara felt like she was an entirely different dancer than she had been before the performance. She felt larger inside and wondered if she had gown an inch taller in the night. She could hardly wait to write to Erin and tell her all about everything.

She put the program back under her pillow and felt the *Concerto Barocco* notes under there. *Oh, that's right*, she remembered. *I still have to get that film back from Robin.* Last night's run-in with her in the dressing room sure wasn't going to help. Then she remembered her injury. She reached down and touched her right foot. The tape was still tight. She wondered if the nurse would let her take it off today. She wanted to feel whole again and healthy and not have to wear the tape when she watched the New York City Ballet perform *Allegro Brillante* tonight.

Sara pretended to be asleep as Mary, Charleigh, Brooke and finally Leah left the cabin for breakfast. Then she whispered for Shannon to wake up. "Shannon, Shannon," she said, touching her arm that dangled from the bunk above.

"Le chocolate glace, merci," Shannon mumbled.

"Shannon, chocolate ice cream is over. That was last night. It's Saturday morning. Wake up. We have to talk."

"Matin?" Shannon asked. "Le week-end?"

"Oui," Sara answered pulling her arm. Shannon had lapsed into French again after being with her father last night. "Saturday morning and we have to talk."

Shannon sat up. "Oh, beautiful *Giselle*. Oh, beautiful flowers!" Oh, good. She was back.

"Shannon. Yes, it was all wonderful. Your father is delightful. The evening was magical. Now we have to get dressed, have breakfast by nine-thirty and get to Dance History class by ten-thirty. After that I have to go see the nurse about getting this tape off my foot. And then we have to discuss how to get that film away from Robin."

"No, no," Shannon said. Today is New York City Ballet Saturday. Today we try to watch rehearsal of *Allegro Brillante*. Tonight we go to the performance in Balanchine Theatre. The same stage we danced on last night!" She climbed down dreamily from her bunk and went into the bathroom.

"Of course, we will do all that," Sara shouted through the bathroom door. "*And* talk about the *Concerto Barocco* film. Believe me, Shannon, as soon as the company leaves we *have* to start rehearsing and we'll need that film."

"No. No. Not today," Shannon answered from the shower. "Today is only for NYCB!" She started singing in French and Sara knew she had lost. She got the blue tin out and put their programs in it, put on her locket, and pushed the tin back under her bunk. She looked over the *Concerto Barocco* notes again to commit them to memory, glanced at the big Nikolais book and thought of all the work ahead. She made up her bunk. She was getting excited about watching the professional company today. But even in all the excitement no one could stop her from thinking of ways to get back the film.

On the way out of the dining hall after breakfast, Shannon grabbed a clean glass. "Take one," she told Sara. "For the flowers. No water. We'll just let them dry." When they got back to the cabin they decided to press some of the flowers in books for a while, with a plan to put them in the blue tin in a few days. As Shannon was putting some yellow rose petals into her dance history book and Sara was putting some of her red and pink carnations into the Nikolais technique book, Leah came in.

"Listen, you guys," she said, taking off her wet raincoat and throwing her dripping boots out on the porch. The boys are all coming over here for the performance tonight and there's going to be a party afterward. We're going to be able to *mingle* with the performers! Look!" She showed them a little flyer that had just been given to her for their cabin. She tacked it to the banner. Sara put her book at the end of her bunk and looked at the flyer: *Afterglow party tonight following the performance by the New York City Ballet. Intermediates and seniors are invited to come and meet the dancers.*

"Wow," Sara said. "They didn't have that last year after the San Francisco Ballet performed *Swan Lake.*"

"Each company is different," Shannon said knowingly. "Balanchine loved children. He always had the studio kids in *The Nutcracker.* As students there today, we are in *Nutcracker* and often welcome to watch rehearsals."

Sara was thinking about what she would wear tonight and if she'd have a chance to talk with Jackson. She thought she might be too scared to actually talk to any company members. "Hey, we're late for Dance History!" Leah said. They all grabbed their rain gear, dance bags and notebooks and ran down the muddy path to class.

Miss Meisner was just about to begin talking when they took their seats. "Welcome, Wilis!" she greeted them. "Wonderful performance of *Giselle* last night. Wonderful." She sighed and applauded and the class joined in. "Today as we are blessed and exhilarated to have members of the New York City Ballet right here on campus with us, we will continue our discussion of George Balanchine." Sara saw the movie screen was pulled down and wondered what film they would see today. How could it be any more exciting than *Allegro Brillante,* which they watched last week and which the company members would perform tonight? But when it came time for the film Sara was astonished that it was *Concerto Barocco!* There it was on the screen: all the dancers in their white skirted leotards dancing quickly to the Bach violin concerto. *There must be two films,* she thought. She looked at Shannon and then at Leah. Shannon was busy taking notes and Leah just shrugged. She got her notebook opened quickly and took as many notes as she could, but when the lights went back on, she saw everything she had written was a mess.

"Notice how this dance epitomizes the Balanchine style of dancing at the speed of light, of flowing arms, bird-like hands, hips thrown into the movement, heels a bit off the floor for fast movement, and, of course, slender dancers." Miss Meisner smiled as the window shades went up. "Balanchine's choreography *is* the music. The dancers are all one as they dance on the floor. The floor *is* the music. The air *is* the music. Did you notice how it's not just the steps in Balanchine's dances, but the 'in-between' the steps that are so important? You have to be a special dancer to perform his choreography, which is why he trained his own dancers." *Just what Shannon told me,* Sara thought. She began to worry that they wouldn't be able to perform any part of the dance for the student concert, but then she remembered she wouldn't have to get that film away from Robin, that there were two films.

As soon as class was dismissed, Sara went up to Miss Meisner. "So, there are two *Concerto Barocco* films," she said. "Could I check this one out?" She held up the box with the film in it.

"Oh, no, dear," Miss Meisner said. "There is only one. Robin was kind enough to give this back to me for this morning's class." She opened her card file. "She has it checked out for almost two more weeks. She's writing her senior ballet paper on it you know." Miss Meisner smiled approvingly, her hair curling uncontrollably in the damp weather.

"Come on," Leah said. Shannon was already on the porch in the rain waiting to go to lunch. Lightning struck somewhere in the near distance and thunder followed. But Sara had an idea.

"When is Robin coming back for it?" Sara asked.

"I think she said tomorrow afternoon," Miss Meisner said.

"Well, could I borrow it until, say, one o'clock tomorrow then? I truly love Balanchine and this ballet," Sara added. "I just really want to watch it again. It is *so* inspiring to me, and your classes are too." She watched Miss Meisner's face.

"I guess it would be OK," she said carefully. "But have it back here tomorrow promptly at one o'clock."

Sara thanked her, grabbed the film and pushed it into her dance bag along with her notebook. "Let's go before she changes her mind," she said to Leah and Shannon. At lunch, Shannon wanted to know when they'd have time to watch it. She reminded them that the studio was closed Sundays and tonight they had the performance and after party. "Well, we have this afternoon. The performance isn't until eight o'clock," Sara said, planning in her mind. She couldn't believe she actually had the film.

"No way," Leah said.

"Yes," Shannon agreed. "No way because perhaps we will be allowed to watch company class and dress rehearsal of *Allegro Brillante* this afternoon."

"And we still don't even know if there's going to be a student concert," Leah said to Sara's annoyance.

"You guys have to trust me!" Sara blurted out. Robin looked over at her from her lunch table.

Shannon and Leah looked at each other. Shannon already took classes in New York and Leah might like swimming better than ballet. "This means everything to me," Sara said. "Doing this Balanchine ballet is the only real chance I have of getting to New York."

"As I have said," Shannon said, "we can't just *do* the ballet we have to look *good* doing the ballet. Even if it's just a part of the ballet. We can't ruin an entire tradition. You can't get to New York that way."

"I *know*," Sara said, gritting her teeth. She whispered the rest so Robin wouldn't hear. "That is why we have to watch the film today. To learn it, to look good doing just a part of it. Three minutes, you guys, that is all we have to do perfectly. Come *on*. We can get started right now." She picked up her dance bag and lunch tray. Leah and Shannon followed her reluctantly. When they got outside the dining hall Shannon spoke.

"All right," Shannon said. "Let's go directly to the dance building and see if the company is taking class or rehearsing and if we're allowed to watch. If we're not, we'll go down to the little room and watch the film." Sara agreed and the three ran over to the dance building in pouring rain. They took their boots off on the porch and heard nothing but silence when they entered the building. No music was playing, the studio was empty and Mrs. Lane was not in her office.

"Come on," Sara said, running down the steps to the lower level. They put their wet rain coats in the old dusty closet of the secret practice room. Sara popped in the film and they sat on the floor and watched the first movement of *Concerto Barocco*. They all took notes. Then they stopped the film and tried the steps in their stocking feet glancing at their notes. But just as Sara thought she was catching on to the opening movements, they heard the studio floor creaking above them. "It's the company dancers!" she said excitedly. Thunder rolled outside the little window as they all dropped their note pads and ran out of the room, down the hall and up the stairs. But the door to the large studio was closed and there was no window in the door. "Darn," Sara said. "Come on!" She led them back downstairs, down the hall to the little practice room again. They would get their raincoats on and go to an outside window and look in at the dancers taking class. But the door to the practice room stuck. "What?!" Sara cried out loud. "This *can't* be! It's the door out in the hallway that always sticks!"

"Let me try," Shannon said, taking the knob. It turned, but the door wouldn't open.

"Here," Leah said, nudging Shannon out of the way. She turned the knob back and forth, pushed and pulled it and shoved at the door with her shoulder, but the door stayed stubbornly shut. "Everybody together," she directed, and all three of them shoved at the door. The door flew open and the girls stumbled over each other with Sara ending up on the floor. Leah was laughing.

"These doors are so awful!" Sara said. "They must all be fifty-one years old like the camp."

"I am not sure at all this is worth it," Shannon said angrily, slamming the door behind her.

"Wait! Don't close the door!" Leah shouted. It was too late. Leah tried the door, but it had stuck again. They all sat on the floor listening to the ceiling creak above them as the New York City Ballet dancers took class.

"I guess we are meant to learn *Concerto Barocco* in this room," Sara said. She did want to learn it, but she also wanted desperately to watch the professional dancers upstairs.

"Yeah," Leah said. "Locked in like prisoners."

Lightning lit the little window and Shannon looked up at it. "I have an idea," she said. She moved the chair across the room, stood on it and tried to open the window. "It's stuck, too," she said sadly. "I thought we could go out the window and leave it open a bit so we could get back in. They each took a turn trying to lift up the old sash, but the ancient paint seemed to glue the window to the frame for good. Then Leah tried it for a second time, pushing her back-stroke shoulders into it. The window opened a crack.

"Help!" Leah said. Sara and Shannon rushed to help and the window opened a bit more. There was no screen on it, so they just needed to get it open enough to let them squeeze through. Sara and Shannon backed away and Leah rattled the window forward and backward to loosen it from the old sticky paint. Then she shoved it hard and it seemed to fly up. One of the dirty old panes in the window broke and glass fell onto the floor. Leah ducked and jumped off the chair. Sara and Shannon ran to the other side of the room.

"Are you OK?" Shannon asked.

"Yeah," Leah answered, pinching her hand to get a sliver out. Rain was coming down hard and some was finding its way into the little room. "Hurry," Leah said. "Grab your raincoats!" They put them on and, one by one, slid through the open window, socks in their pockets. Their bare feet squished into the muddy grass under the window and Shannon screamed. "Be quiet," Leah whispered. Sara looked up at the window. It was wide open, the dance film and their dance bags and notes were in there, and rain was going in.

"Wait a minute," Sara said as Shannon started walking away. Sara stood on her tiptoes but could not reach enough of the window to pull it down. Rain was pelting them as they each tried and failed. "Shannon," Sara said. "Get on my back and I'll boost you up there."

"No," Leah said. "Sara, I'll boost you." Sara climbed on Leah and managed to get the window down almost to the bottom. Then they took off quickly, ducked under Mrs. Lane's office window, sat on the porch under the overhang and put on their socks and boots. They tried the front door and found it unlocked, so they went down to the locker room and dried their hair and faces on paper towel. They came back up and found the studio door still closed. You never opened a studio door. They looked at each other, shrugged and went back out into the rain, walked around to one of the big studio windows and peered in. There was not another soul around. Sara counted ten NYCB dancers in different colored leotards and warm up sweaters and leg warmers. Five men and five women.

"Ten," she whispered, watching carefully as the dancers did adage work at the barre.

"Yes," Shannon said. "That is how many dance in *Allegro Brillante*. Only ten of the company came."

Ten was enough for Sara as she watched their sinuous bodies obey beautifully the commands of each barre exercise. She couldn't wait for them to move to center-floor. The rain was stopping and the sun was making an attempt to appear. She could hear the piano music through the closed window. As the dancers moved from the barre to center, one of them came to the window. The girls quickly ducked down. The dancer opened the window, then returned to the class. Sara's heart was galloping as she stood back up to look in the window. "That was close," she whispered. Leah and Shannon didn't answer. Their eyes were absolutely glued to the dancers. But as class went on and the rain stopped completely, campers came out into the sunshine. They'd have to leave and get back to the little room before anyone wondered why they had their raincoats on and what they'd been up to. They heard voices from the porch at the front of the building.

"Oh, it's a closed class," someone said. "But a sign here says studio rehearsal will be open at four o'clock." Someone must have just posted that.

"Let's go," Sara said. She wanted to get back to practice for a while, then watch the four o'clock rehearsal. But when they got around to the side of the studio they saw Charlie closing the broken window. They hid behind some bushes until he left. "Great," Sara said. "Just great. Now what do we do?" The dance film and their dance bags and notes were in that room and they were not. Sara got back on Leah and shoved it, but the window wouldn't budge. Sara boosted Leah, but she couldn't move it either.

"Follow me," Shannon said, heading for the front of the building. They left their boots on the porch again and silently went downstairs, past the locker rooms, past the costume room, down the long hallway to the little practice room.

Please open, please open, Sara whispered to herself. But it was no use. Nothing could open that door. Then they heard Charlie's big work boots coming toward them. They ran quickly to the costume room door, but it was locked. Their only chance was to make it to the locker room before Charlie got there. They just made it and closed the door quietly. They were out of breath and huddling next to the door when Charlie walked by in the semi-darkness of the long hall. But he wasn't alone. Mrs. Lane's voice came clearly through the locker room door.

"I can't believe someone would break that window," Sara heard Mrs. Lane say. "There is absolutely nothing in that old room. No one uses it at all."

"Well, I'll have a look," Charlie said. "Why don't you just go back to your office? You must have things to do with the New York people here and all."

"I want to get to the bottom of this," Mrs. Lane insisted. "I hope we're safe here."

"Oh, don't worry about that," Charlie said.

Then they heard another voice.

"Mrs. Lane! Mrs. Lane! Are you down here?" It was Miss Sutton.

Suddenly the footsteps stopped. "Yes, Miss Sutton!" Mrs. Lane called out.

"We need you upstairs! Can you come?"

Please say yes, please say yes, Sara whispered to herself.

"Now you get on back upstairs," Charlie told her. "There's nothing to this. I'll have a new pane in that window in no time. Probably got broken in the storm is all." Sara could feel Leah and Shannon holding their breath just as she was.

"Coming!" Mrs. Lane hollered to Miss Sutton. Then there was a long silence. Suddenly the door to the locker room opened. Sara saw Charlie's shoes.

"You better have a good story," Charlie said, looking at the three of them. He must have seen them duck into the locker room.

"We got stuck in there," Sara told him. She wasn't sure if she was relieved or scared.

"What did I tell you last time I caught you in there?"

"You said we couldn't be in there after hours. You were locking up and almost locked me in there," Sara blurted out. She was scared. "But it's not after hours now. We were rehearsing something."

"Sorry," Leah said, sitting on a bench. "We didn't mean to hurt anything. I was the one who broke the window pane."

Shannon said, "We had to get out of that room somehow. My father doesn't pay all this money for me to get stuck in rooms."

Charlie scratched his head and looked down. "Well, I don't want anybody in there while I'm cleaning up that glass. Now go on and get out of here."

"But we left our things in there," Sara said.

"Well, go get them quick before that woman comes back. She's trouble."

The girls rushed to the room with Charlie. Sara watched as he gave the knob a strong upward movement followed by a quick turn to the left. "Darn sticky weather," he grumbled as the door opened.

Sara grabbed the dance film and threw it into her bag along with her notes. As they left the room, she asked Charlie when the room would be open for use again.

"Monday, I'd say," he growled. "I'll have to go to town to get that pane of glass. Should make you girls sweep up in here."

"Well, thank you," Leah said quickly. She herded them out of there. Soon they stood in the sunshine outside the dance building with the dance film and no place to watch it. But Sara had an idea.

"Let's go to the music library," Sara said. "Maybe Miss Meisner will let us rehearse in there."

"But we will miss watching the class," Shannon said.

"We aren't really allowed anyway," Sara argued. "And we will get to officially watch the studio rehearsal at four. We've gotten into enough trouble today."

"It was amazing watching them through the window," Leah sighed. "I want to go back."

"How will we ever learn this ballet?" Sara asked, holding the dance film in the air.

"Hey, where did you get that?" Robin's voice asked. She came up behind Sara and took the film.

"Miss Meisner gave it to us," Sara answered. Leah took the film out of Robin's hand.

"Give me that," Robin said. Hillary was with her and tried to take the film from Leah, but Leah held on tight.

"It is rightfully ours," Shannon said quietly. "Until one o'clock tomorrow. You may ask Miss Meisner."

"Come on," Robin said to Hillary and they headed toward Miss Meisner's classroom. "We'll see about this!"

Leah handed the film back to Sara. "And to think," she said, "there might not even be a student concert."

"Oh, come on," Shannon said before Sara could get angry. "Let's go to the cabin and dry out."

They were alone in the cabin and took their time showering and changing clothes. They used their markers to write "*Giselle* Performance" under each of their names on the banner. They admired the flowers drying in the glasses, then they sat on the cabin porch to talk. Sara wished they had time to go to the secret cabin in the woods to work on *Concerto Barocco*. She wished there was a way to watch the film there. She touched the damp tape on her foot.

"Robin would have been here by now, if she were coming for the film." Shannon said.

"Yeah, looks like we won this round," Leah said.

Sara got up and looked at the clock through the cabin door. "It's only three o'clock," she said. "I am going to the nurse to see if she'll take off this tape. She did, and Sara walked very carefully back to Pavlova.

CHAPTER THIRTY-ONE

"New York City Saturday Night"

There was standing room only for the company's studio rehearsal of *Allegro Brillante.* Leah got the last chair, but gave it to Sara so she wouldn't have to stand. There were so many faces that Sara hadn't seen since the first day of camp at audition class, and some faces she couldn't remember ever seeing at all. There was utter silence except for the recorded Tchaikovsky music that filled the room expansively and propelled the ten New York City Ballet dancers into a flow of perfect movement. Sara was in a trance as she watched. *I mean*, she thought, *the Lakewood seniors are good, but these people are outrageous.* She wondered how old she would be before she got that good.

All the dancers were slender and taut with beautiful turn-out and very high leg extensions. But what Sara noticed more than anything was how they performed the steps with quickness and precision. There was a sharpness to their movement inside a constant flow of motion. She was overjoyed to find that Misty Schaffer had the lead role partnering with a handsome and gifted male dancer. The two danced among and through the other dancers with grace and energy. "I can't believe we took class from Misty yesterday!" Sara whispered to Shannon. Shannon just sighed. When they had completed the ballet, the company stood casually around the floor and Misty spoke to the campers.

She tried to catch her breath as she spoke. "*Allegro Brillante* by George Balanchine had its world premiere by the New York City Ballet on March 1, 1956 at City Center, New York with the principal roles danced by Maria Tallchief and Nicholas Magallanes. Karl Avery and I try to dance it as well as they did; however, every dancer's body is different, so we try to dance it in such a way that expresses our own uniqueness while maintaining the exact choreography. You may have noticed how the ballet requires that we all dance with a vigorous pace. To dance it adequately, and the way Balanchine intended, takes strong dancing with precise timing and great breadth of gesture. Balanchine said that the ballet contained everything that he knew about classical ballet in thirteen minutes. Your teachers have arranged that we teach a few of the steps to some of the seniors. If the first group would please step out."

Courtney, Jackson, Katie and Patrick walked into the center of the studio in practice clothes. Sara wondered when they found out they'd get to take part. *They are SO lucky*, she thought, wishing she were one of them. Misty and Karl taught them a few steps of the principal roles, but it looked to Sara like they had learned much of it already just from observing. She really had to learn to do that. What happened next surprised Sara so much she almost fell off her chair.

"Great. Very good," Misty said after the first group of seniors danced a bit of the ballet to the music. "Second group of seniors come out now." And into the center of the studio walked Robin and Kathy Jacobs, along with two boys from Woodlake.

"*Oh, my gosh, I don't believe it,*" Sara said. The girls around shushed her. She put her hand over her mouth and watched as they were taught intricate steps from the ballet. She was amazed at how fast Robin and Kathy caught on, and mesmerized when Misty played the music and the whole group of chosen seniors performed a part of the ballet.

"Good," Misty said when they had finished. "I hope you will come to dance for the New York City Ballet one day." Sara saw Miss Sutton, Miss Alexander, Mr. Peters and Mr. Moyne beam with pride as they applauded the senior dancers along with the campers. "All right," Misty said. "That's it for rehearsal here. We are off to dinner now and the theatre. See you in the audience!"

"They got an invitation," Sara said on the way to the dining hall. "An official invitation to dance for the company!" She was so envious, especially of Robin, she could hardly stay on the path. She kept bumping into Leah.

"Oh, not really," Shannon said. "They would have to audition for the school like anybody else, then audition for the company. Then they would have to keep up good work to stay in the company and then have to wait their turn for the best roles, too."

"Still," Sara said. "I would give anything to have been chosen to learn part of the ballet like they got to." She was just burning inside with how important it was now to do *Concerto Barocco* for the student concert so she could show that she could do the Balanchine technique just as Robin could. They only had the film until one o'clock tomorrow

265

and no place to watch it. Robin came in late for dinner and made a dramatic entrance. Hillary and the other Tallchief cabin mates cheered for her as she sat down importantly. "Oh," Sara whispered. "It's not like she's dancing it on stage tonight."

"We will have our opportunity to get noticed," Shannon said confidently. Leah was busy munching a big salad.

Sara noticed it was almost six-fifteen. Miss Hess wasn't going to take them over to the theatre with the other intermediates until seven forty-five. "Let's go across to the laundry room with our notes and practice what we have so far of *Concerto Barocco,*" she said enthusiastically. It was all she could think of.

"Sara," Leah said with a tone of voice that was a warning. "We'll just get there and have to come back. Sorry, not enough time."

"Sara," Shannon said with a tone of voice that was wise. "Don't you want to take time to dress in something special for the after party?"

Sara had forgotten all about the party. Now her heart skipped as she thought of Jackson. "Oh, yes," she said. They went to the cabin and joined Charleigh, Mary and Brooke who were trying on different outfits.

"How's this?" Mary asked, standing in the middle of the room in a purple blouse and skirt and matching headband. "It matches my marker color for the banner!" She was pleased with herself.

"Good," Charleigh said. "How's this?" She was in a bright pink knit shirt and dark pink pants with a pink bow in her hair. Pink was her marker color. They had obviously planned this. Next Brooke came out of the bathroom in a blue top, navy pants and blue ribbon around her pony tail. She stood in front of the banner showing that she matched her marker color.

"Yay!" Mary clapped. "We are cool."

"Very cool," Leah smiled. "And you won't lose each other, either." She laughed. Sara and Shannon had to laugh, too.

"You guys should wear your banner colors," Charleigh said. "Do you have anything red, Leah?"

"As a matter of fact I do," Leah said, going to the closet and pulling out a red jacket.

"No, it can't be a jacket," Brooke complained. "Don't you have a red blouse?"

"Nope, nothing else red," Leah said, putting the jacket back. Charleigh threw her a red shirt with sleeves and a collar. "Wow, thanks!" Leah said, catching it. It looked great with her jeans and thick hair.

"OK," Mary said to Shannon. "Now you. Got anything green?"

"I think so," Shannon said, going to the closet. She pulled out a gorgeous fluffy green blouse. From Paris, no doubt. "I'll just throw this on with some jeans." The green complimented her light hair beautifully. "Now, you," she said to Sara. "You have to come up with something yellow."

But Sara had nothing but an old cream colored T-shirt. She tried it on with some light brown pants. The girls all stared at her.

"Ummmm....." Brooke said. "I don't think so."

"Even I don't think so," Leah said. "Wait a minute." She went through her drawer and found a pretty yellow pair of pajamas. Everybody laughed. "Well, you'd be one-of-a-kind," she laughed.

267

"Is that what they wear to parties in Indiana?" Shannon teased with her French accent. She went to the closet again and brought out a soft yellow long-sleeved blouse with a single pink rose and tiny green stem on the front. It was amazing. From Paris, no doubt.

Sara tried on the blouse with her white jeans. It was a perfect fit. The little rose was right over her heart. It made her feel like she was in a beautiful costume, maybe playing the part of Cinderella. "Thank you so much, Shannon," she smiled. She brushed her hair a million times, then Shannon braided it into a loose French weave, leaving some wispy hair around her face. She was just adding a touch of gloss to her lips when Julie Hess's voice came through the screened door. "Let's go, Pavlova!" she yelled.

She had the intermediates from Baryshnikov cabin with her. Soon Sara sat in a seat in the Balanchine Theatre waiting for the curtain to open on the New York City Ballet dancers. When the curtain opened she was so excited she almost stood up. The women dancers were all in a light shade of turquoise with soft skirts to their knees and thin straps on top. The men wore light gray tights and blousy tops in a gray-blue. Of course, the men's ballet slippers were black, and the women's pink pointe shoes and ribbons seemed to glisten. Sara was enchanted from the moment it started and she tried to watch all eight dancers on stage every second. Each woman had a male partner and they danced together seamlessly, the gray and turquoise costumes flitting and flowing everywhere. It was so much more exciting than the studio rehearsal. The dancers were so precise, so well-rehearsed. No one missed a beat of their feet or a twist of a hand in spite of how quickly they danced. Just as Miss Meisner had said, they became the music. The floor became the music. The air became the music. All motion seemed to exist as music. Balanchine was a genius. Then the principals came on stage, Misty and Karl. Misty wore peach and Karl the palest blue. He supported her many turns beautifully and they flowed in and out of the other four partners making intriguing patterns on the stage. Sara's eyes darted here, then there, then here again as she tried to take in every single movement and gesture. In the end she was actually glad that they hadn't learned much of *Concerto Barocco* yet. Seeing a real Balanchine company performing real Balanchine choreography was a terrific eye-opener. It was going to help enormously in her interpretation and performance of *Concerto Barocco*. She saw just how quickly she'd have to move, how thin she'd have to become, how precise she'd have to be. And there was another thing she noticed. Balanchine trained his dancers to go off-center. In some of the movements they would almost fall over to the side, then recover back into a traditional ballet posture. Sara saw that her modern dance training would come in handy for the Balanchine method of dancing.

Suddenly it was over. Sara was filled with the perfection of the length of the ballet. As Balanchine had said, it was everything he knew of classical ballet in thirteen minutes. It started, they danced, the audience was breathless, it was over. Everyone was on their feet applauding and cheering. Sara could hear the boys behind her. She wondered where Jackson was. Then he appeared on stage presenting flowers to Misty. The company dancers took their final bows and Sara walked to the end of the aisle with Shannon and Leah, her heart still beating with excitement, the images of the dancers' movement still flowing in front of her eyes. "Beaucoup

269

congratulations to the company!" Shannon said smiling. "Beaucoup!" When they got outside, she pulled three pairs of ballet slippers out of a flowered purse she had brought. "Now we go to the stage door and get autographs." She gave Leah and Sara one of their own ballet slippers along with their banner markers.

"What?" Sara said. "I didn't know you brought these."

"Yeah, what?" Leah said, putting her marker inside her ballet slipper.

"We go to the stage door and have a dancer from the company write their name on our shoe. Just like in New York. Come on!"

Sara and Leah followed Shannon and they waited in a noisy crowd for the door to open. When it did, everyone cheered. The company dancers were in casual jeans and shirts, some even wore the Lakewood or Woodlake T-shirts. Sara went directly to Misty. She happily signed the inside of Sara's shoe. In the confusion there was barely time to thank her let alone expect Misty to remember her. On the way to the party Sara stared at the yellow writing in her shoe. "Misty" it said with a flourish. Sara smiled. Wow. She would keep this forever. As they walked the path under the tall trees, Leah broke Sara's reverie.

"We have quite a ways to go to be able to do *Concerto Barocco*," Leah said heavily, putting her signed ballet slipper in her back pocket. "I don't know if we should even try it." Oh, great. Sara thought. Sara had the opposite reaction. She felt they were closer to being able to pull it off. She would just die if Leah gave up before they even tried.

"Of course we can do it, Leah," Sara said, handing her ballet slipper to Shannon to put back in her purse. As they walked she could see the late summer sun sinking into the lake painting the trees pink. "I saw how they did everything," she pleaded.

"So did I, Sara, and I don't know if I can do it," Leah answered.

"But you are the best allegro dancer here," Sara said. "You move faster than almost anyone."

"I know. But you have to move from step to step fast, too, and turn your hands and head just so," she said. "That would take a whole lot of practice. I don't know. It could take months to get it right."

"We don't have to decide now," Shannon said just as Sara was going to protest some more. "Let's go to the party."

The campers were all in the dining hall staring at the big cake that said "Thank You NYCB" and talking excitedly. All the tables and chairs had been moved to the sides of the room. Patrick found Sara and offered her some lemonade. "Water, please," she said, thinking of her weight and how she would look in a little white leotard with skirt. While he was gone she spotted Jackson across the room. He was surrounded by senior girls including Courtney, Katie, Hillary and Robin. When Patrick came back they walked over to the group.

"You looked really good at rehearsal today," Robin was telling Jackson.

"What about me?" Patrick kidded. He bowed low in a dramatic gesture.

"You too," Robin laughed.

Then the company dancers came through the door and everyone hollered "Bravo, bravo!" and applauded them. It was the most wonderful party Sara had ever been to. She would write every detail to Erin. She wouldn't believe it. Misty

271

came up to the group Sara was standing with, Keera and Alene behind her and Leah and Shannon on either side of her. She noticed that Misty looked mostly like an ordinary person except for how thin she was in her jeans and light sweater. Her hair was loose to her shoulders. Karl went straight to the bottles of water with some other company members. They all seemed so tall and straight when they walked. Sara looked at Misty's feet that seemed permanently turned-out right from her hips. She turned out her own hips, legs and feet.

"Ah," Misty said. "It's my little leaders from the Intermediate Division." She looked right at Sara, Leah, Shannon, Keera and Alene. Sara couldn't believe it. She did remember her! But then Misty and some of her fellow dancers began to talk about the ballet with Jackson, Courtney and Katie. Patrick, Robin and Hillary leaned in to become part of the group. "Yes," Sara heard Misty say. "*Allegro Brillante* is really fun to perform, but you have to keep up with it practicing all the time."

"Come on," Leah said. "Let's get some cake." Sara sighed. She wanted to be part of the group talking with the professional dancers, but she really couldn't think of a single thing to say. She and Shannon followed Leah and took small pieces of cake and washed them down with water. "Well, we are small potatoes," Leah said. "Misty's little leaders."

"That is how it is at the school," Shannon said. "You have to be around a long time to be recognized. We just have to keep working at it. We are young."

More than ever Sara wanted to make a big splash dancing in a Balanchine ballet. It was the only way. Then Patrick was at her side again. "Good party, no?" he said.

Sara was tempted to say no, but she was busy looking at several of the professional dancers talking to each other and answering questions from the seniors. *Why,* she asked herself again, *why didn't I enrolled as a senior?*

"Come on," Patrick said. "Let's go down to the lake. It's so nice out tonight." Sara looked over at Jackson who was busy talking to one of the professional male dancers.

"Come on," she said to Leah and Shannon. When they all got down to the beach they saw that Julie Hess had built a bonfire and Mary, Charleigh, Brooke and Grace were already there roasting marshmallows with lots of other intermediates. They were singing and having a great time.

"Grab a stick and a marshmallow," Miss Hess said when the song ended.

"Thanks," Sara said. But she wanted to go out on the dock. She nodded to it and Leah, Patrick and Shannon followed. They sat on the far end of the dock and stared down at the cool, dark water. Sara breathed deeply of the cool night air. She thought of Jackson still inside talking with the company dancers. Soon he would probably be one of them. She wondered if he was even interested in girls. Oh well, she thought. He was so nice to me and we did modern dance so beautifully together in the Woodlake studio.

"What are you guys doing for the intermediate student concert?" Patrick asked. They all looked at him.

"Will there be one?" Shannon asked.

"Yes. Don't you know about it?" Patrick seemed amazed that they didn't. "Mr. Peters told us about it yesterday. It's going to be in two weeks and we are invited!"

"So, you're an intermediate?" Leah asked him.

"Technically, yes," he answered. "Although with boys they seem to mix us up and put us where we are needed. There never seems to be enough of us, so if you're good, you can move ahead quickly. I thought you knew about the concert. Robin knew about it and told me she was unhappy about not being able to perform in it."

"I'll bet," Sara said.

"Why do you say that?" Patrick wanted to know.

Sara wished she hadn't said anything. "Well, I know she wants to get out on the stage whenever she can," she said.

"She is a beautiful dancer," Patrick said. "But so are you."

"Really?" Sara said earnestly. "I am?"

"Yes. I think you have a wonderful expression in your dancing. You just have to develop stronger technique. I think you three are all very good."

"We have to find the kind of ballet style that fits us best," Shannon said. "There are many styles that are a bit different with each company." Sara couldn't imagine dancing in any company but the New York City Ballet, especially after tonight.

"Off the dock, please!" Heather Scott yelled over to them from the beach. "The dock is closed after eight o'clock!"

Patrick got out of Heather's chair and walked the girls to their cabin. He sat on the porch with them until their cabin mates returned from the bonfire. Then he stood up and bowed to them making a sweeping gesture like the prince in Cinderella. "I bid you adieu, Ladies," he said, smiling sweetly as he left.

"Adieu," Shannon answered. Sara waved. He wasn't so bad, she thought. But he still didn't make her heart sing.

In the cabin Sara took off the blouse with the rose over her heart and gave it back to Shannon. It felt like part of her own heart and some of her imaginings came off with the blouse. As she lay in her bunk that night, her locket safely under her pillow, she wondered if her legs would ever be as long and thin and turned-out as the professional dancers'. She wondered if she'd ever be in a ballet as wonderful as *Allegro Brillante*. She wondered when her technique would be as strong as her expression. She wondered how they could watch the dance film tomorrow. She had an idea just as she fell asleep.

CHAPTER THIRTY-TWO

"Starting Fresh on Sunday"

S unday morning had a clarity to it. Not only was the air crisp and fresh coming in the cabin window, but Sara's thoughts took on clear edges. The New York City Ballet dancers had gone, her exciting *Giselle* performance was over, master class had been a success, *Allegro Brillante* was an inspirational lesson and the after party good. Especially the part where they were on the dock and Patrick mentioned there would definitely be a student dance concert. There was a blank canvass now for the last four weeks of camp ready for Sara to paint a swirl of colors. She sat up in her bunk, took a deep breath and whispered "Leadership, cooperation, enthusiasm, improvement." She vowed to achieve excellence in each of these qualities and she saw them dancing on her blank canvass in red, blue, yellow and green. She would try her hardest to make a colorful splash in the second half of camp to get the NYCB scholarship. She wanted to write to Erin right away. Then she remembered her last thought before she fell asleep last night. Her idea.

"Well, it's about time you woke up," Leah called out from across the room.

"You don't look so awake yourself," Sara answered. She looked around at all the empty bunks. Even Shannon was gone.

"Come on," Leah said. "We better get some breakfast."

In the dining hall even the chatter seemed fresh to Sara. "Let's start work on a new water ballet," Mary said to Charleigh and Brooke. "We can perform it the last week of camp."

"OK," Charleigh said. "I think Grace wants to be in it again."

"How about you, Leah?" Brooke asked. "*Please* be in it."

"If I'm in it, who will do rescue duty?" Leah laughed. "I don't think so."

"We will watch you rehearse like we did before," Shannon said, sipping the last of her milk. "And we will pass out flyers, too."

Sara was relieved. They had something more important to spend their time on, like *Concerto Barocco*. She thought of her idea again. As soon as Charleigh, Mary and Brooke left for the lake, she told it to Shannon and Leah.

"What?" Shannon exclaimed. "You mean you would risk getting caught going through that window again?"

"After what happened yesterday?" Leah said.

"I can't think of any other way to watch the film," Sara said. "It's already nine o'clock and we have to have it back by one. That gives us exactly four hours to learn and memorize the entire part we're going to perform."

"I have a better idea," Leah said. "Let's see if the music library is open today. Maybe Miss Meisner will let us watch it in there."

Sara hadn't thought of that. "OK," she agreed. The girls finished their breakfast, went back to Pavlova cabin, changed into leotards, grabbed their dance bags, notes and the film and went to Miss Meisner's classroom. The door was locked, the shades were all down and no one was around. "What time is it?" Sara asked.

Shannon pulled her watch out of her bag. "Nine-thirty," she said.

They had already lost thirty minutes. Sara looked around the grounds. Campers were starting to go on the paths and into the lake, but no one was around the music library. The building stood quietly alone. Sara began to walk around the building testing each window.

"No," Shannon warned. "I will not go in or out any window today." The windows wouldn't budge anyway.

"Why don't we go to that little cabin across the lake?" Leah asked.

"You know about that?" Sara was astounded. "How did you find it?"

"Just exploring," Leah said. Sara remembered the day Leah came back from the rain storm in muddy shoes. She couldn't know how special that cabin was to Sara.

"*No*," Shannon said. "That is off-limits and there's muck and snakes. No. No. No. Besides, we can't watch the film in there."

"Well, that leaves the little practice room in the basement," Sara said. She wondered what Erin would suggest. *Help me Erin,* she thought.

Leah started walking toward the dance building. "Let's try the door before going in the window," she said.

It was Sunday. The company was gone. The teachers were off. The door was locked, "Oh, come on," Sara said going around to the window. They hid in the bushes. Sara looked up at the window. It was still broken, but Sara knew Charlie had swept up the broken glass inside and she knew the monitor was in there so they could watch the film. She also knew they had unstuck the window yesterday from years of old paint so it should slide open easily today. "Boost me up there," she said to Leah. "Shannon, you keep a look out." Sara grunted and pushed but the window wouldn't move. She figured Charlie had locked it from the inside.

"We are not supposed to be in that building on Sundays," Shannon warned.

"Keep a look out!" Leah told her.

"Shhhhhh," Sara said. "I'll boost you, Leah. You try." Sara had trouble holding Leah on her back and her foot started to hurt. "Hurry," she said.

"Got it!" Leah exclaimed. Sara heard the click. "I got it unlocked." She had reached through the broken pane.

"Hurry," Sara said again. Leah pushed hard and the window flew up. They scurried in through the window. Leah got on the chair and tried to pull the window down, but it was stuck at the top. Sara tried, then they tried it together, but it was stuck.

"At least it's not raining," Leah said.

"Yes, but if Charlie walks by, he'll notice for sure," Shannon said.

Sara and Leah got off the chair. They'd try it again later. Sara put in the film and they sat on the floor checking their notes against what they saw on the screen. They kept the sound muted so no one would hear them. Sara's notes were a botched mess compared to what she saw on the screen. Leah only had half of what Sara had, and Shannon just had stick figures, but she had a lot of them.

"I need to learn this by doing," Sara said. "My notes are no good and we're running out of time." She stopped the film. "Who's up for trying the steps now?" Leah and Shannon agreed and they quietly moved together as they watched the screen. All they could hope to do was remember as much as they could. Once they had returned the film, they'd have to rely completely on their bad notes and memories to bring the dance to performance level. In two weeks. As they were watching and moving for the third time they heard Charlie's work boots coming down the hall. It was good they didn't have the sound on.

"Yikes," Leah whispered. She pushed the chair to the open window and climbed out. Sara felt panicked and climbed out next. It was Shannon who remembered the dance film. They were crouching in the bushes when they heard Charlie say, "Those girls," and slam the window shut.

Shannon gave the film to Sara who slipped it into her dance bag and they ran all the way to the music library. They sat on the porch short of breath laughing. "Charlie hates us," Leah giggled, lying down on her back.

"I think I hate us," Shannon laughed.

Sara got up and tried the door to the building, but it was still locked. Miss Meisner probably had today off. "What time is it, Shannon?" she asked.

"Time to return the film" a voice said out the window of the building. It was Miss Meisner. She'd been in there the whole time! It was a good thing they hadn't gone in through a window.

"But it is only twelve-thirty," Shannon said.

281

"I know," Miss Meisner said. "But you have to go to lunch and so do I. I want to have the film waiting here for Robin as soon as lunch is over. Hand it over, please."

They had no choice. Sara's head was crammed with all the steps that would fit in it for now anyway. You had to learn a dance from a film over a long period of time, learning some, then checking back against the film over and over until you had the basic steps. Then you had to repeat the process to get the arms and the style right. It couldn't be rushed. They would have to do the best they could with what they could each remember. Sara handed the film to Miss Meisner and hoped that Charlie would keep today's window violation a secret from Mrs. Lane.

After lunch Sara wrote a long letter to Erin telling her about how she practiced Nikolais technique with Jackson at the Woodlake party, about how she had hurt her foot on the mop, about how Hillary was pulled out of *Giselle* and Leah put in, all about master class with Misty Schaffer, the beautiful NYCB performance of *Allegro Brillante*, and every detail about Robin getting the *Concerto Barocco* film and about them breaking the window to the secret practice room. "We have the student dance concert in two weeks!" she wrote. "I don't know what we're going to do without that film." She signed it "Hope all your dance classes are great this summer. I miss you. Love, Sara of Pavlova Cabin."

That evening she talked Leah and Shannon into practicing what they knew of *Concerto Barocco* in the laundry building, but everyone remembered it a different way and Leah seemed more interested in doing her laundry. *What a mess,* Sara cringed as she put her locket under her pillow before falling asleep. *What a mess.*

CHAPTER THIRTY-THREE

"Monday News"

Sara had reviewed Jackson's Nikolais technique book before falling asleep last night, but her head was so full of *Concerto Barocco* that she couldn't remember much of it for modern class this afternoon. Even so, the long sequence of warm-up movements seemed to come easier for her today. Perhaps, she thought, it was because she had sort of given up on the idea of being perfect. Or perhaps she was a more accomplished, self-confident dancer after performing in *Giselle* and watching the New York City Ballet dancers. Today she felt she was more a dancer than she had been last week, that she had expanded inside and it was expressed outwardly.

Miss Lee took the class through a review of the various concepts and techniques she had taught them in the first half of camp. Then she had them sit against the wall and called on them to come out one at a time and perform a movement phrase she had told them to remember. *Oh-oh*, Sara thought. *I hope I remember one of mine.* That turned out to be the least of her worries because, in the end, she had to remember all four of them. Miss Lee kept calling more and more dancers out to the floor so that eventually there was a fascinating conglom-eration of dancers doing different types of movements at dif-ferent levels, different tempos, and different energies filling every space in the studio. Sara was excited to be a part of it. If she couldn't quite remember a certain phrase, she knew enough about the concept to make something up. And when Miss Lee called out for them to stop, she stopped on a dime. They had learned a lot in the first half of camp.

"OK," Miss Lee smiled. Tomorrow we learn a new move-ment concept and homework will begin again. Now I have an announcement." The dancers sat down on the floor to catch their breath. "There will be an intermediate student dance concert in two weeks in the Balanchine indoor theatre." Sara couldn't help looking at Shannon and Leah with an *I told you so* stare. They smiled back. "You can create your own chore-ography or perform an authentic piece in any type of dance style. You choose your own music and costumes. It should be about four minutes long."

"Four minutes," Leah whispered to Sara. "Four minutes, not three."

Miss Lee continued. "The big studio will be reserved for your practice each night Monday through Thursday from seven to eight starting tomorrow night. The costume room will be open for you tomorrow evening, and please talk to Miss Meisner about checking out music or films. I will be the director of the concert and will drop by your rehearsals from time to time. So get thinking about what you'd like to do and who you'll be dancing with. Of course, you can do a solo if you choose. Try to be creative, but also show your highest level of technique and style." Someone wanted to know how many monitors were available for watching films. "Just one,"

Miss Lee said. "You'd have to take turns using it and you'd need a place to watch where you wouldn't disturb the other dancers. You'd be better off creating your own choreography." *Great*, Sara thought, *even if I could get the film away from Robin, we'd barely be able to watch it.*

Miss Lee concluded by saying, "Circle Saturday evening, August 8 on your calendar for the performance and ice cream party. The boys are invited." Sara remembered again how David had kissed her at last summer's ice cream party. It was when they were sitting on the dining hall porch, and she had no idea he was going to do it. Robin saw it and was so mad. *Well*, Sara thought. *Robin had been dancing with Hank.* She sighed remembering the poem Hank had written for her and, again, the kiss he gave her at the end of the final performance. She would never forget.

When they walked out into the hallway Sara grinned at all the shiny black and white *Giselle* photos posted on the walls, a number on each one. "Wow!" she smiled to Shannon and Leah. "Look at these. They're beautiful!" They looked between the heads of some seniors to find any photos they might be in. Sara saw a sign that said, "Give Mrs. Lane the numbers of the photos you want. She will order them from the photographer." Sara chose three group shots where you could at least see her, Shannon chose two, one for each of her parents and Leah chose the only one she could find herself in. Then they had to go into Mrs. Lane's office. It was crowded with other dancers ordering pictures, but Sara thought Mrs. Lane looked at her oddly when she dropped off her order. If she did know about how they broke into the practice room and smashed the window she wasn't say anything for now. A scholarship hung in the balance.

Miss Lee let them out a bit early, but they barely made it to folk class on time. There was a surprise waiting for Sara. Patrick was in the room warming up at the barre. He smiled broadly when he saw her in her character shoes and flowing skirt. "Hurry girls, we have a lot to cover today," Mr. Moyne said. Then he added "Let's have some applause for our three intermediate *Giselle* performers. Congratulations, dancers!" The class clapped and Patrick gave them one of his bows. Then they stood at the barre doing their special folk dance warm-ups. The lively piano music pushed them along while Sara wondered what Patrick was doing in their class. Center-floor, Mr. Moyne passed out tambourines, taught them a couple new steps, and then took them through the folk dance they had learned so far for the final dance concert on the big outdoor stage on the lake. Sara could hardly believe it was just four weeks away. Then she found out why Patrick was taking the class. He was to be her partner in the performance. She would have no solo at all. "Everyone make a half-circle around Sara and Patrick," Mr. Moyne instructed. He gave the two of them intricate steps to learn. They had to dance in a flirtatious way around each other while hitting their tambourines overhead. The dancers around them swayed to the music, hitting their tambourines from side to side. Sara felt embarrassed. Leah kept smiling at her like she was about to burst into giggles. Sara wondered whose idea it was to pair her with Patrick. Finally Mr. Moyne excused the class. "Good," he said smiling. "We're making progress. See you tomorrow morning." Patrick walked with Sara until she got to the stairs. She said a quick good-bye and went down to the locker room.

"How could this happen?" She asked Shannon and Leah. Patrick had gotten his wish to partner her.

"Fate," Leah laughed.

"Oh, stop, Sara," Shannon said. "You look really nice together. It's only about the performance. You are lucky to have the lead. Make the most of it." But Sara could only imagine what it would be like to be partnered in a ballet with Jackson.

After dinner Brooke reminded everyone that they should write on the banner. "I think we should add the New York City Ballet performance and after party," she said getting out her blue marker. "Soon we'll be able to add our final performance. We're going to be in the folk dance with you guys," she told Sara, Leah and Shannon.

"Yeah," Charleigh added. "There will be fifty dancers with both Class A and Class B. It should be spectacular on the big outdoor stage."

Sara wrote "NYCB performance and after party" under her name and drew a picture of a ballet slipper with Misty's autograph. She smiled remembering the magic of the evening.

"Sara, I think you have something to fix on the banner," Shannon said.

"Really? What?" Mary wanted to know.

Sara quickly crossed out "Solo" for the folk dance and wrote in "Duet with Patrick." She threw the marker back in the drawer and got on her bunk.

"Congrats, Sara!" Brooke said.

"Thanks," Sara said, still trying to figure out how it could be happening.

"What are you guys doing for the student concert?" Charleigh asked.

Leah told them about *Concerto Barocco,* leaving out the part about the film. "What are you guys doing?"

"We're thinking of ballet," Charleigh said. "We want to find some good costumes tomorrow night."

Sara wondered again how they could get the film back from Robin. Meanwhile, they could go over to the dance building and try to rehearse what they knew of *Concerto Barocco* if there was space available. Leah and Shannon agreed since they had no homework for modern class. They decided to walk around to the window to the secret practice room first to see if Charlie had fixed it. They were surprised to see the light on, the window fixed and Robin in the room watching the film. She was sitting on the floor taking notes. *Ooooooh,* Sara thought. *I want that film.* Just a thin piece of window glass separated her from it.

"Let's go," Leah said. "Before she sees us."

They went immediately downstairs in the dance build-ing to Studio B, but the door was closed. They could hear the *Tarantella* music inside and Miss Alexander and Mr. Peters rehearsing. Sara wanted to go outside and watch them through the window, but Shannon insisted they go up to the big studio to rehearse. When they got up there it was occu-pied with a few seniors learning solos for a new ballet with Miss Sutton. The music was a rich and flowing waltz. "Oh," Shannon whispered as they watched through the open door. *"Serenade!"* They stood there until Miss Sutton came over and shut the door. She didn't even see them. Sara felt invisible. An invisible folk dancer.

"What is *Serenade?*" she asked Shannon on the way back to the cabin.

"A beautiful, wonderful plotless Balanchine ballet," Shannon said. She stopped and held her right arm out straight to the side. "It opens like this with everybody just standing still holding out their arm with their hand up. Oh, it is a fantastic ballet. They are so lucky to be learning it."

"They must be doing it for final performance," Leah said. "I wonder what the juniors are doing."

Sara wondered only why she hadn't registered as a senior. When she said it out loud Leah said, "Wouldn't you rather have the lead in the folk dance than just be part of ensemble in *Serenade?*"

"Sara," Shannon said. "I hope you can be in reality with the summer. Four weeks left and still a chance to be noticed. You'll see." She put her arm around Sara, Leah put her arm around Shannon's waist and they went to the laundry room and tried to rehearse *Concerto Barocco.* They made no progress at all except for one small step. Their notes were still messy and their memories all different. "But I am sure this is how the opening goes," Shannon insisted, so they practiced it that way. Sara was afraid it wouldn't be like the authentic ballet in the film and they would look stupid, but she had to go along with it. After all, Shannon had seen the New York City Ballet perform it more than once.

In her bunk that night Sara tried to focus on the Nikolais warm-up sequence for tomorrow as well as the folk steps she had learned so far. But she fell asleep next to her drying red and pink carnations hearing the beautiful *Serenade* music in her head.

CHAPTER THIRTY-FOUR

"Things Heat Up"

Sara stood at the barre at eight-thirty sharp for her Tuesday morning pointe class with Miss Sutton. Today would be another chance to make a fresh start. She pulled herself up tall inside her pink leotard and stood in first position between Keera and Alene, new pointe shoes on her feet to break in. Leah and Shannon were still holding down the end positions as leaders. But this would be the week, Sara thought, where she would assume an end position of leadership at the ballet barre. Maybe tomorrow. Today would be exciting enough with more folk choreography to learn, a new modern dance concept and homework, and getting in the costume room tonight. It would be their first official practice for the student dance concert. She made a mental note to go over to see Miss Meisner about checking out the music for *Concerto Barocco.*

"Sara. That tendu foot is to go directly behind your shoulder in back. Don't over cross it. Let's see it again." Miss Sutton's English accent filled the room and everybody was staring at Sara. Shannon's face said: *When you're in pointe class think about pointe class.* Sara quickly corrected and repeated her movements until Miss Sutton said, "Good. That's right." Leah smiled at her and gave her a little thumbs up and the piano music resumed. The rest of class was filled with non-stop turns, bourrées, and arabesques en pointe all done in quick succession. "Come on," Miss Sutton encouraged them. "Only four weeks left to make yourself into a stronger, smarter dancer." It would be harder than Sara thought to be a standout. Just as she felt more self-confident, the work became more difficult. After end-of-class bows and applause for Miss Sutton, Sara took her time in the locker room before heading down the hall to folk class. She wanted to make sure she wouldn't have to speak to Patrick. Dancing with him was OK, but anything romantic was out of the question. But when she got there and expected everyone to be standing at the barre ready for warm-ups, she found Patrick standing by the door. Mr. Moyne was late arriving. The accompanist was playing some lively folk music and some of the dancers were clapping to it and chatting.

"I guess if you're the star you can be a little late for class," Patrick smiled.

"Well, I'm not the star, so I guess I can't be late," Mr. Moyne said as he walked past them into the studio. "Sorry, dancers. Sit down, I want to talk for a moment." When everyone was quiet on the floor he said "We really have to get a push on this dance for final performance. A decision has been made that Class B will dance with us, so not only will I have to set permanent steps on both classes, you will need to memorize the dance as we go. There will be no time for revising or forgetting. And we will be scheduling a time on Saturday in the big studio upstairs for both classes to rehearse together. Your friends and family will be watching you on the big outdoor stage very soon. So, I promise to keep the steps the same and you need to promise not to forget them. OK, everybody up. Let's get started."

The pressure was on. Sara hoped she would remember the steps Mr. Moyne had taught her and Patrick the day before. Shannon gave her that look again that said *concentrate*. She didn't have any trouble remembering the entrance step to the dance and the part that followed, but she kind of fell apart in her mind when the semi-circle formed around her and Patrick. "Toes, heels, in-out, toes, heels, in-out!" Mr. Moyne coached. "Tambourines over your heads!" Patrick was quick and sharp and hadn't forgotten a thing. They learned a new part where they held hands and danced in and out of the line of corps de ballet dancers who swayed and hit their tambourines. Each time they passed a dancer, that dancer would turn to face the back. Then Sara and Patrick stood in the middle of the stage while the other dancers held hands and did quick slide steps in a circle around them. Their backs were toward Sara and Patrick but their heads were turned over their shoulders to smile at them. Somebody dropped a tambourine. "Stop! Stop!" Mr. Moyne shouted. He turned off the recorded performance music. "It really isn't that hard to hold hands and hang on to a tambourine. You are dancers, not kids playing on the playground. And you are Lakewood dancers. You would not have been accepted to this program if you weren't capable of performing my choreography. Now again, please." He turned the music on and Sara quickly snapped back into her stage presence. She could feel Patrick alert next to her. That helped keep her kinetic and ready for the next step. Finally Mr. Moyne taught Sara and Patrick to twirl around each other holding each other's waists with the tambourine hand overhead while the corps de ballet circled around them in the slide steps. Sara could feel an excitement about the dance now. Maybe it would be OK. Then all the dancers were dismissed for lunch except Sara and Patrick. "I'll be keeping you late from now on, but you'll still have a half hour for lunch."

Wow, Sara thought. *The pressure is on. Things are heating up.* They learned several more steps that were pretty difficult, then had to perform everything they had learned so far. She was very tired when Mr. Moyne finally excused them. Patrick was perspiring and said a quick good-bye as he hurried out the door to get lunch at Woodlake. Sara collapsed into her chair with her lunch tray. Leah and Shannon had already left. She couldn't remember being so tired from dancing. Folk dance took a *lot* of energy and quick thinking, especially after a difficult pointe class. After lunch she would have an hour before ballet technique class. She wanted to rest so she could dance better for Miss Sutton this afternoon. She smiled remembering that Misty Schaffer's autograph was in one of her ballet slippers.

"Hey, you guys!" Charleigh smiled to two dancers from the Baryshnikov table who came over. "Everyone! Meet Amy and Lexi. They're in Grace and Catherine's cabin." She smiled at them. "Ready for our first practice?" Charleigh-the-Friend-Machine had apparently rounded up more swimmers for their second water ballet. Colorado snow-skier or not, she was totally into the synchronized stuff now. Grace and Catherine joined them.

"Yep, let's get going," Grace said. "It's a nice, warm day out there." Mary and Brooke got up. When they had all left, Sara walked to Pavlova cabin. Her muscles felt a bit sore and she was still tired. She meant to look through the Nikolais book to prepare for modern class, but promptly fell asleep. The next thing she knew Shannon was touching her back and saying her name. She just had time to jump into the shower and change her leotard.

Ballet class was good. Sara could tell again that she had somehow improved both her technique and expression by being in *Giselle* and by taking class from Misty and watching the company dance. She felt exhilarated doing the big leaps across the room at the end of class and she saw Miss Alexander watching from the doorway. Sara felt she had been noticed again. She felt clear-headed for modern dance, her last class of the day. *Then dinner*, she thought, *followed by their first* Concerto Barocco *rehearsal*. But Miss Lee's class required Sara's full attention. The instructor sat on her high stool in front of the long mirror with her drum. Sara looked down at her bare feet and willed them take her correctly into every movement today. The announcement of the scholarship winners was getting closer each day.

"OK, everybody, five weeks into camp my expectations are higher," Miss Lee said. "You now need to show me in every class that you deserve to be here. Show me that your body and mind can remember what I give you so I can add on to it as we go without your forgetting what came before. This is what is expected of dancers. This is what you would have to do to make it in New York. Write down all the movement phrases that I've asked you to remember so far. Write down all the movement phrases I ask you to remember starting tomorrow. If I haven't yet asked you to remember a movement phrase, maybe this technique is not for you." Then she simply said "And..." and began beating her drum. The pressure was on, things were heating up and Sara could not take the chance of making a mistake in the warm-up sequence, so she placed herself in the middle line so she could follow other dancers if she needed to. But, just as in ballet class, if she were to be a standout, if she were to be a contender for the NYCB summer scholarship, she would have to place herself in the front line very soon.

"Now," Miss Lee began when they had finished the warm-ups. "We have four weeks left of camp and we have four major principles of dance to explore more thoroughly: space, time, shape and motion. We have been using these concepts as we have gone, but now you will learn to refine each one, to express these in a clearer way in your movement. By the end of camp, you will need to show me that you can express each one in an extremely distinct way. Today I ask you to visualize the space in the room as blank canvass. We will revisit the idea of carving volume in space, only now we will carve three-dimensional *square* volume instead of round as we did in the first week of camp."

Sara couldn't believe Miss Lee was talking about a blank canvass, just as she had been thinking of it. She felt excited to try carving squares of volume in space as the first way of splashing color onto her blank canvass. They had to create a simple arm pattern carving square volume within their own personal space. Sara chose a spot on the floor and began to work in the concept. "Keep your focus in the movement," Miss Lee coached the class as she gently beat her drum. "Follow every gesture with your eyes. If you don't see it, I won't see it." She walked around the room watching carefully. "Don't let your arm be too stiff or too limp. You can't carve volume with a wet noodle." Sara stiffened her arm a bit and figured out a way to look like she was cutting squares of space. She was careful to keep her focus within her movement every second. "Focus not just inside your personal space, Sara," Miss Lee said next to her. "Focus on the volume your arm is carving." Sara shifted her eyes to her imagined square of volume. She felt it become her very own small piece of space. "Yes," Miss Lee said, as she walked away.

Next Miss Lee had them combine their carving movement with a locomotion movement across the floor. Sara saw many interesting ways of fulfilling this creative problem. Some dancers had their arm above their head, some jutted the arm directly in front, some put it behind them all while carving squares in space and sliding, walking, running or doing leg swings or curves across the floor. The next time they crossed the floor Miss Lee beat her drum faster and the third time she changed the tempo twice. The result was fascinating to Sara. "Keep your volume alive!" Miss Lee shouted above her drum. "Don't carry around dead volume. Let it lead you!" The last time they crossed the floor they had to combine carving round volume with square volume and use two different body parts. "Whoa," Miss Lee hollered. "Remember your boundary. Be *clear*. Don't try to do more than what I asked for. Keep your focus on the carved volume." Sara found it hard to do everthing at the same time. She thought it could take many years of practice to get it right. She wondered what a professional dance company would look like doing it on stage.

For the last exercise Miss Lee designated half the class as "movers" and the other half as "boundary makers." The boundary makers leaned together and made spaces like arches and holes for the movers to pass through. The movers had to pass through them shaping themselves to the space without touching or changing the boundaries. Now and then the boundary makers were free to reshape the volume spaces. Sara was first a boundary maker and then a mover. In both roles she found it challenging to be a reliable part of a team and a sensitive part of those dancers around her.

Homework for Wednesday was to choose a partner for a volume duet phrase. The first person was to create a volume of space for the second person to move into and then walk away, creating a path allowing for the first person to create a new volume space. The first person was to move closely in reaction to the second person and the result was to become the duet. *Wow*, Sara thought. *This should be interesting.* They would have to spend from seven to eight tonight working on *Concerto Barocco*, and work from eight to nine on their duet for modern. As she planned this in her head, Keera ran over and asked Sara to be her partner. Alene had already paired herself with someone else. That left Shannon and Leah to be partners. It was all happening quickly. "OK," she said, and the four of them went down to the locker room together. At dinner Sara and Keera made plans to get together at the end of student concert rehearsal to decide where to practice.

As soon as Sara, Shannon and Leah got to the dance building at seven o'clock, they threw their dance bags with their *Concerto Barocco* notes on the floor under the barre and ran downstairs to the costume room. Sara made a beeline for the white leotards. "You two look for soft white skirts," she told Shannon and Leah. She grabbed four white leotards off the rack in different sizes. The girls around her were going for the red and blue ones. She ran up and down the aisles calling out for Shannon and Leah.

"Over here," Leah shouted from a few rows over. Sara got there to see many skirts in a variety of colors. Several girls were touching them and looking them over.

"These black ones are nice," Sara said, trying to sound casual. No need to let people know what they were going to choose.

"I like the yellow ones," Leah kidded. Sara watched as a couple of girls came up and took the yellow ones off the rack. "Oops," Leah said. "Guess we'll take the white." She laughed as Sara held the white leotards up in front of each of them and Shannon held up the white skirts in front of the leotards.

"Perfect," Shannon said. "Let's go into the dressing room and try them on. She led the way to the large room that was just behind the raised fitting platform. Charleigh, Brooke and Mary were there in flouncy yellow and orange tutus along with some other girls. "Ah, belle, belle!" Shannon exclaimed. She touched the stiff skirts that came above their knees. "Very beautiful, Shannon said. What dance will you do?"

Mary twirled in her costume while Brooke tried a flow-ered matching ribbon in her hair. "I think we'll make up our own ballet," Charleigh said. "We only have two weeks." Shannon looked at Sara as if to say: *Now that is sensible.* Sara ignored her. Her heart was set.

They quickly tried on the white costumes and looked into the mirror between other girls looking at themselves. Leah had to switch to the smaller sized extra one Sara had brought.

"OK, good," Sara said. "Let's sign these out." She didn't want too many people to see them. She loved her imagination and liked a surprise. It would have more impact when they performed it. When they got back up to the studio, they put

299

the costumes in their dance bags and took their dance notes out.

Then Miss Lee appeared and made an announcement. "Dancers! Miss Meisner is holding the music library open for you right now. It might be a good time to go and check out your music and the portable players." Sara, Shannon and Leah dropped their dance bags again and ran over to the music library. They had to stand in line. When they finally got up to the desk with the *Concerto Barocco* music, Miss Meisner hesitated.

"I hope Robin won't need this for her research," Miss Meisner said importantly.

"There's music in the dance film," Leah quickly reminded her.

"Oh, that's right, dear," Miss Meisner smiled. She wrote on one of her cards. "That's who now?" she asked.

Sara felt invisible again. "Shannon, Leah and Sara," she said. "St. Pierre, Bennett and Sutherland."

As she handed them a player for the music, Miss Meisner said, "Such a difficult ballet. Are you sure you can do it? I mean the right way. The Balanchine way. I mean in such a way as to honor Balanchine?"

"Perhaps," Shannon said, as she took the player and the music from Miss Meisner.

"Merci beaucoup," Sara found herself calling out as they walked out the door. Leah laughed all the way back to the dance building. When they entered the studio to begin practice they saw it was already quarter to eight. "Great," Sara said. "What can we do in fifteen minutes?" The seniors were already starting to gather at the doorway for their rehearsal.

"We can simply repeat the opening part," Shannon said. "The same as we set it in the laundry room. But this time to the music." So they spent fifteen minutes going over and over the first two steps. Sara was inspired by the exciting Bach violin music and would just have to be happy with what they had done so far.

"Ok, dancers," Miss Lee said at eight on the dot. "Intermediates out, seniors in."

Sara had to walk right past Robin on her way out of the studio. "What is that you guys are doing?" Robin asked.

Like she doesn't know. Like she can't say 'Wow, I'm impressed' or something nice, Sara thought. "We're not really sure yet," she said.

"If it's *Concerto Barocco*, good luck," Robin said, walking past her.

Keera found Sara in the hall. "Where are we going to practice our Nikolais assignment?" she asked.

"Let's all run downstairs to Studio B," Leah suggested. She and Shannon had to practice, too. When they got down there it was already filled with dancers trying to create the assignment. "Let's try Studio C," Leah said. So they ran down the hall to Mr. Moyne's tap and folk class room. Nobody was in there. Sara wondered where Miss Alexander and Mr. Peters might be rehearsing *Tarantella*. It took Sara a while to get used to dancing with Keera. She looked over at Leah and Shannon who seemed to fall into their duet easily. They had theirs done and left the studio by eight-thirty. Finally at ten to nine, Sara decided what they had was good enough for tomorrow and Keera left her in the locker room. Sara could hear the wonderful Tchaikovsky *Serenade* music upstairs and could

301

feel the studio floor above creaking as the seniors leaped and danced. She went upstairs and stood watching them through the doorway for a few minutes, then walked back to Pavlova alone. She sighed thinking she would give anything to be in a Balanchine ballet. Before she went to sleep she reviewed the Nikolais warm-up sequence focusing on parts where she always forgot what came next. As she fell asleep a dried pink carnation fell off its stem and softly landed next to her cheek.

CHAPTER THIRTY-FIVE

"Patrick in the Boat & Sara in the Woods"

Tap class was the highlight of Wednesday morning. Sara loved all the music they danced to and every step they learned. It was great fun, and Mr. Moyne chatted afterward with some dancers who wanted advice on music for their student concert piece. Then he turned to Sara. "Have you memorized everything I've taught you for your duet with Patrick?"

Folk class wasn't until after modern this afternoon. Sara had planned to take some time after lunch and think about both classes. "I hope so, "she smiled, wishing they were discussing *Concerto Barocco* or *Serenade*.

"You know," Mr. Moyne said. "This is a good opportunity to show your talent. Try to remember to take every part someone gives you and make it as big as you can. Have fun with the folk dance, but make it yours and convince the teachers and the audience that you are the very best dancer in the world."

"Thank you," Sara said. As she walked away she realized Mr. Moyne really cared about her dancing.

She decided to row a boat out after lunch for an hour and write down the folk steps and rehearse in her mind the modern dance warm-up sequence. If she had time, she'd think about her Nikolais duet with Keera and the *Concerto Barocco* steps. The lake was calm but there was enough wind to bring out little sail boats from both the girls' and boys' sides. She remembered the first time she had seen Hank last summer as he was drying off the Will-O-Way. She had told Hank she thought winning was important, and she still thought so. She had to believe she could win that scholarship to New York. She smiled and the sun shined on her through the clouds and poured light on her paper as she jotted down every step to her folk solo and every step in her duet with Patrick they had learned so far. It came flowing into her mind like the sun streaming out of the clouds. When she looked up Patrick was in a rowboat next to her. *Did he just stand by the shore,* Sara wondered, *and wait for her to appear on the lake?*

"Hey, Sara," he said as he threw his anchor overboard. "Mind if I join you?" He climbed out of his boat and into Sara's. "What are you doing?"

Oh, no, Sara thought. *He's just going to have to leave.* "Patrick, I'm busy," she said. "I'm very busy."

He peered at her notes. "Oops, you have that backwards," he smiled. "First we do heels-toe, then we twirl." He took her pen and made the correction. "Saved by the bell," he laughed, "or by the boat."

Sara felt stupid, but she still thought she had remembered it all correctly. "I think I am right," she said confidently.

"Now you'll have to leave because I have a lot to think my way through before my modern class."

"I don't have class for an hour," Patrick said, his blue T-shirt matching the water. "I can help you for a while." Sara saw past him to the girls creating their water ballet and to Leah doing her backstroke laps. They looked so far away. She wasn't sure what to say to Patrick. She didn't want him for a boyfriend, but he was from New York and he did know some things she didn't.

Sara decided to let him stay and help her go through the Nikolais warm-up sequence. She said them out loud, and he corrected her or helped her if she got stuck. By the time she had said them twice, she thought she had mastered them, but she'd have to successfully translate them all to her body for class. She looked at Patrick's watch. "Gotta go," she announced. "Haul up anchors." He drew hers up and clunked it into her boat then jumped into his own boat. "Thanks!" Sara said as she rowed away quickly. He gave her a naval salute. She would have to tell him the truth about her feelings soon.

Everything in the boat paid off. For good measure she placed herself in the middle line for the Nikolais warm-ups again, but Miss Lee changed the lines so that hers became the front line. She took a deep breath and really focused her mind to blend with her body and she made it through the entire sequence without one glitch! She wasn't sure Miss Lee noticed any difference. Maybe she thought Sara had been doing them correctly all along. Maybe she hadn't noticed that Sara had been failing certain parts of it and sneaking looks at other dancers to get by. But now Sara felt triumphant.

The important thing was that *she* knew she had mastered the sequence. She vowed to stay in the front line each day and show her self-confidence. She smiled to herself. The homework assignments were totally intriguing to Sara. *Very inventive,* she thought watching Leah and Shannon's volume duet. Shannon started out standing on Leah's shoulders, then Leah put her down in front and Shannon went through her legs on her knees, then Leah turned on her back and Shannon went between her legs in the air. They just kept changing volume shapes that way and somehow kept moving across the floor. Another couple changed their shapes and showed volume all the while hopping or jumping. Keera and Sara's was more lyrical with smooth gliding movements almost in slow motion. They took turns being the creator of the volume space and the mover through the space and they made sure to change levels while moving across the floor in many directions. Miss Lee called all three duets back out to the floor after the entire class had performed their phrases. She offered suggestions to make them better and said to remember them. *I am really going to have to write all these down,* Sara thought.

Next Miss Lee brought everybody back to the floor and introduced the concept of moving in different types of space. First they pretended to be submerged in water and had to respond to the pressure on the body. Then, they had to pretend that lightning bolts were striking around them as they moved across the floor. "Don't act afraid like a bolt could kill you," Miss Lee yelled above her drumming. "It's just something in the air. Be neutral about it. Just focus on how it changes your movement." Sara kept pretending to dodge make-believe lightning bolts in a neutral way. The homework assignment for Thursday was to create a phrase to do alone that showed movement in a make-believe space. Sara thought maybe she could create it in her bunk that night and spend more time on *Concerto Barocco*. As she headed out the door Miss Lee said knowingly, "Good job on warm-up sequence today, Sara." Their eyes met and Sara smiled. She had been noticed.

Patrick stood next to Sara at the barre for folk dance warm-ups, then stood at the side of the room waiting for his part with Sara. The class was starting to perform the choreography pretty well. Sara liked the opening where they all danced in from the sides, one line coming in from each direction onto the stage. It reminded her of *The Skaters* ballet from last year, but, of course, the steps and music were much different. And instead of snow muffs, they had tambourines at their sides. After the two lines joined up center-floor, they broke into four circles spaced around the room, tapping the tambourines above their heads. Then they danced facing the outside of the circle with their arms linked and the tambourine ribbons falling down their skirts. The music was so fast and lively it pushed Sara on and made her smile. Now that Mr. Moyne wasn't changing his choreography all the time and she was remembering it, things were improving. Then the circles changed into a curved line around Keera, Shannon, Leah and Alene and Mr. Moyne gave them special steps and special ways to use their tambourines. Then the curved line became a circle around the four and as they danced the four became part of the larger circle. Then it was time for Patrick and Sara. The circle opened up and made a curved line again with the dancers dropping to one knee. The music came to a loud crescendo and stopped, then the melody changed. Sara danced forward in a lively step and Patrick danced out from the side to join her. The music was very light and playful and matched perfectly the steps Mr. Moyne had taught them. Sara was astonished to find that Patrick was right. The heels-toe step came before the twirl where they held each other's waist. She felt dumb, but was glad that Patrick had saved her from looking bad in front of Mr. Moyne.

Mr. Moyne stopped the music, made some corrections for the whole class, and then dismissed everyone but Sara and Patrick. "Now," he said. "The steps are good, but you don't convince me. I mean, you need to show the audience that you care about each other. Like this." He danced Patrick's part with Sara, gazing into her eyes and smiling sweetly. All Sara could think of was that if she were in *Serenade* with the seniors she wouldn't have to be dancing and smiling with Patrick. She did the best she could while Patrick seemed to enjoy it immensely. Mr. Moyne added some new steps then let them go to dinner. In the locker room Sara quickly wrote down the new steps they had learned and wrote down the movement phrase Miss Lee had asked her to remember. There would be no more going out in a boat to write down these things.

At dinner Sara got her mind back to *Concerto Barocco*. They would have a full hour to practice in the big studio tonight. Her only big part was going to be in folk dance, so her performance in the Balanchine ballet in pointe shoes was the absolutely only way she'd ever qualify for a summer scholarship to the New York City Ballet school. She just had to pull it off and look great. But, again, when they tried to go on to the next part of the dance, they were in total disagreement. "I know for sure this is what it is," Leah said. But Shannon's stick figures disagreed and Sara's notes were too messy to figure out. Sara pictured her white leotard and skirt in the closet back in the cabin and worried she'd never get a chance to wear them.

Miss Lee came over and asked them why they didn't get the film to learn the dance. She just nodded her head when they explained it to her. "Well, I am no help," she said. "I certainly don't know the choreography. Pray to Balanchine," she laughed. She moved on to another group. Sara looked across the room at Mary creating original ballet movements. It looked nice, but too simple to win any scholarship. She looked at Keera and Alene trying to make up a Nikolais modern dance piece. She sighed and looked at the clock. They had to agree on something.

"I say we go with Shannon's stick figures," Sara said. "She's probably right." She looked at her notes again. "I think my notes agree."

"OK," Leah said. "But don't blame me when it turns out I'm right." They taught themselves the next part and by the end of the hour had the first three steps rehearsed. But that still left two over minutes of the music. When Miss Lee excused them Robin was looking at Sara from the doorway. She shook her head as if to say *you have it all wrong.*

Sara was so frustrated that she took off by herself and went up the path to the lookout bench. *Oh,* she thought. *How could this happen? How could my plan be failing? By the end of next week we have to be ready to perform* Concerto Barocco. *We just have to.* She pictured Robin sitting on the floor in the secret practice room watching the film. She pictured Robin giving her that look that said they had it all wrong. She pictured Robin turning in an excellent paper on *Concerto Barocco.* She pictured Robin dancing in the great Balanchine ballet, *Serenade.* She pictured Robin on the big outdoor theatre on the lake after the final performance winning the NYCB scholarship. She pictured Robin dancing with Jackson in New York. She pictured herself dancing with Patrick in the folk dance. She heard someone coming. Girls were laughing and talking and getting closer to her. She threw her dance bag over her shoulder, got up and went into the clump of tall pines. The trees smelled heavily sweet and mosquitoes were swarming. She started running down the path into the woods and didn't stop until she came to the black muck and the little plank across the creek. She took it to the other side, jumping off almost onto the snake again. She screamed and began crying as it wriggled away. She wanted to run away from dance camp. She suddenly envied her little brother at soccer camp. She wished she were there. She wished Erin were here. She wished she were taller. She wished she were thinner. She wished she were smarter. She wished she had a ballet solo for the final concert. She wished there was a way to get that dance film back from Robin.

Sara trudged up the path to the Woodlake side and hid behind trees until she had made her way to the dance barn, the windows glowing from the studio lights. She heard piano music and Mr. Peter's voice instructing a class. She wiped the tears from her face and stole a peek in the window. There was Jackson leaping across the room with Patrick and some other boys. Sara felt herself leap with Jackson. Her eyes became bright as she watched his exquisite technique. "Control your finish," Mr. Peters said. "Pull up as you land. Land softly. Try it again." Sara's heart filled with the music, with the boys' effort and artistry, with how much she loved ballet. She couldn't believe a minute ago she was wishing she were at a soccer camp. The boys took their end-of-class bows, applauded Mr. Peters and the accompanist and began to leave the dance barn. Sara quickly ran toward the secret cabin. The boys wouldn't be going in that direction. She'd find her way back to the girls' side from there. But the boys had worn several little paths into the woods and she didn't know which one led to the cabin. She looked up to find a clearing in the tall fir trees and then took the middle path, remembering the cabin was in the center between the girls' and boys' sides of the lake. She made her way through thick fern and poison ivy, walking on dried pine needles. A chipmunk scurried off the path, its mouth gorged with an acorn. Suddenly she came into a small clearing and as she looked around for the cabin she saw a mother deer and two fawns standing motionless just a few yards away. If she moved they might run off scared. Then she saw the cabin directly behind them. It was growing dark. She took a silent step and the deer leaped off toward the cabin, the white of their tails bobbing in the trees. It was as if they had been waiting for her to remind her of the beauty of movement, the grace of motion. Sara thought of her assignment for modern class tomorrow. She would create a movement phrase in an imaginary atmosphere of forest. She would be neutral in it and as natural as a deer standing and running and leaping through trees.

She went into the old cabin, divided the floor in half with acorns so she would stay on the girls' side, and made up her phrase. It was dark when she got back up to the look-out bench. She stood staring up at the sky full of silver stars and knew she wasn't ready to give up. Tomorrow would be a new day with another chance to somehow learn the authentic

Concerto Barocco. She ran down the path to Pavlova and just said "Nowhere," when the girls asked her where she had been. She fell asleep with her fingers touching her lucky locket and her toes touching the Nikolais book.

CHAPTER THIRTY-SIX

"Hope and Fear"

In pointe class Thursday morning Miss Sutton seemed to push them beyond what they could actually do, combining échappés with double pirouettes, bourrées while bending backward, and relevé arabesques. When she finished the class with fouetté turns en pointe Sara thought she had them mixed up with the seniors. This was the difficult step ballerinas did to prove their mettle. This was the whipping turn with the leg out to the side Odette did zillions of in *Swan Lake*. Sara might be able to do six good fouetté turns to the right and maybe four to the left, but Miss Sutton pushed them to do as many as they could by making it a contest. They were to stop and stand still in first position once they made a mistake until everyone had stopped but the last dancer. Shannon was the last dancer, and she did eight more than anyone else. When she had finished everyone applauded for her. Sara was perspiring, but Shannon seemed cool and organized. "It was not so much," she said on the way to folk class. "I am used to it. We do it in New York." *Well*, Sara thought. *Looks like we do it at Lakewood, too*. It was as if the teachers had a meeting and decided the second half of camp would be a lot harder than the first half. She was going to have to up her game in every class. It was becoming more and more difficult to be a standout.

Sara stayed in the locker room by herself during the short break before folk class to look over her notes on the steps to her duet with Patrick. Then she stood up and practiced them before going to class. Patrick was waiting for her. "Try to get here a bit early so we can rehearse a little before class starts," he said.

"I really can't do that," Sara said. "Besides, Mr. Moyne keeps us after class."

"Sara," Patrick said. "I get the feeling you don't understand how important this is. I mean, this is our special part in the final performance."

"Look, it's not like it's *Swan Lake* or something," Sara said.

"You have a lot to learn, Sara," Patrick said. "In the real dance world you are happy to get something special, anything special, and you for sure take it seriously and make the most of it. That is how you get bigger parts."

"OK," Sara said. "Sorry." But she knew there would be no bigger parts for her this summer at Lakewood. And every moment she spent dancing in folk rehearsal were moments away from learning *Concerto Barocco*. Time was running out. Besides, she didn't want bigger parts in folk dance; she wanted bigger parts in ballets. She let Patrick take her hands and they quickly practiced the steps they knew before Mr. Moyne entered the room. He had an announcement.

"This weekend will we begin rehearsing every Saturday with Class B in the big studio upstairs from one-fifteen to

314

two-thirty. The juniors have the studio before us and the seniors have it after us, so please arrive on time. We only have three Saturdays to work together. The following Saturday is the final performance." Sara pulled her Class A schedule out of her dance bag. Just as she thought, there was a blank square after lunch on Saturdays. She had been thinking they would practice *Concerto Barocco* in that time slot.

"OK," Mr. Moyne said, nodding to the accompanist. "Let's begin." Sara's face must have been showing that she was thinking of something besides folk dance because Shannon was giving her that *Please focus on folk* look. Sara couldn't help it. She was thinking: *Let's see, this is Thursday. We have to find a place to work on* Concerto Barocco *tomorrow night since intermediates are not scheduled for the big studio on Friday evenings.* She thought of the secret practice room and wondered if Robin would loan them the film just for tomorrow night. After all, she probably had something else planned for a Friday evening.

Sara managed to get through all the steps to the folk dance without a mistake, but Mr. Moyne was still not pleased with her expression. "We will move on to new steps and come back to that later," he told her. Sara could not deny loving the music. It was rousing and fast and fun to move to. She liked using the tambourine, too, and was getting better at it. By the end of class they had learned the rest of the duet, Patrick moved back to the side of the room, Sara rejoined the corps de ballet and enjoyed dancing through many patterns on the floor from zig-zagging lines to squares to more circles. But Mr. Moyne kept her and Patrick after class again and taught them the beginning of what he called "Duet Number Two." The music slowed down to an adage and Sara had to wear a little red kerchief on her head tied under her chin. She would have to tuck it into her skirt pocket at the beginning of the dance. She was to look shy, but flirtatious as she put her hands behind her back and swayed gently back and forth. Patrick walked gracefully around her, then clicked his heels together and extended his hand to her. She was to take it and walk around with him. "We'll learn the rest in class tomorrow," Mr. Moyne said. "Don't forget what I have taught you."

On the way out Patrick said maybe they should start rehearsing their part together somewhere alone. "Oh, no," Sara said. "I'll do better if I just write it down." She ran off to the locker room, then to lunch. *Duet Number Two*, Sara thought. *Wasn't Duet Number One enough?* At lunch Sara kept sneaking glances at Robin trying to get up the courage to ask her for the film just for tomorrow night, but felt frightened each time she thought she might do it. Then Robin and her friends left and Sara went to Pavlova with Shannon to hang out. Charleigh, Mary and Brooke were practicing diving off the raft and Leah must have gone swimming.

Sara and Shannon wrote their Nikolais remembers on the banner. Leah had already marked her fourth one. There were five for Sara now and one for Shannon. But Shannon didn't think it actually counted because she did the movement phrase with Leah. "Leah totally got me through that one," Shannon said, climbing onto her bunk above Sara.

"YMCA-Leap-Year-Life-Saving Leah!" Sara smiled. There was a letter on Sara's bed from her mom. She read it on her bunk quickly, then pulled out the blue tin and put it inside.

"What does she say?" Shannon wanted to know from her bunk above.

"Only how my brother is the star of soccer camp and how much Miss Abbey liked *Giselle*."

"Wait," Shannon said. "Let's put our dried flowers in the tin before you put it back."

They picked the dried yellow roses and red and pink carnation blossoms off the stems and put them in the tin. "What about the ribbons?" Sara asked.

"Let's hang them from our bedposts," Shannon suggested. She tied hers into a white bow and hung it from the side of her bunk, the ribbons streaming down. Sara hung her pink bow just under Shannon's so the long ribbons hung down the side of her own bunk. She thought it was probably something very French. She put the tin back under her bunk behind her pointe shoe boxes, two empty now. *There's no worry this year about running out of pointe shoes without a final performance in ballet,* she thought sadly.

"Oh, wait," Shannon said from her bunk. "Let's put our pressed petals in the tin, too." She shook her French dance history book upside down and all the flat yellow rose petals came floating out of the book onto her bunk. As she gathered them up, Sara got Jackson's Nikolais technique book from the end of her bed and turned it upside down. She swung it from side to side and ruffled the pages and all the pink and red blossoms fell out onto the floor. As she bent over to gather them up, a piece of paper floated out and landed on top of the dried blossoms. She was amazed when she opened it: *Best of luck in your Nikolais class. It's an adventure you can handle. I think you are a fine dancer and I am rooting for you. Jackson.* Sara could barely speak.

"Here are my petals, Sara," Shannon said, her hands cupping them. Sara silently raised Jackson's note up for Shannon to read. "C'est bon!" Shannon declared. "It is good!"

Sara brought the note back down in front of her eyes. She smiled. He liked her dancing! He really did. He was almost a professional dancer and he liked her dancing! He probably wondered why she hadn't thanked him for the note. She would have to do that the first chance she got. Maybe Saturday after Dance History when he came out of the girls' dance building after partnering class. Out of the corner of her eye she saw the girls coming back from the raft. She grabbed the blue tin and held it up for Shannon to put her petals in, put her blossoms in it along with Jackson's note and quickly put it back under her bunk. She smiled all the way to ballet class. She smiled all through ballet class. She smiled all the way to modern class. She was extra confident in the front line for the modern warm-up sequence and thought she saw someone following her lead.

Miss Lee didn't ask anyone to remember their home-work assignment, and she taught them to combine what they learned about moving on the periphery, like carrying spar-klers through space, with volume phrases. They were to prac-tice moving on the periphery tonight and think some more about the concept of volume and creating another unusual environment to move in so that tomorrow they could work with all three concepts. *Wow*, Sara thought. *That means we really don't have to actually create a movement phrase for tomor-row. We are free to concentrate on C.B.* That was her new way of referring to *Concerto Barocco*, her ticket to New York. She wondered if Jackson meant he liked her dancing in ballet or modern. She had danced modern a bit with him, but he had seen her dance in *Giselle.* She smiled again.

Sara couldn't remember ever enjoying baked chicken so much for dinner. She sipped iced tea and stole glances at Robin knowing now that she would find the courage to ask her for temporary use of the film. She would do it right after *C.B.* rehearsal tonight. But when she went back to Pavlova after dinner there was a flyer from Julie Hess under their door announcing that for the next three Fridays, beginning tomorrow night, intermediate dancers were to attend "Friday Fun Nights" sponsored by their counselors. Tomorrow's "Friday Fun Night" for Pavlova and Baryshnikov cabins would be an overnight cookout-camp out. The flyer said: *Meet under the "Welcome to Lakewood" sign at 6 PM Sharp! Bring your bedrolls!* Sara was staring at it when the other girls came in.

"Wow!" Mary said in delight. "Friday Fun Nights!"

"And with Baryshnikov cabin!" Brooke said, smiling.

"That's Grace, Catherine, Amy and Lexi!" Charleigh said excitedly. "It's our whole water ballet team!"

"Keera and Alene, too," Mary smiled. "The whole cabin!"

"Do we absolutely have to go?" Shannon wanted to know.

"Just what I was wondering," Sara said gloomily.

"Are you kidding?" Leah said sarcastically. "Does Indiana have corn? Like Miss Hess is going to let anyone sleep alone in their cabin when she is away camping."

"Well, how do you camp?" Shannon asked.

"Easy," Leah said. "Just get in your bedroll inside a tent and wait for the mosquitoes to bite you."

"No," Charleigh said. "It's fun. Maybe we'll have s'mores. I love those chocolates and marshmallows!"

"Just what a thin dancer needs," Shannon said. She took the flyer and tacked it up on the side of the banner. "Oh well. We aren't scheduled for rehearsals on Friday nights, anyway."

On the way to rehearsal they ran into Julie Hess. "Does every single person have to go camping tomorrow night?" Sara asked.

"Every single one," she answered with a smile. "Do you have a problem?"

Sara certainly did not want to be known as a person with a problem. *Leadership, cooperation, enthusiasm, improvement*, she reminded herself. She bounced back with a feeling of cooperation and enthusiasm. She knew they did not just apply to the classroom. Miss Hess would have some input to the scholarship winners, for sure. "Oh, no," Sara said. "I just wondered. I am looking forward to it." Julie Hess nodded and walked on.

"This stinks. This really stinks!" Sara said, sitting on the floor in the big studio. It wasn't helping that they had agreed to follow Shannon's stick figures for *C.B.* and it wasn't even helping that Misty Schaffer's name was inside her ballet slipper. By this time next week they had to have the dance finished and polished to perfection. That left only four more rehearsals in the big studio and still no film or any place to watch it.

"I think we should quickly make up our own ballet," Shannon said, sitting next to Sara.

Leah plopped down next to them. "We still have a half hour tonight," she said, looking around at all the other dancers busy creating their dances.

"Yeah, but why keep doing it over the wrong way?" Sara said. She lay back on the dull wood floor and looked at the posters of *Serenade* that were on the walls to inspire the seniors. *It must be so wonderful*, she thought, staring at the dancers in their pale aqua costumes, *to learn real Balanchine dances in a professional studio and have time to rehearse properly.*

"Any suggestions?" Leah asked.

"Maybe we could ask Miss Alexander or Miss Sutton to help us," Sara said.

"That would not be fair," Shannon said. "We are supposed to make it up ourselves or learn from a film." That

320

was true and Sara didn't want to risk having their piece thrown out. She glanced over to Keera and Alene who were still trying to put together a Nikolais piece. They were struggling. *How can all the best intermediate dancers be looking so bad,* she wondered. It was like they were all downing in a bad water ballet.

"I don't know how we will do this," Shannon finally said. "We haven't even tried it in pointe shoes. It's going to be much more difficult."

Sara didn't want them to give up. She got up and decided to try leadership and enthusiasm. "I say we go over the first three steps that we all agree on and try to find a space to learn more of it on Saturday afternoon."

"But we have Dance History on Saturday, then lunch, then our first folk rehearsal with Class B," Leah said, standing up. "And I promised the water ballet kids that I would watch them after that."

"Leah!" Sara raised her voice. "C.B. is *much* more important than the water ballet."

"Well, it's not to those swimmers!" Leah shouted back.

"Shhhhh......" Shannon whispered. It was too late.

"What's the problem?" Miss Lee asked, standing above them holding her clipboard. Shannon stood up.

"Oh, nothing," Shannon smiled. "We are at a slight impasse on our choreography."

"That's normal," Miss Lee said. "I am writing down the types of dances people are doing and the names and performers," she added. "Then I will decide on the performance order for the concert and have the programs printed. I see you're doing ballet. What's the name of it again?" She held her pen poised.

This was it. They were going to have to commit. "It's *Concerto Barocco*," Sara answered quickly, locking them into it. Leah and Shannon looked at the floor.

"Oh, I guess you've been praying to Balanchine," Miss Lee laughed. The girls laughed with her. "Make sure I have your names spelled right," she said, showing them the clipboard. She had them all right. She walked away.

"Thanks, Sara," Leah said. "Now we're stuck. S-T-U-C-K." Shannon headed for the drinking fountain.

Sara was scared. She was scared that Leah was going to drop out. She was scared Shannon would suggest easier choreography. She was scared she'd never be able to watch the film again. She was scared they would look like frazzled, dumb dancers. She was scared Jackson would see that. She was scared the teachers would see that. She was scared she'd go home with nothing. No scholarship to anything. She was scared. She looked at the *Serenade* posters. She was determined to look like one of those dancers. She was determined to dance an authentic part of *Concerto Barocco*. She was determined to do it in pointe shoes. She was determined to get that scholarship. She just had to be dancing in New York next summer. She took a deep breath. "Look, Leah," she began as Shannon returned to her side. "I'm sorry. Of course you should help the synchronized swimmers. You are a swimmer."

"Yeah," Leah said angrily. "Swimming is just as important as dance." She picked up her dance notes and walked out. Sara could have cried.

"Well," Shannon said. "We have no dance without Leah."

"I *know*," Sara said, tears welling in her eyes. She had caused this herself. There was no one else to blame.

"Come on," Shannon said gently. "Let's practice what we have and try to add another step." They did the best they could until Miss Lee announced intermediate rehearsal time was up. Of course Robin had been watching from the door. Sara walked quickly past her like a Nikolais dancer avoiding lightning bolts.

CHAPTER THIRTY-SEVEN

"First Friday Fun Night"

Friday was the day of five classes: ballet, tap, pointe, modern dance and folk. When it was over, Sara found that she was actually happy to be standing with her bedroll and her dance bag with a flashlight and clean underwear under the "Welcome to Lakewood" sign waiting for Miss Hess. Miss Sutton was still pushing them in ballet and pointe, Miss Lee was tough as they learned how to improvise, Mr. Moyne was still on her about memorizing everything, Patrick was still flirting with her and Leah was still not talking to her. Geez, Sara thought. *Maybe all that will burn up in the bonfire.*

Julie Hess showed up with Leah and the last of the campers and she led them across the road and onto the path Sara had taken into the forest. "Oh," Shannon said. "I've been here."

"Me, too," Sara said. But she wouldn't have remembered which fork in the path to take. Eventually they found themselves in the clearing with the old hammock strung between the pine trees. The tents were already set up and the pit was filled with firewood.

"Choose your tent, girls," Julie Hess instructed. "Three to a tent."

Sara looked over the four tents and ran to a red one near the fire pit. Shannon followed her and they threw in their bags and bedrolls. "Can I be in your tent?" Alene asked, standing at the entrance.

"Sure," Sara said, sorry it wasn't Leah.

They cooked hot dogs over the fire and ate the carrot sticks and coleslaw Julie Hess had brought from the kitchen. As it got dark they made s'mores, sang and told scary stories. The only scary story to Sara was the one that ended in not being able to perform *C.B.* and not getting to New York. She looked over at Leah who seemed like a girl who had already forgotten she was ever in *C.B.* Sara wished she could forget it, too, but it just made her heart sink to think of not winning. In the tent Sara and Shannon kept their flashlights on to write down notes from modern dance and folk. Alene left hers on to read a book. When she closed it, she said. "What is that dance you are doing for the student concert?"

"We're doing a small part of Balanchine's *Concerto Barocco*," Sara answered as she put away her notes.

"Oh, that's why it looked familiar. We saw that film in Dance History class. It's so beautiful!"

"It actually looked familiar to you?" Shannon said. "I mean, you could tell what we were doing?"

"Yes. I think it looks pretty good so far. Keera and I are really struggling trying to create a modern piece using Nikolais technique. Miss Lee doesn't offer any help. We've only got four practices left before the concert next Saturday. We're in a jam."

Sara realized everyone must feel the same way. The teachers might be doing it on purpose to test their mettle. "We're just going to have to do our best," she said. She turned off her flashlight and settled into her bedroll. She would not be weak, she would not give up. She would not lose without trying. When Shannon and Alene turned off their flashlights it was pitch black in the forest. She could only hear crickets and the wind in the pines. After swatting at a couple of mosquitoes she slept peacefully under the sparkling stars until she heard big shoes clomping through the brush next to the tent.

"Let's go!" Charlie shouted. Sara sat up and looked out to see Julie Hess and some girls already packed up. It was a bright morning. "Let's get this show on the road. I got things to do today." He began taking down the tents.

Miss Hess blew a whistle. Alene jumped up. Shannon yawned and rolled over. "Come on," Sara said to her tent mates. "Time for breakfast." They quickly got their things organized and stood with the group. Miss Hess doused the embers of last night's fire and they started the walk back through the deep forest to the other side of the road. Leah hung back with some other girls and avoided Sara at breakfast.

"I thought sleeping in the cabin was rough," Shannon said on the way to Dance History class. "I wonder what the next "Friday Fun Night" will be like. Sleeping in trees?"

Sara was delighted to find that the film Miss Meisner was showing them today was *Serenade.* She showed the film first, then told them about it. "I just wanted you to be able to get lost in the charm of the choreography, the flow of the long, pale aqua costumes, the lilting waltz music." Sara was definitely lost in it. It was as if all the posters on the studio walls came alive. She loved it so much she wanted to see it right away again. She couldn't wait to see how well the senior girls performed it. She longed to be in it, especially when Miss Meisner told them *Serenade* was the first ballet Balanchine presented in America. "It was 1935 and came about when a dancer came into class a bit late and then fell onto the floor during rehearsal out of frustration. Balanchine thought it would be wonderful to compose a dance showing young dancers that way. Did you notice a few girls with their hair down dancing with the boy?" That was very different for ballet in those days."

Sara wondered if Jackson would be dancing in Lakewood's version of *Serenade*. How romantic, she sighed, wishing and wishing that she had enrolled in the Senior Division. Not a thing she could do about it now. Time was racing to the student concert and the end-of-camp final performance. She felt like a steam roller was coming straight at her and if she jumped out of the way or even flinched she would be out of the running for a scholarship to New York. She had to meet that steam roller and turn it into a beautiful carriage. She looked around the room and saw the sayings from famous dancers. She read Balanchine's again: "To be romantic about something is to see what you are and to wish for something entirely different. This requires magic." Then she saw a quote from Alwin Nikolais: "The dancer does not practice failure. The dancer's challenge is to effectively act..." Then she read more of the one from Martha Graham: "You have to keep open and aware directly to the urges that motivate you. Keep the channel open." *Magic, don't practice failure, stay open,* she thought. Then she heard Miss Lee laugh and say *Pray to Balanchine*. She had that wispy feeling around her neck, but when she felt for her locket she wasn't wearing it. Somehow at that moment she knew she would triumph. She wasn't sure how, but she knew she would. It would take magic.

After class Sara wanted Shannon to go past the dance building with her to see if they could meet up with the boys. "No," Shannon said. "We only have an hour for lunch then we have rehearsal for folk dance." She said she'd rather have time to eat a salad then see the boys, so she went to lunch. Sara hurried down the path toward the dance building and saw Jackson and Patrick coming out with some other boys. Robin, Hillary, Courtney, Katie and Kathy Jacobs were just behind them. They all stopped to say good-bye, then the boys started down the path to Woodlake. Sara started to go after them so she could thank Jackson for his note, but Mrs. Lane came out onto the porch.

"Robin! Robin! Go right over to the music library. Miss Meisner wants to see you," Mrs. Lane shouted. Sara wondered what it could be about. She watched the boys disappear into the trees. Her curiosity and vivid imagination took over. She would thank Jackson later. She followed behind Robin and Hillary carefully then ducked below an open window when they went into Miss Meisner's classroom.

"Hello, Robin," Miss Meisner began. "Hillary, would you mind waiting outside?" Sara moved to a window farther away from the porch so Hillary wouldn't see her.

"Robin, I have read the draft of your paper on *Concerto Barocco*," Miss Meisner said. "I am sorry to say that it's just not where it needs to be. You are watching the film, aren't you?"

329

"Yes, I am," Robin said.

"Well, your paper does not reflect that. I mean, you have the history of the dance written nicely and have interesting background information on Balanchine as a choreographer, but you express little of the actual images of the ballet. I expect you to describe many of the steps and patterns and write about which ones might be the highlights of the dance for you. After all, one day you might want to be a dance critic or even a dance history teacher."

"Oh, no," Robin said. "I am going to be a performer, a professional ballet dancer."

"Well then being able to write, to absorb what you are seeing in a ballet will help significantly toward meeting your goal. Now, Robin, you have only a few more days to make this paper worthy of yourself and worthy of Balanchine. It is due next Saturday. That is the absolute final day. Miss Alexander wants to see all the senior papers next Monday."

Miss Alexander is reading the papers! Wow, Sara thought, *Robin couldn't possibly be in the running for the NYCB scholarship with a failing paper on Balanchine. I mean,* she exclaimed to herself, *City Ballet was Balanchine's company!* She heard the door shut and then heard Robin and Hillary on the porch.

"Wow, Robin," Hillary said. "I'm glad I chose a simple ballet. Do you want me to help you with your paper?"

"No. You have to finish yours," Robin sulked. "I don't know what I'm going to do." She sounded ready to cry. They jumped off the porch and Sara crouched down more. After she was sure they had started down the path to the dining hall, she followed them.

It was all she could do not to look at Robin during lunch. It was clear to Sara now: If she performed *Concerto Barocco* exceptionally well in the student concert and Robin wrote an unacceptable paper, her chances of getting the scholarship to New York were much better. On the way to rehearsal she told Leah and Shannon about Robin's paper. "I am more excited than ever about doing *C.B.* well," she told them.

"But you are forgetting one thing," Shannon said. "Robin will never give up the film now."

"Not even for one day," Leah said. At least Leah was talking to her again.

"We need to practice today," Sara said, then suddenly remembered that Leah had promised to watch the water ballet after folk rehearsal. Shannon nudged her. Leah might get really mad again. "I mean tomorrow. We can clean up our dance notes tonight, then find some place to practice tomorrow," She said quickly.

"We'll see," Leah said.

Folk rehearsal in the big studio with Class B was messy. Mr. Moyne had to keep stopping the music to make corrections. Sara didn't get a chance to look over the dance notes she had scribbled in the tent Friday night, but Patrick led her through everything. Some of the younger dancers in Class B kind of snickered when Sara put on the red kerchief, but Mr. Moyne explained that it was an authentic folk dance he was teaching them and the kerchief was part of it. He asked them to take it seriously and to learn from it. *Nobody will laugh at me when I do those quick little steps in my pointe shoes dancing Concerto Barocco,* Sara thought. Dancing with Class B did make the folk dance more interesting, with double lines leading in for the entrance step onto the stage and with eight circles at the beginning instead of four. They would fill up the entire huge outdoor stage in front of a big audience. Mr.

Moyne didn't add any new steps, just went over what they knew a zillion times. True to his promise, he did not change any of the steps. It was a bit after two-thirty when he let them go. The seniors pushed past them into the room. Robin looked upset and didn't say a word to Sara.

Sara and Shannon wanted to support Leah and the water ballet, so they went to the beach to see what the girls looked like. They sat out on the dock, applied sunscreen and drank bottled water. Sara actually wanted to see if she could get Leah away early to rehearse *C. B.* somehow, but the girls kept asking her opinion of their choreography. It was going to be good, Sara thought. Their underwater chain took much longer and was more exciting with seven girls in it. She wondered if they'd ever come back up to the water's surface. "Be careful!" Leah hollered. "Make sure everyone can hold their breath that long." Sara fell asleep on the dock and when she woke up everyone had gone. Someone had put a towel over her face.

Heather Scott laughed. "You've been out for a while."

"Wow," Sara said. "What time is it?"

"Five o'clock," Heather said, looking at her watch. Sara gathered her things and ran up to the cabin.

"Well, if it isn't Rip Van Winkle," Leah said.

"You were really out," Shannon said. "So we didn't want to disturb you." Sara felt like she had missed a whole day or something.

"Where is everybody else?" Sara wanted to know.

"Probably standing in line to get in the dining hall," Shannon said. "They worked so hard in the water, they were starving."

"What do you want to do after dinner?" Sara asked.

"I'm going to do my laps in the lake," Leah said with a look that said *and don't ask me to rehearse.*

"I am going to finish my dance history book tonight," Shannon said. Sara must have looked angry or sad or frustrated. "Don't worry, Sara," Shannon said. "We will find a place to practice *C.B.* tomorrow."

Sara noticed mail on her bunk. A letter from Erin!

"We're going over to dinner," Leah said. They let the old screened door slam behind them. Sara hardly noticed. She jumped in the shower, threw on some clothes, brushed her hair, grabbed the letter and ran off to dinner. She knew what she would do tonight.

CHAPTER THIRTY-EIGHT

"An Idea"

Erin's letter said her ballet classes were going well and that her parents had taken her to a performance of the New York City Ballet. "They did *Allegro Brillante*!" she wrote. Sara could feel her excitement between the lines. "That was my favorite," Erin added. She wrote some things about her Graham modern dance classes, but didn't seem all that thrilled with them. Sara understood that; after all, ballet was Sara's highest love in the world. Erin couldn't believe they took Hillary out of *Giselle* and that Sara had tripped over the mop. "I assume it's all healed now and that you are dancing at your best. I hope *Concerto Barocco* is coming along." She said she laughed so hard when she read about them going in and out the window to the secret practice room. "Another sticking door!" she wrote. "And Charlie!" She said that Misty Schaffer was a great dancer and that Sara was lucky to get master class with her and her name in her ballet slipper. She closed by saying "Oh, that Robin. Wouldn't you know she'd have the dance film you need? Remember last summer when she and Hillary took the same costumes we did? What a mess. But you took the chance to suggest we dance together and it worked."

Sara had so much to tell Erin. She settled into her bunk while Shannon read above her. The cabin was quiet with everyone else gone. She told her how difficult pointe and ballet classes had become, how she had earned five remembers in modern dance, how they had camped out Friday night, how she had been partnered with Patrick in folk when she yearned to dance with Jackson and how they were struggling with *C.B.* for the student dance concert. She told Erin all about Robin's possible failing paper on *Concerto Barocco*. "She's been watching the film and can't write about it. Boy, if we had that film we could not only write about it, but dance it!" She told her how full the banner was getting, and about how the seniors were doing *Serenade* for final concert. She saved for last the news that she had found the note from Jackson in the Nikolais book when they were saving their pressed flower petals. "He said he liked my dancing and was rooting for me!" she wrote, adding a smiley face with "LOVE" written above it. She finished with "Questions and Mysteries: What will the next Friday Fun Night be like? How will I ever win a NYCB summer scholarship dancing in a folk dance? How can I make a splash dancing *Concerto Barocco*? How can I get that film away from Robin? As Balanchine said, 'This requires magic.'" She signed it "Magic Sara at Lakewood with Three Weeks to Go." She read it over, then licked the envelope shut. The stamp was already on it, thanks to Erin. But something stuck in her mind. Balanchine had talked about magic, Martha Graham had talked about staying open and following your motivation, but Alwin Nikolais had talked about taking action. She grabbed the Nikolais technique book and looked for the complete quote. She turned page after page, but couldn't find it.

"Sara," Shannon said. "You better get the tin out now while everybody's gone if you need to put something in it. I have something to put in."

Sara got out the blue tin and held it up. Shannon took a paper out from under her pillow and put it in the tin. Sara looked down at it. It was her stick figures for *Concerto Barocco.*

"Shannon, what are you doing?" Sara was shocked. They were using these exclusively to learn the ballet.

"I just want to save them," Shannon sighed. "There is no way now we can learn it properly by the end of the week. We have no chance of getting the film now that Robin will fail her paper without it." She lay back on her pillow and stared at the ceiling.

No, no, Sara thought. *We still have five days! We still have five days!* Her mouth was open but she didn't know how to express her fear and disappointment. No words would come out. She was afraid if she spoke, the words would be flaming red anger. She was frozen holding the tin looking at Shannon's stick figures. All she could think to say was, "Well something could happen. Why don't we post this on the banner instead of putting it away in the tin?" She just couldn't lock it away. Not without trying. She felt her determination welling up inside. She had to get Shannon to agree there was still hope before Leah got back to the cabin and sided with Shannon.

"I don't care," Shannon said wistfully. "It makes no difference."

"Shannon," Sara began, "*Please* don't give up. We've already learned the first three steps. And Alene said it looked good. Two more minutes is all we need. We can finish learning it by Tuesday and practice it in pointe shoes Wednesday, Thursday and Friday. It will work." *Please, please,* she thought.

"We have *more* than two minutes left to choreograph, Sara. And there would be nothing wrong with making up our own ballet." She sat up and looked at Sara's tense face. "Sara, if you are meant to go to New York to dance, you will. You have to work hard and see what happens."

"Working hard is what I am trying to do, Shannon," Sara said angrily as she tacked the stick figures to the banner. She put Erin's letter in the tin, then put her lucky locket in for safe-keeping until the end of camp. It didn't seem to be helping under her pillow. Besides, she kept feeling that wispy necklace of pearls around her neck like she did last summer. The spirits of dancers past. They didn't seem to be helping either. She shoved the tin back under her bunk.

"Don't get angry," Shannon said, closing her dance history book with a bang.

"We have to do *C.B.,* Shannon. *I* have to do C.B. to change my life. You are in New York half the time and Leah seems to have no ambition to go there. But it means magic for me. The kind of magic that makes you something entirely different."

"Quoting Balanchine will not help," Shannon said. "There is just the film, and Robin has it."

"Please give me until Monday, Shannon. Don't say anything to Leah. If something doesn't happen by end of the day Monday, we will still have five days to make up something different and we could even use some of the steps we have. We could just change the music."

338

"All right, Sara," Shannon said reluctantly. "But give me back the stick figures so everyone won't see them. And we won't have five days left, only four."

Sara could feel her heart slow as she handed Shannon the paper and watched her put it back under her pillow. Then Leah came in dripping water from the lake. "What's going on?" she asked, looking at Sara then up at Shannon.

Sara took a chance. "Nothing," she said. "We were just going to ask you if we could go to the laundry room tomorrow to try to pull together *Concerto Barocco.*" She looked at Shannon with her best *Please go along with this* look. Shannon came through on her promise to stick with it until the end of the day Monday.

"Yes, Shannon said. "Only for an hour. What do you say?"

"OK," Leah said, going into the bathroom. "I'll do my laundry, too. But I don't want to do it until evening. I am helping with the water ballet." She got in the shower. As Sara heard the water rushing out, she smiled. Shannon gave her a strange look and left the cabin with her book.

Sara wasn't at all sleepy because of her afternoon nap on the dock and she didn't want to talk to Leah when she came out of the bathroom, so she grabbed the only book she had to read and went out onto the porch. Then she put the Nikolais book under her arm and went up to the lookout bench. What a glorious evening! The sky was awash in pink as the sun started setting over the lake. Sailboats seem to float gently in the wind and she could hear the voices of swimmers still splashing. Then Heather Scott blew her whistle signaling the closing of the beach. *It must be eight o'clock,* Sara thought. She had about an hour of waning sunlight left for reading. She opened the book and wondered if she really wanted to read it or if it was just an excuse for company. But as she picked up reading where she had left off, she became more and more interested. Nikolais had written a lot about all the concepts and techniques Miss Lee had taught them so far. Sara felt it expanding her understanding and she went on reading about the concepts they hadn't learned yet. *Wow*, she thought, *it's going to be interesting, to say nothing of challenging, to learn to move well in the concepts of time, shape and motion.* She was thinking of giving the book back to Jackson, maybe with a note in it for him, but now decided to keep it longer. A chipmunk ran out from under the bench and frightened her. She dropped the book in surprise and when she picked it up, there was the page with the quote: "The dancer does not practice failure. The dancer's challenge is to effectively act within the confines of his specifically allotted space and time. His fundamental practice is that of achieving consonance. The impulse, the motivation to move, the follow-through and the ending are an absolute fulfillment of his desire." She thought she understood most of it. She thought consonance was a word like harmony, a blending of everything. She read it again, changing the word *his* to *her.* Then something clicked. She had to *act* to bring about her desire. A-C-T act. In this space and this time she needed to act on her motivation to move *Concerto Barocco* to the ending she desired. She felt an impulse, an idea. She looked up at the darkening sky. What was it that Erin said in her letter? "Oh, that Robin. Wouldn't you know she'd have the dance film you need? Remember last summer when she and Hillary took the same costumes we did? What a mess.

But you took the chance to suggest we dance together and it worked." Her idea came completely into focus. She closed the book and went back to Pavlova bursting with it.

CHAPTER THIRTY-NINE

"Robin & the Film"

The highlight of Sunday was Julie Hess dropping off mysterious envelopes for Sara, Shannon and Leah. "Oh," Shannon exclaimed. "Our *Giselle* pictures!" They ripped open the envelopes and compared. "They are all beautiful," Shannon said, looking over the shiny black and white photos. Sara didn't think her own were very good. She was just a little part of the corps de ballet. You could hardly tell who she was.

"Big deal," Leah said. "You should see the ones they get of me winning the swim meets. The water is splashing all around and everything."

Sara wondered how Shannon could always look like a ballet angel with her graceful poses and wispy light hair. She looked at the photos of herself and saw an earthier, grounded dancer. Inside she felt light as a sprite. She was still working on how to express that on the stage in a tutu. She'd have to do it better in *C.B.* They put the photos up on the banner and as Sara stood back and looked at them she thought of the inspiring picture she had on her bedroom wall at home of Mr.

Moyne lifting her overhead in *Les Sylphides* last summer. She had hoped that this summer would bring her more special roles and a new kind of scholarship.

Sara hadn't told Leah and Shannon her idea. She was holding it a secret until after the laundry room practice tonight. When evening came she told Leah to bring her *C.B.* notes along and she brought her own. Shannon had her stick figures in her pocket. They sat on the laundry room porch with their bags of soiled clothes waiting for washing machines to become available. There was a steady stream of dancers who needed clean leotards and pajamas. Julie Hess would come to lock the building at nine o'clock. Sara looked at the clock on the wall above the dryers. It was already eight. "Why does everybody wait until the last minute to wash their clothes?" she asked as another dancer walked past them.

"Why does everybody even wear clothes?" Leah asked, throwing up her hands.

"Why does everybody else practice in the studio at regular hours?" Shannon asked. Three girls came out with clean laundry. Shannon got up. "Come on," she said. They threw their laundry in and as it was washing the last girls took their clothes out of the dryers and left. Sara pushed the big folding table to the side of the room and got out her notes.

"OK," she said. "Leah, get out your dance notes. From now on we begin with Shannon's notes but then compare them to mine and Leah's for a more complete picture. We'll see where are our notes agree and ignore where they disagree." They all put their dance notes on the big table. Sara took the portable music player out of her laundry bag and they got in their opening positions. The lovely Bach violin music was inspiring and Sara felt even more inspired when they made it smoothly through the first three steps. She looked at the minute hand of the wall clock. Yep, they still had over two minutes to go in the piece. "Now we look at Shannon's figures for step four, then compare to mine and Leah's." Shannon's figures showed arms over head, three bounces up on pointe with ankles crossed, then going off pointe into plié with the right foot pointed out to the side and the right arm opening to the side, then repeat to the other side. "Do a total of four times" it said. But Leah's notes indicated they were to do arabesques sliding a bit backward first. Sara's notes said that two dancers were to hold hands while a third dancer went underneath them, but said maybe a part came first where they a dancer was to leap over the legs of two other dancers posing in low arabesques.

"I know mine is correct," Shannon said. "The bounces come as step four."

"No," Leah said. "This time I know I am right. I was very careful when I watched the film."

"Does that mean I don't know how to watch a film?" Shannon said, annoyed.

"Well, maybe yours is wrong, Leah said. "I am getting tired of doing it your way even though I know I am right."

"I'm sure I was watching the film carefully," Sara said. "And my fourth step is different from both of yours. I absolutely know *mine* is right."

"You know what?" Leah said, sitting on the table. "I don't care. I really don't care. If swimmers on my team disagreed on how to get to the other end of the pool we would *never* win. What is wrong with you guys? Who cares what comes next? We only have about two minutes to fill. That's about the time it takes to swim from one end of a pool to the other. Can't we just dive in and swim? Let's do something. We've got like four days left and I am getting sick of this."

"I told you from the beginning that I would only be in it if it were good," Shannon said. "It has to be authentic. All the teachers will know if we say it's Balanchine's *Concerto Barocco* and it looks like a hodge-podge we made up."

Sara was terrified. It was time to take a chance. To try her idea. To act. A-C-T. "Listen," she said with authority. "Promise me you'll both stay here for a minute. I have an idea. I'll be right back. Do you promise?" She looked at Shannon to remind her that she had promised Sara until the end of tomorrow. Shannon nodded.

"What's up?" Leah wanted to know.

"You have to trust me," Sara said. "Just stay here. I'll be right back." When they looked like they weren't going to bolt, Sara took off for Robin's cabin. She knocked on the door. Hillary answered.

"What do you want?" Hillary asked.

"I have to see Robin," Sara said importantly.

"She's not here."

"Where is she?"

"At the music library."

"On Sunday?"

"Special permission."

Sara ran over there. She heard music coming from the Dance History classroom, but the door to the building was locked. She knocked, but no one answered. She jumped off the porch and looked in a window. There was Robin watching *Concerto Barocco* and taking notes! Sara knocked hard on the window. Robin looked at her. Sara yelled through the window to let her in. Robin got up and went to the door. Sara ran around and jumped onto the porch. Robin unlocked the door and stood there letting the film run behind her in the darkened room.

"What do you want?" Robin said. "I am very busy."

"I know," Sara said. "You have to write a good paper on *Concerto Barocco.*"

"How do you know?" Robin said, putting a hand on her hip.

"Never mind," Sara said. "Leah and Shannon and I are trying to dance part of it for our student concert. It's a mess. We need your help."

"What? Why should I help you? It's no secret we are both after that scholarship to New York."

"Because unless we help each other, neither one of us will get it."

"How in the world could you ever help me?" Robin asked.

Time was running out. She had to get Robin over to the laundry room. She took a chance. "Shannon will help you write your paper if you'll help us choreograph the ballet. We need to share that film." Robin just stood there thinking. "Come with me!" Sara grabbed her hand.

"Wait a minute," Robin said. She ran over and quickly turned off the film. Then she jumped off the porch with Sara and ran they back to the laundry building.

Leah and Shannon looked surprised. Shannon finally spoke. "Hello, Robin." Leah just stared at her.

"What are you guys doing in here?" Robin asked.

"Not much," Leah said sarcastically.

"Well, a lot is going to start happening now," Sara said. "Robin is going to help us choreograph *C B.* and Shannon is going to help Robin write her paper on it." She looked at

Shannon as if to say *I took a chance. Pleeese go along with this. You must do it for Balanchine. You just have to. You must do this for me.*

"Oh. Good idea," Leah said.

"Will you let us watch the film?" Shannon asked.

"OK," Robin said. She seemed resigned that it was the only thing left for her to do.

"Let's go, girls!" Julie Hess was there with her keys jangling. "Time to lock up. Move the table back. This isn't a dance studio."

The girls moved the table back, grabbed their laundry bags and left. It was nine o'clock. Lights-out wasn't until ten. Sara thought quickly. "Robin, can we begin by watching the film with you tonight? We still have an hour. I mean, we'll hear your paper first."

"I guess," she said and led them to the music library. They shoved all the classroom chairs to the sides of the room and sat in a circle on the floor. Robin read her paper out loud. It was still pretty bad.

"Well, I think you have a good history of the dance," Shannon offered.

"Yeah," Leah said. "But what about the dance itself? The actual steps?"

"I know," Robin said. "I need to learn the dance by heart almost and then write about the three different sections of it. The whole thing is almost nineteen minutes long and the steps go real fast."

"We know," Sara laughed. "Try dancing it."

"I have an idea," Shannon said to Robin. "You watch the film and help us rehearse it each day this week and I will read your paper each day to see how it progresses."

"You see, Robin," Sara said. "You will know how to write about the first part of the dance by helping us. Then you'll be off and running."

"We still have over two minutes more to go to have a four minute dance," Leah added. They stood up and danced what they knew for Robin.

"Well, you have a problem," Robin said. "You aren't even doing the opening right. Also, the first section of the dance is five minutes long and you think you can chop it into a four minute piece?"

"But Miss Lee said it had to be four minutes," Leah said.

"No, she said *about* four minutes," Sara said. "We just thought four minutes would be hard enough."

"But you can't do the beginning wrong or chop off the end. The teachers will know. If you can't make it through all five minutes on pointe, then you're going to have to do it in ballet slippers," Robin said.

"Oh, no," Sara insisted. "We are doing it on pointe." She just had to get that scholarship.

"I thought we had been doing the opening correctly," Shannon sighed sadly.

"I told you," Leah said.

"I think I can straighten out your dance if you can straighten out my paper," Robin said.

"Oh, my gosh," Shannon said. "It's ten o'clock!"

"OK," Robin said as they quickly shut off the lights and locked the door. "I'll watch the first section of the film carefully tomorrow, then come to your rehearsal. What time do you start?"

Sara was already running down the path to Pavlova with a smile when she shouted "Seven o'clock!"

CHAPTER FORTY

"Stepping Up in Everything"

Seven o'clock seemed forever away. Monday morning Sara had to get her mind back on ballet and tap. She pushed herself in front of Miss Sutton by finally placing herself at the end of the line for the barre work, so she could lead the class. She almost messed up the quick degagé exercise, but Shannon was behind her and whispered the correction. When they faced the other way to repeat the exercise, she could follow Leah. On the way to tap class Leah said, "You should have taken my end of the barre, Sara. That way you could have watched Shannon first and been the second leader." But Sara did it on purpose. She wanted to jump in as a leader in a big way. There were only three weeks left to impress Miss Sutton.

In tap Sara placed herself in the front line for the whole class. She was so relieved about *C.B.* that she just seemed to fly around the room to the rhythmic music. In modern she had no trouble with the long warm-up sequence. It was etched in her mind and body now. It was so exciting to move right through it to Miss Lee's beating drum without looking at anyone else. They reviewed the concepts and technique

351

from last week in the Nikolais principle of space: working in the periphery, with volume, and creating an environment or atmosphere to move in. Then Miss Lee taught them their first movements in the principle of time: stop and go, syncopation, sensing duration and pulsing. Sara had already learned to stop on a dime and she found it intriguing to combine that with going immediately into a locomotion movement. And she loved moving in the concepts of double time and half time. Now she could use a body part to control volume, she could stop suddenly then begin a locomotion movement, then speed up, slow down or infuse all that with expressing moving on the periphery. "For tomorrow," Miss Lee said, "come in prepared to work in groups using improvisation to show that you understand these concepts."

"How can we be so lucky?" Sara asked Leah and Shannon on the way to folk class. "We don't have to make up a movement phrase for modern tomorrow. We can concentrate on *C.B.* tonight!"

"Well, that's going to be enough to concentrate on," Shannon said. "We still have so much to learn."

"Yeh," Leah said. "And now we have to trust Robin. I'm not quite sure I do."

Sara didn't say anything, but she was thinking of all the ways she mistrusted Robin last year.

"I will know if she tries to teach us a wrong step," Shannon assured them. "But I don't know how lucky I feel. I mean, I should probably spend some time practicing modern tonight. I'm not as good at it as you two are."

"Not until eight o'clock when *C.B.* rehearsal is over," Sara said. "Then I'll help you with it if you want."

Mr. Moyne seemed happy to have Class A by itself this afternoon. As usual, Patrick seemed happy to be dancing with Sara. Sara was happy Patrick remembered all the steps perfectly, but annoyed at how he seemed to keep flirting with her. They ran through everything Mr. Moyne had taught them from the lines meeting each other in the middle of the room for the entrance step to making the circles, through the special part for Keera, Shannon, Leah and Alene. Then it was time for the corps de ballet to drop to one knee and for Sara to walk into the middle of the room and meet Patrick who made his entrance from the side. Patrick said out loud "Toes, heels, in-out, toes, heels, in-out." Then he whispered to Sara for her to put her arm around his waist and put his around hers. He was holding her so close that Sara could hardly hold her tambourine above her head. During the next part where they had to hold hands and dance between the other dancers, he held her hand too hard. She was going to say something but it was time for him to leave and stand off to the side and she had to focus on dancing with the whole class as they danced in zig-zag lines, squares and more circles. When it was time for her second duet with Patrick, Sara found she was dreading it. She took the red kerchief out of her pocket, put it on, and pretended to be romantic while the slow music played. Patrick laid it on thick, flirting and smiling. She tried to just look shy, but Mr. Moyne stopped them. "Be convincing, Sara," he said. "The audience will know if you are not sincere and all the other dancers are depending on you to make a good performance. Now do it again." From then on Sara tried her best to pretend to be romantic so she wouldn't have to do it twice. When it was over Patrick left and went off to the side again smiling at her. "Today was a good review," Mr. Moyne said. "Tomorrow morning, new steps. Come prepared."

Sara couldn't wait to get to *C.B.* rehearsal, but Robin came a bit late and Miss Lee stopped her. "Come on," Sara said just loud enough for Leah and Shannon to hear. "What is the hold up?" Everyone else was already practicing. Finally Robin came over. "What was that about?" Sara asked.

"I had to get permission to help you. I told her you wanted to learn from the film, but that I need it. She said there really isn't any monitor available any way." Sara thought of the one in the secret practice room downstairs, but not many people knew about that.

"Well, let's get to work," Leah said.

"OK," Robin said. "Let's see what you have again." She turned on the music and watched them carefully, glancing at her notes now and then. "Pretty good, really," she said. "After watching the film again today I realized you weren't that far off." She made some quick corrections and had them stand in a straight vertical line for the opening step instead of in a horizontal one. "That will be more like what the choreography really is," she said. Sara remembered that in the film the ballet started with two vertical lines on either side of the stage. Of course many more dancers were in it.

"I like that better," Shannon said.

"All right," Robin said with authority. "You have to remember everything I teach you. There is no time to forget. I will teach you the rest of the dance by Wednesday, then you'll have to start practicing it in your pointe shoes. And remember: if you can't do it well on pointe, you'll have to do it in your ballet slippers."

Sara cringed at the thought of not dancing it in pointe shoes. That would be no help at all in getting a scholarship to the New York City Ballet school. But if they couldn't muster it, they would be stuck doing it in ballet slippers because they would have nothing else prepared. Stuck. They would be totally S-T-U-C- K.

She loved the next parts Robin taught them with quick arabesques sliding backward then going up on pointe and the wonderful part where they held hands and went under each other's arms. Robin made sure they understood how to move precisely and quickly the way Balanchine dancers did. At eight o'clock when Miss Lee ended their rehearsal Sara thought they had accomplished a lot. But Robin had timed them and said they still had almost two minutes left to learn of the dance. "Now write down everything you have learned so far. See you tomorrow." She handed Shannon the paper she was writing on *C.B.* and left to put her pointe shoes on for *Serenade* rehearsal.

Sara wanted to go right to Pavlova, throw her old notes away and write down clearly everything she now knew of *C.B.*, but Shannon said she still wanted Sara to help her with modern. Then Keera and Alene came over and asked Sara if she would help them with the modern dance piece they were doing for the student concert. "See you at the cabin," Leah said as she left.

Sara led the girls down to Studio C, but Mr. Moyne was in there creating new steps for the folk dance. They went to Studio B and found Miss Sutton rehearsing the Junior Division dancers in a little waltz. Sara thought they were cute and very good. "Must be for the final performance," she whispered to Shannon. They watched for a minute until Miss Sutton excused the class. When they cleared out, Sara and Shannon watched Keera and Alene perform their Nikolais piece. It wasn't bad, but Sara coached them in making their movements a clearer expression. "When you carve volume, focus your eyes on the volume you are carving," she advised them. "Show the difference between drawing lines in space and carving volume in space." She asked Shannon if she could see the improvement the second time they did it. It was a way for Shannon to understand the technique better. Then Shannon tried some movements she was confused about and Sara was able to help her. From watching that, Keera and Alene added some new movements to their piece.

On the way to the cabin Shannon said, "You really understand that stuff, don't you?"

Sara was surprised. "Are you kidding?" she said. "I have had so much trouble in that class just trying to remember the warm-up sequence. You're the one with the memory."

"Yes, but you have more remembers than anyone," Shannon reminded her. Sara wasn't sure what that was worth in the scheme of things. She was happy to get on her bunk with her paper and pen. She started fresh writing down all the steps for *Concerto Barocco*. When she finished that she made sure all her notes were up to date for the folk dance. In her mind she reviewed the day and decided she had done a good job of stepping up in everything. Then it was time for lights-out and she lay on her pillow thinking of Nikolais technique. She thought of space, time, shape and motion. She thought of making lines, carving volume, moving through different atmospheres, stopping and going, syncopation, sensing duration and pulsing. She dreamed she was on stage doing modern dance in a fluffy tutu, one foot bare and the other in a pointe shoe.

CHAPTER FORTY-ONE

"Things Come Together, Things Come Apart"

Tuesday and Wednesday Sara thought of nothing but learning the rest of *Concerto Barocco*. Robin was watching the film every day and came prepared to teach them the steps at rehearsal. Shannon was reading Robin's paper and making suggestions every day. "OK, this is it," Robin said at Wednesday night rehearsal. "These are your last steps, then you go into the bow that ends it. That's it. Five minutes. Tomorrow you start doing it in pointe shoes."

Sara was excited. So far so good. She had been writing all the steps down and reading them to Leah and Shannon each night before lights out. It just had to be perfect. The last steps that Robin taught them were mostly steps they had already learned earlier in the ballet, so it was just a matter of keeping energy up to the end. Sara was perspiring when Miss Lee came over and wanted to see the whole dance. "Wait," Robin said. "They just need to learn the bow." She had them take little turned-out steps into a straight line, bend over from the waist, put both arms back and lean over a pointed toe. Shannon was in the middle with Leah and Sara on either side of her. "In the film," Robin said, "half the line bends over their right toe and the other half over their left toe. Since there are only three of you, Sara will bend over her left toe, Leah her right toe, and Shannon will bow in the classic position with her right foot behind. Let's see it." Although Sara thought the bow gave Shannon the spotlight, she had to admit it probably was best since Shannon was the tallest.

"OK," Miss Lee said. "I need to see it from the beginning." Sara wiped her forehead with her small rehearsal towel and got in the opening vertical line with Leah and Shannon. She took a deep breath and tried to get her face to look as serene as Shannon's. The instant the fast-tempo violin music began, she could feel they were going to do it perfectly. The music drove them on and on without stop from one step and position into the next, flowing, constantly flowing. They were up on the balls of their feet over and over, their arms were up and down and up again, to the side, to the back. They went quickly under each other's arms, danced around each other, took little jumps and kicked a leg out to the front, then to the back, the music driving them without stop for the full five minutes. By the time they took their little steps into a straight line for their ending bow, everyone in the room had stopped to watch them. Now they broke into applause, Miss Lee included. "Bravo!" she smiled. They had pulled it off. They had done it. Sara smiled as she tried to catch her breath. Miss Lee was writing on her clipboard. "*Concerto Barocco* will have the honored position of opening the second half of the concert," she said. "Good job, dancers." Everyone went back to practicing their own dances. Sara's heart was singing.

"Tomorrow night I'll see you in pointe shoes," Robin said. "Shannon, do you have my paper?" Shannon walked wearily to her dance bag, pulled out the paper and gave it to Robin. Sara could see Shannon's writing all over it. "Really?" Robin said, looking at the marks. "I thought it was getting good."

"Oui," Shannon said. "It is. Tomorrow I will wear pointe shoes for you and you will have a final draft of the first two movements of the ballet for me." She smiled. Robin actually smiled back.

When they got back to the cabin, they found a flyer for this week's Friday Fun Night. Sara was too tired to read it. "Looks like a Woodlake wild night," Leah said. She put the flyer on the banner wall.

"What?" Sara said, peeling off her sweaty leotard.

"Friday Fun Night this week is at the boys camp," Leah said as she went into the bathroom.

"You will have the chance to thank Jackson for his note," Shannon said as she pulled back her bedroll.

Sara had forgotten about Friday Fun Night. She had been thinking they would rehearse *C.B.* in their pointe shoes Friday night. Tomorrow was already Thursday. Saturday they would have folk rehearsal with Class B in the big studio and Saturday night they had to perform. She fell asleep with the last pair of new pointe shoes she had, bending them back and forth trying to break them in.

She wore the new shoes for pointe class Thursday morning. They felt stiff and hard. Everything she tried to do seemed to be half-fulfilled when she was trying to be a standout for Miss Sutton, but she had no choice. Her other shoes were too soft to get her through the remaining practices and performance of *Concerto Barocco.* "Do lots of bourrées in those shoes, Sara," Miss Sutton told her at the end of class. "Get them broken in. I hear *Concerto Barocco* is going to be good." Sara thanked her and bourréed all the way down the hall to the locker room.

"You should break in all your shoes ahead of time," Shannon said as they changed for folk class. "Then they are ready to go." So that was why Shannon's shoes always seemed perfect. Leah never had trouble, either. She had the kind of toes that were all the same length that fit into a new pair of pointe shoes immediately and off she went. Everything about ballet seemed harder for Sara. But in the afternoon ballet technique class she took Leah's place at the end of the barre and was the second leader. It worked. Second would have to do for now.

Miss Lee worked them hard in modern class, piling on new movements across the floor, expecting them to combine locomotion with stop and go and repetition. In center-floor they learned to move with an awareness of duration, trying to sense how long to continue a certain movement. "For tomorrow," she said, "I want you to compose a movement phrase that expresses 'dancer time' solving the problems of repetition, duration, pulsing, stopping and going. You should express your Nikolais knowledge of how to move through space at the same time." Sara winced. *Homework tonight? Tonight? Really? How could Miss Lee do that tonight of all nights when they were going to have their first rehearsal of C.B. in pointe shoes? Great,* she thought. *Just great.*

After dinner Sara did bourrées in her pointe shoes all over the cabin until it was time for rehearsal. She hoped all the other girls would mind their own business and not watch them tonight. When they got to the dance building the first thing they saw was a note posted that said tech/dress rehearsal for the student concert would be at six o'clock Saturday in the theatre followed by the concert at eight o'clock.

"Here's my paper," Robin said as soon as they entered the studio. She handed it to Shannon. "I think you'll like it." Then she told them to get in their opening poses and in the same breath started the music. There was no time to think. Sara was just plunged into the dance and never seemed to get on top of it. It was impossibly difficult to do en pointe. Shannon seemed a bit ahead of the music to Sara, and Leah seemed right in time with it. "Wow," Robin said when they had finished. "You guys have a *long* way to go. I'm not sure you can do it. You have to stay together. Stay right inside the music." She looked at Shannon. "You'll see I have written that into my paper. You must *be* the music. Balanchine dancers *become* the music."

"What you are missing," Shannon corrected Robin, "is that Balanchine dancers actually arrive a split second late to the music. This gives the impression of breathlessness, a bird-like quality of flight." She looked at Sara and Leah. "That is what we should aim for."

Robin looked embarrassed. "Again," she said, clicking on the music. She watched them carefully, nodding her head and moving her lips, saying the steps to herself. "I don't know," she said when they were posed in their final bow. "I think you're going to have to do it in ballet slippers. I wish I could slow down the music for you."

Shannon shrugged and rolled her eyes. "But that is the whole point of the dance," she told Robin, "the fast tempo. How can you write a paper on the dance if you don't understand the dance?"

363

"How can you dance the dance if you can't do it?" Robin said angrily. "You are on your own now." She took her paper out of Shannon's dance bag and left.

Leah plopped on the floor. Shannon walked over to the drinking fountain. Sara felt like screaming. What would they do now? Then Keera and Alene were at her side. "Would you help us with our modern piece?" Alene asked. "It's not there yet." Sara was still dumbfounded by what had just happened. Shannon came back and Leah stood up. Sara and Leah looked at Shannon.

"We must do another couple run-throughs of our dance," Shannon said to Alene. "Then Sara can help you. Meanwhile, could you please turn on our music?" Alene did, and they practiced the whole dance looking into the mirror. There were times when they didn't have to be exactly together and other times when they were supposed to be exactly together. The second time they did it Shannon asked Sara to speed up and promised that she would try to slow down just a bit. Leah was fine, but not too stylish. They watched themselves doing it in the mirror again and Shannon said she thought it looked better. But Sara thought it was far from how it should look. Leah didn't seem to have the flit of the hands right at all and she, herself, lacked confidence and kept slipping off pointe in her hard new shoes. Miss Lee looked at them, then looked the other way. Sara was very worried.

At ten to eight Leah said that was all she could do. She headed downstairs to the locker room and Shannon followed. Sara sat on the floor and took off her pointe shoes. Her feet were throbbing. Bits of blood stained the feet of her pink tights. At least she knew where to put the Band-Aids. She made her way over to Keera and Alene and helped them refine

364

and add a couple of movements to their Nikolais piece. She incorporated the concepts for their homework assignment and that, she told herself, would become her assignment for tomorrow. She had no energy left to prepare anything beyond that. On her way to the cabin she was oblivious to the torches over the lake, the stars, the moon, and the tall pines swaying in the breeze. All she could see was the image in the mirror of three intermediate dancers struggling to look like they knew what they were doing. They desperately needed tomorrow night to rehearse, but she knew there was no way out of Friday Fun Night.

CHAPTER FORTY-TWO

"Second Friday Fun Night"

Patrick was all about Fun Night in folk class. "You're coming over to our side tonight!" he reminded Sara.

"What do you guys have planned?" Sara asked as they began the barre warm-ups.

"Surprise," he smiled.

Sara was dreading the time away from *C.B.* rehearsal, but eager to see Jackson again. She planned to read over the sections on shape and motion after dinner and write some notes on them, then return the Nikolais book to Jackson tonight. Studies on shape would be the topic in modern class for next week and motion would be the topic for the last week of camp. She wanted to be prepared. After Mr. Moyne stood and watched the class do everything they knew of the final performance dance, he made some corrections and added new steps. The class was divided in half, dancing to either side of the room. Facing each other, the lines danced toward the center, meeting in the middle of the room and forming one vertical line. They learned a couple steps to do together, then continued to pass through each other, dancing to the other side of the room. Then they skipped backward, meeting again in the middle with tambourines overhead. From there, they split into four lines and danced in a big circle making a pinwheel. The music became almost frantic. "Keep your lines straight!" Mr. Moyne shouted over the music. "Keep your spacing!" Then he turned off the music. "That's all for today. And there will be no rehearsal tomorrow because of the student concert. I wish you all well in it." The dancers who were doing the tap routine in the concert stayed after to ask Mr. Moyne some questions. Sara left the room with the others.

"Hey, we can rehearse *Concerto Barocco* tomorrow afternoon now," she said excitedly to Shannon and Leah in the hall.

"It's not like we need to or anything," Leah laughed. Sara wished she would take it more seriously. She looked at Shannon who just shrugged. Sara wanted to cry. She wished she could make them both feel how important this performance was. It was everything to her. A scholarship to New York City. Miss Sutton, Miss Alexander and Mr. Peters just had to notice her and give her high marks toward a scholarship.

After dinner Sara spent time on her bunk reading over the Nikolais book. She put a note inside for Jackson thanking him for lending it to her and for his great comments on her dancing. She ended by saying she hoped to join him in New York one day. "New York–city of dancers!" she wrote. Then, before she changed for Friday Fun Night, she bourréed around the cabin in her pointe shoes to break them in more and she put new Band-Aids on her sore spots. It was a little chilly outside, so she decided to wear some black stretch pants with a white long-sleeved T-shirt. It felt good to be comfortable. Besides, she didn't want to glamour up and have Patrick think it was for him. At the last minute she put a pretty white ribbon around her pony tail.

"Charlie, Charlie, pipe down," Leah said as Charleigh kept up a steady stream of chatter about the water ballet, the student concert and the boys.

"But I'm so excited about everything," Charleigh giggled from her bunk under Leah's.

"Yeah," Mary said as she brushed her hair. "We love our water ballet, we love our costumes for student concert—"

"And we love the boys!" Brooke laughed, sitting on her bunk under Mary's.

Sara looked at everybody. They were all wearing blue jeans and camp sweatshirts.

"Let's go, Pavlova!" Julie Hess yelled through the screen door. Sara grabbed a sweater and the Nikolais book and headed out to the porch. Baryshnikov cabin was all there, including Keera and Alene who walked with Leah, Shannon and Sara behind Julie Hess on the official path to the boys camp. As they walked past the music library, Sara saw the light on. She looked in the window and saw Robin watching the *Concerto Barocco* film and taking notes.

"How was Robin's paper last time you looked at it?" Sara asked Shannon.

"Not good enough for her to turn in tomorrow," Shannon frowned.

"At least she got through all the steps with us," Leah said. "It's her own fault she won't be getting Shannon's final comments."

The lights were on in both the boys' dining hall and the dance barn. Julie Hess led them directly to the dance barn.

As they got closer Sara could see some boys dancing in the upstairs studio. Ballet music drifted out the windows. Mr. Peters greeted them, asked them to leave their shoes in the hall, and took them into the downstairs studio. An accompanist sat at the piano. "Welcome! Have a seat," Mr. Peters said, motioning to some soft mats on the floor in front of the mirror. When they were all settled he said that they had prepared a small dance performance for them. "Since you will be dancing for us tomorrow night," he smiled, "we will return the favor tonight." Sara could hear the boys rehearsing upstairs. She wondered what Jackson was wearing and what he would be performing. "First," Mr. Peters said, "a short ballet from the younger boys." A group of seven boys who looked to Sara about ten or eleven years old entered the room in practice clothes. They got in position and danced a lively folk dance with jumps, spins, twirls and heel clicks. It ended with them on one knee, one hand on a hip and the other overhead.

"Bravo!" Julie Hess yelled among the applause. "Bravo!" It was wonderful, Sara thought. She could see the good New York training the boys were getting from Mr. Peters.

"Next we have something from the intermediates they choreographed themselves," Mr. Peters said, looking to the doorway. Twelve boys came into the room in black tights and white T-shirts, including Patrick.

"Look! Boyd, Hudson, and Camden," Charleigh whispered to Mary and Brooke pointing at the boys.

"Quiet about your boyfriends," Leah whispered.

Sara recognized the Russian music from *Nutcracker*. She was enchanted as the boys danced their own version of the famous Russian dance, including the high jumps with legs apart and the low tumbles on the floor. "Hey!" they yelled as they clapped their hands and jumped up with their legs bent behind them. *Wow*, Sara thought. *Pretty impressive.* She had to admit that Patrick was the best.

As he took his bow, he gave Sara a special smile. She pretended not to notice. She really was going to have to let him know he was only her friend. When the applause ended, Mr. Peters announced the seniors would be next.

"Excerpts from *Sleeping Beauty*," Mr. Peters smiled as the tall boys entered the room. Though they only wore practice clothes, Sara pictured them in the beautiful white and silver beaded costume the prince wore in *Sleeping Beauty*. She looked at Jackson and pictured him on stage in New York dancing with Misty Schaffer in the wedding scene at the end of the ballet. She sighed as the beautiful Tchaikovsky music played and Jackson performed perfect pirouettes and leaped across the room with the other five boys. He was more than the best one in the room. He was nearly professional. Her eyes followed each move he made, every step he danced, and each breath he took until he stood perspiring, taking his bow. She clapped hard and smiled at him looking straight into his eyes, but Jackson was entirely professional, smiling at the whole audience as he strode tall out of the room. Sara felt like she had just danced with him. She wanted to stand and bow and receive flowers. She wanted to be on the stage with him in New York City. She wanted him to bow to her in front of a velvet curtain. She wanted to give him a flower from her princess bouquet.

"Sara!" Shannon said. "I am talking to you."

"Oh. Sorry," Sara said, coming back to reality.

"Do you want to take part?"

"What?" Sara asked.

371

"Mr. Peters has just said if we want to dance with the boys to sit on the other side of the room."

"There's nobody over there yet," Sara said, looking around.

"Everyone is scared," Leah said.

"Come on," Julie Hess said, standing up. Then she pointed to Shannon, Sara and Keera. "I volunteer you," she smiled. "And you," she said, pointing to Alene, Catherine and Lexi. Sara looked at Mr. Peters. She did want him to notice her, but not this way. She wanted to be prepared. She wanted to do something perfect and wonderful. But now she was sitting under a ballet barre waiting to see which boys would come back into the room for some mystery dance with her. As she stared at her socks she heard Patrick's voice above her.

"Sara," he said, extending his hand to her. Other boys chose other girls and they all stood in the middle of the floor. Mr. Peters asked the accompanist for music and led them in some simple partnering, the boys supporting the girls as they took deep penché arabesques, turns under the boys' arms and did small leaps across the floor. Jackson had not come back into the room. Sara did her best with Patrick hoping Mr. Peters would notice her. When they were done, he asked Shannon to stay out on the floor. Patrick bowed his stupid prince charming bow to Sara and she sat back down on the floor. Mr. Peters led Patrick and Shannon through some more sophisticated partnering that even included a lift overhead.

"Ah," Mr. Peters smiled. "Nice, even in blue jeans." Everyone applauded. Shannon blushed and sat down next to Sara. Then the boys left and Jackson came back into the room. He picked up a small drum and handed it to the accompanist, setting a tempo for him. Then he walked over to Sara and asked her to take off her socks. She nearly froze in surprise, but managed to pull off her socks and leave them next to Shannon. The drum beat out its rhythm and Sara walked out onto the floor with Jackson, her heart beating double time. "Some Nikolais movement!" Mr. Peters announced. Sara smiled. She saw Leah give her a thumbs up from across the room.

"Round volume study," Jackson announced. Sara joined him in moving around the room pretending to carve round volume. "Square volume," he said next, and Sara switched to carving make-believe square volume as she moved through space. "Turning and spinning!" Jackson said, and Sara flew into turns and spins. "Slow time walking through flowers," Jackson called out, and Sara pretended to be barely moving through a thick field of flowers. As she picked up her knees slowly Jackson came next to her and said, "Body parts!" He touched her knee with his elbow. Sara responded by touching his back with her head. He responded by touching her forehead with his hand. She touched his thigh with her foot. He touched her back with his finger, then said, "Carving duet." He opened his arm to the side and Sara went through the space then opened her legs. Jackson crawled through then got on his knees putting both his arms out. Sara slid under, then lay on her back with her legs open. Jackson stepped backward through her legs, pulled Sara up and said, "Moving on the periphery changing levels!" The drum increased in tempo and intensity and Sara ran around the room pretending to be streaking it with a sparkler. Then she rolled with it, then she walked on her tip-toes with it. She pretended to write her name in the air with it until the drum stopped with a bang. She stopped and froze. Jackson stopped and froze. "Thank you," he said, walking over to her. They bowed together and he smiled at Sara and actually said, "Good job." Then he left the room while applause filled the studio.

Sara could not believe it happened. "Now join us in the dining hall," Mr. Peters said. Sara grabbed her socks and joined the group. She was so shaken up she almost put on the wrong shoes in the hall.

"Dynamite," Leah said to her on the way to the dining hall.

"Thanks," Sara said. But something fell in her heart when she had to admit that she had just danced modern with Jackson instead of ballet. She had trouble shaking the image of herself as Sleeping Beauty giving her prince a flower from her bouquet in front of a velvet curtain. She looked at Shannon across the room putting some watermelon on her plate. She was her best camp friend, but Sara wished she had got to do the special ballet partnering instead of Shannon, even if it had to be with Patrick. She didn't eat any of the watermelon and popcorn the counselors had put out for them. She just had to get as thin and wispy as Shannon.

When it was time to go, Mr. Peters announced another surprise. Some of the boys would take the girls home in their rowboats. "Patrick, Hudson, Boyd, Ross, Gabe to the boats!" he smiled. "Save one for me. Two girls to a boat." Charleigh, Mary and Brooke made a mad scramble to get to the boats they wanted.

"Boyfriend boats," Leah said. She and Sara jumped quickly into Hudson's boat.

Sara looked up at the bright stars as the oars squeaked in the locks. She heard laughter from the other boats. Nothing seemed funny to her. *Odd*, she thought. Everything seemed *odd.* When they reached the other side, the boys pulled the rowboats onto the sand and the girls jumped out. Sara could see a bonfire on the senior girls' beach. Mr. Peters sat on the sand with Julie Hess, and the rest of the group followed. Sara felt like being alone and walked out onto the end of the dock, but Patrick followed and sat down next to her. "Very cool," he said to her. "Most cool you were this fine evening in the studio." *Why does he always act like he's Romeo?* Sara wondered. It was starting to get to her.

"Thanks," she said, staring across the lake thinking of Jackson.

"I think we dance wonderfully together," Patrick said, brushing his arm against hers. Sara moved a bit away from him.

"Are you cold?" he asked.

"No," Sara said, "I have my sweater." She wished he'd go out to the group on the sand and leave her alone. She had things to think about.

"I think it's cold out," Patrick said, trying to put his arm around her. Sara stood up and started to walk away. Patrick caught her arm. "There's only two weeks of camp left," he told her.

"So?" Sara said, turning toward him. She looked him straight in the eyes in a way that said, *I am not your girlfriend.* He leaned forward and tried to kiss her and Sara pushed him away. Patrick careened backward into the lake. Everyone on the beach turned when they heard the splash. Mr. Peters shined his flashlight on Patrick and when he surfaced everyone laughed. Sara took off for the cabin, angry, embarrassed and confused about the evening. She tried to sort out what had happened. How Shannon had been in the ballet spotlight that she, herself, had wanted, how Mr. Peters surely noticed Shannon's ballet dancing. *Oh*, Sara thought angrily, *Shannon already dances in New York. What about me? What about me?* Concerto Barocco *just has to be perfect tomorrow night, but now we don't have Robin to help us.* She started crying as she stepped onto the cabin porch. Through her tears she noticed a piece of paper taped to the door. She grabbed it and went inside.

After a long shower and getting into her favorite pajamas Sara got on her bunk and read the note. It was from Robin! It said: *I'm sorry for acting like a goof at rehearsal. The final draft of my paper is under your porch mat. Please have Shannon look at it, put it under my porch mat tonight, and I promise to help you with C.B. tomorrow.* Wow! Sara went to the porch and got the paper out from under the mat. She ran in her pajamas to the grass above the beach and yelled for Shannon and Leah. They waved to her and started up the stairs. She got cold and ran back to the cabin. As soon as they came in she showed them the note and gave Robin's paper to Shannon. Shannon got right on the floor with Leah and they went over the paper together. "Hurry. Hurry," Sara said. "We have to get it under Tallchief cabin porch by lights-out."

"Well, I can't believe it," Shannon said. "She finally got what I was talking about."

"Yeah," Leah said. "She wrote about the flow between steps and flitting like birds and the quick up and down on pointe and everything."

"I will just write 'Good' on it," Shannon said.

"Also write that we'll meet her in Studio A tomorrow at 1:15 to rehearse," Sara said excitedly.

"OK," Shannon said.

As soon as Shannon finished writing Sara grabbed the paper and flew out the door in her pajamas and bare feet. She heard Leah shout that they could return it in the morning, but she knew that Robin had to turn in the paper in her Dance History class at nine o'clock. She ran to Tallchief cabin and put it under the mat. "There," she said out loud. "See you tomorrow!" On the way back to Pavlova she saw everyone coming up from the beach and quickly got inside.

It wasn't until lights were out and most everyone was asleep that Leah said from across the room, "Didn't you forget something, Sara?"

"What?" Sara whispered.

"The Nikolais book," Leah said. "I picked it up off the floor and gave it to Jackson."

Sara was startled that she had forgotten to give it to Jackson, that the book had gotten lost in the shuffle.

"Thanks," she said, picturing Jackson reading her note.

CHAPTER FORTY-THREE

"Student Dance Concert"

Sara dreamed all night that she was still dancing with Jackson. Twirling, spinning, touching body parts, carving volume, and running with make-believe sparklers moved like a movie in her head. It was so exciting that when she got up she walked straight over, got her yellow marker out of the drawer and wrote under her name on the banner, "Danced Nik with Jackson!!" She stood back and smiled at it. It had been a sort of performance. It counted. She put the marker back and shut the drawer, then decided to open it again to get Shannon's green marker. The drawer squeaked and Shannon sat up. Sara looked around at all the empty bunks, then she looked at the clock. Twenty minutes left of breakfast.

"We slept in, Shannon. I had *wonderful* dreams all night," Sara said.

"I wonder if Patrick did," Shannon said as she climbed out of her bunk.

"Oh, you two were great together last night," Sara said. "I was just going to write it on the banner. Do you mind?"

"I don't mind," Shannon said, going into the bathroom. "But I was talking about how you pushed him into the lake." She shut the door.

"No. I didn't." Sara shouted through the door. "I mean I didn't mean to push him in the lake. He tried to *kiss* me, Shannon. So I shoved him away."

The toilet flushed, then Shannon came out. She took the green marker from Sara and wrote under her own name, "Did partnering with Romeo. ICK!" They both laughed. "You take the shower and go to breakfast," Shannon said, getting back on her bunk. "I'll see you at Dance History. I have a pear in the drawer." She opened her book on dance history to the part on modern dance. Of course in class she had all the answers.

Miss Meisner had a big chart on the wall that showed the history of modern dance in America. There were so many names and descriptions on it that it looked like the map of the world to Sara. It started with a box labeled 1880 to 1923 with names Sara had never heard of like Isadora Duncan, Ruth St. Denis and Ted Shawn. Martha Graham was in the second square on the chart in the years 1923 to 1946 along with Doris Humphrey and some other people she'd never heard of. The next box on the chart included the names Merce Cunningham, Paul Taylor and Alwin Nikolais! Murray Lewis was up there, too, and Twyla Tharp and Alvin Ailey. Miss Meisner talked for a long time about many of the pioneers of modern dance and their particular influence on those who came after them. "We won't be able to spend too much time on any one of them," Miss Meisner said. "There are lots of books on my shelves if you'd like to read in depth about any of these giants of modern dance." She spent the remainder of class speaking in general about the differences

380

between ballet and modern. "It was shocking at first for the public to see dancers without tights and corsets dancing with bare feet, long hair, with no turn-out and with flexed feet. Does anyone know how Isadora Duncan finally gained an audience?"

"She went to Europe!" Shannon answered, raising her hand. "She was never well received in the States and she died in Paris in 1927."

"Very *good*, Shannon," Miss Meisner smiled. She spent some time talking about Martha Graham and all the dancers she trained who started their own companies and styles. "Unlike ballet," she explained, "modern dance emphasized being grounded to the floor rather than fighting gravity. Modern technique came from the center of the body, rather than from the limbs." She gave examples of Martha Graham's contraction and release and Doris Humphrey's fall and recovery. She explained that in some early modern dance, emotions and stories were emphasized, then evolved into abstract dance. "Alwin Nikolais is an example of this abstraction. He loved pure motion, shape, color and sound. He said theatre was a magical panorama of things, sounds, colors, shapes, lights, illusions and events. Since you are taking classes in Nikolais this summer, next week we will focus on Nikolais and see a film. That will be our last class together because the following Saturday will be your final performance."

Sara's head was jammed with this new information about modern dance. She found she was eager to see the Nikolais film. She couldn't believe there was only one more Dance History class.

"I wonder how Robin's paper turned out," Leah said at lunch. Sara had forgotten all about that.

"Miss Alexander will see it Monday. I think she'll do well," Shannon said confidently. "Now we need to do well."

"Yeah," Sara said. "We need to get over to the dance building like *now* to rehearse *Concerto Barocco.*"

Robin was waiting for them in the big studio. Other intermediates had the same idea and the place was filled with last minute rehearsals. Sara tried not to look at anyone else while she put on her pointe shoes. *C.B.* had to be the best. This was her very big very important chance to be a standout. They had to get it perfect by six o'clock tonight. "No looking in the mirror today," Robin said when they were in opening position. She clicked on the violin music and sat on the floor to watch them. Sara took a deep breath and tried to let the music push her through the movements. *Become the music,* she told herself. But her toes were sore and her pointe shoes still weren't broken in enough to let her move smoothly. She felt stiff. She could sense Shannon dancing like a wisp all around her and saw the look of confidence on Leah's face.

"Sara!" Robin called out. "Faster. You're lagging." Sara tried to catch a glimpse of herself in the window pane, but only saw billowing sail boats on the lake. She hoped her feet and energy would take her to the end of the five-minute piece. It was the most challenging dance she had ever been in. When the three of them posed in their bows Robin turned off the music and stood up. "I don't know what else I can do to help you," she said. "You know all the steps, but you're not getting the crispness, the quickness of tempo, the Balanchine style. And Sara, you look stiff as a board in those pointe shoes. Let's try it again in ballet slippers."

"No!" Sara blurted out. "I can do it. I just have to break these shoes in more." But she wondered no matter how soft her shoes, she'd always look stiff. She needed more practice time to relax into the flow of the dance. Everyone agreed to do it again in pointe shoes. Miss Lee stood by the door and watched them. Sara pushed herself, but sensed the three of them weren't a cohesive group. She saw Miss Lee write something on her clipboard. *Please don't move us into the middle of the program*, she thought. *I can do it. I just need more time.* She pictured the Balanchine dancers in the film, every one of them dancing precisely, quickly, pertly and making it look easy. *If only Robin hadn't hogged the film for two weeks, I would have this down perfectly by now,* she thought angrily. Now Robin seemed to have lost interest.

"I think it's getting worse," Robin said when they had finished. She looked at the clock on the wall surrounded by *Serenade* posters. "I need to get ready for my rehearsal," she said. "Good luck tonight," She left. Sara looked at Leah and Shannon. Her toes were sore and she was about to cry.

"I think we have done all we can do," Shannon said.

"Well, I hope her paper isn't perfect," Leah said. Shannon stared at her. "I mean, you did a lot more work on her paper than she did on our dance." Then Miss Lee came over.

"I'm no ballet expert," she said. "But I thought it looked excellent when you did it in your ballet slippers."

"We'll get it by tonight," Sara smiled, but she felt a lump in her throat.

"You only have ten minutes left here to rehearse," Miss Lee said. "I think it is what it is. I can keep the honored spot for you to open the second half of the concert if you wear ballet slippers. If it still looks rough in pointe shoes at dress rehearsal tonight, I'll have to move you to the middle of the second half regardless of the printed program. Good luck with it." She went on to another group.

383

"Looks like ballet slippers for us," Leah said, taking off her pointe shoes.

"Don't you want to do it one more time?" Sara pleaded.

"Sara," Shannon said, "I agree with Miss Lee. It is what it is. I said I would be it in only if it were good. It is good only in ballet slippers."

"But it's not you," Sara cried. "It's not Leah. It's me. I'm the one who's messing it up." The truth hurt so much that she ran downstairs with tears streaking her cheeks. She took off her pointe shoes and threw them carelessly into her dance bag. She opened her locker, took a sip of water from her bottle, put the bottle back into the locker, grabbed her street shoes and slammed the locker door. She ran up the stairs holding back sobs as dancers walked past her. She heard Miss Lee saying, "Show your highest level of technique and style." She had not had the opportunity to arrive at her highest level yet.

"Sara, wait!" Leah hollered after Sara as she ran out of the dance building. But Sara kept going. She charged down the path through the tall pines. Maybe she'd go up to the lookout bench.

"Sara!" Shannon called behind her.

I'm sorry, Sara thought. *I got us all into this and I don't know how to get us out.* She walked angrily past the music library. *Darn Robin*, she thought. *She would have to choose C.B. for her paper.* She was so upset she broke into a run. Maybe she'd throw her dance bag in Pavlova and go to the secret cabin. But when she got to the Pavlova door she thought of the note Robin had left taped to it last night. *The film*, she thought. *She must have returned the film!* She leaped off the porch and ran back toward the music library. She ran into Leah and Shannon in front of the dining hall. "The film! Sara shouted. "The film! We can watch it now. Come on!" She bolted for the music library and Leah and Shannon followed. The door was locked. Sara shoved at it. Leah knocked and tried it. Shannon looked in the window.

"Miss Meisner isn't here," Shannon said. "It is no use. Besides, what good would it do?"

"A *lot* of good, Shannon," Sara said. "I need to watch that film again. If I could see it one more time I know I could get it!"

Leah looked at the clock inside the Dance History classroom. "It's already going on three o'clock," she said. "We have dinner at five and dress rehearsal at six. I'd like to rest. Besides, Miss Lee will take away our good spot unless we dance in ballet slippers."

"Leah!" Sara would not have her plan dashed. "If we can spend just half an hour watching the film and doing our five-minute dance twice, we can get this on pointe shoes."

"OK," Leah said. "But only a half hour."

"Yes," Shannon said. "There is no shame in doing it in ballet slippers anyway."

"You know," Leah added. "I came here for fun." She plopped down on the porch.

"We just have to get the film," Sara said.

"It's right there on Miss Meisner's desk," Leah said. "I saw a stack of films there when I checked the time."

"Maybe there's a window open," Sara said. She ran around and checked them all, but they were all locked. She had to think of something fast before Leah and Shannon changed their minds. Mrs. Lane probably had a key to the music library. She cringed thinking about having to ask her for it. She had been trying to avoid her in case she knew about the broken window and she was already in trouble about trying to practice in a studio without permission and losing her locket. But she had no choice. A scholarship to New York City hung in the balance. She'd have to take a chance.

"Follow me," Sara said. Leah and Shannon followed her to the dance building. They took off their shoes on the porch and walked down the hall. Mrs. Lane's door was open and she was talking to someone across her desk, but she saw them.

"Yes?" Mrs. Lane said, looking at Sara.

Sara felt herself turn red. *Here goes.* "We were wondering if you have a key to the music library," she said, trying to sound confident.

"Of course I do," Mrs. Lane said. "Miss Meisner doesn't want anyone in there except during her scheduled hours." She paused to look at the person across her desk. "Isn't that right, Miss Meisner?"

Miss Meisner? Miss Meisner was right here. She appeared in the doorway. "What do you need, Sara?" She asked.

"The *Concerto Barocco* film," she answered. Her heart felt like it stopped.

"Oh, yes. You're performing it tonight," Miss Meisner said warily. "I look forward to seeing that." Her tone implied it would be a failure. Sara felt like walking away. "We were just discussing Robin's paper," Miss Meisner continued. "It's quite good." She looked at the three of them. "Did any of you help her with it?" Sara didn't know what to say.

"I did," Shannon said, "in exchange for her helping us with our performance. We all learned better that way. In all of dance history," Shannon smiled, "it's the most spectacular ballet."

Miss Meisner and Mrs. Lane looked at each other. Mrs. Lane shrugged. "Well, if you're going to dance it, you should probably watch it." Miraculously, she took the key out of her pocket and gave it to Shannon. "Leave the key under the mat when you're done."

"Thank you!" the girls said at once. They made a bee-line for the music library, unlocked the door, switched on the lights, grabbed the film and brought out the equipment to watch it.

"Hurry!" Sara urged as they put on their pointe shoes. Leah pushed all the chairs to the sides of the room and Shannon pulled down the movie screen.

First they sat on the floor and watched the whole film. The dancers seemed almost life-size on Miss Meisner's big screen. Sara felt she was dancing with them. She understood the tempo, the crispness, the perfect ensemble work. When they turned off the film Sara felt ready in a new way. Leah clicked on the music and ran to take her place in the opening position. As they progressed through the piece Sara felt a fresh flow and cohesiveness. She knew they were dancing in sync as they hadn't before. It was because *she* was finally getting it! Though her toes hurt during the part where they had to do the fast bounces up on pointe followed by the point of one foot to the side, she did it better than she ever had. As they repeated the step first to one side, then the other, she knew she'd be able to do it in the concert and that everything would come together. When they took their bow at the end she wanted to laugh out loud, but was too tired. They hugged each other and smiled. They had it.

"Let's do it again with the film on," Sara said, wiping her forehead with her dance towel.

"I think we better save our feet," Shannon said, looking up at the wall clock.

"Why don't we do it in our ballet slippers with the film?" Leah said. But Sara left her pointe shoes on just to get in one more honest practice. It was like being in another world to dance in the darkened room along with the Balanchine dancers projected on the big screen. Sara was invigorated, inspired, enthused, and self-confident. It was only when she took off her pointe shoes that she realized the softening shoes had given her new blisters.

"Let's have a quick dinner," Shannon said. "Then put our feet in the cold lake."

"And then put on new Band-Aids," Sara added.

At six o'clock they stood at the portable barre on stage for warm-up exercises in their classic white skirted leotards and their make-up. Sara thought they all looked thin enough. By six-thirty the run-through of the show had begun. Sara sat in the twelfth row of the theatre with Leah, Shannon, Alene and Keera watching the dance pieces. "I can see why Miss Lee chose the tap number to open with," Leah smiled. Sara had to admit it was a smashing piece with twenty girls in red costumes and red bows in their hair. Mr. Moyne cheered for them and clapped loudly when they finished. About half way through the first half of the program, Mary, Brooke and Charleigh did their ballet, which was sweet in the yellow and orange costumes, and rather simple to do. Sara thought they were graceful and had chosen well. The camp photographer was snapping photos of each group of dancers.

"We're in the second half right after you guys," Alene told them. "I hope you like it."

"You helped us a lot, Sara," Keera said.

"That's OK," Sara smiled. Miss Lee spent some time talking to the lighting and sound technicians between the two halves of the program. When it was finally time for *Concerto Barocco*, Sara stood on stage in the vertical line between Leah and Shannon, arms overhead and took a deep breath. *Please let everything go right*, she thought. The music began and her body seemed to take her by itself through the entire dance. When she bent forward over her foot for the bow, she heard instantaneous applause. "Good job," Miss Lee said. The photographer posed them for a few pictures.

Back in the dressing room they took off their pointe shoes and kept their feet up on the make-up counter under the mirror and lights. They ate the apples and cheese they had brought with them for energy and they kept quiet in the midst of all the excited girls around them. Sara looked over the printed program and was pleased to see the placement of *Concerto Barocco* opening the second half of the concert. She was thrilled to see her name there. At seven-thirty, Miss Lee called them all to the Green Room for photos and a pep talk.

"There you are!" Leah said. She pointed to the poster from last year with Sara, Erin, Robin and Hillary in their modern dance costumes.

"Look up here," the photographer shouted from high on top his ladder. "I need to get all fifty of you in this. Say 'Lakewood fifty-one years!'"

Sara repeated the words and could imagine the poster on the wall next summer. She smiled picturing herself in

New York next summer. Miss Lee interrupted her thought. "OK, dancers," she said. "Everybody looks good. You can be proud." Sara thought she was looking at her. "Let's hear it for intermediates," Miss Lee said, raising her hand in the air. Everyone hollered, "Intermediates, intermediates!" then they walked back to the dressing rooms.

As the show began Sara could hear the audience reaction through the intercom speaker on the wall. She could hear the boys cheering and pictured Jackson sitting somewhere out there. As she stood on the stage waiting for the curtain to open on *Concerto Barocco*, she thought of him, but also of Miss Sutton and Miss Alexander. When the curtain opened just before the music began she became fully aware of the full house of all the junior and senior dancers, of Mrs. Lane and Miss Meisner, of Mr. Peters and Mr. Moyne. Everyone was out there watching and waiting. She took a deep breath and took off with the music. She became the music, she was the air, a flitting bird. She was crisp and quick. She sensed Shannon even quicker, and making it all look so easy. She felt Leah's self-confidence. Her pointe shoes felt perfect and she flowed through the entire dance. She heard whistles and cheers and endless applause when they finished. Her smile was huge and her heart pounded happily as she ran off stage into the wings. "Stop!" she whispered to Leah and Shannon as they headed toward the dressing room. "We have to watch Alene and Keera."

They went back to watch. Sara was amazed as she saw the Nikolais method come to life. They changed directions, changed levels, went from percussive to lyrical, from carving volumes to touching body parts, showed thick and thin, and ended with spinning and turning, all to the beat of Miss Lee's drum. "Hurray!" Sara said out loud as Alene and Keera ran breathless into wings. She gave them each a hug. Then they all ran to the dressing room.

"I have never been so glad to have something over with," Leah said, sinking into her chair. She looked exhausted as she threw her pointe shoes onto the make-up counter.

"You came for fun," Shannon smiled. "It was fun."

Fun wasn't how Sara would describe it. Challenging, difficult, hard, really hard was more like it. She took off her pointe shoes, rubbed her feet then began to take off her costume and make-up. Too tired to talk, she listened to the intercom for the remainder of the show. The audience seemed to applaud wildly for each dance, so Sara couldn't really tell if theirs had been the best. Then it was time to leave for the ice cream party. They came out of the stage door to a crowd of junior and senior dancers.

Robin found her way to Shannon. "Nice performance," she said. It seemed to be meant for Shannon only. Then a little junior dancer came up to Shannon holding out a ballet slipper.

"Would you sign my shoe?" she asked. When she left, Miss Meisner came over to them.

"Balanchine would be proud," she said to Shannon. Then she smiled at all of them and walked away with Mrs. Lane. Sara was hoping for some response from Miss Sutton and Miss Alexander but they were nowhere to be found.

The boys were already in the dining hall when they got to the party. Sara saw Jackson eating ice cream with some senior girls. She saw Patrick by himself and went over to him. "Well, it's Miss Concerto Barocco," he smiled. At least he didn't do his sweeping bow with a pretend hat.

"Patrick," Sara said. "I am sorry you fell in the lake. I didn't mean for that to happen."

"I didn't mean for that to happen, either," Patrick said. "I thought something else was going to happen."

"No," Sara said. "That isn't going to happen. I think you are a good dancer and a nice person, but we're just dance friends." She waited for his reaction.

"Then let me just say that it is good to be friends with Miss Concerto Barocco," he said. "I thought you were pretty good. "

"Pretty good?" Sara asked, dismayed that his critique seemed reserved. She needed her performance to be great.

"Yes. You have a certain stage presence. A Miss Concerto Barocco aura," he smiled. That was the best he could give her. But Sara knew if she had performed just OK, *C. B.* was such a high level ballet that his comment meant she had done well enough. She thought of Lin last year unhappy with her performance of the Sugar Plum Fairy variation and how she had won the summer scholarship to the San Francisco Ballet for her excellent try.

"I'll have to turn into Miss Slavonic Folk Dance next," Sara laughed.

She suddenly felt relieved that *C. B.* was over, that Patrick knew where she stood with him, that now she could just concentrate on the folk dance. She ate ice cream with Leah and Shannon and felt the magic of their performance. Jackson made his way over to them and smiled. "Pretty good, you guys," he said. "That's a tough ballet. I wouldn't want to be your toes right now." He gave them each a little hug and wandered away. On the way to Pavlova Sara felt the warmth of his hug.

Leah and the water ballet team went down to the beach for a while and Shannon and Sara put their dance programs into the blue tin and wrote "Successful C.B. performance!" under their names on the banner. Sara added "ON POINTE!!" *Two more weeks until the final concert and the scholarship announcements,* she thought. *Just two more weeks.* She kissed her perfect pink pointe shoes and slept with them under her pillow for good luck.

CHAPTER FORTY-FOUR

"Camp is Almost Over"

Monday morning Sara took the leadership position at the ballet barre with Shannon just behind her. It was scary with no one to watch. She had to memorize each exercise the first time Miss Sutton gave it and do it exactly right. Once she pointed her foot to the side when it was supposed to be to the back, but Shannon did it correctly, so all the girls behind her did it correctly. She didn't think Miss Sutton saw her mistake. She was in a count-down to winning points toward the scholarship and wanted to show improvement. She had to keep pushing. The *Concerto Barocco* performance was pretty good, but so was Robin's paper, and no one important had told her that her performance was great. After class Miss Sutton told Shannon that she enjoyed her performance. "I guess I didn't do too well," Sara sighed to Shannon on the way to tap.

"Why do you say that?" Shannon asked.

"Everybody seems to be complimenting you."

"Miss Sutton only said that she enjoyed the performance. She didn't say she enjoyed *my* performance," Shannon said.

"Besides, it wouldn't have been much of a performance by myself. I think we all did well. It was a lot to take on. A difficult ballet for us."

Sara tried to think positive thoughts and remain enthusiastic in tap. Mr. Moyne surprised them by asking all the tap performers from the student concert to repeat their dance in costume for the class. Sara love the spunky music and was delighted when Mr. Moyne had the class stand behind the performers and learn the steps. She felt relaxed during lunch. At the Tallchief table Robin was comparing her dance history paper to others. "Robin got an A!" Hillary bragged for Robin. Robin smiled at Sara and Shannon but didn't thank them.

"I am so happy that we did *Concerto Barocco* in pointe shoes!" Leah said loud enough for Robin to hear. "And we did so well!" Sara and Shannon tried not to laugh.

After lunch Sara stayed on her bunk and thought about modern dance class coming up at two-thirty. It seemed like weeks since she had been in that class. Without Jackson's book, she was on her own. She looked over her notes for remembered dance phrases and the movements seemed to rush fully into her head. Then she thought about what she had read in the Nikolais book about what was to come this week. It would be all about making shapes. "Shape is the skill of sculpting the body," she remembered from the book. She closed her eyes and imagined herself turning her whole body into a perfectly round shape. Then she tried to imagine how she could turn into a square. At two o'clock Leah suggested they leave for the dance building so they'd have time to return their *C.B.* costumes. "Oh, I don't want to return it," Sara sighed. But she got the pretty white leotard and skirt out of the closet and went down to the costume room with Shannon and Leah.

"Thank you," the seamstress smiled as they checked them in at the front table. They were not allowed into the huge room today, but Sara glanced around at all the long and short tutus, gauzy gowns, leotards, tap and modern dance costumes. *Fifty-one years' worth of costumes*, she thought. She wondered who wore her *C.B.* costume before she did. She wondered who would wear it next. She saw the folk costumes hanging nearby and the long, filmy pale aqua costumes for *Serenade*. She wished one of the *Serenade* costumes was for her.

Miss Lee beat her drum at a slower tempo for the long warm-up sequence today, but seemed to do it to give herself time to observe each dancer's technique carefully as walked around between them. Sara was sure she was making mental notes and giving points toward a scholarship. She took them through some fast locomotion combinations across the floor, then settled them into their first lesson in making shapes. It called for the utmost inner awareness to imagine what shape the audience would actually see. An intention for a shape began within the body and manifested outwardly, but only pure clarity in the body would allow the audience to see the shape the dancer was trying to express. Sara had no time to think of anything else as she learned to shape and sculpt her body inventively. She tried to feel her energy radiating outwardly so Miss Lee would see the shape. She was perspiring by the time they finished going across the floor for the rest of class combining shapes with a variety of locomotion movements. At the end they had to change shapes every four counts as they moved to Miss Lee's quick drum beats.

"For tomorrow," she said, "create a shape dance using your whole body. I don't want you to move across the room, just dart from shape to shape. You can change levels to make it interesting."

"At least we don't have *C.B.* rehearsals anymore," Sara said on the way to folk class. "We can find time and space to do our Nikolais homework." But after folk class, instead of keeping Sara and Patrick to rehearse, Mr. Moyne informed them that he would be rehearsing them each evening now from seven to eight in his classroom. So again Sara would have to find time to squeeze in her Nikolais homework preparation. "You have much more to learn," Mr. Moyne told them. "We'll begin tomorrow night." They had learned nothing new in class. The review of old steps had been good. Now Patrick smiled at her and left for dinner on his side of the lake. Sara went down to the secret practice room to create her shape dance for tomorrow. When she was satisfied with it she did a few stretches on the floor, put her shoes on, shut off the light and breathed easily when the doors opened to let her out into the cool evening. She sprinted back to the cabin laughing at the torches, the lake, the stars and all her possibilities. *Just two more weeks,* she thought.

After that, time seemed to speed up. Tuesday the student concert pictures were posted. After pointe class Sara, Shannon and Leah walked up and down the hall until they found photos of themselves in their white costumes. Sara was disappointed to see that she didn't look very much like the Balanchine dancers in the *Concerto Barocco* film. She wasn't tall enough or thin enough and the photographer certainly hadn't caught her in any great positions. She jotted down the number on a picture of herself alone and another one with the three of them. "This one's good," Leah said, pointing to one where she looked good, Shannon was a blur and Sara looked awkward. Shannon chose a nice one of herself in arabesque and one of the opening pose, and they went into Mrs. Lane's office to order them. Sara was sure the performance must have been much nicer than the photos.

Tuesday evening Sara rushed to Mr. Moyne's studio for rehearsal with Patrick. They spent a lot of time perfecting what they already knew before learning anything new. Sara found it easier to pretend to flirt with Patrick since her honest talk with him. *He probably doesn't want to risk another accidental shove into the lake*, she laughed to herself. When they took a break Sara heard the *Tarantella* music from the studio next door and felt inspired imagining Mr. Peters and Miss Alexander darting around with tambourines smiling at each other. *Enthusiasm, improvement*, she told herself. After practice, she stood with Patrick for a while watching the *Serenade* rehearsal upstairs. The dancers had ensemble work, duets, trios and pas de quatre. They moved in and around each other in a graceful waltz Sara yearned to be part of. The Tchaikovsky music was incredible in its luscious flow. "Where's Jackson?" Sara asked.

"He's not in it," Patrick answered. "Girls only. Miss Alexander is staging her own version of it. The actual ballet is over a half hour long, so she's taking lots of movement from the original to make it about six minutes, but no boys. Besides, we're busy learning a Nikolais piece for the final concert."

"You guys will be dancing in our concert?" Sara asked, surprised.

"I don't think Miss Lee is teaching us a performance piece for nothing," he answered.

When Sara got back to Pavlova, she found all her cabin mates on the floor making flyers for the second water ballet. "Yuk, you guys," she frowned. "It smells like wet markers in here!"

"Help us," Charleigh said, handing Sara a red marker. And that was Tuesday. Wednesday she got a letter from Erin.

"Patrick can be silly," she wrote. "But he's a good dancer. Just let him know you're only dancing. And I hope C.B. turned out OK. That is *so* hard. So exciting about the note in the Nik book from Jackson. Wow, the camp-out in the woods sounds fun! Be sure to tell me about the last Friday Fun Night. Congrats on all your remembers in modern class. The banner must look full by now. Write me back right away. Getting bored in New York. Wish I were there."

After dinner Sara wrote back telling Erin about getting to do modern improvisation with Jackson at the last Friday Fun Night at the boys camp, about how she helped Alene and Keera with their modern piece for the student concert, about Robin helping them with *C.B.* and them helping with Robin's paper, about how the *Giselle* photos were up on the banner and about how disappointed she was with the *C.B.* photos. "But the performance went OK," she wrote. Just next week to go before the final performance and the announcement of the scholarship winners. I'll let you know what happens." She signed it, "Sara who wishes she was in *Serenade*."

She forgot to tell Erin that ballet and pointe classes were getting harder each day. Miss Sutton was adding barre exercises and steps center-floor that Sara had never done before. She expected perfection, too. "I want to see that you are incorporating all the things I have taught you this summer," Miss Sutton said Thursday morning. "Not just the steps, but your expression." Sara was sure Miss Sutton was watching them more closely now to see who deserved a scholarship. They had to make the decisions next week.

Sara found time to create her homework phrases for modern dance right after dinner before her evening folk rehearsals with Patrick. The door was always open to Mr. Moyne's studio and sometimes Patrick came early and gave her feedback. Making shapes seemed to Sara like the easiest Nikolais movement to do, and she got another remember Friday when she showed her ability to combine a locomotion movement across the floor with changing shapes. And she excelled at making shapes center-floor with pauses in between. She seemed able to pause until she sensed she had a good shape that the audience would clearly see. She hoped next week's lessons in motion would come just as easily to her. She had to continue to keep Miss Lee's attention. She had to be a standout in everything she did now in every class.

After dinner she added her sixth remember to the banner and rested before the water ballet Friday Fun Night. She wondered where everyone was.

"Can you help us get this down to the beach in one piece?" Leah asked, coming into the cabin holding one end of white mural paper. Shannon came in holding the other end. The names of all the girls in the water ballet were written in bright marker colors on the paper and there was a large hole under each name.

"Come on," Shannon said. "We have to get this down there. It's part of their opening." Sara realized she had been so busy that she hadn't been to the final practice of the water ballet let alone distribute flyers. She knew Leah and Shannon had been helping them with it and that everyone was excited. She stood up and held the middle of the paper and they walked it carefully down to the beach. A crowd was already gathering, including some juniors with their counselors and lots of seniors. Soon Miss Hess was making an announcement.

"Welcome to our last Intermediate Friday Fun Night!" she shouted. "Seven intermediates will present a water ballet. That will be followed with a free-swim until eight o'clock and then a bonfire with some of our favorite songs. Let the fun begin!" She nodded to Leah and Shannon who stood on the beach in front of the audience with the paper mural. At Miss Hess's cue they stretched it out between them. Miss Hess announced each swimmer's name, then went over to the side and turned on the music. Charleigh, Brooke, Mary, Catherine, Lexi, Grace and Amy ran through the crowd, down to the beach and jumped through the holes in the paper under their names. It was a spectacular opening. Once they were through, Leah and Shannon ran off to the side with the paper and the swimmers performed a short ballet on the beach then swam out with fancy hand movements toward the raft. The performance was excellent with classical music, synchronized kicking feet, churning legs, ballet arms and a long scary underwater chain. They finished by bowing together on the raft, swimming into shore and bowing again. The crowd cheered and filled the evening sky with applause.

Miss Hess built the bonfire as the swimmers went up to change into dry clothes. Before long the sky was dark with a slice of moon. As everyone sang songs around the fire, Sara looked across to the boys' side and wondered what their modern dance piece would be like.

If Monday through Friday had gone fast, Saturday seemed to happen in the blink of an eye. First there was Dance History class. On the way in, Leah dropped off the *C.B.* music tape. Miss Meisner seemed more enthusiastic than ever on her last day with them. She quoted Alwin Nikolais as saying, "I am excited by things very old and also very new, and by so many things in between." *Old and new and in between*, Sara thought. It made her think of old ballets like *Swan Lake* and *Giselle* and newer ones like *Allegro Brillante* and *Concerto Barocco*, the old stories and the new plotless, abstract dances. "I see things best in abstract terms," Nikolais had said. Sara thought of how she loved the Balanchine abstract ballets and saw for the first time that the Nikolais method she had learned this summer was also abstract. Perhaps that is what she liked about both. It was OK to be a swan or a Wili in the forest, she thought. But there seemed to be more freedom and an endless opportunity to create in the abstract.

She helped pull down the shades for the movie and settled in her chair. Sara was delighted that the last film she would see in Dance History class was of Nikolais teaching small boys in a school gym. How wonderfully they moved, totally focused. She recognized their walks in thick and thin, heavy and light, their percussive and volume movements, their studies in time and in body sculpture. They were very inventive in pairs going in and out of space volume and making shapes together. There seemed no end to their imaginations. When it was over she had a fresh understanding of the method and a renewed enthusiasm.

Miss Meisner said she hoped they had learned a lot in her classes and said she looked forward to seeing their final performance. After class, she stopped Shannon and told her

403

how nicely Robin's paper turned out. "And your performance was good too!" she smiled. Sara couldn't tell if it was meant for all three of them.

It was their last Saturday rehearsal with Class B for the folk dance. There was still so much to learn and to get right. Halfway through rehearsal, the seamstress wheeled their costumes in on a rack and called their names to try one on. She guessed right with Sara. Hers fit perfectly. She twirled, looking into the mirror. The layers of net petticoats under the skirt billowed out and the green, yellow and red ribbons danced out from the flowered circle on her head. The front of the dress had a red flowered apron over the big white skirt and the tambourine ribbons matched all the costume colors. Patrick danced across the room to her in wide black cropped pants, a blousy white shirt and a long red scarf around his waist. When everyone had put on a costume, the photographer came in. Mr. Moyne posed them in some of the positions from the dance and placed Sara and Patrick in front of the ensemble. Then he arranged Shannon, Leah, Alene and Keera in poses by themselves. Before he was done Mr. Moyne made sure the photographer got a couple of shots of Sara in her red kerchief smiling back at Patrick while he held her on his knee. The class applauded for that one and Sara felt stupid. Everybody knew the story by now of how she had shoved him in the lake. She was trying to enjoy being in the dance and having a special part, but as she glanced up at the *Serenade* posters again she wondered how sitting on Patrick's knee would get her to New York.

They worked intensely on learning new steps to the dance. After the skipping back and forth part and dancing in the pinwheel, Mr. Moyne gave parts to small groups of dancers while the ensemble swayed and hit their tambourines in the background. Mary, Charleigh and Brooke got to hold hands and run in a circle in the center of the stage. They kicked their legs up behind them and Sara imagined they wore tall shiny black boots and were running in snow. More circles were added until the floor was filled with them and everyone had joined in. Then the circles became straight lines and Sara and Patrick danced out to the center. Shannon, Leah, Keera and Alene danced around Sara and Patrick while they held each other and swayed. Sara had the red kerchief on and felt dumb looking sweetly at Patrick. Finally they were alone in the center of the stage. The music became frantic while they twirled around each other holding one hand on each other's waist and one hand overhead with the tambourine. Faster and faster the music went until they had twirled around six times. Then all the dancers came running out, stamped a foot and hit their tambourines overhead to the long, loud chord that was the end of the music. That was when Sara had to sit on Patrick's knee. "Big smile!" Mr. Moyne cried out. "Big smile for the end of the dance!" The seniors who were waiting their turn to come into the studio burst into applause. Robin gave Sara a thumbs-up. But she was laughing and Sara couldn't tell if she meant it or not.

"It's just a dance, Sara. It's just a dance," Shannon said to Sara in the locker room when she complained about the kerchief and sitting on Patrick's knee.

"It's just a dance I am glad is almost over," Leah said, taking off her character shoes. "I'm going for a swim." She pushed her way through the dancers to the stairs. "See ya."

When they got to Pavlova, Sara and Shannon saw large envelopes on the chest of drawers. There was one for each person. Sara opened hers to find black and white photos from *Concerto Barocco*. After feeling trapped in the folk dance, she was happy to see the photos of herself in pointe shoes and the lovely white costume. She put her best picture on the banner next to Shannon's and noticed that Leah had already put hers up. Mary, Brooke and Charleigh came in and, bubbling with excitement, wrote their special folk dance part on the banner, drew stick figures of their second water ballet, and compared photos from the student concert. When they finally put their favorites on the banner and went for a swim, Sara stood back and stared. "The banner is overflowing," she said to Shannon who was reading on her bunk.

"Don't worry," Shannon said. "Camp is almost over."

CHAPTER FORTY-FIVE

"Miss Lee's Surprise"

Monday Miss Lee had the class review shape studies, trying some new shapes with partners. There seemed to be endless ways of making interesting shapes this way. Then they switched to the study of motion. "Motion is the sensing of what you are doing," Miss Lee said. "You must sense the shape, time and space you are creating along with your interior senses of graining and the use of gravity. In using motion you can be still, you can create a disturbance or unexpected movement, and then you release from that. That is what you do when you move and dance. Motion gives your phrasing an identity." She looked at them. "Do you understand?" Sara thought she did. She took a chance and raised her hand.

"So movement is the choreography, and motion is the way a dancer brings it to life," she said. It was sort of a question.

"Exactly, Sara," Miss Lee said. She picked up her drum. "Everybody stand and make a floor pattern. Slowly add details of body parts. Keep trying to reveal the quality of motion in your movement," she instructed. After they worked in their movement phrases for a while she stopped drumming. She had them move across the floor in lines using almost everything they had learned in the preceding weeks of camp. They moved heavy, light, soft, smooth, slow, erratic, hard, and fast. They moved low and high and at medium levels. They paused to create shapes and they ran with pretend sparklers. They carved volume in space moving backward and sideways. When they finished Miss Lee had them sit on the floor. "You see how much you have learned?" she asked. "Homework for tomorrow is to create a phrase using contrasting time qualities. I want to see nothing else added. Keep it simple and use motion to bring your phrase alive. Good work today."

In folk class Sara found she missed dancing with Class B, but they were able to get through the dance three times without stopping. She needed the practice of getting the kerchief in and out of her skirt pocket and using the tambourine while dancing with Patrick. He was excellent and Sara was starting to feel like they were dancing well together. After class she saw him waiting for a girl. When she came, he took her hand and they walked down the path toward the beach. "Oh, that's good," she said to Leah on the way to dinner. She felt more relaxed with Patrick at their rehearsal that night.

Tuesday was muggy and cloudy. Everyone seemed a bit on edge from the heat. Sara had prepared a solid movement phrase for Miss Lee's class, but was getting tired by four o'clock when warm-ups started. By five o'clock when it was time to perform her homework assignment, her energy was dragging and she was wet with perspiration. She decided at the last second to slow the overall tempo of her phrase so she could focus on expressing pulsing, rhythm, syncopation, resting in place, accelerating, stepping out of time, and then coming back into dancer time. The class applauded when she finished, but Miss Lee did not ask her to remember it. She gave a homework assignment for Wednesday to show motion while using an emphasis on body parts for movement.

Sara watched Miss Sutton leading the *Serenade* rehearsal for a while after her rehearsal with Patrick, then went back downstairs to Mr. Moyne's studio to do her modern homework. But Mr. Moyne was locking the studio behind him. She waited until the *Tarantella* rehearsal was over in the other studio, and when Mr. Peters and Miss Alexander came out, she asked if she could use it. "Well, technically you aren't supposed to use it. We are supposed to lock up," Mr. Peters said. He turned the knob a certain way so it would lock when she left it. "But go ahead. By the way, Sara," he continued, "I need to speak to Miss Lee tomorrow. What time is your class?"

"Two-thirty," Sara told him.

Sara was surprised when Mr. Peters stayed and watched the whole modern class on Wednesday. After they did their homework assignments, Miss Lee announced that Thursday would be their last class. "Friday evening is your final performance," she smiled. I think you will only have morning classes that day. And for the rest of class today, I want you to perform all the movement phrases I asked you to remember. Start at the beginning and keep going until you have performed each one once. Whoever is left standing has obviously earned the most remembers and is to be congratulated." Once they were all standing in a personal space in the big studio, she began to beat her drum. At first Sara was self-conscious because Mr. Peters was watching, but then she got so involved in her phrases nothing was real to her but the movement and motion. She got so lost in it that she didn't realize that she was the only one left as she started performing her final phrase making shapes as she traveled through space. She tried hard to make them come alive through her sense of motion. When she finished it was very quiet, then everyone stood and applauded for her. Miss Lee and Mr. Peters were smiling. "Congratulations, Sara," Miss Lee said. "No homework for tomorrow class, but come prepared to work."

After class as she was taking a drink from the hall fountain Sara saw Mr. Peters talking with Miss Lee. All the dancers were going past her to go down to the locker room. It was still muggy and hot and she wanted to go for a swim or take a cold shower, but she had folk class next. "Sara," Miss Lee called to her. She walked back into the studio. "The boys are performing a Nik piece for the final concert," Miss Lee began. "And Mr. Peters thinks it would be more interesting with a girl in it. How would you like to be in it?"

Sara was totally surprised. *No,* she thought. This was supposed to happen in ballet, not modern. She wanted a special part in a ballet. She wanted to be in *Serenade.* She wanted an "A" on her *Concerto Barocco* performance. She wanted to be a ballet standout. She suddenly saw the words she had written across the top of the Pavlova banner: "Leadership-Cooperation-Enthusiasm-Improvement." She couldn't fail now. "OK," Sara answered. She patted her face with her little dance towel and looked down at her bare feet. They still had blisters from all the pointe work.

"Great!" Mr. Peters said.

"You'll need to be over in the boys' dance barn at quarter to six tonight," Miss Lee said. "Don't worry. I won't give you any new material to learn. You can pretty much use your remembers and there will be some improv." *And there will be Jackson*, Sara thought.

Mr. Moyne had only small corrections for the folk dance. At five o'clock Sara was the first one out the door. "I have to go to the boys' Nik rehearsal!" she shouted over her shoulder to Leah and Shannon. She'd explain later. She ran down the path to Pavlova to get a cold shower. She grabbed an apple in the dining hall and headed over to the boys' side using the secret path. It was quicker. Everybody was in the upstairs studio and welcomed her warmly. Miss Lee instructed all the dancers to establish a personal space in the room. Then she told Sara just to perform her remembered dance phrases from class and to ignore everyone else.

"Just don't crash into anyone," Miss Lee laughed. She sat on a stool, beat her drum and Sara fell right in with the boys, moving comfortably in her bare feet on the floor of the dance barn. When Miss Lee stopped them to make some suggestions for more clarity of movement and changing levels, she also asked Jackson and Sara to move to center after their first four movement phrases. "Just go into some body part improvisation like you've done together before," she said. *Mr. Peters must have told her about that.* She beat the drum again and after four phrases, Sara and Jackson made their way to each other in the middle of the dancers. They worked well together using elbows, hands, shoulders, toes, heads, moving apart and coming close. Miss Lee seemed pleased and Jackson smiled down at her.

Sara got back to the girls' side just in time for her rehearsal with Patrick. When it was over Mr. Moyne said they would have no more duet rehearsals. As she said good night to Patrick and walked wearily down to the locker room, Sara could hear the *Serenade* music. How she loved it. How confused she felt. She trudged down the path to Pavlova picturing herself on stage for the final performance doing folk and modern. *Why didn't I enroll as a senior?* She thought. *Why didn't I get a special part in* Giselle*? Why aren't I dancing in* Serenade*? How can I possibly win the scholarship to the New York City Ballet?* It seemed entirely out of reach.

CHAPTER FORTY-SIX

"Dress Rehearsal"

"You have to put that on the banner," Leah said after lunch. "That is pretty cool."

"Yes," Shannon agreed. "Dancing with the boys is special."

"Here's your yellow marker," Mary said, handing it to Sara. Charleigh and Brooke stood waiting.

Thursday morning had been difficult with pointe class not going as great as she had hoped. In folk class Mr. Moyne had been rough on them, raising his voice and demanding they do each step over and over. "This is our last class. Tonight is tech and dress rehearsal!" he had reminded them. "Tomorrow evening you perform. There is no time left to forget steps or to forget to smile or to forget the pattern. I'll see you in the outdoor theatre tonight. Be there at six-thirty to warm-up. We stay until everybody gets everything right."

Sara had just eaten a large lunch to make up for only having an apple last night for dinner. She didn't have to care anymore about getting super thin. Her chances for looking like a real Balanchine dancer were over. She had done what she could do and now was staring at a banner that did not mention any special parts for her in *Giselle* or being in *Serenade*. But *Concerto Barocco* was up there! Her chance to get the scholarship she wanted. She thought of Misty Schaffer noticing her in the master class. She closed her eyes and made a wish as she walked up to the banner heavy with the summer's memories. She wrote, "Nikolais performance with boys" under her name and stepped back feeling disappointed. She handed the marker back to Mary, grabbed her dance bag and left with Leah and Shannon for ballet class.

To make things worse it was still hot and muggy outside. No breeze off the lake at all and a heaviness in the late summer air to match how Sara felt. It was hard to get herself high in jumps and leaps in ballet and when she did manage it, she left her heart near the floor. She would have just one more class to look like a standout in front of Miss Sutton. In modern class, despite the awful weather, Miss Lee took them through their long warm-up sequence with more intensity than usual. She seemed to be pounding her drum as though it were her last time ever. Center-floor, she took them through every concept and movement they had learned all summer demanding clarity and expressive motion. "Show me what your intention is! Focus! Don't add anything extra! Higher! Lower! More percussive!" she yelled over her drumming. At the end of their last Nikolais class of summer, they bowed to Miss Lee and gave her long applause. Sara was exhausted, but realized how much she had learned. As the class walked slowly toward the door Miss Lee came over to Sara. "Wear a black leotard and tights for the performance with the boys," she said. "See you at the theatre tonight." Sara nodded.

414

When Sara got to Pavlova cabin after dinner Julie Hess was stepping off the porch. "Mail and envelopes!" she said, walking away. Sara had a letter from Erin and an envelope with photos. She sat on her bunk with them and tore open Erin's letter. "Dear Sara: OMG you are doing so well there! You have been in Giselle, got through C.B. on pointe, got a lot of remembers for modern, and had some good Friday Night Fun nights! My life is boring compared to yours. I miss the lake and the trees. The water ballet girls sound so nice. I wish I could meet Leah. This is just a wish for your great final performance. Break a leg!! Ura! Ura! for Pavlova!! Let me know what happens. And remember: Try to have fun. Whatever happens will be cool. Love, Erin."

Sara took out her last stamped envelope and a blank piece of paper. She put the blank paper inside the envelope and addressed it to Erin in New York. She put it in her dance bag unsealed and opened the envelope of pictures. There were three pictures from Saturday's folk dance rehearsal. The photos hadn't been posted. She hadn't gotten to choose. There were two of her and Patrick and one group shot of her with Shannon, Leah, Charleigh, Mary and Brooke. *From Mr. Moyne* a note said. She was wearing that stupid red kerchief in the photos with Patrick. The group shot was full of excitement and joy. She put it on the banner. Everybody came in then.

"Wow!" Mary said. I *love* that picture of all us! She ran and opened her note. "This says that the proofs of the photos are in Mrs. Lane's office and we can go and order them. They will be sent to our homes."

"You are so lucky, Sara," Charleigh said.

"I want that same one," Brooke smiled. They left to go to Mrs. Lane's office.

415

Leah and Shannon looked at their notes. "Same message," Leah said. "Guess yours was a gift from Mr. Moyne."

"Yeah," Sara said, shoving the other photos under her pillow.

"That is special," Shannon said.

Stop saying everything is special, Sara thought. It was nice that Mr. Moyne liked her dancing and made her the star of the folk dance, but character shoes were not going to get her to New York.

Pavlova cabin arrived at the big outdoor theatre on the lake at precisely six-thirty. They found the dressing room with their names on the door and went in to find their folk costumes hanging on racks and the tambourines in a box. Sara could hear the little juniors chattering in the dressing room next door. She knew the seniors had the one closest to the stage. She wondered where the boys were. She got into her black leotard, pink tights and character shoes for tech rehearsal and laid out her make-up for the dress rehearsal that would follow. Then she found a program posted on the wall near the door. Blue this year with black printing. Leah looked over her shoulder. The juniors were first in *Poupée Valsante,* a waltz choreographed by Mr. Moyne with music by Poldini/ Kreisler played by Fritz Kreisler on the violin. Second were Miss Dana Alexander and Mr. Michael Peters in Balanchine's *Tarantella* with music by L. M. Gottschalk. Next came the intermediates in *Slavonic Folk Dance* with music by Antonin Dvořák, choreographed by Mr. Moyne. Duet: Sara Sutherland and Patrick McCracken, it said. *Modern Dance Nikolais Improvisation* with the Woodlake Boys and Sara Sutherland was next with drumming by Miss Diane Lee. The last piece was the seniors in *Serenade* by Balanchine staged by Miss Dana

416

Alexander, music by P. Tchaikovsky. "Your name is in there twice," Leah said.

"You can have a program to take," Shannon said, waving the blue programs from across the room. Sara took one, sat in her chair in front of the make-up mirror and opened it. A couple of spaces down from the listed performance pieces Sara read, *Scholarship Announcements and Lakewood Song*. She held her breath and made a wish. She felt the wisp on her neck and remembered she had left her locket in the blue tin. The last thing on the printed program advised that parents and friends were not allowed backstage after the performance, that they should pick up the dancers at their cabins.

Suddenly Miss Sutton's voice came over the intercom speaker: "All dancers on stage for warm-up, please!" Patrick appeared and took a place next to her for the barre exercises. She spotted Jackson across the stage on a different portable barre. Robin was next to him. When they were finished and she helped Patrick push the barre off stage into the hall, she asked him where the boys' dressing room was.

"In the wings," he laughed. "We don't really need one." That's when Sara realized the modern piece directly followed the folk dance. How would she and Patrick make the change from folk costumes to the black leotards? Then everything started happening quickly.

"Go to your dressing rooms during tech rehearsal and stay there until called," Miss Sutton said. "You can watch dress rehearsal from out front if you want." There was no air conditioning in the dressing rooms, and the evening air was still warm and getting heavier.

417

"If it's going to rain," Leah said, "I certainly wish it would." She was perspiring and wiped her forehead with her dance towel. "I wish I were in a cold swimming pool."

"I know," Shannon said. "The clouds are just hanging around waiting for us to faint. I can hardly breathe when I dance." But they got through the tech rehearsal without incident. The lighting technician was efficient and the music was all recorded this year with no live orchestra, so what could go wrong? They soon found out. It was almost dark outside and the junior dancers were on stage in lipstick and frothy pink costumes with long ribbons in their hair. They had their hands on their hips and were turning in circles when it happened. Thunder crashed over the lake, lightning struck nearby, the music screeched to a halt and the lights went out. The little girls screamed.

"Stay right where you are!" Mr. Moyne yelled to them from in front of the stage. Heavy rain was pelting the roof, and the wind was blowing some of it onto the plastic seats near where Leah, Shannon and Sara were sitting. The trees shook and waved. More thunder and lightning. More screams. Mr. Moyne got on the stage and led the girls off into the wings.

Miss Sutton stood on the stage talking to the music and lightning technicians for a while. It was useless. "All right," Miss Sutton finally said. "We will have to cancel and have dress rehearsal tomorrow." But just then orange torches appeared on the path to the outdoor theatre. As they got closer, Sara saw Julie Hess and several other counselors in hooded raincoats and rubber boots carrying the torches toward them. Everyone cheered. The counselors stood around the apron of the big stage lighting the rest of dress rehearsal. The teachers hummed the music and gave corrections. *The show must go on,* Sara thought. When Miss Alexander and Mr. Peters took the stage in their lively white, yellow and red *Tarantella* costumes, Sara was surprised to see that Mr. Peters wore a big red kerchief on his head. *Oh,* she thought. She felt less conspicuous with hers on during the folk dance, and it went well with few corrections. After her bows with Patrick, she rushed back to the dressing room to change as quickly as she could for the modern piece, but even with all the thunder and lightning and blowing wind, she heard Miss Lee calling for her.

When she finally got on stage Miss Lee said that she wouldn't have time to go back to the dressing room to change. "There will only be a short break between the folk and the Nik piece," she warned. Sara's heart was pounding from all the excitement and rushing and she missed coming to the center of the stage to meet Jackson. "Sara!" Miss Lee shouted over the weather and her drumming. "You're late!" Sara had trouble getting it get together for the rest of the piece. When Jackson was near her he whispered for her to relax and focus. She was glad when it was over and she could stand in the wings and watch *Serenade.* It was even more wonderful in front of the torches, though Miss Alexander counted out the steps for them all the way through. The pale aqua long and gauzy skirts filled every inch of the stage and made wondrous motion as the dancers lifted their legs high into the air. Sometimes the skirts caught on the girls' arms and seemed to float forever. Sara closed her eyes and saw herself dancing in *Serenade.* She felt her feet moving in perfectly broken-in pointe shoes and the soft, frothy costume billowing around her. She felt herself standing at the end of the dance as still as a statue with her right arm out to the side, hand up, the dance ending in the same pose as the opening. When she opened her eyes the seniors were practicing their bows. The curtain closed in front of them and Miss Sutton gathered all the dancers as another burst of thunder made them shudder.

"Once the curtain closes," Miss Sutton shouted, "the risers will be brought out. Seniors stand at the top, intermediates in the middle and juniors in front. Boys will stand with the intermediates. Then the curtain will open, I will announce the scholarship winners and we will sing the Lakewood song. Let's hope tomorrow we have sunshine. See you here at six-thirty."

The counselors ran the dancers to their cabins in the rain, then returned the torches to their proper places along the bluff overlooking the wild lake.

CHAPTER FORTY-SEVEN

"Final Performance"

Gray clouds hung over camp Friday morning and there were so many deep puddles everywhere that the girls had to wear their tall rubber boots to walk the path to the dance building for their last ballet class. "Watch out!" Leah shouted as she jumped over a fallen tree branch. It was strangely cool after the heat of the last few days.

Sara wore her pink wool leg warmers and sweater to class over a dark blue leotard. Her black one was drying out for the modern dance performance tonight. She stood alert in first position in front of Shannon in the leadership position. She was ready to make this her best class of the entire summer. But Miss Sutton was ready to make it the most difficult class of the summer. She combined many of the barre exercises and kept the tempo fast. She had them changing directions, and dancing away from the barre and back. She gave them combinations with quick turns ending in relevé. Halfway through the barre Sara felt like giving her position to Shannon, but just kept trying her best to look sharp. When they turned to the other side, Sara saw a lot of worried faces. But Shannon appeared poised, as usual, and Leah did a perfect job as second leader. Center-floor, Miss Sutton created combinations that seemed to incorporate everything they had learned in the last eight weeks. She started with lots of bourrées, added chugs across the floor, threw in some port de bras while kneeling, and taught them a long and complicated waltz combination.

"Shannon, Keera, Alene, Leah and Sara first group," Miss Sutton said for the waltz movement. Sara smiled doing the waltz steps, the pirouettes and the leaps in the air. She finished exactly with the group in a nice steady arabesque at the end of the room. *Ballet is so exciting*, she thought. She was sure she had been pretty much outstanding in class today. She couldn't wait for tonight. By the end of class everyone was warm and all the leg-warmers and sweaters were on the floor under the barres. Sara felt good and wished she could perform on stage right away. She took a deep bow to Miss Sutton with the rest of the class and joined in the heavy applause for all she had taught them.

"Thank you, girls," Miss Sutton said. "It was a pleasure to have you as students. After lunch be sure to clean your cabins and roll up the mattresses. Make sure you pack all your belongings and get to the theatre by six-thirty. The program will begin at seven-thirty. I promise you will have lights and music." Everybody laughed and then curtsied to Miss Sutton on the way out. Sara suddenly felt like crying. The magic of dance camp was almost over.

Mr. Moyne made tap class fun and let them choose their favorite combinations from the summer. Then he helped them make up a dance using all the combinations. "Thank you, class," he smiled at the end. "See you tonight." He motioned to Sara to stay for a moment. "You looked good in the folk dance last night," he told her. "I hope you will smile more tonight. It's supposed to be fun."

"Oh, I think it's fun," Sara smiled, garnering enthusiasm. "And I like how the *Tarantella* comes right before us in the same colors." It was true. She felt inspired last night watching Miss Alexander and Mr. Peters dancing their precise and sharp Balanchine movements, flirting and buoyant.

"Well, turn your stage presence on tonight for the performance," he smiled. "You know I believe in you, Sara."

"Thank you," Sara said. She felt herself blush as she walked away. She counted him as one of her votes for the scholarship. But she needed Miss Sutton's vote and Miss Lee's and Miss Alexander's and Mr. Peter's and even Misty Schaffer's.

The sun came out of the clouds on her way to the dining hall and by mid-afternoon the water on the grounds had begun to dry up. "I'm going to do my laps," Leah said. "When I come back I'll sweep the cabin, OK?" They had put cleaning jobs in a hat and drawn them out with their eyes closed. Shannon got rolling up all the mattresses and Sara got checking all the drawers and wiping them out. Charleigh and Mary got different jobs in the bathroom and Brooke was to sweep off the porch. They all had to do their laundry so the afternoon was kind of helter-skelter.

In the laundry room with Shannon, Sara thought of the last practice for *Concerto Barocco* they had there when she had to run to get Robin to keep the whole thing together. It felt exciting and scary all over again. When they got back to Pavlova no one was there and the jobs were only half done. They started to pack their suitcases, then Sara thought of something.

"The blue tin," Sara said. "We have to divvy up the stuff in the tin." She brought it out from under her bunk.

"OK," Shannon said. "I'll just throw my part in my suitcase."

"No," Sara said. "It's a secret filled with our entire summer. We have to take it to the secret cabin in the woods to do it. Hurry before someone comes back." She put on her boots and went out the door with the tin heading for the path to the lookout bench. Shannon just had to come. She looked back to make sure she was following.

"I guess it's OK now that we probably can't get kicked out of camp," Shannon said, pulling up her boots and catching up to Sara. "At least I hope we can't."

They walked quickly, sinking into the wet earth on their way down the path through the tall pines. Everything smelled fresh after the rain. The door to the old cabin opened easily and they sat on the girls' side of the floor and opened the tin. They made a pile for each of them with letters from home and from Erin, flower petals and dance concert programs, the note from Patrick. "Here's your note from Jackson and your locket," Shannon said, putting them in Sara's pile. Sara put on the locket, read the note and put it on the top of her pile.

"What is your favorite memory from the summer?" Sara asked.

"The New York City Ballet's performance of *Allegro Brillante*," Shannon said without hesitation. "Definitely. What is yours?"

"Dancing with Jackson at Fun Night in the boys' dance barn," she said without even thinking. "Definitely." Then the whole summer seemed to flow in front of her. She saw herself auditioning for class placement, performing in *Giselle*, doing homework assignments for Miss Lee, practicing *Concerto Barocco* in the music library, breaking the window in the secret practice room, Charlie almost catching them, dancing with Patrick in the folk dance, watching films in Dance History, camping out across the road, the water ballet shows, and the rehearsal last night in the storm with torches.

"What about shoving Patrick in the lake?" Shannon said. Their laughter filled the cabin right up to the rafters. "We better get back," Shannon finally said. "What do we do with the tin? Why don't you take it since Erin sent it to you?"

"Oh, no," Sara said. "She sent it for us both. We leave it up in the rafters here, then whoever comes back next summer gets it."

"What if neither of us comes back?" Shannon asked, picking up her pile.

"Someone will get it," Sara said, remembering Robin and Hillary walking away with the red tin this summer. She climbed up on the creaky table and carefully placed the blue tin in the dusty rafters. It shined like a symbol of their friendship. She jumped down, picked up her pile of memories and they left. As soon as they had put their blue tin memories in their suitcases, Leah came back and began to sweep.

"Did you guys get that blue tin that was under Sara's bunk?" Leah asked.

Sara looked at Shannon, then back to Leah. "You knew about that?"

"Well, duh. I think I saw it the first week when I was on the floor putting fruit in my pointe shoe box. No big deal." Sara and Shannon laughed.

"Yes, we got it," Shannon said. She took the white and pink ribbons off their bunks and they put them in their suitcases. Then the other girls came in and wanted to know if they should take down the banner.

They all stood looking at it. It was filled with words and stick figures in different color markers of all their achievements and with the photos of *Giselle, Concerto Barocco*, the folk dance and the ballet Charleigh, Mary and Brooke performed in the student concert. There were also the class schedules, and the flyers for the boys' party, the New York City Ballet after party, the student concert, the Friday Fun Nights, the water ballet shows, and all their remembers from Miss Lee. Sara stared at the top where she had written in different colors, "Leadership-Cooperation-Enthusiasm-Improvement." She smiled knowing there were moments in the long summer where she had performed well in each category.

"Ura! Ura!" Charleigh yelled. "Hoorah for Pavlova cabin!"

"Ura! Ura!" they all shouted together raising their arms in the air. Then they dismantled the banner, ripping it up to divide what was under each name and putting the pieces in their suitcases. They left the top part for next summer's campers. Everyone completed the cleaning jobs and when all the bedrolls were wound and placed on top of each suitcase, Shannon rolled up all the mattresses. It looked so final.

"Camp is really over," Charleigh said.

"Not until after the performance tonight," Brooke said, putting the broom in the closet.

"Cabin check," Julie Hess shouted from the clean porch. "You guys better have dinner, get cleaned up and get to and the theatre. Let's go!" Sara's stomach jumped in excitement.

Across the aisle at dinner Robin never looked Sara's way. Sara could hear her talking with Hillary about who would win the Lakewood senior scholarships. She heard Hillary say that Courtney could not win because she was going to college in the fall. Robin said that left Katie Easton, Kathy Jacobs and Jennifer Kent in the running. "Along with you," Hillary smiled. Sara saw Robin shake her head. A scholarship back to Lakewood wasn't wanted she wanted. Sara knew Robin wanted the same thing she wanted. She looked away and pictured herself standing on the stage tonight with the audience applauding and cheering for her as she accepted the scholarship to the New York City Ballet school.

Soon Sara stood in front of the dressing room mirror in her folk costume and make-up. She made sure the red kerchief was in her skirt pocket and that she had a tambourine ready to go. She glanced up at the clock. It was seven-fifteen and she knew her mom was probably already sitting out in the audience along with hundreds of others. "Oh my gosh!" She said to Leah and Shannon. "I haven't figured out a way to change quickly for the modern piece!" She felt herself panic.

"Take off your costume," Leah said. She helped her get it off. Shannon hung it up and held her pink tights. "Now put your black leotard on under your costume." Shannon handed it to her and she put it on. "Now put your pink tights on over the leotard," Leah instructed. Shannon handed her the tights and she slipped them on over the leotard. "Now, when you run into the wings after the folk dance, we'll be there to take off your headpiece and your costume. You will take off your shoes and the pink tights and put on the black tights." Everybody was nodding and talking and moving quickly. She put her headpiece back on and adjusted the ribbons. "Don't forget to drop your black tights off in the wings," Leah warned. *Good old YMCA-Leap-Year-Life-Saving-Leah*, Sara thought as

427

she grabbed her black tights and put them on the make-up counter.

Miss Sutton's voice beamed through the intercom: "Juniors on stage. Juniors on stage!" *Here we go*, Sara thought. She looked in the mirror one more time. Her locket shined at her under the lights. How could she have forgotten? She quickly took it off and put it in her dance bag. She pulled the envelope with the blank paper for Erin up to the top. "Intermediates in the hall!" Miss Sutton's voice said. "Intermediates in the hall!" Sara ran out the door and took her place in the line.

"Where are your black tights?" Shannon asked. Sara stared at her. Shannon ran back and got them. "Here," Shannon said. She took them and placed them carefully on an old folding chair in the wings. "Go right over to that chair after the folk dance." Sara nodded. She was getting nervous. The juniors were already taking their bows. The audience sounded excited and their applause was a roar. She looked across the stage to see Patrick in his folk costume giving her a wave and a smile. The audience died down, the little girls came running past them, and Miss Alexander and Mr. Peters took the stage. Sara could barely see them from where she stood, but the audience kept breaking into applause. When the dance took them over to Sara's side of the stage she saw how energized and professional they looked. *Balanchine was so great*, she sighed to herself. She was suddenly so proud to be part of Lakewood. When they took their bows Sara saw Jackson take a bouquet of flowers out to Miss Alexander. There were more bows and then she saw Miss Alexander give Mr. Peters a rose from her bouquet. She thought of *Romeo and Juliet* last year and how she, herself, had given Hank a flower from her own bouquet. She almost cried. She had never felt happier to be a dancer. She straightened her skirt and her head piece as the *Tarantella* dancers ran off the stage. It seemed forever before the folk music started. Then, right on cue, the fifty intermediate girls danced onto the gigantic stage. As soon as the audience saw the colorful costumes they began to clap, and each time they liked a step or a pattern they burst into applause. As she skipped backward, then forward in her line, Sara began to relax.

In her duets with Patrick, Sara remembered to smile at him. It was mostly for the audience, but she could feel how calm he was and it helped her. She was able to remember all the steps without thinking and had room to express her stage presence. As she danced near one side of the stage she caught a glimpse of Mr. Moyne watching them intensely and counting the steps to himself. When they did the pinwheel going in a circle to the pulsing music, the audience got to their feet and cheered. It was amazing. Sara smiled even harder as she watched her friends dance their special parts. Mary, Charleigh and Brooke were energized as they held hands running in a circle kicking their legs up behind. Shannon, Leah, Keera and Alene danced around Sara and Patrick with fervor while they held each other and swayed. Finally the music became frantic and Sara and Patrick held each other's waist and twirled around and around, one hand with the tambourine overhead. Faster and faster they went with the ensemble dancers twirling behind them. Then all the dancers came running forward, stamped their feet and hit their tambourines overhead to the last beat of the music. Sara dropped onto Patrick's knee and smiled up at him. He astonished her by giving her a little kiss on the cheek. The audience loved it. Sara found she didn't mind. She was so happy the dance was over and had gone so well. The kiss was to congratulate them both. She saw Mr. Moyne beaming and clapping in the wings. They stood to take their bows, and Jackson came out with a bouquet for Sara. *My mother is out there somewhere watching this*, she thought excitedly. They all rushed off stage. Sara started back to the dressing room, but Leah quietly called out to her.

"Sara! Over here!" Leah and Shannon were standing in the mix of boys ready to go on for the Nik piece. She ran over and put her flowers on the floor. Leah and Shannon got her headpiece and costume off while Sara peeled off her pink tights and pulled on her black ones. Miss Lee started beating her drum from a stool at the side of the big stage.

"Let's go," Patrick said. She had no idea how he got out of his folk costume so fast. Now he took her hand and led her onto the stage. Sara took a personal space and when Miss Lee stopped her quiet steady beating and gave one loud bang on the drum Sara went naturally into all she had learned. She began with carving and carrying volume, both round and square, going high and low and making her way through the boys who were focusing on their own movement, some percussive, some lyrical. Then she switched to moving on the periphery, pretending to run around the circle of boys with lit sparklers. From there she spontaneously immersed herself in expressing in time, out of time, slow time and fast time, and into changing direction and making shapes. Then she saw Jackson moving to the center and danced to him. They spent several minutes doing the body parts improvisation, touching back to head, toe to knee, elbow to thigh, wrist to hand, foot to shoulder. They changed levels and tempo.

Jackson was fabulous to work with and took her into body sculpting on the floor. The audience was looking at a kaleidoscope of movement, studied but spontaneous. Miss Lee began to slow her drum and the dancers slowed their movements. Jackson danced away from Sara, and Sara went into drop swings, her favorite part of warm-ups. Over to her feet she dropped, head and arms loose. Up she swung, down she released, and up she swung, higher each time. She felt her feet leave the stage on the fourth one, her arms high overhead, but she stopped on a dime when Miss Lee gave the final beat. The audience broke out into loud applause when they all froze. Sara was perspiring as she took a quick bow with the boys and ran off stage. The seniors were lined up in the hall in their frothy pale aqua gowns and soft pink pointe shoes. Sara's heart nearly broke as she passed them. *That is where I should be*, she thought, nearly crying. "Break a leg!" she shouted out to them as they walked quickly past her into the wings.

In the dressing room, Tchaikovsky's majestic *Serenade* music flowed from the intercom. Sara felt tears in her eyes as she started to take off her black leotard. "No, Sara," Leah told her. "Mr. Moyne came by and said to tell you to leave on your black leotard for the award ceremonies. Leave that on." Sara looked at her folk costume on the rack behind her. *What's the difference*, she thought. If she couldn't be in pointe shoes and the *Serenade* costume, bare feet would do as well as character shoes and she could stand with the boys on the risers. Shannon and Leah had put her bouquet on the counter in front of her chair. She picked it up and smelled the fresh roses, carnations and lilies. She stood in front of the mirror with the long green ribbon hanging down and turned out her

431

legs like a gracious ballerina on stage in front of a massive audience in New York.

"Come on," Shannon whispered. "Let's sneak into the wings and watch *Serenade*." So the three walked softly out of the dressing room, Shannon and Leah in their folk costumes, flowered headpieces and character shoes, and Sara in her black leotard and tights and bare feet. Sara's eyes grew wide as she caught glimpses of the long legs arcing high in the air, the lithe bodies in graceful arabesques and flowing waltz steps. They *were* the music. They *were* the movement. They *were* Balanchine! *I should be in this,* she thought. *I should be in this.* She closed her eyes and pictured herself dancing in Misty Schaffer's master class and dancing in *Concerto Barocco* in the little Balanchine theatre. She wished as hard as she could that that would be enough to get her the scholarship to New York.

Charleigh's voice crashed her thoughts. "We have to line up for the award ceremony!" she said. "Come on!" She led them away into the hall where the juniors were at the front of the line, the intermediates second, followed by the boys. *Serenade* dancers would be last and stand at the highest level of the risers. Patrick waved her over to the boys' group. Shannon and Leah hugged her and wished her luck, then took their places with the folk dancers. Sara heard the last long chord of the *Serenade* music and heard the swell of applause. She imagined the dancers taking ballerina bows in their gorgeous gowns. Then they ran quickly past her to their place at the end of the line.

"OK," Miss Sutton said, appearing at the front of the line. "The curtain is closed, but the audience can hear you. Move quietly to the risers and wait for the curtain to open."

She looked at the little girls. "No fidgeting up there," she said. "Keep your arms at your sides and stand tall like dancers. I will be at the podium near the front of the stage." Sara stood taller and her heart beat faster.

CHAPTER FORTY-EIGHT

"Closing Ceremonies"

The curtain opened on the last evening of Lakewood's fifty-first summer. Sara felt the wood of the riser under her bare feet and gazed out over the huge audience. It was starting to get dark and the sky was twinkling with stars. Her heart seemed to sway with the wind moving the pines as she looked at Miss Sutton at the podium across the stage. She felt the seniors breathing behind her and the juniors standing at attention in front of her. She felt Patrick on one side of her and Jackson on the other.

"Thank you for coming!" Miss Sutton said to the hundreds before them. "Our summer has been filled with fun and friendship and the growth of challenges met. These dancers have learned so much from their wonderful teachers and from one another. They have felt what it is to be committed dancers and to reach for the best they can be. While so many of them deserve the honor of a scholarship, we could only choose three from each division." But Sara knew about the special surprise scholarship. Miss Sutton read from her paper. "The Junior Division winners are…" As she announced each girl's name, they walked to the center of the stage, the audience cheered, and Mr. Moyne presented a small bouquet to each one. When the applause died down Miss Sutton said, "The Intermediate Division winners are: third place Leah Bennett." Oh, wow. Leah so deserved it. Leah kind of shrugged and walked out to receive her bouquet from Miss Alexander. She stood proudly next to the junior winners as Miss Sutton said, "Second place: Alene Kay." Sara could hardly stand still as she watched Alene accept her flowers. The announcement of the special scholarship was getting closer every second. "First place: Shannon St. Pierre." *Shannon!* Sara wanted to run right onto the stage and hug her. *Wow*, she thought. She and Leah will be back here next summer.

"Now the Senior Division," Miss Sutton smiled. "Third place goes to Kathy Jacobs." Kathy curtsied in her long gown as she received her flowers. "Second place, Jennifer Kent." Jennifer had the most turned-out legs and pretty feet Sara had ever seen at Lakewood. She stood with her bouquet next to Kathy. "And first place scholarship back to Lakewood goes to Katie Easton," Miss Sutton announced amid wild applause and cheering. The photographer moved in front of the winners and took pictures of the happy dancers. Sara remembered exactly how she felt last year when she accepted the flowers and smile from Madame for second place. "Now Mr. Peters will announce the Woodlake winners." Miss Sutton gave the podium to Mr. Peters. Sara felt Patrick hold his breath.

"The boys' dance program is new this year," Mr. Peters said. "We have boys here from a few different states on scholarship and I brought some of my dancers from New York. They found dancing in the woods quite conducive to learning. Indeed, they have grown in many ways and I think enjoyed themselves." *Hurry*, Sara thought. "We have only one scholarship to award this year," Mr. Peters continued. "But as we grow into a bigger program we hope to add more. Our scholarship back to Woodlake next summer goes to Patrick McCracken." Patrick gasped and ran down the risers onto the stage. Mr. Peters met him and handed him a rolled certificate with a red ribbon. Patrick bowed and waved to the cheering audience. Sara was happy for him. She had to admit she had learned some things from him. Now her heart beat faster and the photographer moved in for more pictures. Miss Sutton took the podium again. Sara closed her eyes and made her wish.

"Congratulations to all our scholarship winners," Miss Sutton said. "Now I have a surprise. The New York City Ballet visited us this summer, and I'd like to introduce Misty Schaffer from the company." *Misty!* Sara was so excited she almost fell off the riser. Misty liked her dancing in the master class. Misty remembered who she was at the after party. Misty watched her dance tonight! Misty might have suggested that Sara should win the NYCB scholarship.

"Thank you. You were all wonderful tonight," Misty said, looking at the dancers. "You all deserve a scholarship, but I can only give one." Sara held her breath. "The scholarship for next summer at the school of the New York City Ballet goes to Robin Stewart." Sara's heart pounded and tears filled her eyes as Robin brushed past her down the risers. She felt a lump in her throat watching Robin's long legs take her to Misty in the center of the stage. Robin's strawberry blonde hair wisped around her cheeks as she smiled graciously and curtsied in her flowing gown to Misty Schaffer who handed her the largest bouquet. Robin smiled self-confidently and took an extra bow to the audience as everyone continued to cheer. Then Jackson put his arm around Sara and gave her a little smile.

"And now before we sing the Lakewood song," Miss Sutton said, "Miss Lee will take the podium." Sara tried to control her breathing. *Everybody can't win*, she told herself, holding back sobs. She'd come back to Lakewood next year. Leah and Shannon would be here. The blue tin was in the rafters. She bit her lip and tried not to let disappointment overwhelm her. *Whatever happens will be cool*, Erin had said.

"Congratulations, dancers," Miss Lee began. "I have taught a unique method of modern dance to these dancers all summer. I have put obstacles in front of them to solve problems and to grow. It was difficult. A few dancers stood out, but one kept coming up as someone who deserved to be in New York to continue Nikolais training. That person is Sara Sutherland. Come down here, Sara!" Miss Lee smiled. Sara's mouth fell open. Jackson hugged her. She dried her eyes, caught her breath and made her way through the juniors and across the stage to Miss Lee. In her black leotard and tights and bare feet she curtsied and took her bouquet from Miss Lee. "Good job," Miss Lee smiled down at her. Sara was so surprised and nervous that first she turned her legs out, then turned them back into a modern dance parallel position. She felt the wisp around her neck of the old dance spirits. She knew now that they included modern dancers. The audience kept applauding and cheering for her. It was almost as if they knew how much she wanted to go to New York and their applause would lift her there. She stood next to Robin for pictures. Robin went up on her pointe shoes and held her flowers in front of her elegant gown. But she said to Sara, "Congratulations, dancer."

"Same to you," Sara said. She swallowed the lump that was still in her throat as the music began for the Lakewood song. She could hardly sing, she was so filled with surprise and confused feelings.

> *Lakewood, Lakewood nestled fair*
> *Among the leaves and northern air.*
> *We come to you to dance and share,*
> *to grow and learn, to teach and care,*
> *to make new friends and build new paths,*
> *which lead us on to dreams that last.*
> *And when the summer's days are through,*
> *we'll think of our return to you*
> *and never once throughout the year*
> *forget our friends made steadfast here.*

As the curtain closed in front of them, Shannon and Leah put their arms around Sara. Brooke, Mary and Charleigh came running down from the risers and joined them. They screamed in joy and jumped up and down. "Charlie, Charlie, that's enough," Leah laughed, untangling herself. Then everyone went off in all directions, hugging, saying good-bye and crying. Eventually, Sara made it to the dressing room. She put her second bouquet next to her first bouquet and smiled. "Double winner," Leah said behind her.

"Yes," Shannon said. "Félicitation." She took off her folk costume and hung it on the rack.

As Sara was taking off her black leotard Brooke yelled to her from the doorway. "Someone's here for you, Sara!" Her mother was supposed to meet her at Pavlova. She pulled her leotard back up and went to the door. Jackson stood there with his Nikolais book.

"I thought you might want to keep this," he said, holding the book out to her, "until next summer."

"Thank you," Sara said. She took the book and smiled up into his eyes. He smiled back.

"See you in New York," Jackson said, walking away.

Sara could hardly believe it was going to happen. She looked down at her bare feet that had won the scholarship. She walked over and picked up her dance bag from under her chair. She went to the back of the dressing room, opened the door to the balcony and walked out into the night air. She breathed deeply of the pines towering over the dark lake. She looked up at the stars. She opened the Nikolais book and found a note from Jackson. "Best wishes for the rest of your wonderful dance life," it said. He had drawn a heart. "Jackson" it said under the heart. She laughed out loud in joy. Then she found the pen she had put in her dance bag and took out the blank letter to Erin. Under the Lakewood moon she wrote:

"See you in New York!

Sara"

440

Glossary of Dance and Theatre Terms

Adage — Slow and graceful movements performed with control and ease.

A la seconde — To the second.

Allégro — Brisk, lively steps.

Apron — The part of the stage nearest the audience. The dancers generally do not dance on it.

Arabesque — A pretty pose. The dancer stands on one leg with the other leg in the air behind.

Attitude — A pose with the back leg bent at a 90 degree angle.

Balençoire — The leg is thrown up high forward, then to the back like a seesaw.

Barre	The horizontal wooden or metal bar fastened to the walls of the ballet studio that the dancer holds for support.
Battement	Beating step.
Battu	Crossing or passing of the ankles.
Body positions	Movement through poses in different positions.
Bourrée	Quick, tiny running steps on pointe.
Chassé temp levé	A slide into a hop in the air.
Choreography	Dance steps or movement phrases.
Choreographer	A person who composes dance steps or movement.
Contraction	A contracting of the muscles of the diaphragm.
Corps de Ballet	Same as ensemble. The group of dancers who do not solo.
Degagé	Disengagement of the foot. Point away from standing leg & off floor.
Demi	Half or half-pointe.

Derrière	Behind, back.
Développé	Developing movement. The gesture leg points to the knee, then extends out away from the body.
Downstage	Toward the audience.
Échappé	Escaping, level movement of both feet to second or fourth position.
Emboité	A little jump turning, with boxed, tightly fitted feet.
En pointe	Dancing on pointe
Ensemble	The dancers who do not have solos. Same as corp de ballet
En tourant	In turning. The dancer turns while dancing.
En diagonale	In diagonal. The dancer movers on a diagonal.
Frappé	A striking movement of the foot at the barre.
Fouetté	A sharp whipping movement of the raised foot in a turn.

Gesture leg	The leg that moves.
Grand or Grande	Large or big movement.
Grand Révérence	Large curtsie.
Grand battement	The gesture leg is raised quickly from the hip and lowered with control. Like a high kick to the front, side, or back.
Jeté	A jump from one foot to another from a brush.
Passé	The gesture leg passes in front or back of the supporting leg.
Pas de bourrée	Bourrée steps. Or, for example, moving one foot back, the other side, then the other front.
Pas de deux	Dance for two.
Pas de quatre	Dance for four.
Penché arabesque	Leaning forward, inclining.
Petit	Little, small.
Piqué	The dancer steps directly onto pointe or demi-pointe.

Pirouette	A turn on one foot.
Plié	Bent, bending. A bending of the knees to make the joints and muscles pliable and soft, and the tendons flexible.
Port a bras	Movement of the arms.
Relevé	Raised. A raising of the body onto the balls of the feet or onto pointe.
Retiré	The dancer brings the toe of one foot to the knee of the other foot.
Rond de jamb	Circular movement of the leg on the ground or in the air.
Sauté	Jumping. In a sauté arabesque the dancer leaves the floor.
Scrim	A thin curtain stretched across the stage to produce a mysterious or shadowing effect when the dancers are behind it.
Spotting	The movement of a dancer's head during a turn. The head is the last to leave and the first to return to a spot in front of the dancer on a directed path.
Stage-left	The dancer's left when facing the audience.

Stage-right	The dancer's right when facing the audience.
Supporting leg	The leg that holds the dancer's weight when the other leg moves.
Sur le cou de pied	The foot is between the base of the calf and top of the ankle.
Tendu	The gesture foot slides out to the front, side, or back, and back again.
Tombé	The weight of the dancer falls onto one leg.
Upstage	Away from the audience.
Variation	A solo dance in a classic ballet.
Wings	The sides of the stage out of the audience's view.

What Do You Think?

Point of View
1. From whose point of view is this story told? (Which character?)

Setting
1. Where is the setting of the story?
2. Why is the setting important for the main character?
3. What are two ways the setting challenges the main character?

Description
1. Find a description of how the author describes what a character looks like.
2. Find an example of how the author describes the personality of a character.
3. Find an example of how the author describes the setting, such as a cabin, the dance building, the music building, the secret practice room, the woods, or the lake.

Symbols

A symbol in a story is something that has a deep meaning, such as the locket.

1. Give examples of two symbols in the story and tell what they mean to the main character.

Plot

A plot is what happens in a story.

1. Briefly tell the beginning, middle and end of this story.
2. Tell when the plot takes an important turn that might change the outcome of the story.
3. In what way was the ending expected? In what way was it a surprise?

The Characters

1. Who are the most important characters in the story?
2. Who is the main character?
3. Which character is in most competition with Sara?
4. Which character is most supportive of Sara?
5. Do you think Sara is more mature at the end of summer than at the beginning? Give two examples.
6. Why do you think the author had Leah, Sara and Shannon use the window to get into the secret practice room?
7. Why do you think Sara made a deal for Shannon to help Robin with her paper?
8. In what ways did Sara show her passion for ballet?
9. When Sara accidentally pushed Patrick in the lake, what did they say about her personality?
10. Were all the teachers in the book equally supportive of Sara's dancing? Who was most supportive and how did this show?

11. Why do you think Robin won the scholarship to the school of the New York City Ballet? Why didn't Sara?

12. Why do you think Sara won a scholarship to study the Nikolais method of modern dance in New York?

13. Do you think Leah really wants to come back to Lakewood? Why or why not?

14. Do you think Shannon really wants to come back to Lakewood? Why or why not?

15. What influence did Jackson have on Sara during the summer?

16. Do you think Sara will be happy in New York studying modern dance? What might happen?

Made in the USA
San Bernardino, CA
09 December 2016